EMMALINE

EMMALINE

A NOVEL

ASHLI O'CONNELL

Published by Briar & Ash Books
An imprint of Briar & Ash Publishing, LLC
Harrisonville, Missouri

BRIAR & ASH
BOOKS

ISBN: 979-8-9948075-0-7 (Paperback)
ISBN: 979-8-9948075-1-4 (EPUB)

LCCN: 2026905971

Book design by Stewart A. Williams
Author photo by Greenbox Photography

Printed in the United States of America.

For my father, Larry, who first told me the story.
For my mother, Phyllis, who has always supported my dreams.
And for Lydia, who lived it.

NOTE TO READERS

Emmaline is a work of fiction inspired by true events. The broad historical arc and public figures in the novel are grounded in the historical record with scenes that have been dramatized. The central characters are inspired by the author's ancestors and drawn from documented accounts by the pioneers of that era.

The author has also used informed imagination and composite storytelling gleaned from primary sources. The goal is not to reconstruct history verbatim, but to share a story that is emotionally resonant and historically sound. For more on the intersection of storytelling and the historical record, please read the Author's Note at the end of the novel.

DEFINITIONS AND HISTORICAL CONTEXT

For readers unfamiliar with Mormonism, the following terms may be helpful. These definitions reflect how the terms were commonly used during the time in which this story takes place.

Emigrant: Though *immigrant* may be more common in modern usage, European converts to the Church of Jesus Christ of Latter-day Saints were referred to as *emigrants* during the nineteenth century.

Endowment ceremony: A religious rite within Mormonism during which members make sacred covenants to God. In the mid-nineteenth century, endowments were typically performed in the Endowment House in Salt Lake City. Women often received their endowments immediately before marriage.

Gentile: A term used by Mormons to refer to non-members of the LDS Church.

Mormons / Latter-day Saints / Saints: Used interchangeably to describe members of the Church of Jesus Christ of Latter-day Saints, founded by Joseph Smith in 1830.

Plural marriage: Used interchangeably with *polygamy*, meaning the practice of one man having multiple wives. This is the preferred term historically used by the LDS Church.

Priesthood: Divine authority believed to be granted by God to worthy Mormon men, giving them the authority to act in God's name.

Promised Land / Zion / New Jerusalem: Terms used interchangeably to describe the Utah Territory, which was being developed as a theocratic society outside US borders and viewed by believers as a gathering place for the faithful.

Sealing: A religious ordinance performed by a priesthood holder to bind individuals together for eternity. In the nineteenth century, sealings were commonly performed in the Endowment House. The term is sometimes used interchangeably with marriage. Today, sealings take place in LDS temples.

PROLOGUE

OCTOBER 19, 1856

NEAR PRESENT-DAY CASPER, WYOMING

The Platte had been our lifeline for weeks. We'd followed the river all through Nebraska and into Wyoming. It was our source of water and our guide. We were alive because of the Platte.

But on the nineteenth of October—a day so bitterly cold that the winds bit straight through our bones—the river became our greatest foe.

It ran wide and swift, with ice chunks bobbing over the rough waters. The river cut straight across our path. We had to get to the other side. And the only way past it … was through it.

There was no bridge. No ferry. No choice.

I stood next to Gideon and considered the unforgiving threat before us, our breath hanging like clouds around our heads as we spoke. "There has to be another way," I said.

Then with more urgency, "Don't we have to turn back?"

"We can't," Gideon answered softly, drawing a deep breath as he brought his trembling hands to his face. It was the first time I saw him scared. "If we go back, we'll starve to death. Our only hope now is that the supply wagons will meet us on the other side of the river."

PART ONE

EMMALINE KENDALL

CHAPTER ONE

SPRING 1854

never talked about William because he wasn't so much a brother as he was a ghost, a shadow that covered my mother and father in grief during most of my childhood and, I supposed, rendered me nearly invisible to them.

I was so young during those years in Wiltshire, but I remember a doctor whispering about a fever, and neighbors saying things like "Nothing they could do" and "So sudden" as they dropped off stews and mincemeat pies. I think my mother sang before the darkness came. I think my father whistled. But my memories from that time are like dreams. I question the very ground beneath my feet when they come.

What I know for certain is that William's absence reshaped everything that came after. It started immediately and didn't stop, like water seeping through the cracks slowly and then all at once. With Father too grief-stricken and lost in drink to work dependably, the jobs stopped coming. And then so did everything else.

He had worked as a carter, hauling produce for farmers and merchants. But as time passed, his grief consumed him more, not less. I knew when I woke to the sounds of him stumbling through the house at night, I would likely not eat the next day.

I wondered if he knew that.

By the time we left Wiltshire for Liverpool in the spring of my twelfth year, William's name seemed already forgotten in our home, if not our hearts. If I ever spoke it aloud, no one answered. He lies there still in Wiltshire—unvisited, I am sure. We have no people there.

We went to Liverpool because Father had been told there was good work at the docks. He found a home at the courts on Pembroke Place. It was to be a new start, and oh I had such excitement to move to a city where Father would have a steady income and there would be no ghost of William. But ghosts do not stay so easily where you leave them.

I had thought of Liverpool as something grand. A place of ships and trade and men in good hats and women in smart dresses. The kind of place where fortunes were made and dreams come true. But reality collides with your dreams quickly, even when you are twelve. I wasn't prepared for the smoke, for the filth in the gutters, for the way the buildings closed in on each other, leaving no room for the sky.

My nose detected the court housing first. We rounded the corner, and an unending expanse of red brick tenement housing with slate roofs and muddy, cobbled roads came into view. It was awash in the scent of crowded, filthy bodies, coal smoke, seaweed from the docks, and—worst of all—the shared outdoor privies and chamber pots emptied into a communal ash pit. The smell stung my eyes, and I wiped a lone tear falling down my cheek.

"This is to be our home?" I asked.

Mother and Father did not answer. They just kept moving toward it. At first they didn't notice that I wasn't following. My feet were heavy with dread, my legs frozen. I couldn't fathom that we'd traded Wiltshire for … this.

I found my feet and ran ahead to them just before they got lost in the crowd. I reached for Father's arm. He pulled me close and kissed my head.

Father was a good man, but a weak one. And a broken one. He drank to forget William, but in doing so, he forgot us too. He was not the type to get mean under the influence, not the type to rage. He was the kind who disappeared. In spirit first, then in body.

When he wasn't drinking, he sometimes shared his dreams with me. "Emma," he'd say—he was the only one who ever called me Emma. "Emma, things'll be better in Liverpool. I can get good work at the docks. We'll be startin' fresh. There's nothin' but possibility when you start fresh." He and I shared that kind of naive optimism in those days. And when he wasn't drinking, there was a twinkle in his eye that made me believe him.

But this was not the Liverpool of our dreams. I tried telling myself that somewhere in this city was the promise Father spoke of. I trusted his dreams because I needed them to be true, not because I had reason to believe.

I understood my mother less than my father, even though I was almost always at her side. She was constant and steady. Always moving, always working.

She took pride in our home, even when we had almost nothing, cleaning and tidying our few possessions as if it made a difference. She never let herself be beaten down, but she never let herself soften either. It was only when I heard her quiet tears at night that I knew her heart was still broken. By William? By Father? By me? I didn't know.

There were no tears in the mornings. She was industrious and pragmatic and spoke to me mostly about what needed doing.

"Tomorrow we'll settle our home and talk to the merchants about taking in their mending. Always there's mending to be done," she said the day we arrived. "Your stitching's coming along. You're good enough to help now. We can double our pay."

I understood that to mean I would not be going back to school, and I wanted to protest. But I didn't have the courage. I almost never had the courage in those days. I nodded instead, eager to please her. To reach her. To break through her carefully built walls.

If I could know her, or she could know me, I thought I wouldn't miss school so much. But I didn't know how to break through.

Father, Mother, and I squeezed into one room, all of us, with only the pump in the courtyard for water. At night I could hear the groan of its handle as neighbors filled their pails in the dark. I heard the uneven, clomping footsteps of drunken men. I heard the cries of children, suffering from things I imagined but couldn't know.

Each night that first week, I curled up in my narrow cot and pulled the covers tightly around me, the thin fabric inadequate against the cold dampness of the dark room. I counted the sounds of the *drip, drip, drip* as rainwater fell into a bucket by the door. A drip for every minute I would not sleep.

I despaired at our circumstances and expected the darkness to settle upon us again, and it did—for a while. Work at the docks was not always guaranteed, even when Father was sober and eager to work.

Liverpool held the same sadness as Wiltshire, just covered in filth.

I had been right about not going back to school. This saddened me, but I knew it happened to many poor girls my age. Still, I was determined that I would not forget how to read. I was a good reader, earned the best marks in my class in Wiltshire, and reading was my only escape.

In the evenings after supper, I sat on my cot and brought out the four possessions beneath my mattress: a copy of *The Poetical Works of Felicia Hemans* that had once belonged to Mrs. Harcourt, a widow from our parish in Wiltshire who often lent me books and told me a girl should never be without poetry; a royal primer from the years I attended school; and a leather-bound journal and pen I received for my eleventh birthday.

Father had carved "E. Kendall" into the leather. I couldn't control much, but I would still find ways to read and write.

The journal was still blank. I wanted to have beautiful words for its lovely pages, but I was still waiting for the right thing to say. I dreamed of a life that might one day be worth recording. I didn't know it then, but the events of the next five years would fill those journal pages.

In the meantime I practiced my writing in the margins of my primer and on scraps of newspaper used to wrap fish or line our shelves, flattening them when no one was looking. I sounded out shop signs as we passed them, silently spelling each letter in my head. Liverpool would not take reading from me.

Mother and I walked the cobblestone streets early each morning to spend one or two shillings on food. She would send me to the baker's for day-old bread while she haggled over the price of fish or mutton.

"I'll not pay more than four pence, I won't," she'd tell the fishmonger before she walked away. He always called her back. Mother was something to watch. She did the best she could to feed us on our meager income.

After shopping we worked on the mending, had tea and bread for lunch—with butter on the good days—and mostly stitched silently. What Mother thought about, I never knew, and that was my greatest sorrow.

Vegetables like carrots and cabbages were bought when Father had a full week's wages. If he worked a whole fortnight, we might have tea, milk, butter, and even eggs. One morning at market, I watched a girl my age sink her teeth into a crisp apple. My mouth responded before I could stop it, watering as if I'd bitten it myself. It had been months since I felt the flesh of an apple on my own tongue. My mind wandered to a summer memory of Grandmother helping William and me pick all the apples we wanted from the trees in her garden. How I longed to taste that tartness or to feel the juice of an orange dribble down my chin.

Longing. That was what I knew best in the years since William's death. Longing for food. Longing to be known. Longing to be enough for my parents.

Still, I held on.

Liverpool was not the first place to try to break me, and it would be far from the last.

CHAPTER TWO

The men in the courtyard were causing quite a stir. Father had just come in from the docks, his dark brown curls dusted with coal and his freckled face still streaked black. He said it looked like some missionaries were outside. Mother and I silently scraped skins off potatoes for supper, but the noise was becoming too much to ignore. Father went out to investigate, and Mother and I set down our paring knives and followed.

We saw two well-dressed street preachers who had drawn a small crowd in the twilight. The setting sun broke through the clouds, casting golden light on their heads—as if God himself had placed them there.

The men looked almost identical to one another. They wore starched white shirts with crisp, dark gray waistcoats and smartly pressed woolen trousers. With trimmed brown hair and beards, I guessed them to be about my father's age.

They had polished leather shoes, fancier than anything I had ever seen, and the one who spoke carried two leather-bound books. One of the books looked like a newer version of our old family Bible. I couldn't tell what the other book was.

I had never seen such gentlemen standing in our soot-covered court-yard. They stood out from the crowd of dockworkers who all wore scuffed leather boots, patched-up woolen trousers, and dirty linen shirts covered with grime and sweat from a hard day's work.

The ministers' presence commanded attention, and they spoke with eloquence that captivated the swelling crowd gathered around them.

"You have prayed many times for blessings. Blessings of shelter and plenty on your table for your children and yourselves. There is a Holy Spirit ready to pour out temporal and eternal blessing upon you even at this time."

The words of the minister drew my father closer. I watched my mother follow him. Though her dark brown cotton dress and white apron were well worn, they were clean, and she walked with quiet dignity. I watched her untie her rose-colored headscarf to reveal her neatly pinned-up chestnut hair, a small gesture that felt like an act of deference to the preachers.

It was not the first time we had heard about prayers and blessings. We were members of the Church of England, like everyone we knew. But there was something charismatic about these preachers, about the way they spoke of blessings. I continued to watch from the doorway of our home.

They began to tell the most curious story.

"Many of you are faithful Christians. You know how the Lord has, in every age, raised up prophets. Did he not call unto Noah? Did he not speak from the burning bush to Moses? Did he not appear to Paul on the road to Damascus?

"And now, in our day, the Lord has again stretched forth his hand. He has called a prophet—a humble boy named Joseph Smith. This boy knelt in a grove of trees in New York, seeking to know which church was true. And lo, a pillar of light descended, brighter than the noonday sun, and in that light stood the Father and the Son!"

The crowd thinned as the men continued to speak. My stomach growled, and I wished my parents would come back inside. But they only looked more engaged as the preachers droned on.

"'Join none of them,' the Lord said, 'for they draw near with their lips, but their hearts are far from me.'"

I tried to make sense of what I was hearing. A boy prophet had seen Jesus Christ? On the American continent? I had never heard of such things. As I pondered the words, I watched my father inch closer toward the ministers.

Suddenly, the crowd turned violent.

"Filthy Mormons!" someone spat.

"How many wives do yer Joseph Smith have?" yelled another.

Someone hurled an egg at the ministers. It hit one of their shoulders. A wet slap against his fine coat. My heart jumped to my throat, and I took an instinctive step backward. Shouts filled the courtyard.

And then someone threw a rock. I had never seen men inspire such rage. I ran inside. But my parents did not. I watched from our one small window as my father reached for the minister who'd been hit with an egg, lightly grasping the man's arm with a hand that usually held a bottle of ale. Most of the crowd had scattered by now, but my parents and several others continued talking with the ministers.

Back in our dark, damp home—the entirety of which was smaller than our kitchen in Wiltshire—I finished peeling the potatoes. The sermon echoed in my mind. It was unlike anything I'd heard at parish churches before.

"There is a Holy Spirit ready to pour out temporal and eternal blessing upon you even at this time."

I doubted it. By the age of twelve, I had learned not to expect blessings. I saw this entire encounter as little more than an entertainment to liven up my dull existence.

But I wondered what kept Mother and Father out there so long.

I put the potatoes on to boil and set three plates on the small round table. The rough pine surface was scarred by years of faint knife scores; the wood darkened by years of spilled broth and candle wax. I sat down on a chair that wobbled if you didn't adjust your weight just so, cradled my head in my folded arms, and rested my eyes. Sleep came dear in these conditions.

My parents did not say much when they came in for supper. I was used to quiet meals, but this felt different. The silence was almost deafening, as if the words not being said were overtaking the room. I didn't know what those missionaries had said to my parents in the courtyard, but whatever it was must have been deeply impactful. Something was happening inside of my home.

The next morning before the sun rose, my father prepared for his day at the docks. I heard the most peculiar sound. Something familiar from when I was a little girl: He was whistling.

Later, Mother and I sat together having porridge before our daily mending began, and she related to me the events of the night before.

"Emmaline, I have never heard such truths spoken. The Bible was explained to my understanding like never before."

I had seen Mother negotiate the price of fish with the confidence of Queen Victoria, but never had I heard her speak with such awe. It startled me, like the way thunder does when the sky is blue.

The men, she said, were elders of the Church of Jesus Christ of Latter-day Saints. The Mormons. It was the first time I ever heard the name of that church. They had given my parents a new book of scripture, the Book of Mormon.

As I tried to work out how my parents had been so enamored with new spiritual ideas from one conversation, she explained they'd been invited to go to a special service with the elders that very evening. I would stay home until my parents understood more about this new religion. But one thing was certain: It had already begun to change our little family.

Later that night, my parents went to the service, leaving me behind. At twelve, I was old enough to be left alone but unaccustomed to it.

I was used to the kind of loneliness you felt in the presence of another person, and I was not sure what I thought about this new independence. The constant din of neighbors and passersby penetrated the thin walls and only increased my sense of isolation.

Sitting on my little cot, I unbraided my hair and brushed my long, dark brunette curls—a trait I inherited from my father, along with his freckles. Our single room, dimly lit by two oil lamps, was both my sanctuary and confinement. It felt especially cold and damp, so I took a woolen shawl from a nail on the wall and wrapped it around my muslin nightdress.

The room held space only for my cot, my parents' narrow bed on the opposite wall, the time-worn kitchen table with three wobbly chairs, a small set of shelves, and two rocking chairs that we brought from Wiltshire. My father's old steamer trunk sat at the foot of my parents' bed and held most of our earthly belongings.

Near the entrance of the room, a small stove provided the only warmth. Its heat barely warded off the pervasive dampness. The walls were stained with years of unsanitary living.

I needed to use the privy, but that would have meant a trip outside to the courtyard, and I dared not go alone. I decided to wait for Mother and Father.

I shivered as a rat scurried across the floor. For a moment I considered blowing out the lamp so I wouldn't have to see another one, but the thought of hearing a rat without seeing it felt worse. I pulled my shawl tighter and tried to keep still, listening for my parents' return.

Just then they burst through the door with great excitement, full of incredible stories of people being healed by the laying on of hands. The elders claimed if they administered consecrated oil to the sick and also prayed, they would recover. And many did, my parents said.

My father told of a ganger at the docks who'd crushed his hand bad. Pinned it right under a crate of coal.

"I was there, Emma, seen it happen meself! His hand, trapped tight— just last week, just last week it was! Doctor said plain as day, he'd never bend them fingers again. But he come tonight, and the elders anointed his hand with oil, prayed over him, and, Emma, by God, the swellin' went down right before our eyes!"

Mother nodded, eyes bright. "Aye, and more besides. Sick little ones burnin' with fever, now right as rain. And an old woman, blind for a year, now she's up and seein' clear as ever."

I wasn't sure what to make of it all. Maybe this was what it looked like when people found light again. I wanted to ask questions but didn't know exactly what to ask. I knew I was grateful that something had ignited my parents, had them really talking again—to each other and to me. I listened intently when they told me the new things they were learning.

The next evening while my parents were at another service with the Mormons, I pulled out our old family Bible and flipped through the Psalms, which had always been my favorite. My grandmother used to read them to me when I was a little girl. She passed several years after William did, but I remembered well reading with her. I stopped when I found what I was looking for in Psalm 103: "Bless the Lord, O my soul, and forget not all his benefits: Who forgiveth all thine iniquities; who healeth all thy diseases."

The Bible did foretell of great miracles. It was right there in the Psalms. I still didn't understand everything, but I felt comforted. I couldn't find anything about Jesus on the American continent, but maybe the missionaries were right about this new prophet. It was true, after all, that there were many prophets in the Bible. Why couldn't God give us one for our day? Why shouldn't he?

Over the next several months my parents became so zealous with these teachings that they decided to join the church and be baptized. My mother and father made many friends, and my father stopped drinking altogether. Just like that. I liked these Mormons. They were kind to me and good to all who were in trouble.

I may not have been certain of the truth of all I was learning yet, and I sensed that my parents' zealousness had less to do with revelation and more to do with filling the void William had left behind. Still, the joy it brought into our home was enough for me.

If my parents needed me to be a Mormon, a Latter-day Saint, for us to be whole again, I found that to be a modest sacrifice. So I devoted myself to prayer and study, hoping the truth would be revealed to me as well.

And only once, in the quiet of a sleepless night, did I let myself wish—wickedly, fleetingly—that it had been me who made them this happy.

CHAPTER THREE

almost yelped as the cold water filled my boots, but I silenced myself in reverence. As I descended farther down the bank, my cotton dress darkened with the industrial silt and coal dust in the River Mersey. Water filled my bloomers, and a light current caught my unsteady legs. I gripped the elder's arm tightly. Sunshine warmed my face, but my teeth still chattered.

It was my baptism day: May 29, 1854.

Three months had passed since my parents were baptized, and I knew they'd eagerly been awaiting the moment when I, too, would make this decision.

By that time the mission house had become a second home to us. I was getting well acquainted with other young people, and I even sang in the church choir.

Baptism among the Mormons was unlike anything that had happened in the Church of England, where I'd been sprinkled as a baby. Many Saints from our branch gathered at the river for that sacred day. I was one of twelve who would be baptized. Each one of us immersed in the filthy river and made clean.

Before we began, an elder had spoken words of blessing to all who were gathered: "This is the gate, my brethren and sisters. Through baptism, you take upon yourself the name of Christ and enter into his covenant. You bury the old life and arise in newness of spirit."

Then, as I stood in the river, he held me steady and spoke, "Sister Emmaline, are you prepared to follow Christ all your days?"

"Yes," I said solemnly.

And I meant it. Even if I wasn't certain whether I believed, or if I was just following Mother and Father, I rejoiced that this church had transformed my family and my home. I had prayed and sought the Lord. I had not yet felt the "burning in my bosom" the elders spoke of—they said it was a tingling in your chest that testifies of the gospel's truth—but I was sincere in my desire to feel it. I trusted it would come if I obeyed. The elders and my parents promised that it would.

Straightaway, all I felt was water. Over my head, in my ears, in my mouth, which I had forgotten to completely close. My last thought was, *Will this be my death?*

Before I could complete the thought, I was standing again, shaking water from my ears. The first thing I saw was my parents' smiles. Every other feeling melted away.

I wondered if something magical had happened to me. Was I simply overwhelmed by my parents' joy? Would the burning come now? I still didn't fully understand, but I saw that I had made my parents proud. That was all I needed.

As the elder helped me out of the water, he declared, "Rejoice, for today you have become a child of the covenant."

I stood shivering on the shore of the Mersey, and Mother wrapped a faded quilt around my shoulders. It had been hand-sewn by my grandmother's nimble fingers decades ago. The dusty blue-and-green fabric enveloped me, almost like Grandmother was giving me a warm hug. I wondered what she would think of all this—her daughter and granddaughter stepping into a new faith, leaving behind the church she had so loved.

My new friend Eliza was to enter the waters next. As her name was called, she looked back and searched my face. I believe she was looking for the courage to proceed. I knew Eliza was excited to be baptized, but she was even more frightened than I of the river. I smiled and nodded, trying not to let her see my body quake with chills.

Eliza walked slowly. Her blonde, almost white hair was pulled into one long braid, and her porcelain skin was pale with fright. Her naturally wide smile was hesitant today, but she walked forward confidently.

When the baptisms had finished, my heart felt oddly weightless, as if the river had rinsed a year's worth of worry from my bones, if only for an afternoon. For once, I wasn't the girl counting stitches by candlelight, worried about her next meal; I was simply twelve, alive in clean sunlight, sprinting beside my best friend.

We tore up the riverbank toward the meetinghouse, braids flying. We laughed about the way our skirts had billowed in the river and tried to shush each other when a cluster of boys glanced our way, but we couldn't stifle the giggles.

That evening I slept at Eliza's house. Her mother made mutton, stewed vegetables, and apple hand pies. I loved Eliza's house. It was a two-bedroom cottage on the outskirts of Liverpool. You could neither hear nor smell the city from her bedroom.

Best of all, she had her own bookshelf with more than twenty books. She let me borrow a new one each time I visited. Eliza still attended school, and she was generous with her lessons and school texts as well.

They bored her while they excited me.

I pulled a delicate volume from the shelf and ran my hands over the cover. *Lyrical Ballads* by William Wordsworth and Samuel Taylor Coleridge. "We had this at school," I said, looking through the pages to find my favorite.

The thin paper crackled as I gently turned the pages. I quickly found what I was looking for: Wordsworth's "We Are Seven." I touched the corner of the page as if it might vanish. I hadn't read it since we left Wiltshire, but I had recited it often in my mind, especially when I thought of William.

The poem began with a child. A cottage girl who looked like me. Thick curls, fair eyes, mother close by, death even closer.

"And when the ground was white with snow,
And I could run and slide,
My brother John was forced to go,
And he lies by her side."

"How many are you then," said I,
"If they two are in Heaven?"
The little Maiden did reply,
"O Master! we are seven."

"But they are dead; those two are dead!
"Their spirits are in heaven!"
'Twas throwing words away; for still
The little Maid would have her will,
And said, "Nay, we are seven!"

I felt the familiar sadness as I read the lines that felt like they'd been written for me. The little girl with curls like mine had known the death of a brother and a sister. But she did not forget. They were counted. Her family was still seven even though two died. My family was still four even though one died. No one ever spoke it, and I had always thought our sorrow hid in the silent spaces.

I didn't tell Eliza what Wordsworth meant to me. That he understood.

It would have been too hard to explain. I simply slipped the book into my satchel and told her I would bring it back next time.

She just shrugged. "You can keep it," she said, already brushing her hair for bed.

Eliza's life seemed more grand than it really was. Her father had been a spice merchant, but he died the previous year, leaving her mother with enormous debts. I knew they feared losing the house every day. Each time I visited, another piece of furniture had been sold.

"Did you feel the burning in your bosom yet?" Eliza whispered that night as we drifted to sleep.

"No," I whispered.

She giggled.

"Why are you laughing?"

"You don't even have a bosom yet."

I threw my pillow at her. After the laughter died down, I grew serious. "Do you even understand what they mean?"

"I think," she said, pausing to choose her words carefully, "maybe our bodies have a telling in them when we know the gospel is true."

I still didn't really understand, but I didn't want to say so.

Eliza and I walked to the mission house for choir practice one sunny afternoon in July. The streets were noisy with the sounds of Liverpool. The hum of ship horns was such a constant backdrop we almost didn't hear it anymore, but the *click-clack-click-clack* of carters on the muddy cobblestone was deafening.

Fishmongers hollered at each passerby. "Fresh herrin'! Fine haddock! Cod fer yer supper!"

You could buy near anything on the streets of Liverpool. There was the baker, the butcher, the florist, and the greengrocer, all with their enticing colors and smells. Newsboys cried out as they darted between carriages, hawking the latest broadsheets—"*The Liverpool Mercury*! *The Albion*! Shipping news from America!"—their voices rising above the clatter.

I watched a gentleman buy a paper and discard it quickly after scanning the headlines. "Be right back," I said, darting off to rescue it from the rubbish heap.

We passed a group of girls jumping rope in their soot-stained dresses, each one too short for their growing legs and knobby knees.

My heart was full, and my mood was light. I felt I understood my parents' decision better every day. Eliza and I talked excitedly about the upcoming Pioneer Day festival at the mission to celebrate the Saints arriving in Zion—that was what they called the Utah Territory in America.

We were within sight of the mission house when it happened.

I was jarred out of my pleasure by the feeling of a rock hitting my back. One, then another. I almost fell as I struggled to catch my breath. I reached for Eliza, but she also got hit. No, they weren't rocks. They were eggs. The cold slime penetrated my dress and began to run down my backside. Hot tears burned my eyes.

We searched the road, looking for our assailants. In the alleyway just behind us, a group of boys several years older than us howled with laughter.

"Oy, little Saints! Where's yer prophet now?" hollered one. "Bet them Yankee preachers dipped ya in pig water!"

The harassment of the Saints was common in Liverpool, as it was for our sisters and brothers in America. I had heard similar taunts while walking with my parents, and I had seen a missionary pelted with an egg and a rock that first night in the courtyard.

We knew they did not like us—for we were children of the covenant. The scriptures foretold that we would be a persecuted people. But I had never been the one wiping yolk off her dress.

Eliza was sobbing.

"Stop it," I said, grabbing her hand as we ran. "Do not let them see you cry."

Inside the mission we were safe. Sisters there gave us each a clean, dry dress and a cup of warm tea. We dried our tears. The scratchy, woolen borrowed dress was too large, clothing me in the memory of the humiliation I had endured.

Brother Joseph Young, observing our distress, sat down with us and spoke gently. "My dear sisters," he began, "remember that the righteous have always faced persecution."

He reminded us how much the Savior endured and how the Prophet Joseph Smith was jailed and killed by wicked men in America.

"But take heart, for such trials refine our faith and draw us closer to God." He patted my shoulder and offered a reassuring smile.

His words comforted me, turning my tears into determination. If the prophet could die a martyr, I could handle taunts and egg-throwing.

Persecution grew in the city, but so did the number of Saints. And with the growth the talk of sailing to America to join our brothers and sisters in Zion became more frequent.

Ships full of Saints regularly departed Liverpool, bound for the "Promised Land." In Zion there was a home for every family and food enough for everyone. It was said to be a "land flowing with milk and honey."

We were eating Sunday supper one rainy summer evening when I first heard Father speak of Zion like it was becoming his own dream.

"Brigham Young's built it up, he has—out there in the mountains, one o' the finest cities in all the West," he said. "A place where Saints can live their faith without fear. No jeerin'. No stones. Just peace. And every family gets their own home, Ruthie—think of it."

I stopped chewing and watched Mother closely.

"I can't see as how we'll be affording that," she said, shaking her head at him.

Rain leaked through the roof by the door, and my father got up to move the bucket to catch the stream of water.

"Not tonight, we won't," he said, then laughed.

Mother and I joined him. Never before would we have found lightness in such a moment.

If I had any skepticism left about the truthfulness of Joseph Smith's story, I'd buried it and replaced those thoughts with love for the church that brought my parents back to me.

The Pioneer Day festival held on July 24 was a joyous occasion. Dancing and singing and games lasted all day. There was also a grand feast, and oh, what a meal it was. The tables stretched the length of the hall and were covered in white linen. There was roasted lamb and meat pies, fresh-baked wheat and rye breads, potato cakes, roasted vegetables, berry tarts, plum pudding, and even lemonade. Never had I felt so full or satisfied. After the feast Eliza and I sang with the choir.

In six months' time my life had gone from longing to belonging.

CHAPTER FOUR

"It is a damnable practice! Thousands will reject the gospel, and it'll be the end of the church."

My mother's desperate voice woke me up as my parents returned late from a meal they'd been invited to that evening with visiting elders from the States.

"What is it?" I asked, rubbing the sleep from my eyes. "What's going on?"

"That Elder Stowell—he spoke to us tonight about the principle of plural marriage," my father said.

"Plural marriage?"

"Polygamy!" my mother shouted, her body shaking, her green eyes burning with anger. "Men havin' more than one wife. And they're practicin' it in Zion!"

"Now, Ruthie," Father said gently, "calm yerself for a moment. Don't be forgettin' what the elders said. David and Solomon practiced it, and they were men after God's own heart."

"I s'pose this idea doesn't bother *you*. Sounds right appealin' to the husbands, eh? But the womenfolk won't stand for it. They won't."

He softly took hold of her shoulders, but I noticed his hands were trembling. He kissed her forehead. "You know I want no wife but you."

She began to weep. "He said it's a commandment. A commandment!" She collapsed on the bed, sobbing.

That night Mother barely spoke another word. By morning she had taken to her bed ill and would not rise again for a fortnight. We could not compel her to eat.

"I shall not take a bite again, Emmaline, until Heavenly Father himself reveals the answer to me," she said.

Our little home felt darker than usual. She didn't like lanterns lit, for they hurt her eyes. And the brightness of her countenance, which for the past year had warmed us, had vanished beneath a pile of quilts.

Father said I should stay with her each day and try to get her to eat and drink. I brought her water and weak tea, which she sometimes sipped. She spoke little, only fasting and praying, begging the Lord for an answer about polygamy.

For his part, Father spent longer days at the docks and late evenings at the meeting house. He was troubled, that was easy enough to see, but he didn't seem to know how to help her, and he didn't want to talk about it with me.

"Do something, Father," I pleaded one evening. "You're the only one who can help her."

"I can't help her, Emma," he said softly. "She must work it out with the Lord."

"Have *you* worked this out with the Lord?" I asked, needing to know if he accepted it.

"I trust the prophet." His tone told me that the conversation was over.

One evening he brought Elder Stowell to offer a blessing. The elder anointed Mother's head with oil and prayed aloud, saying he knew she was an earnest sister and that the Lord would convince her of the holiness of the principle. If she remained faithful, he said, the Lord would show her.

As he left, I followed him out the door.

"Brother Stowell," I began.

"Yes, child?"

I stuttered. I couldn't find the courage to speak the questions burning inside me: *Why? Why is this a holy and pure principle? Why must this be asked of my mother?*

Instead, I said, "Thank you," and my eyes filled with tears as he walked away.

My heart ached for my mother. I knew she was zealous in her belief of the Prophet Joseph Smith and the restored gospel. I had watched her devote everything to it. And in return it had brought her back to life. We had heard whisperings of polygamy—accusations shouted by those who taunted us on the streets—but she had not believed them. Neither had I. We couldn't avoid it anymore now that the elders were teaching it here in Liverpool.

I wondered if this would be the end of our membership in the church. I thought of Eliza, of the choir and pageants. I thought of the mission house and the meals. I didn't want to lose any of it. But I agreed with my mother about this so-called principle: It was a damnable practice.

On the fifteenth day my mother rose from bed early, two hours before Father was to leave for the docks. She woke us both and said she had a vision to relate.

"In the night the heavens were opened to me, and I was shown that Joseph Smith is truly called of God and that the Saints walk in the only faith leading to salvation. I beheld angels descending from above, gathering near Brother Stowell as he spoke. The sky itself bore witness that the words he carries are meant for all the children of this earth. I was made to understand that those who receive it will be preserved and that sorrow awaits those who turn away. Woe to any who reject this principle."

I watched with awe, and not a little confusion. A chill ran from the top of my head down to my toes. I couldn't reconcile her words with her appearance. Her chestnut hair was tangled and oily from a fortnight in bed. Her flannel gown hung askew. Her voice was calm, even certain. But her lifeless green eyes betrayed her.

She said it was the Lord, but I believed she had surrendered—to the elders, to the weight of expectation, to our family's need to belong. But I didn't speak those thoughts aloud. They stayed hidden in my heart. So many of my thoughts remained concealed in those days. I was thirteen by that time, and I would not find my voice for several more years. My outward self was merely a reflection of the choices made for me.

What my father thought, I never knew. He never spoke of it again.

Life returned, for the most part, to the way it had been before the words "plural marriage" were first spoken by my parents. Father went to the docks each morning. I helped Mother with the mending. I committed large portions of scripture to memory. The principle of plural marriage was still whispered about, but I never heard much fuss about it again.

Not while we were in England.

CHAPTER FIVE

Life had settled into a gentle rhythm, and the year that followed was the happiest I could remember. But just after my fourteenth birthday, February 8, 1856, I began to feel something shifting. Nothing had changed outright, yet there was a restlessness in the air. I sensed the coming of a new season, but it wouldn't reveal itself to me.

Father worked longer hours at the docks, and Mother took in more mending and even some washing. I saw how hard they were working and knew they were making more money, but it didn't change the way we lived. We still ate our standard meals—porridge in the morning, and simple suppers of fresh fish and bread, smoked haddock with potatoes, or stewed mutton with barley. Indulgences were rare unless we were at the meeting house, and even then, only on special occasions.

Mother softly sang hymns as she worked late into the night, rocking in the oak chair Father had built for her when I was a baby. It creaked against the rough wooden planks of our floor. I felt comforted by her melodic voice and the familiar rhythm of the chair. Sometimes she asked me to read to her from the Book of Mormon while she stitched, and sometimes Father read to us both.

My parents' faith had only deepened in the year since the crisis over plural marriage, and my father had been ordained a priest.

I had begun to think that they were saving money for a better home. On lonely nights I would lay on my narrow cot and imagine us moving into a little stone cottage with a thatched roof and honeysuckle that climbed up the side.

There would be a garden out back, with rows of cabbages and carrots and daffodils just for me. Daffodils were my flower, Father always said. They were often the first flowers to bloom each year, and they sprung from the earth the day I was born. When we had a warm February, he would cut a bouquet for my birthday. I loved the way the bright yellow petals were sometimes dusted by a late snow. Yes, there would be daffodils outside my window at our new house.

I'd have my own room of course. Eliza would come for tea parties, and we would gossip and read books under the shade of our own maple tree.

It was a silly dream, and I should have known better.

In late April I learned the truth. The news that would alter the course of my life forever. My parents had not been saving for a home. They had been saving for our passage to America.

We were going to Zion.

"We'll be takin' the last ship of Latter-day Saints to sail this year," my father said proudly when he shared the news after supper one evening. "The *Horizon*."

I knew from their faces that they expected me to be excited, and perhaps a year ago I would have been. But now it was different. I had become contented with our life in England, and I feared the plural marriage practiced in Zion.

We were no longer struggling so much. I had friends at the meeting house. I had the choir, the place where I felt most like myself. My parents were happier now, and their joy filled our dank little home with more warmth than I had ever known in Wiltshire.

"Wait until you see it." Father leaned forward, eyes alight with excitement. "We're going to the Promised Land, the New Jerusalem. There's land and homes and food for everyone. They say it's the most beautiful valley you've ever seen, Emma."

"What's more important," Mother added, her green eyes serious, "is that the Lord is calling us there. He commands that the Saints gather." She expected no argument.

I nodded. It was all I could do. But I felt like I was drowning.

If they said any more words, they were distorted by the waves of emotion coursing through my head and my heartbeat throbbing in my ears.

All I could hear in my mind was what my mother had said: *"Polygamy! Men havin' more than one wife. And they're practicin' it in Zion!"*

Anger rose inside me, my cheeks burned, and my hands clenched in my lap. I didn't know what the feeling meant, only that it consumed me. I wanted to throw a Book of Mormon at somebody.

Would Father have another wife? Would I have two mothers, or even three? I couldn't comprehend it.

Land and homes … and extra wives for every man. Had they forgotten? Father wanted blessings. Mother wanted obedience. Nobody had ever asked me what I wanted. Nobody ever did.

The next morning we walked the familiar cobblestone streets to the meeting house for Sunday services. The din of the city was a little quieter. I saw other families dressed in their Sunday best walking to church, the solemn toll of church bells calling them to worship at St. John's, where we would have gone before my parents found the restored gospel.

I watched a small boy kick an old sardine can down the road, and I pondered my parents' announcement, with thoughts tossing around in my head like the sardine can bouncing against the cobblestone. It wasn't as if I had a choice. I couldn't stay alone in England. I would be setting sail, crossing the sea, and gathering with the Saints in the Utah Territory. If I had reservations, what place did a fourteen-year-old girl have to voice them? The decision was already made.

As we approached the mission, I saw Eliza and ran ahead.

"I have to tell you something," we both said.

"I'm going to Zion," we cried, again in unison.

We collapsed to our knees, each sighing in relief. Whatever happened now, Eliza and I would have each other.

"I don't really want to go," I confessed. "But I'm so glad you're going with me."

"Maybe it won't be so bad," Eliza said. "I'm just praying my mama will be happier there. She cries every night here. It can't be worse than our life now." Eliza was ever the optimistic one. I hoped she was right.

The next few weeks were alive with activity as my parents got their affairs in order and we prepared to leave. There were tickets and paperwork and medical checks to be completed. Each evening Mother and I worked on packing the steamer trunk. One steamer trunk. That's what our life in England had to be reduced to.

In addition to our clothing and scriptures, we carefully wrapped my great-grandfather's pocket watch, a handmade butter dish that my grandfather had carved before Mother was born, a small wooden box of letters, a tin of dried medicinal herbs, and a length of lace my mother had once sewn into her wedding dress. My great-grandmother's silver brooch, wrapped carefully in linen, would be the only piece of jewelry we carried.

One evening when Mother thought I was sleeping, I watched her pull out my christening gown. It had also been William's christening gown, and I suspected that was how Mother thought of it as she ran her fingers gently over the delicate lace and tiny buttons. She placed it in the trunk, along with a small doll that she and I had both played with as little girls.

Each treasure, small as it was, made my throat tighten and my eyes water. These things were us. I didn't know what "us" would mean in

Zion. The thought scared me, and I couldn't tell anyone. Not even Eliza.

The next morning I took my books from under my bed. I couldn't take them all. I carefully tore Wordsworth's "We Are Seven" from Eliza's book, folded it, and tucked it into the pages of my leather-bound journal. I stuffed the journal and pen toward the bottom of the trunk. I still had never written in the journal, but perhaps I would start by keeping record of our voyage.

Maybe it was because I had become resigned to my fate, but as the day of our departure drew near, I couldn't ignore the tiny glimmer of hope inside me. I had to admit that the church's promises and my parents' faith and dreams were enticing.

Zion awaited. I wanted to believe in a land of plenty, where the Lord was gathering his people. Where every Saint would have a home and no one went hungry. No more stench of Liverpool's streets. No more nights lying in musty court housing listening to the rats scurry across the floor.

But even as I let the dream in, whispers of doubt found me in the night. *Will it be everything they promised? And what about polygamy?*

CHAPTER SIX

The morning air stirred with a warm, salty wind from the east on May 25, 1856.

"'Tis a right perfect day for sailing, Ruthie," Father said as he and Mother hoisted the steamer trunk onto a small wooden cart.

As we began our short walk to the docks, Mother smiled at him. "Aye, Heavenly Father is with us today."

The city was alive with its usual activity, oblivious to the fact that today would change everything for me. Fishmongers and carters filled the streets, with newsboys darting in and out of their paths. The markets were open, and mothers were about their morning shopping. Dirty children played or ran about trying to beg a ha'penny off passersby.

I drank in every sight but heard none of it. My thoughts were louder than the thundering sounds of the city. We were going to America. To Zion. I would board a ship and leave England forever. While the world I knew receded behind me, an unknown land full of both terror and possibility lay ahead. In that moment I longed to run both backward and forward, to laugh and to cry, to stay and to go.

I wore a simple cotton dress, navy blue with a small white floral pattern in the bodice. The fabric was faded but sturdy. Over my shoulders I had wrapped a brown woolen shawl fastened with a small brass pin, though the sun was already warm on my back. My curls had been brushed and gathered behind my head with a bright yellow satin ribbon that Father had given me the night before.

"Like a daffodil," he'd said. "You'll look right beautiful for the journey."

He pressed it into my hands, and I thought I saw tears in his eyes. Mother had sighed at the indulgence, but I thought it the most beautiful thing I had ever owned. A straw hat with a plain, modest brim sat atop my head, and a few rebellious curls framed my face.

As we approached the docks, I was taken aback by both the sounds and the scent. I couldn't count the number of ships and sails I saw. It was a towering skyline of vessels, all waiting to carry emigrants, travelers, and cargo across the seas. Dockworkers and seamen moved everywhere with purpose, hauling ropes, freight, food, and coal. Families clung to one another, while a few panicked parents searched frantically for lost children. I grabbed Mother's hand, and she squeezed mine tightly.

The stench of saltwater, fish, tar, and coal smoke nearly knocked me over. I had thought the smell strong in the city, but it was unnerving this close to the water. I heard dozens of languages as this mass of humanity converged in one place—everyone either departing or arriving, saying goodbye or greeting loved ones, or going about their work to make it all possible. There were as many seagulls squawking overhead as people scurrying below.

And then the whole world grew quiet as I saw it: the *Horizon*. Our ship. Our home for the next five weeks. A three-masted, fully rigged sailing vessel. The hull looked sturdy and freshly painted, with the word *Horizon* emblazoned on the bow.

The next few hours were a blur of dizzying chaos of lines, inspections, and jostling crowds. I remember mostly a desperate feeling of wanting to escape the madness. I clung to my parents and tried to block it all out. The next thing I remember was Father guiding me up the gangplank. I took one look back. And then I stepped forward into the unknown.

The ground immediately rocked beneath my feet. We weren't even sailing yet, but I felt the loss of my land legs at once. A porter took our trunk and guided us to our quarters in steerage. We descended below deck into a dimly lit, poorly ventilated compartment that smelled like wet wood and sweaty men. Father's six-foot frame stooped to avoid grazing the ceiling. Narrow bunks were stacked three high in rows of three.

Stewards shouted, moving people forward but mostly causing confusion.

Locating our berth, my parents and I stood together and took it all in. There was a small space at the end for our trunk, and a bunk for each of us. Mother on bottom, Father in the middle, and me on top. No one had room to fully sit up, the space was so tightly packed. There was a small shelf at the head of each bunk for personal belongings. The beds were covered with thin straw mattresses. We unpacked a quilt for each bunk. I placed my journal and pen underneath my mattress.

The bunks didn't bother me so much. I was used to sleeping on a small cot. But the idea of sleeping in the ship's hold with hundreds of people was another matter. I ran my hand along the rough wooden wall, suddenly aware of how deep below deck we were. I wondered how many layers of planks separated us from the sea. If water started seeping in, how would we escape in time? Would I even know before it was too late? I prayed I was not staring at my own watery grave.

I looked at Father and tried not to cry. "Is it safe?" I asked.

He placed a strong hand on my shoulder. "It's right safe and sound, Emma. The *Horizon* has already made several safe voyages across the sea."

He spoke confidently, but I watched him swallow hard. I saw the fear in his eyes too.

Mother clapped her hands together and said, "Let's go explore the deck and say goodbye to England." Her voice cracked as she reached the end of the sentence.

As we made our way out of steerage, I searched each bunk for Eliza and her mother. They were supposed to be here somewhere. *Please don't let them change their minds*, I prayed. I couldn't survive this without Eliza.

Mother seemed to understand. "They be here somewhere, Emmaline. Don't fret."

Back on deck we found a spot near the stern railing, and I held on tight as the ship groaned and pulled away from the dock. A strong gust of wind caught my shawl, whipping it against my back. I turned my face toward Liverpool. It was grand from this distance—church spires and smokestacks reaching toward the sky. It appeared more like the prosperous city I had imagined as a young girl. You couldn't see the hunger that gnawed at bellies, or the filth that spread disease and death. But I knew. And I would not soon forget.

We waved to the teeming crowd gathered to bid the ship farewell. Unlike many others, we had no family there. Most of the people we knew were aboard the ship.

Horizon carried about eight hundred passengers, all fellow Saints. They had come from all over England and places like Scotland, Wales, and Ireland. Many were from our own mission. I scanned the deck but still didn't see Eliza.

I turned back to my parents, and together we watched silently as Liverpool shrank behind our wake. Father looked proud and excited, but I saw that Mother's stoic face was wet with silent tears.

"William—" she choked out, reaching for my hand.

I squeezed it tightly, understanding what she couldn't say.

"We are four," I whispered.

They didn't hear me, and if they had, they wouldn't have understood.

Father, standing between us, wrapped his strong arms around our shoulders and pulled us close. We stood that way for a long time, watching England disappear. Before long we were surrounded by the slate-gray expanse of the Irish Sea, its restless waves carrying us toward an unknown future.

Our company was under the direction of Edward Martin and Elders Jesse Haven and George P. Waugh. They soon called all the Saints to gather on deck.

President Martin began his address: "Brothers and sisters, today we embark on a journey over sea and land—a journey of great significance to reach Zion, our Promised Land. Our faith in the Lord will be our guiding light as we stand united, assisting one another in time of …"

He kept talking, but I quit listening. I had spotted Eliza. She hadn't seen me yet. She stood with her mother about ten feet away. Eliza and I were the same age, barely fourteen, but we looked nothing alike.

Her satin-blonde hair was pulled into two tight braids, and she wore her prettiest calico dress. Lavender with deep purple flowers. It hung longer than mine, covering the tops of her black leather boots. The bodice was gathered and trimmed with lace. Her sky-blue eyes were set off by a matching bonnet adorned with delicate blue flowers and tied beneath her chin with a wide lavender ribbon. She looked like a girl who belonged in first class, not steerage.

But I knew the truth behind the lovely dress and bonnet. Eliza's father could afford fine clothes, but once the business debts had been settled after his death, most of their belongings were sold. These clothes were the only things of value she had left. Eliza and her mother were as poor as we were. They were placing all their hopes in this new faith and in the Promised Land across the sea.

I tugged at Mother's sleeve. "May I go stand with Eliza?"

"Yes, child. Go."

I snuck up beside Eliza and tickled her side.

"Emmaline!" she shrieked.

We giggled, and her mother had to shush us. President Martin was still speaking, currently outlining the daily schedule and explaining that work assignments would soon be handed out.

"Have you seen steerage yet?" I whispered to Eliza.

She nodded, wide-eyed. "It already smells like death down there," she said, wrinkling her nose.

I didn't like the sound of that, but I didn't disagree.

President Martin's voice drew my attention again as he finished his remarks: "Though challenges may arise, let us remember the promise that 'If God be for us, who can be against us?' Our destination is Zion, and with faith we shall arrive in safety."

Faith. Safety. Zion. I prayed every word was true. What else could I do?

CHAPTER SEVEN

The wind was still, and the sea lay like glass on the second Saturday in June 1856, making it terrible for sailing but perfect for playing a game of marbles on deck.

Eliza and I, along with several other children on the ship, were taking advantage of the calm while the adults worried about the wind needed to carry us toward Boston. If I'd learned anything in my weeks at sea, it was that the weather could change in an instant—and more marbles were lost to the sea than to other players.

I rolled a marble between my hands. "Alright now, who's ready to lose a cat's-eye?"

A red-headed boy named Thomas crouched low. "Not I," he said. "I've the steadiest hands in steerage." Thomas was only eleven, but he'd won my best marbles nearly every time we played.

He knelt lower and focused, the tip of his tongue sticking out a bit, and then flicked a clay marble into the circle, knocking out my polished stoney.

"Blast!" I cried. "You got my lucky one."

I had to laugh. It was impossible to be mad at Thomas, with his

39

crooked smile and silly swagger. At dinner he was usually the first to share an extra piece of bread.

"Me have it! Me have it!" A tiny boy with chubby cheeks and bright red curls had wandered into the middle of the game.

"Willy," Thomas groaned. "Go find Mummy. This is a game for big kids."

It was Thomas' little brother, William. The name stuck in my throat each time I heard it, but he had eyes as blue as the sea and his skin smelled like toffee. I laughed every time he ran around deck with his arms stretched out hollering, "I fly'n like a bird!"

"Oh leave him be, Thomas," I said. "Come sit with me, William." I pulled him into my lap and handed him a clay marble.

As Eliza began to make her move, the ship rocked, and the marbles went rolling. We dove for them, and I hoped Mother wasn't watching. I knew how unladylike I looked, but for one dizzy moment I didn't care. I just wanted to be a girl playing marbles. Not someone sailing toward a life I hadn't chosen.

Three weeks ago the ship rocking would have meant something else entirely. The whole company had been taken by seasickness for days, and we were more likely to lose our breakfast than our marbles.

By now the worst had passed, and we'd settled into a routine. Eliza and I had been assigned to assist with meal preparation. Each morning and evening, we hauled water to the cookhouse, swept floors, tended stoves, and piled plates with rations.

Between meals we were mostly free, except for scripture study and prayers in the late afternoons. Evenings were often cheerful, with music and dancing on many nights.

Daytime belonged to fresh sea air—to laughter, friendship, faith, and family.

But nighttime in steerage was another world. Snoring, coughing, and the wails of children echoed off the wooden walls. The stench of seasickness remained. My father had developed a cough that rattled the boards beneath me. I bore each night with great dread.

That's when the questions rattled my mind and the fears soured my belly. What awaited us on the other side of the sea? What if the promises weren't true? And what of polygamy? Sometimes when I looked around our company and saw the poverty among us all, I wondered if it wasn't faith, but desperation, that took us all across the sea. Yet I dared not say it aloud.

Mornings on deck were a relief from the endless nights. As soon as we finished our breakfast duties, Eliza and I sat near the stern, reading or writing.

A week after we set sail, I made my first journal entry:

June 10, 1856.

I am Emmaline. Fourteen. Of Wiltshire. Of Liverpool. Of the sea. I have a brother, but he is dead, and I am not supposed to talk about that. I go now to Zion, to the Promised Land across this ocean. My parents and my church say I will be happy there. What do I say will make me happy? I have never been asked.

Each day I wrote about things that happened on the voyage and tried to work out what I thought would make me happy. The first part was easy; the second was not. What I didn't understand then was that, at fourteen, I did not know who I was. And you cannot know what will make you happy until you know who you are—and who you are not.

Eliza and I were on deck one morning when I glanced up to see the ship's captain headed our way. Captain Reed was a kind man and a gentleman. Everybody liked him. He was as tall as Father, with a tuft of white hair and a trim white beard. His brass buttons sparkled in the sun.

"Girls, I've something to show you," he said. "If you're keen for a little adventure."

Eliza raised her eyebrows at me as I shut my journal and stood. I was curious enough to follow.

Captain Reed led us up a narrow staircase to the quarterdeck, where we would never have been allowed otherwise. Salty wind whipped my curls, and my blue scarf nearly flew off my head. It would have been a terrible day for marbles. I held tightly to the railing as the captain pointed out to the horizon.

"What do you see?" he asked.

"A ship," we squealed in unison, as if our words had been scripted.

"Would you like a better look?" Captain Reed asked, handing me his brass spyglass.

I nodded eagerly. I had seen ships from a distance, their white sails like ghosts on the horizon—but never through a spyglass. I stepped closer to the rail and held the cool brass to my eye, adjusting the lens as the captain had shown us. The sea jumped into focus. Blue waves rolled gently, and there in the distance was a grand ship with full sails billowing in the breeze. It looked close enough to touch.

"Where is it headed?" I asked, handing the spyglass to Eliza.

"From Boston back to England. Opposite of us."

"It's beautiful," Eliza whispered. "Like looking into a mirror. Do you suppose they're watching us?"

"Somebody on that ship is watching," the captain said thoughtfully. "It can be lonely out here."

"Sometimes the sea feels endless," I said. "Like we're just drifting or even going backward."

Captain Reed gestured toward the ship on the horizon. "But you see that vessel? When the sea swallows the world around you, look for another traveler. You may not feel yourself moving forward, but if you fix your eyes on a ship sailing the other direction, you'll begin to feel the motion."

After Eliza had a look, she handed the spyglass back to me, and I lifted it to my eye again. Captain Reed was right. The ship slipped slowly away, and in that moment I could feel it. We were the ones moving forward.

"Thank you, Captain," I said. "Thank you for showing us."

I still don't know why he picked us. Maybe he took other children to the quarterdeck whenever he had the chance. I was just grateful that he chose us that day.

His words lingered as I stared out over the sea. How many times had I felt alone in a sea of sorrow? How often had I felt like I'd never move forward? I couldn't wait to write about it.

If you fix your eyes on a ship sailing the other direction, you'll begin to feel yourself move forward.

"Run along now," he said. "Before your mothers think you're lost overboard."

Eliza and I had only started down the narrow staircase when I heard the word I most feared hearing while at sea.

"Fire!"

The captain cursed, pushed past us, and nearly knocked us over as he leapt down the stairs. I slammed into the wall, and Eliza slid down the steps on her backside. I picked myself up and followed quickly.

"Did they say fire?" I shouted.

"Yes!" Eliza cried. "I've got to find my mother!"

Chaos had erupted on deck.

"Fire! Fire!"

People were shouting, and fear ripped across the deck faster than flames.

The crew was already in action. Some sailors ran for fire buckets; others clambered up the rigging. A few flung open hatches, searching for smoke below deck.

Mothers clutched their screaming children. Men shouted over one another, some running toward the danger, others away, but it was hard to tell which was which.

I stopped and spun around. Where was the fire? Where was the smoke? I smelled nothing but salt air.

Then, through the noise, I heard a small, desperate cry.

"Mummy, Mummy, Mummy!"

I whipped around, nearly losing my footing as a man shoved past me.

I heard it again.

"Mummy, Mummy."

I followed the voice behind a stack of crates, my pulse pounding. Wedged between two barrels was a little boy. A red tuft of curls.

"William!" I gasped.

I had to be brave. I knelt in front of him and placed a trembling hand under his chin. His face was wet with tears. His arms were wrapped tightly around his knees. He looked so small, so defenseless.

I scooped him up. "Come with me, little lad. Let's find your mummy."

His hands locked around my neck, his tiny nails digging into my skin. I pulled him close, smelled the faint toffee on his skin, and felt his racing heart thudding against mine. Around us the shouts were becoming less frantic, more uncertain.

Then a familiar voice cut through the noise: "Emmaline! Where have you been?"

Father came running, flushed and breathless. He coughed deeply into his sleeve as he reached us, then bent over to steady himself.

"Your mother's half crazed with worry," he said, his voice rough but relieved.

"Is there a fire?" My voice cracked. I held William tighter, stroking his curls. "What's happening?"

Father exhaled and pulled us both into his arms. "It was a mistake. A misunderstanding," he said, laughing in disbelief. "A sailor aloft was shouting, 'Hoist higher! Hoist higher!' The wind twisted it, and someone thought he yelled 'Fire!' Then everyone lost their heads, Emma."

I leaned against him, my whole body exhaling. "So we're safe?" I whispered.

He kissed the top of my head and tousled William's curls. "Safe as can be, love. No fire. No danger. Now come. We've got two mothers to set at ease."

I nodded, loosening my grip on William as we crossed the deck. "We're safe, Willy. Let's go find Mummy."

All around us panic faded into sheepish murmurs and relieved laughter. Sailors shook their heads. Mothers wiped their eyes. Children looked around in confusion.

Captain Reed passed by and stopped to shake my father's hand. "Carry on, then," he said, giving me a wink and a pat on the shoulder.

I glanced up at the towering masts above us. No smoke. No fire. The sea was still calm. The sun still shone.

And, at last, I could breathe again. Everyone was safe for now.

CHAPTER EIGHT

I was sweeping in the cook room on a Tuesday morning after breakfast while Eliza scrubbed soot from a kettle with salt and an old rag. It felt so routine by then, I could hardly recall a day we hadn't done it. We both jumped when the door burst open and Thomas shouted, "Willy ain't breathin' proper. He's dyin'. I know it!"

William, who usually couldn't be kept still, had been coughing for a few days and had barely been out of steerage.

Eliza and I jumped up and followed Thomas down. There, William's mother cradled him. His eyes—usually bright with mischief—were sunken and gray. His chest heaved and drew in raspy breaths. He coughed so hard, he turned purple.

"Do something! Help him!" Thomas cried.

Eliza pulled Thomas to her side while I knelt down to William's face and stroked his forehead. His skin was clammy and his red curls dripped with sweat. He was delirious with fever. His mother tried to calm him and offered him water between coughing fits.

He turned away from the cup, but she pleaded, "Come, love, just a little sip."

My mother, who had followed us down, went to our trunk and pulled out our little tin of herbs. She sprinkled them into a cup of hot water and offered it to William's mother.

"These always help. Let him breathe the steam if he won't drink it."

His mother's voice broke as she begged, "Please, sweetheart. Just a sip."

My mother sat beside her, placing a steadying hand on her arm.

"His lungs have always been poor," she told my mother. "But I've never seen him so weak."

Thomas and William's father arrived with Elder Haven, who brought the anointing oil. Elder Haven's voice sounded confident as he asked us to make way, but I noticed sorrow in his eyes. Or was it fear? He closed them for a moment, as if in silent prayer, and then dipped his fingers into the oil and gently touched William's forehead.

"Our Father in Heaven, we come before thee with humility. We seek thy mercy and thy will. We place our hands upon thy son, William, and ask thee to look upon him with kindness. We ask for his healing. That his lungs may be strengthened. That his breath may come easy once more. And, Father, we ask that he may be restored to his mother's arms in health and joy."

Thomas stood between Eliza and me. He sniffled and rubbed his sleeve across his nose. "He's gonna be alright, ain't he?"

"Yes, of course," I whispered. "My parents told me all about the healing services. The Lord does great miracles when the elders pray." I was convinced we would see a miracle in little William's lungs—just like the children healed in Liverpool.

William's mother let out a quiet sob. Her husband placed a firm hand on her shoulder.

Elder Haven wavered slightly. But he continued, "Yet, Lord, if it is thy will to call him home, we pray that thou wilt receive him in love and light."

Call him home? They said the elders could heal. That miracles came with faith. That we were safe now. We didn't have our faith and the restored gospel when our William died. But we had it now. Why was Elder Haven giving up?

"Let angels bear him up that he may know no more pain or suffering. And grant comfort to those who love him, that they may feel thy peace in the midst of sorrow."

For once, steerage was silent. I could hear only the sound of William's labored breathing.

"Thy will be done. In the name of Jesus Christ, amen."

A chorus of amens followed.

I waited for the miracle, but none came. We all watched helplessly as William drew his last breath and went limp in his mother's arms. And then her low, guttural moan filled steerage. Thomas collapsed into his father's arms. Little William was gone.

I could see nothing through my tears, but I took off running through steerage, up the narrow stairways to the deck, and across the ship. I did not stop running until I found the barrels William had hid behind the day of the fire scare. I collapsed there, and my grief erupted. I pounded the deck with my fists.

Why? Why did you let him die? We prayed. They anointed him with oil. We're going to Zion just as you commanded! We did everything right.

I remembered a verse I had memorized from 3 Nephi 17:7 in the Book of Mormon: *"Have ye any that are sick among you? Bring them hither. Have ye any that are lame, or blind, or halt, or maimed, or leprous, or that are withered, or that are deaf, or that are afflicted in any manner? Bring them hither and I will heal them."*

I trembled with anger. I could not comprehend what I had witnessed. *Why? Why? Why?* I stayed there for what seemed like hours, but no answers ever came.

The sea had nearly swallowed the sun when my father found me. He did not say a word, but sat down beside me and shared the silence.

"I don't understand," I finally said.

"Truth be told, I don't either, Emmaline. The Lord's ways are not our ways. He sometimes asks us to accept his will over our own. Faith means trustin' even when we're not understandin'."

I nodded, but I did not accept it. I didn't know if my faith could withstand such pain and sorrow.

A piece of me died with little William that day. I was not so sure I wanted to cross an ocean for a God who broke my heart like this.

Later, I learned about burial at sea. William would not even have a grave.

I watched with my parents as they lowered his little body into the water, wrapped in a sailcloth and weighted down with stones. I'm sure it couldn't have been real, but I felt I smelled toffee in the breeze. The entire company of Saints had gathered. We sang a hymn, the words of which I could not remember. I listened but did not join in the prayers said as his body was committed to the water.

Several more children would die before we reached Boston. Pneumonia, dehydration, fever. Each body buried at sea. Each one ripping a bigger hole in my faith.

During our five-week voyage, we experienced more than just death. There was also new life. Two babies born, three couples married. We grieved. We celebrated. We carried on.

But after little William's death, I felt more like a spectator than a participant. It was difficult to accept that the Saints could move forward while some families still mourned. I knew the sorrow of losing a brother, the impact that losing a child had on a family. I didn't know how to reconcile such deep grief with such joyous occasions. The adults around me modeled the faith they wanted me to have, but no one told me how to find it for myself.

A week before we were due to arrive in Boston, I rose one morning to find Eliza crying on deck. I ran to her.

"What is it? What's wrong?"

"My mama," she sobbed, unable to finish.

"Is she sick?" I asked.

It took Eliza a dreadful long time to answer. "No. She is … She is to be married."

"Married?" I cried. "Has she been … keeping company?"

"No!"

I didn't understand. Who would she marry?

"It's Elder Monson. The missionary from Utah," she said, then sobbed uncontrollably.

I glanced behind my back to see if anyone else was listening to us. "But he's married," I whispered. "He has a wife in Zion. They have children."

She nodded and wiped away her tears. "They say Mother and I shouldn't travel alone. The journey to Utah will be too difficult. He can take care of us."

My blood ran cold. I had known, in some distant way, that this would become real to us, that plural marriage was not just a doctrine whispered about in England but something we would have to face. But now? Like this?

"Does your mother want to be wed?" I asked.

"She will only say that the Lord commands it, that it's her sacred duty, and that he provides. I think she's quite addled, but she won't admit that to me."

I swallowed hard. "When will it happen?"

"Once we reach Iowa City," she said, barely above a whisper.

Iowa City was where the Saints were gathering to prepare for the journey by foot to the Utah Territory. It was our next destination after Boston.

And there it was. The arrangements had already been made. Perhaps even before we left England. Perhaps Elder Monson had written ahead to Utah to receive approval.

Or maybe Brigham Young himself sent a message commanding it. Perhaps Elder Monson's wife didn't even know. I imagined her waiting for her husband to return, never suspecting he would bring home another woman as his bride.

Everything inside me felt wrong. I wanted to run to my mother. But I remembered her vision. "Woe to any who reject the principle," she had said.

Was there really anyone I could turn to with these thoughts?

I hugged my friend. "I am so sorry."

I didn't know what else to say. Every day brought us closer to the life they had chosen for us. A life I wasn't sure I could bear.

CHAPTER NINE

We arrived in Boston on June 30, 1856, after five weeks at sea. The weather had been unusually kind to us throughout the voyage. There were a few mild rainstorms, but we never faced rough seas. The only real storm was the one brewing in my heart.

I stood near the bow with my parents, Eliza and her mother, and Thomas' family as the ship approached Boston Harbor. Regardless of what had come before or what lay ahead, my chest ached with wonder as my eyes settled on land once again.

The first thing that came into focus was a tall, stark white lighthouse. The land beneath it was rocky and jagged, but this towering beacon had guided ships safely to shore for generations. Now it guided me toward my new life.

Beyond the lighthouse, the city emerged. Steeples and spires, ship masts and smokestacks rose against the sky, not unlike Liverpool. But here we could also see green spaces. Grass. Trees. Though the harbor bustled with life, it was quieter, calmer than Liverpool had been.

We gathered as a company of Saints, and Brother Martin spoke to us about the journey ahead. The Utah Territory lay more than two thousand miles away—nearly two-thirds the span of the American continent. That very day we would board the rail cars to Iowa City, which was as far as the railroad could take us. That would get us about halfway. As other Saints before us had done, we would push our belongings on handcarts.

The plan, which had sounded like an adventure when we spoke of it in England, now seemed absurd. For the first time, I considered what it truly meant to walk more than a thousand miles. To cross plains and mountains on foot. It occurred to me that we would have no ready shelter, no protection from wind or rain. We had never slept outdoors. Never cooked over an open fire. We were not frontiersmen.

Beside me, Thomas whispered, "My father's changed his mind. We ain't going no more."

"What?"

His family had decided to stay in Boston or perhaps eventually go to New York. The trek would be too arduous for his mother, who had taken ill after little William's death.

"Stay on with us," I heard Thomas' father urge mine. "We'll find work here, no trouble. We know the docks well enough. Zion can wait till next year."

Brother Martin's voice rang out over the gathering: "This journey will not be an easy one, but the Lord has commanded it. Woe to you who consider disobedience. The Lord has delivered you from England, from the very depths of Babylon. He is gathering up his people in Zion. The Prophet Joseph Smith prophesied that those who do not gather will be afflicted by the devil, you and your children."

My father shook his head at Thomas' father. My mother looked on with scorn.

Truth be told, part of me wanted to stay. To go to New York and begin a life in America now instead of trudging across the wilderness on my own two feet. To end up in a place where my father might take another wife. But I also feared the poverty of the city. And more than that, I feared having the devil loosed upon us.

"We will do as the Lord commanded," my father finally said.

I knew my parents' faith was unshaken, their loyalty to the church sincere. But what was I to think of a God who asked this much of us? A God who threatened us with the devil if we faltered?

Had the Lord not been contented with me for being baptized into this faith? Had he not been contented with those who crossed an ocean for him and buried their babies at sea? Would he not be contented if we worshipped in Boston, or New York, or Iowa City?

It occurred to me for the first time that perhaps the Lord would never be contented with me.

Eliza and I fell in step behind our parents as we walked to the train station. We were dressed as we had been the day we first boarded the *Horizon*—in our Sunday best. My skin was tanned and wind-chapped from weeks at sea, and my curls were more unruly than ever. Mother had pulled them into a single braid and fastened the bottom with my yellow satin ribbon.

Eliza's skin was as fair and beautiful as ever. On the outside she appeared untouched by the voyage, but I could see what was on the inside. She, too, had been forever altered. She now walked toward a future as another man's daughter. A man she and her mother barely knew. And then there was the matter of having a second mother. My heart ached for my friend.

As we walked, I asked how she was feeling.

"I miss my papa. I wish he hadn't died," she said, her shoulders slumping and her feet dragging. "I wish we hadn't had to leave. But I do believe the Lord found us and that he has saved us. If we follow him, he will see us through."

She said the right words, but her voice trailed off, and she looked back toward the sea. It was hard to believe she felt more at peace about this than I did.

I didn't wish to make this more difficult for her. I wanted us both to find joy in the Promised Land.

"Yes," I said. "He will see us through." I hoped I sounded more certain than I felt. The words were for her, not for me.

Some in our company, like Thomas' family, had decided to stay in Boston, either because they lacked the funds to go on or because they no longer wished to. Others had been detained for quarantine due to illness. But most were devoted to following the call to Zion, and our company was still at least six hundred strong as we moved through Boston like a bedraggled army.

Everything we owned, we carried with us. Trunks and carpetbags, crates full of provisions to last us through a week on the train.

Boston's streets were not unlike Liverpool's, but they were cleaner. The *clip-clop-clip-clop* of horses and buggies was loud at first but soon edged out by the sheer number of us filling the road.

I found that instead of observing Boston as I walked, Boston was observing me.

The streets were lined with fine ladies in coats and bonnets, men in suits carrying leather satchels, street vendors, newsboys, children skipping rope, and even dirty little ones who might have been transported straight from the streets of Liverpool, begging for their dinner.

All stood aside, watching as the Mormons paraded through their city toward the railroad.

I felt terribly conspicuous. And, for reasons I didn't quite understand, ashamed.

What a spectacle we must have been.

We soon learned that the Saints attracted the same ridicule here as we had in England. Men with American accents heckled and jeered, just as the English had done.

As the jeering grew louder, my mother pulled me close and we walked arm in arm. She whispered, "'Blessed are they which are persecuted for righteousness' sake.'" It was a verse we had heard often.

In that moment I didn't understand all my feelings, but I was very anxious to board our train and leave Boston behind.

I didn't have to wait long. The ground soon rumbled beneath my feet, and the air filled with the piercing wail of a steam locomotive. My hands shot up to protect my ears from the roaring engine. The sound reverberated off nearby buildings and engulfed my body, drowning out whatever thoughts I was having.

Then came the smell. My nose and eyes burned from the acrid scent of coal burning in the firebox, along with the sharp tang of grease and oil on the rods and pistons.

We all spread out for a better look as the train approached the station. A wrought iron fence lined the perimeter of the building, which was long and made of soot-stained red brick with a gabled roof. Wooden eaves lined the front to protect passengers from the weather, and a central clock tower marked the main entrance, which was alive with activity.

Like the docks, the train station was a place for hellos and goodbyes, endings and beginnings. People scurried like ants in their comings and goings, and few had time to gawk at the large gathering of salt-stained, sea-worn Mormons who had drawn such attention on the road.

We didn't have to wait in line at the ticket counter, as our passage had been paid ahead by elders in the Boston mission. Brother Martin led us around the side of the building to board the train.

That was when I found out we would not be riding in passenger cars but cattle cars. This was also the first time I witnessed my mother question or complain about the journey.

Her shoulders dropped, and her tired eyes glared at my father as the reality of our situation settled in.

"We're to be treated as livestock," she muttered.

"Lord, give us the strength to endure what we must," Father

whispered, just loud enough for Mother and me to hear.

Even as they spoke, we were jostled into the car and shoved next to others in conditions more cramped than steerage had been. There was nowhere to sit, except atop our trunks and crates. It smelled of manure, and there were no windows. The only ventilation came through the open slats in the sides of the car.

A short, dark-haired woman with a warm smile and a clean calico dress of deep blue with bright yellow sprigs sat across from my mother and noticed her distress. She reached out and lightly touched Mother's arm, speaking in an American accent.

"I know it seems terribly dreadful," she said cheerfully, "but I've made the trip before, and it's not so bad. We'll be there before you know it."

My mother looked confused. "Why? That is … how did you come to do it twice?"

The woman smiled kindly. I liked her already.

"I come from Boston," she said. "I traveled with the Saints last spring and have been in Iowa City, planning to go west with a handcart company. But my brother took ill, so I came back to settle his affairs and bring his girls." She motioned to two small children sitting beside her primly. "We're ready to head west now."

Mother nodded but did not look convinced.

"My name is Cordelia Hathaway," the woman continued. "But please call me Delia. And these are my nieces, Ellie and Olivia."

Sister Delia appeared to be about my mother's age. She had thick hair the color of well-steeped tea, pinned up in a chignon. Ellie and Olivia appeared to be twins, about six years old. They both had Delia's dark hair and brown eyes. Each sat with folded hands, as if in a schoolroom rather than a cattle car. They looked like girls who had already learned to endure hardship in silence.

My mother introduced our family, and then Eliza's mother did the same.

"I have something," Delia said, digging into a carpetbag. "These might cheer us up." She brought out about ten apples and passed them to us and the others sitting in our corner of the car.

Apples! It was grand. I hadn't had fresh fruit since we left England. We all cheered at the treat, and smiles and laughter returned to faces that had been soured by thoughts of the journey ahead.

About that time, the train lurched forward, and I covered my ears again in anticipation of the piercing wail of the whistle.

As the cattle car began a rhythmic rattle down the tracks, I took a bite of my apple. The sweet taste melted into my tongue, and pleasure spread through my body and soul. My father and I locked eyes, and he gave me a wink.

"There's no going back now," he said.

Indeed there was not.

And though all my doubts remained, they would now travel with me across the continent.

CHAPTER TEN

woke with a start on the floor of the rattling cattle car after a short and uncomfortable nap between Pittsfield and Albany.

My heart raced, and sweat dripped down my neck as I peeled my sticky back away from the side of the car, where I'd propped myself after eating a lunch of salt pork and dry bread. My small ration of water had been warm and nowhere near enough to quench my thirst.

How long had I been asleep? Judging from the crick in my neck and ache in my backside, it felt like hours.

But golden afternoon light still filtered through the wooden slats in narrow bands, just as it had at lunchtime. I couldn't have been asleep long. Maybe an hour. I'd learned that one does not sleep in a cattle car until her body gives her no other choice.

As miserable as steerage had been on the *Horizon*, it was pure luxury compared to the train. The smell alone was torturous. I was overcome by fifty human bodies, most of whom hadn't bathed in five weeks, packed into a car recently used to haul cattle. With the stench of chamber pots and motion sickness, it was almost unbearable. But there was nowhere to escape.

Even if I managed to drift off, I'd be jolted awake by a screaming child, the wail of the train's horn, or the retching of a passenger who couldn't keep down the last meal.

My parents sat next to me on our trunk. Mother's head rested on Father's shoulder, both of them snoring lightly. I rejoiced that they could rest, but I didn't understand how they managed it.

Across from us, Sister Delia quizzed Ellie and Olivia on their letters. Her voice was soft and patient. The girls sat obediently on a quilt laid over the filthy floor, their identical dark heads bent over a battered primer. Ellie held a rag doll and Olivia a small stuffed lamb made of worn flannel. It was almost never out of her hands. The normalcy of it felt comforting, but I had a twinge of jealousy. They made it look so easy, carrying on as if the world weren't shaking beneath them.

Eliza and her mother sat in silence beside Elder Monson. My friend wiped away tears as her mother rubbed her temples—always a sign her head ached. I watched Elder Monson lean forward as if to say something to Eliza, but her mother raised a hand without looking up and shook her head. He closed his mouth.

I wanted to comfort Eliza. To reach for her hand, say something gentle, remind her I was still here. But my body was paralyzed with heat, misery, and confusion.

When I thought I couldn't take another moment, the train lurched to a halt at the Albany station. The wheels shrieked, a long, earsplitting wail as sparks flew where iron met iron. Dust and soot swirled in the air, blocking the sunlight and seeping in through the slats.

My father coughed as the soot filled his lungs. Others stirred, waking children, stretching stiff limbs, gathering belongings.

A voice called out above the din: "Albany! Albany Station! All passengers for Albany, disembark here!"

Brother Martin's voice boomed next: "Make haste! Use the privies and wash up while you can. Then make your way to the ferry slip. We'll cross the river by boat and board the westbound train on the other side. Be ready to depart in thirty minutes!"

The Hudson River reminded me of the Mersey—lined with docks and ships—but it lacked the salt air and scent of the sea. I couldn't imagine leaving our car behind and crossing a river in the open air, but Delia assured me passengers had crossed this way for years.

"There's nothing to fear, Emmaline," she said.

Olivia and Ellie watched her closely as she said it. Their wide, unblinking eyes told me they were afraid too.

I stood and reached for Eliza's hand. "Let's drink all the water until it's gone!" I cried, thirst driving my excitement.

But she jerked away. "Don't touch me! Don't talk to me!"

She ran from the car and disappeared behind the station. I froze.

A glance passed between her mother and Elder Monson. I heard him say, "I'll go," before hurrying after her.

Tears stung my eyes. Why was she angry with me?

I stood rooted in place, helpless. This man she barely knew had gone to comfort her, yet I was the one she pushed away.

Sister Delia put an arm around my shoulders. "Come with us to the fountains," she said gently. "Eliza will be alright. She's not angry with you."

I wiped my face and nodded. There was nothing I could do for her now. But I could drink. I could wash the soot from my skin and cool down.

Grabbing Ellie and Olivia by the hand, I said, "Let's go, girls!"

My parents and Sister Delia followed behind. We took turns cupping water from the pump and gulping it down. It was cool and clean, like a magic elixir. Nothing like the miserable stale water from the ship or the sour barrel in the cattle car. It shocked the heat out of my body.

Suddenly, water poured down my back. I gasped and spun around to find my father grinning, tin cup in hand. He poured the rest over Mother's head.

"James!" she squealed.

And then she did something I hadn't heard her do in a long time. She laughed.

She cackled and howled and grabbed the cup to fling water over Father's head. I snatched it next and flung water at Olivia, then Ellie.

They squealed with delight, yelling, "More! More!"

Sister Delia shocked us all by dunking her whole head under the pump. We giggled and followed her lead, taking breaks from our play to drink again and again.

It was like drinking joy itself. The water reached beyond my body, into some dry and hollow place I didn't know I had.

As we walked toward the Hudson to board the ferry, a gentle breeze touched my damp face. For the first time in weeks, I felt refreshed. Almost content. But that peace didn't stretch far.

Eliza pouted on the boat and avoided my eyes. I doubted Elder Monson could ease her sorrow; he was the source of it. But maybe that's how it had to be. He was going to be her new father, after all. She would have to learn to face him. I only wished I could make it easier.

Delia caught up with me and gave me a gentle squeeze. "Some burdens are not yours to carry," she said as we stood watching the Hudson. "Eliza has a heavy one just now. Heavenly Father will sustain her. Just be her friend when she's ready."

Though she'd only met me, Delia always seemed to know my heart. She saw me like no one else ever had.

"I don't always understand," I said quietly.

She smiled. "Faith doesn't always mean understanding. Sometimes it just means obeying."

She sounded like Father. I admired their faith. I wanted desperately to believe as easily as they did.

After a brief ferry crossing, we boarded the train waiting on the other side. It was another dark, breathless box that felt exactly like the one we'd left behind. I sat on the floor in front of my mother as she worked a comb through my damp, tangled curls. Her fingers were gentle, and I leaned into the rhythm of it, wishing I could stay there forever.

Our water play had crossed a barrier between us, if only for a moment. I longed to lay my head in her lap and let my tears fall. Tears for Eliza. Tears for my confusion. Tears for this strange and demanding religion.

But I knew she wouldn't abide such weakness. So I stayed quiet, stiffening my spine, and swallowing everything down.

Tomorrow, I told myself. *Tomorrow I'll be stronger.*

CHAPTER ELEVEN

"Buffalo! Buffalo Station! All passengers for Buffalo, disembark here!"

I jolted upright and tugged at Father's sleeve. "Come! Let's go!" I said.

Mother caught my arm before I could push forward. "Mind yourself, Emmaline," she scolded. "We shan't go anywhere until the way is clear."

I couldn't stand to wait. Buffalo meant three whole hours off the train. Three whole hours to stretch my legs, breathe fresh air, and escape the stench of the cattle car.

And today wasn't just any day. It was July 4, 1856—Independence Day.

Sister Delia had told all the children about the holiday. "America's birthday," she called it, the day they celebrated their freedom from England. We hadn't learned much about that in school, but I did know America had fought a war about a hundred years ago and won.

"Yes, and they make rather a grand show of it, don't they?"

Delia's story had been cut short by a sarcastic voice from the other side of the car. It was Gideon Ashford leaning against the wall, arms folded and smirking.

"A whole day to celebrate sticking it to the British, eh? How very American." His voice was laced with scorn.

A tall, blond boy of about seventeen, Gideon had been on the trip with us since England, but he was none too happy about it. He seemed to have some of the same reluctance about the church that I did, but he said things out loud that I barely dared think.

Gideon had the kind of face that could be charming—if he had ever smiled. Perhaps his lack of manners was because he didn't have a mother. Gideon traveled with his father, Eli Ashford, and gave him grief the entire voyage. But his father didn't have much patience for Gideon carrying on about America this way.

"It's your home now," snapped Brother Ashford in a tone that shut Gideon's bravado right down.

"It will never be my home," Gideon muttered.

That had been the end of that. But Gideon's attitude didn't dissuade me. My heart had been stirred by the idea of an American holiday. I was excited to see this new country, its people, and how it would be different from England.

We exited the train and went first to the water pumps, as we did at every stop. I was still gulping down water when I heard music.

A band was playing somewhere nearby. It was a familiar tune, and I began slowly following the sound. What was it?

It sounded like "God Save the Queen."

Yes, they were indeed playing "God Save the Queen."

How peculiar. But why would Americans honor Queen Victoria on their country's birthday?

I figured perhaps they had known a train of British emigrants was arriving.

I sang the familiar words softly under my breath as I searched for the band.

"Send her victorious,
Happy and glorious,
Long to reign over us,
God save the Queen!"

Around the backside of the train station, I saw a sprawling park with a large oak pavilion in the center. It was decorated with red, white, and blue bunting and American flags. The band was playing, and a choir was preparing to sing.

I walked closer to the park, along with many in our company who had also heard the music. We saw horses and wagons tied up along the edge of the park, families seated on quilts with picnic baskets that filled the air with the smell of roasted meats. I hungrily eyed a spread of chicken, cornbread, and several pies laid out by a family near me.

And then the choir began to sing. It was the melody I knew so well, but the words were different. This wasn't "God Save the Queen."

"My country, 'tis of thee,
Sweet land of liberty,
Of thee I sing;
Land where my fathers died,
Land of the pilgrims' pride,
From ev'ry mountainside
Let freedom ring!"

Liberty. Freedom. I turned these words over in my head, wondering what they meant in this country and what they meant for me.

If liberty looked like this park, I wanted it.

"Let music swell the breeze
And ring from all the trees

Sweet freedom's song
Let mortal tongues awake
Let all that breathe partake...."

I longed to have the freedom of running around with other kids in the grass—playing tug-of-war or contending in sack races like these American children. I longed to lie in the shade of a maple tree, listening to music and feasting on a picnic basket full of food.

The families looked so happy and carefree. Laughter rang out from every corner of the park. I couldn't help but notice how clean they looked, dressed in their Sunday best. How long had it been since I had a bath and a clean dress?

"Let all that breathe partake."

Suddenly, I felt a tickle at my waist, and Eliza was at my side.

"I'm sorry. I have been horrible to you. It's only—"

I cut her off with a big hug. "You don't have to explain."

A huge smile lit up her eyes. I hadn't seen her happy all week. She held out her hands, something mysteriously cupped inside them, then asked, "Can you guess?"

"What?" I asked, curious about what had put such a smile on her face.

She pulled me behind a tree and opened up her hand, revealing a large coin.

"Elder Monson gave it to me. It's for us. You and me. He said we can buy anything we want from the food carts."

"Truly?" I squealed. "How much is it?"

"It's a fifty-cent piece!"

If Eliza had any reservations about accepting such a gift from Elder Monson, I imagined her rumbling stomach had outweighed them. Mine certainly did.

I turned my attention to the outskirts of the park, where food carts were gathered. The proprietors were hollering:

"Lemonade!"

"Popcorn!"

"Hand pies!"

They seemed to have everything. Roasted nuts, sandwiches, grilled sausages, sarsaparilla, candy. How would we choose?

We walked among the vendors and considered our choices. I noticed we had attracted the attention of a group of boys about our age.

"Phew! I reckon them girls smell worse than the cows in those cattle cars," one said intentionally loud enough for us to hear.

"Mormons don't believe in baths, it seems," said another.

Heat rose inside of me. Why were people cruel to us everywhere we went?

A woman at a lemonade cart rebuked the boys and then said to us sternly, "Food costs, girls. You got American money?"

Eliza's face went red with shame. She looked like she might run.

I grabbed the coin and held it out to the woman. "This will do?" I asked.

The woman's tone changed. "Why yes, dear. That will work."

"We'll take two lemonades—*with ice*." I looked at the boys when I said the last part, to let them know we could afford the extravagance.

The boys kicked the dirt and walked away at this development, our presence no longer an amusement.

We also bought two sausages, two apple hand pies, and a bag of salted peanuts. Eliza wrapped the change in Elder Monson's hanky. I could tell she wanted to return the change to him, to show him she was responsible with the money. She appeared to be coming around to her situation.

We found a place to sit down under the biggest maple tree in the park.

"Well," Eliza said, brushing invisible crumbs off her lap. "I suppose those boys never had a meal so grand."

We giggled.

I knew it wasn't true, and so did she. But it was fun to pretend.

I carefully ate half of my sausage and half of my pie, then wrapped them in my scarf and hid them in my skirt to save for my parents. We slowly ate peanuts and drank our lemonade. I sucked the salt off each peanut and let every piece of ice sit in my mouth until it melted all over my tongue. My senses were alive with the tastes and sensations of the meal and the fresh breeze at my back.

On the other side of the podium, a man with a deep baritone voice began to recite something called the Declaration of Independence: "'We hold these truths to be self-evident, that all men are created equal, that they are endowed by their Creator with certain unalienable rights, that among these are life, liberty, and the pursuit of happiness.'"

"'Life, liberty, and the pursuit of happiness,'" I repeated to Eliza. "Don't you think that's beautiful?"

"Um-hmm," she responded absentmindedly.

"Do you believe we are pursuing happiness?" I asked her. "I mean this journey. Is it a pursuit of happiness?"

She shrugged. "It's Zion," she said as if that was an answer.

I stared at her, and she finally said, "We're following the Lord. That is our happiness."

I had no answer for that.

"My parents will be wondering where I am," I said, fingering a large maple leaf that had floated to the ground in front of me. I intended to save it and press it in my journal. I wanted a piece of this park with me forever. I wasn't sure what Zion held for me, but I would hold this version of America in my heart always.

Eliza nodded. "We'd best go find our parents now."

We walked toward a larger gathering of our company. I spotted Mother and Father on a park bench, sharing a cup of lemonade. I was glad they had treated themselves to a small indulgence, though I noticed there was no ice.

I ran to sit with them and brought out the rest of my lunch for them to share.

A look passed between my parents. Mother's face showed love, pride, and a little sadness. She placed her hand on my knee and softly patted my leg.

"Emma, love, that's for you," Father said. "We don't want to be eatin' your food."

"Oh, I'm stuffed full," I lied. "I couldn't possibly eat another bite."

Mother nodded at Father, and he took out a pocketknife to slice the remaining sausage and hand pie in two. It wasn't more than a few bites for each of them, but I recognized the pleasure on their faces as their bodies registered the sensations of the food.

"Emmaline, did you thank Elder Monson proper?" I knew Eliza's mother had explained the gift to my parents.

"Not yet, but I will."

The train whistle sounded, reminding me that our stay in Buffalo was coming to an end. Brother Martin was weaving through the crowd, reminding the Saints it was almost time to board the cattle cars again.

I noticed Gideon sitting at the train station, slumped against the wall, chewing a piece of grass. His blond hair half covered his royal-blue eyes. I felt it silly to miss the celebration out of bitterness, but I supposed it was his choice.

We lined up at the outhouses to take care of business, then we washed our hands and faces one more time before climbing into the train to finish the long ride to Iowa City.

Back in the car I noticed a great variation in the moods of our people. Some had clearly had the means to spare a few coins for a treat at the park; others had not. Some, like me, looked inspired by the American celebration of liberty and freedom. Others looked like they had soured over the offense to Britain. Most just looked weary.

Once we got moving, Sister Delia passed out penny candies to all the children. I saw her stop in front of Gideon, her hand outstretched. He hesitated, but he took it. Lying back against the wall of the car, I felt more satisfied than I had in weeks. I drifted off peacefully, not knowing this would be my last happy moment for years.

71

CHAPTER TWELVE

We arrived in Iowa City on July 8, 1856, weary from travel and in need of rest. It should have been a brief stay. But the handcarts weren't ready.

Instead of covered wagons like most westward travelers used, Mormon emigrants walked across the country pushing their belongings in handcarts. It was a prophetic plan meant to allow thousands of Saints like us to move affordably and efficiently. We should have camped only a handful of days in the large Mormon quarters where everyone gathered for final preparations before the westward trek to Zion.

But something had gone wrong—I was never told what—and the handcarts were not built for our company. What should have been several days at the Iowa City camp turned into several weeks.

By then we had spent five weeks at sea and ten days by train, an experience that had been at times adventurous and at times miserable. I had endured discomfort, hunger, and exhaustion. There was both sorrow and happiness in the memories I had made thus far.

Though we slept on the ground and cooked over open firepits—a skill Mother and I learned as we went—I felt relief at camp. The air was fresh, the nights warm, and the earth solid beneath me for the first time in two months. We could bathe in the river and wash our clothes, a luxury after the weeks aboard the ship and the cattle cars.

I did not despair over the lack of solid shelter. The conditions were mild, and nothing felt more inviting than the fresh, open air. Not since Wiltshire had I breathed so freely.

While many in our company grew frustrated by the delay, I welcomed the respite. We gathered in the evenings for hymns and prayers. Music always steadied my soul. My spirits rose when we sang "Come, Come, Ye Saints" together:

"Come, come, ye Saints, no toil nor labor fear;
But with joy wend your way.
Though hard to you this journey may appear …
All is well! All is well!"

I wasn't sure yet if it was faith, but I finally felt a measure of comfort. There were moments when I could almost understand why we had endured so much to be here together. I found solace in the community. Nobody bothered us here. I went to sleep each night with a growing admiration for the faith and sacrifices of the Saints.

When the first whispers of fear finally found me, I realized how little I had thought about what lay ahead.

~

"Emmaline, we're making soap this morning," Sister Delia said. "Would you join us?"

She posed it as a question, but I knew it was an expectation. President Martin had asked Sister Delia to organize the women and children in domestic tasks.

Mother looked up from mending a canvas tent to give me a nod and look that said, *"Do as you're asked."*

I enjoyed making soap, especially when I worked with Sister Delia, so Mother need not have worried. I preferred it to helping watch the children, which I was sometimes asked to do. This morning a girl named Julie Ann had that duty. She was taking Ellie and Olivia, along with several other little ones, swimming in the creek before going on a hunt for twigs to help start fires. Everybody helped; every effort mattered.

"Emmaline," Sister Delia said, "please help Gideon at the fat-rendering station while we set up the ash hopper."

Gideon stood near a chopping block, sleeves rolled, knife glinting in the sunlight. The day was already sweltering, and beads of sweat ran down his face from the fire he had built for the cast-iron melting pot. A pile of raw pork fat sat beside him, thick, yellow, and putrid, waiting to be melted into tallow. He worked methodically, his blade slicing through with a sound both wet and solid.

Suddenly, this day promised to be less than idyllic. Working with the surly, sour-faced Gideon while inhaling the rotting smell of fat sounded dreadful.

But I was not one to argue in those days. I did as I was told.

Gideon handed me a large stirring stick, and I silently began working while he chopped. The fat melted slowly and then had to be strained for impurities.

We worked silently for a while, him chopping, me stirring. My mind wandered in the quiet, and I scanned the camp. Eliza—dressed in her Sunday best, the lavender calico and bonnet that she wore on our first day at sea—was climbing into a buggy with her mother. I could not see who else, if anyone, was with them. The driver cracked giddy-up, and they took off in the direction of town.

I wondered what that was about.

"Watch yerself," Gideon hollered. "You're burning yer skirt!"

I jumped back. He was right. In my carelessness, I had moved too close to the fire and singed my skirt. Fortunately, I had not burned my legs.

Gideon scowled, grabbed my stick, and stirred the pot with unnecessary force.

I smoothed my skirt, still shaken from the near mishap, and glanced at him warily. I was accustomed to his gloomy attitude, but something seemed different about him today. His lips were pursed, and his eyes were cross. He worked angrily.

We returned to our jobs in silence. The fat popped and sizzled in the heat. The smell was worse now, thick in the air. I choked it down when I breathed.

"She oughta be careful," Gideon muttered.

I looked up. "Who?"

"Eliza." He flicked his knife in the direction of the buggy, now a distant speck on the road. "Off to town, dressed up all fine. My pa says she and her mother have been seen with Elder Monson more than's proper. You know what that means."

I frowned. "It's not improper. Elder Monson is a leader in the church. He looks after the Saints."

Gideon snorted. "Is that what they tell you?"

"What is your meaning?" I asked.

He shook his head. "Just watch out. It's her and her ma now. It'll be you next."

I blushed as understanding came over me. *This must be the sealing day.* That's what we called celestial marriages—sealings. I didn't realize it would happen in secret. I had expected a wedding in camp one evening, with music and dancing, like the weddings on the ship.

"Eliza doesn't have a father anymore," I said in retort. "I do."

After a pause I continued, more sharply than usual, "They will not seal my mother to another man."

His eyes narrowed like he was thinking on how to respond. Thinking up something cruel to say. "Your pa's got a bad cough, ain't he? That's not so good for cold weather."

Cold weather? We were standing there sweltering in the heat of July.

"My father is as strong as an ox," I said. "He's building handcarts every day."

Gideon wiped his brow, then lowered his voice. "I heard my pa talking to some of the elders last night. Some of 'em don't think we should leave yet. They asked President Martin to wait until next season."

I stilled. "And?"

"He won't." Gideon's grip tightened on the knife. "He says we've got to go. No matter what. Brigham Young has commanded it, and he ain't goin' against the prophet."

I swallowed. Tried to make myself look confident. "The Lord is calling us to Zion," I said. "We're under his protection. Besides, we are the fifth company to go this year. They know what they're doing."

He scoffed, leaned forward, and looked directly into my eyes. "We ain't ready, Emmaline," he whispered. "And if we go now, some of us ain't gonna make it."

I glanced around the camp. The hymn from the night before still echoed in my mind: *"All is well! All is well!"*

But despite what I had said to Gideon, I felt a shift. A crack in my confidence. I'd been trying hard to believe in the plan, in the Saints, and in our purpose. But if the men—the ones building our carts, the ones guiding us west—were uncertain, should we not be as well?

Gideon saw my hesitation. He wiped his knife clean on his apron and leaned in. "You want to know what they said? They said it's too late in the season. They said we'll never make it before the snow."

I sighed and thought about what Sister Delia would say. "Surely President Martin knows best."

Gideon looked at me for a long moment, something unreadable in his expression. Then he spat in the dirt. "Guess we'll find out, won't we?"

It took me a few minutes to gather my thoughts and come up with a response. "May I ask you something?"

He didn't answer.

"Why do you stay? You're old enough to ride the rails to Boston. You could work for passage back to Liverpool. Why are you still here if you're so unhappy?"

His shoulders slumped, and he looked stricken at the question. He put down his knife and wiped his eyes. "My pa believes deeply," he finally answered. "He's determined to go. I won't let him go alone. Me and this church are all he has left. My mama and my sisters …" His voice cracked, and his eyes flickered with sadness.

He did not finish the sentence, and I did not press.

I was shocked at this revelation, this show of vulnerability. I found myself wanting to comfort him but didn't know how.

"I lost a brother," I said, surprising myself.

Had I ever said that out loud?

"My parents," I went on, "they could not move past the sorrow, not until the missionaries came."

He turned around and looked at me. I had piqued his interest. But I didn't know how to finish. I'd never talked about this with anyone.

"I think it's good you're helping your pa," I finally said.

After that we worked together more easily. But the worries he had introduced stayed with me.

That night after supper, I looked for Eliza but found that her things had been cleaned out from the tent where she and her mother slept. What if she didn't come back?

It wasn't until we began to gather for our evening prayers that I saw her. She was exiting a wagon with her mother. Elder Monson helped them each out of the wagon and then linked her mother's arm with his in a gentleman's escort. The three of them walked together toward us, looking like … a family.

It was beautiful—if you didn't consider his wife and children waiting for him to return in Utah. As I watched them approach, I wondered how this could be of the Lord. I wondered how Eliza felt to be such a spectacle. All eyes watching them walk toward camp.

President Martin addressed us that night before evening prayers. His expression was grave and his voice heavy with warning: "The spirit of apostasy has crept into our company," he declared. "Some have already departed under the cover of darkness, turning their backs on the Lord's will. And some, yes, some who now stand among us are entertaining the same wicked thoughts."

A hush settled over the crowd. People shifted uneasily, searching their neighbors for signs of doubt. I, too, scanned the gathering, trying to discern if anyone I knew was missing.

Was this about the conversation that Gideon overheard?

"Who has deceived you? Who has led you to forget the mercies of God, who has carried you across the sea and brought you safely here? Do you not see how he gathers his people to Zion? Do you not feel the weight of this calling?"

He let the silence linger, his gaze sweeping over us like the judgment of God himself.

"Woe unto those who turn away. They shall know sorrow and affliction, for they reject the blessings reserved for the faithful. The Lord will pour out his favor upon the Saints under the guidance of his prophet, Brigham Young. But to those who waver, to those whose hearts are already divided, I say this: If you intend to leave, do so now.

"We depart for Zion on Thursday next, and I will not have the spirit of apostasy among us. Let no man or woman bring the Lord's judgment upon this company."

The camp was silent. Nobody moved. Nobody said anything for what seemed like ages.

Finally I heard the sound of a fiddle, sweetly playing "Come, Come,

Ye Saints." It was Eli Ashford, Gideon's father. He had often played the fiddle on the ship when the Saints gathered to sing hymns or to dance.

He played reverently, a look of determination on his face.

We all sang, a little more sadly than usual, and then we broke to prepare for bed.

I ran to Eliza and pulled her behind a tent. "Are you well? What happened?"

She looked at me with knowing eyes. "I'm not really supposed to talk about it," she said. "But it was …" She paused as if unable to continue. "It was nice," she finally said. The distant look in her eyes betrayed her. She nodded anxiously and twisted her hair around her fingers.

"Are you to call him 'Father' now?"

She answered with more nodding. One tear rolled down her cheek. "My mother was sealed to him as a wife, and I as a daughter. We are a family now." She looked faint.

"Do you feel well?"

"It is a blessing to follow the prophet's command."

Eliza was not looking at me anymore. I followed her gaze and saw her mother and Elder Monson driving back toward town in the dusk.

"Where are they going?"

Eliza shrugged uncomfortably. "Mother said I should sleep in your tent tonight. She already talked to your mother about it."

It seemed strange, but I was glad for the company. We lay together on my bed pallet, and I tried to sleep.

But rest would not come. Gideon's words echoed in my mind all night. *"If we go now, some of us ain't gonna make it."*

CHAPTER THIRTEEN

Father rolled our handcart into camp on July 21. Like all the others, it was built hastily of green wood. I did not understand at the time how unfit raw lumber would be for the long journey ahead, but I would learn.

Mother and I stood looking at the handcart for several minutes. "That will do nicely," she finally said, eying every inch of it with more than a little consternation.

She wouldn't have voiced her complaints aloud, but her face said she was thinking what I was: The handcart looked even more absurd than we had expected.

Two large, spoked wheels sat on a wooden axle with a shallow box attached to the top. The box was about three feet wide and five feet long. A wooden yoke extended out front.

"How does it work?" I asked my father.

"It's right clever," he said, demonstrating how one or two people would stand behind the yoke and push the cart.

I took the cart from him and practiced. The cart felt light and rickety, bumping along behind me and bouncing over the uneven terrain. We hadn't yet loaded it, but I already felt the discomfort of being yoked like oxen and burdened by a load behind me.

We had to push these carts 1,300 miles across plains, through rivers, and over mountains. It was difficult to comprehend what an arduous task lay ahead of us.

"Seventeen pounds!" hollered President Martin. "Every man, woman, or child may have seventeen pounds of personal effects only. Line up at a weigh station to have your belongings weighed and inspected."

We'd heard it a dozen times. I didn't see why he had to shout about it again.

I lined up with my stack of belongings. One extra dress, my woolen shawl, my journal and pen, my grandmother's quilt, and a bedroll. I figured I was well under seventeen pounds, having left nearly everything in England. But we also had to add our cookware and utensils, which increased the weight quickly.

My mother had the family Bible and Book of Mormon, the christening gown, the rag doll from her childhood, the butter dish carved by her father, and the box of letters to add to her stack. She had sewn the pocket watch and brooch into her dress.

Once we distributed our belongings among the three of us, we felt we could travel lightly. We would have to leave only our trunk behind. Though I felt sorrow at parting with it—the one constant through all our travels, the keeper of our past—I was relieved we wouldn't have to abandon any of the precious items inside.

We lined up for inspection behind Gideon and Eli Ashford.

"No!" Gideon shouted. "I will not do it. I will not put my pa through this indignity and make this ungodly trek and then discard my books too. I will not do it! And my pa will not leave his fiddle!"

"Son, you'll have to choose," said a kind elder. "Seventeen pounds only."

Brother Martin came to diffuse the situation. They would not be the first family who required his intervention.

"Mind your tongue, boy. We'll not tolerate such talk. Now calm yourself, and we'll speak on it."

We moved through the inspection process while they talked. I overheard Brother Ashford kindly explaining that they had tools, a rifle, a tin flask of gun powder, and a bundle of shot.

"These items will be for the benefit of all the Saints," he said, trying to negotiate. "Perhaps they could be carried on a supply wagon so that we could take some personal effects."

"No, we'll not be partin' with them, Pa!" Gideon cried. "We'll never get them back."

Brother Martin cut in, "You'll not need a hunting rifle. The Lord has provided for all the Saints. There are rations enough for everyone."

Gideon tried one more time: "Please," his voice breaking with desperation. "I'll give up my books if you'll let him take the fiddle. That fiddle has been in our family for three generations."

"Seventeen pounds," said President Martin.

He spoke without compassion, and my cheeks burned with anger.

Brother Ashford stared at the fiddle case a long while, his hands clenching around the leather strap. For a moment the silence held nothing but grief.

"The tools," he finally said, his voice hoarse. "And the rifle. The rest can be left."

Gideon stomped back to camp, defeated. Around us a flurry of activity continued. Mothers tended to restless children, men tightened cart wheels, the last few Saints weighed their belongings. No one else seemed to notice what had happened. No one but me.

I couldn't stop watching Brother Ashford. He lingered, shoulders hunched, staring at the instrument that had been his for so long. Then, without a word, he picked up the fiddle and carried it out of camp.

I followed at a distance, slipping between trees until I found a place to sit, unseen.

Before long I heard the most sorrowful version of "Amazing Grace" cry out from Brother Ashford's fiddle.

The low, mournful notes caused an aching in my chest I couldn't understand. I watched as this gentle and loving man—who had used his beloved fiddle to bring joy to the Saints on board the *Horizon*, at weddings, at dances, and hymn sing-alongs—now played his last song. He played it as if he didn't know where his fingers ended and the fiddle began.

And then I watched him set it down on a rock and kiss the case softly. He walked away sadly, his grief palpable. I ducked behind the tree, ashamed to have witnessed something so raw and personal. I don't know if Brother Ashford was crying, but tears were streaming down my face.

All afternoon and into the evening, I watched similar scenes with other families. Desperate Saints negotiated and pleaded for exceptions to the weight requirements. A growing pile of goods was left at the weigh stations, the ground cluttered with books, heirloom tea sets, china, portraits, toys, clothes, and boots. All symbols of lives being left behind.

The cost of faith seemed so high.

Early the next morning, July 22, we had a quick breakfast, cleaned up camp, and packed our cart. Mother and Father secured our tent, bedrolls, Dutch oven, and food rations. We had flour, cornmeal, rice, beans, salt pork, lard, and hardtack that the women had been making for weeks. Was it enough to last four months? I hoped and prayed so.

My mother worked with excitement. I knew her faith was deep, and her motivation to show herself worthy to the prophet was her guiding light. "Today is the day the Lord hath ordained, Emmaline," she said to me, her eyes bright with anticipation.

"Mother, are you sure it's safe to leave now?" I hoped she would look past my impertinence and see my fear.

"My daughter," she said, placing her hands on my cheeks and pulling me into a hug, "we are the most safe when we are living in obedience."

I swallowed my fear and clung to her faith. That was the only thing left to do. Camp bustled for hours as Saints packed and secured the last of the handcarts.

We lined up, facing west. Our company consisted of 576 pioneers, 145 handcarts, eight supply wagons pulled by oxen, and a small head of cattle.

President Martin prayed a final prayer of blessing on us. "Our divine Heavenly Father, have mercy on these, thy obedient servants. As we set forth, we trust in thy hand to guide and sustain us. The road is long, our burdens heavy, yet we walk in faith, seeking Zion.

"Bless our steps, that we may not falter. Strengthen our hands, that we may not fail. Let the little ones be carried in thy care and the weary find rest in thee.

"Grant us fair skies, food for our hunger, and water for our thirst. Should trials come, let them refine us. Should loss be our portion, let it draw us nearer to thee.

"Now, in thy name, we go forth, trusting that thou art our shield, our light, and our deliverance.

"In the name of Jesus Christ, amen."

The 1,300-mile trek had begun.

As we departed Iowa City, the sun was already warm on my back, and the morning dew soaked the hem of my skirt. The wind was still as we sang our way out of camp:

"Ye saints who dwell on Europe's shore
Prepare yourselves for many more
To leave behind your native land
For sure God's judgments are at hand
For you must cross the raging main
Before the promised land you gain
And with the faithful make a start
To cross the plains with your handcart"

CHAPTER FOURTEEN

We left Iowa beneath an unforgiving sun. Sweat soaked my clothing as we pushed our carts through clouds of dry dust. My daily water ration was never enough to clear the grit from my throat.

If suffering had a season, I would have sworn it was summer. I had no idea how bitterly wrong I would turn out to be.

It wasn't until I stood next to Father, pushing the cart through the unrelenting August heat, that I realized how severe his cough had become. I hadn't seen him much at camp. He had been too busy building handcarts. And I supposed the open air and the night's sounds had masked it.

But with every jolt and strain of the cart, there was no missing it.

Day after day we pushed and pulled. Sometimes Mother and I leaned into the yoke in front while Father braced from behind. But we rotated often, trading places to balance the wear on our bodies.

I tried to ignore Father's gasps, the times he doubled over on the side of the trail. But as they grew in intensity, ignoring them became impossible.

"Let me push for you a while, Father," I said one afternoon. "Why don't you look out for rocks for us?"

If we could avoid taking the wheels over large stones, we could spare the axle from further wear. Already, a week into the journey, nearly every family had suffered a broken wheel or cracked frame, slowing our pace. The prophet expected us to make ten to fifteen miles a day, but at this rate, we would never reach Zion before winter.

Father didn't seem to hear me. His gaze was fixed westward.

I followed his line of sight and felt my stomach drop. A dark, rolling wall of midnight-colored clouds was pushing toward us, stretching from horizon to horizon.

We had experienced rains so far, and despite the cumbersome mud we had to push through, I welcomed a cooling shower. But this … this did not look like a shower.

About the time I noticed the clouds, gales of wind were swirling about us. Tents, clothing, and utensils flew about my head. A Book of Mormon flew past us and hit the ground, cover flying open, pages tearing away. People were running about everywhere, trying to salvage belongings and secure their loads.

Thunder roared.

Lightning split the sky.

For a heartbeat the world turned white, the vast darkness illuminated ominously.

And then the rocks began pelting us.

No, not rocks. Hail.

Wind roared in my ears. My eyes stung as they were pelted with ice and blinding rain. I turned just in time to see Father stumble.

One hand gripped our cart; the other clutched his chest.

The world slowed. Or maybe my mind simply couldn't keep up with the terror.

I turned in all directions, seeking shelter, any shelter. But the truth was inescapable. There was none.

We were alone on the prairie, surrounded by hundreds of miles of emptiness. No trees. No rock outcrops. No safety. We were at the mercy of the sky.

Father collapsed beside the cart, gasping like he did so often now. I fell beside him, hands trembling as I reached for him. Mother joined us, her arms shielding my head even as hail struck her back.

There, beneath the furious sky, we did the only thing we could.

We prayed.

We slept in fits and starts that night as hail gave way to driving rain, then awoke the next morning covered in mud and starving as the downpour continued.

After several more hours of storms, the sky finally calmed, but Brother Martin decided we should do our best to make camp. The damage had been done.

I was soaked to my bones, and so was every scrap of wood that could have been used for a fire. We ate only a little hardtack before trying to sleep again.

But sleep never came. Not for any of us.

I lay between my parents, shivering all night. Every inch of me was cold, but worse than the cold was Father's coughing. Consumption. I was sure of it now.

Fits that came sudden and hard, racking his whole body.

I reached for him. "Father."

He straightened too fast. "I'm fine," he snapped between gasps, as if saying it could make it so.

But he wasn't fine. I could see it, plain as the streaks of blood that had mixed with the rain on his sleeve.

I should have said something. Comforted him. Insisted that he rest.

But I was afraid. Afraid that if I said it aloud, if I admitted that he wasn't well, I would make it real.

We toiled on in this manner for weeks. Pushing. Pulling. Breaking down. Father growing worse by the day.

Mother and I exchanged glances during his coughing fits. I searched her face for reassurance, but all I found was helplessness.

We were moving along the Oregon Trail, passing other pioneers headed west. But they all had covered wagons.

Nobody else walked without ready shelter or protection.

As we negotiated our cursed carts through dirt, rocks, and mud, we sometimes heard taunts from passing travelers.

"Brigham Young's got a fine carriage in Salt Lake. Why don't you ask him to pull your cart?"

"Is this what your God promised you? A death march?"

We were counseled to ignore them. President Martin reminded us that persecution was a blessing. That it meant we were the chosen ones.

But as the trail stretched on, as my father weakened, as my arms ached from pushing, and as my stomach growled from hunger, I did not feel blessed.

I did not feel chosen.

I felt scared.

~

One evening in early August, we camped near the Missouri River. We would cross by ferry in the morning.

The air was damp, smelling mostly of mud. In the distance I heard voices, the scrape of iron against wood as the ferrymen prepared for the next day's crossings.

I sat beside our cart with aching legs, watching the last traces of the sun paint the sky the color of my grandmother's copper tea kettle. Father lay inside the tent. His cough was quieter now—not because he was better, but because he was too weak to cough as hard.

Mother was with him, kneeling at his side, pressing a damp cloth to his forehead. I could not bring myself to go in.

I wanted, for just a moment, to be alone with the illusion that everything was still okay. That he was still strong as an ox.

Footsteps crunched in the dirt behind me.

"How's your father?"

I didn't turn at first. I knew the steady, familiar voice. Gideon, once a foe, had become something of a friend on the trail, fixing our broken wheels and axle. Sharing his paltry rations when he could.

I shook my head. "Not good."

A pause. Then the soft thud of him lowering himself beside me. The silence stretched between us. Not heavy, not awkward, but understanding. Eliza soon joined us, offering me a precious cup of water and sharing our silence.

"I heard him coughing earlier," Gideon finally said. "It's getting worse, isn't it?"

I nodded, staring at my hands. My fingers curled into fists, then released. "I think he's dying."

The words settled among us.

Gideon and Eliza didn't offer false reassurance. They just stayed with me as the Missouri River flowed dark and endless before us.

In the morning Gideon lifted Father and placed him on the Ashfords' handcart. Gideon and Eli pulled him the rest of the way to the ferry dock.

By the next evening we had arrived in Florence, Nebraska. Ferrying across the Missouri River wasn't difficult, but it had taken all day to get everyone across.

Florence was the first real outpost we'd seen in nearly a month, and it would be the last until Fort Laramie, still four hundred miles away.

We would camp in Florence for several days to rest, trade, and resupply before the long push west.

I had high hopes that a doctor might be available, someone able to help folks like my father who had taken ill.

Mother and I worked over the firepit the following morning, making porridge and salt bacon, while Father lay in our tent, burning with fever.

Despite my hunger pains, I had no appetite.

I couldn't keep quiet one more minute. "We have to get him to a doctor," I said harshly, determined to be heard.

Mother removed her bonnet, running her fingers through her hair, which had fallen out of its tightly wound bun. For the first time, I saw her break.

Tears ran down her cheeks. She looked me straight in the eye. "Emmaline, we do not have enough money for a doctor, even if there is one here."

"We have the pocket watch," I said quickly. "We have the brooch."

Her face brightened a little. I could see that she hadn't considered this.

She jumped up and said, "Finish breakfast and try to get your father to eat. I'm going to talk to President Martin."

Hours passed.

I sat with Father. He wouldn't eat, but I got him to take a little water. I held his hand, stroked his forehead.

"You're going to be better tomorrow," I whispered. I didn't know if it was a lie or a prayer.

Mother came back late in the afternoon with President Martin.

He was holding the anointing oil.

My heart sank.

The last time I saw this happen, little William died on the *Horizon*.

I felt like I would be sick.

"Where's the doctor?" I demanded, looking at my mother in anger.

She didn't meet my eyes. She only whispered, "There's no doctor. I tried."

We all walked into the tent together. Mother. Me. President Martin. Several elders. I knelt at my father's side. I prayed. Prayed that the anointing oil and the priesthood blessing would make him well. Prayed harder than I'd ever prayed before.

I waited for the answer.

But in the tent we were met by silence. The coughing had stopped. At first I thought that meant he was finally sleeping.

But then I realized … there was nothing.

No labored breathing. No sound at all.

I grabbed his hand. Willed him to live.

Nothing.

The world outside kept moving. Boots tramping in the dirt, families murmuring around campfires, prairie grasses rustling in the wind.

But in our tent the world had stopped.

CHAPTER FIFTEEN

We buried seven people in Florence.

Several had consumption like my father. Most had likely been sick since the *Horizon*. The other two were a mother and her baby who had passed within hours of a difficult birth.

We stood around shallow graves in the grass while President Martin prayed. The warm wind whipped at my curls, and my cheeks were chapped from the tears I cried at night. Most in our company seemed impatient at the delay; others paid the deaths no mind at all.

Mother and I were surrounded by Elder and Sister Monson; Sister Delia and the girls; and the Ashfords. Eliza held my hand. Olivia offered me her lamb. I wanted to feel comforted by their presence, but I only felt numb.

"O God, our Eternal Father, we commit the souls of these faithful Saints into thy hands. May their journey to thee be swift, and may we, in your time, be reunited in the eternities."

The prairie wind carried his words away, lost to the vast emptiness of Nebraska.

When we pulled out of Florence, Mother and I looked straight ahead. Though our grief was shared, and though we stood side by side at the yoke, we did not know how to find our way to one another. The cart was heavier, the ground was rougher, and my heart was shattered like the broken pieces of rock along the trail.

Gideon said we shouldn't go. That we should winter in Florence as Saints before us had done. Several families were of the same mind and decided not to move forward. Often they disappeared overnight while the camp slept. Brother Martin said these families were weak in the faith.

"Woe to those who have gone," he preached one morning after the absence of several more families was noticed. "For they are faint of heart and feeble of spirit. The protection of Zion is only for those who endure."

I could see that Gideon was incensed at these words. He looked as if he might spit on President Martin. But many others nodded in agreement and said, "Amen."

We sang "Come, Come, Ye Saints." I barely mouthed the words. Even if my heart had felt like singing, my mouth was too dry and my tongue too sticky.

In the end, Gideon chose to stay with the company. "I won't leave my pa," he said, then hesitated before adding, "or my friends."

There was more talk from President Martin about the danger of disobedience, about the Lord's will, about the glory that awaited us in Zion.

I didn't care. My heart was buried in Florence, and they could do whatever they wanted with my body.

I pushed and pulled, moving forward like a shell without a soul.

We were five days out of Florence the first time I saw Indians—Lamanites, the Mormons called them. At first they were just shadows on the horizon, black dots against the sea of golden grass.

Then, as the sun dipped lower, the figures took shape. Riders on horseback, moving along a distant ridge. There were six, maybe seven, of them. They didn't come closer. They only watched.

I kept my eyes on the trail ahead, pretending not to see. But I could feel them, their presence as heavy as the weight of my cart.

Someone behind me muttered a prayer. Another man reached for his rifle.

President Martin raised a hand. "We are a peaceful people," he said. "They have no reason to harm us."

The riders lingered a moment longer, then turned their horses and disappeared into the grass.

That night, as we gathered for evening prayers, President Martin spoke of what we had seen. "My dear brothers and sisters, as we press forward to Zion, we travel through lands that belong to a people the Lord has spoken of in the scriptures. Those whom the Book of Mormon calls the Lamanites."

We all knew the Lamanites were a remnant of the House of Israel, a once-great people who had inhabited this land. Through transgression they had fallen from the Lord's favor.

"The darker skin you saw today is the mark of Cain, a sign of their separation from the covenant."

At this, many around me straightened their shoulders, standing a little taller in quiet superiority.

"But lo, the day will come when children of Laman will once again embrace the gospel, and they will take their rightful place among the faithful. In time they shall be numbered among the Saints, and we, as their brethren, have been given the sacred task of setting an example of righteousness before them.

"Fear them not, but neither provoke them. We are to travel in peace, keeping our covenants and trusting in the Lord."

That night, as I lay awake beneath the vast Nebraska sky, I turned his words over in my mind. Though I had heard this all before, it took on new meaning now that I had seen them.

I thought about the Lamanites' dark skin and wondered how it could be a mark of sin.

Were we not all sinners? Had we not all transgressed? And if we had, why should the color of my skin make me better than anyone else?

I wrestled with these questions for a while, certain that I was the only one awake.

Then, beside me, a sound. A quiet, broken weeping. My mother's body trembled. I didn't know exactly what she felt, but I thought her feelings must certainly be something like mine.

Grief. Fear. Uncertainty. Hunger.

All of it threatened to suffocate us in the darkness. I wanted to comfort her. I wanted her to comfort me. But I lay frozen, caught between the weight of my own grief and the fear that she would resist me.

My mother—who had always been beside me, who worked so hard to care for me, who desired so purely for her works to be pleasing in the Lord's sight—simply did not know how to reach for me.

Something in her had been lost when William died. And now, with Father gone, I feared she wouldn't ever find her way back to me.

For a long moment I did nothing. Then I made a choice. If she could not find a way to me, I would find my way to her. She was all I had. We needed each other.

I reached through the quilts and found her hand. She briefly stiffened. Then, slowly, her body softened at the touch. Her fingers laced through mine.

She held on.

Grasping my mother's hand, I finally slept peacefully. It became a habit for us to fall asleep clutching one another this way. Our hands saying what our words could not.

We continued for the next couple of weeks through Nebraska. The land was unique and more beautiful than I expected. Tall prairie grasses swayed in the summer breeze and took on an iridescent hue. The grasses stretched as far as I could see. The view only broken by the deep blue sky. It reminded me of being on the ship, only the waves were made of prairie grasses rather than water.

Perhaps I could have appreciated the beauty more if I had been in a covered wagon or even on horseback.

But heaving these carts through the dirt clods and the mud was no way to enjoy the journey. I often forgot to notice the view.

Our food rations were running low, and hunger became our greatest trial. My belly ached, and my arms and legs trembled with weakness. At this point in the journey, Mother and I were both allowed one-half pound of flour a day. Each week we were also allowed two ounces of rice, three ounces of sugar, and one-half pound of salt pork. Some days there were beans.

I saw how quickly the food supply was being emptied. We were using up our barrels faster than we were covering ground.

Mother's face had become hollow and gaunt. Her dress hung much more loosely around her frame. One evening while changing my dress, I looked down and saw that I was able to count each of my ribs.

I found myself thinking less of my grief because the hunger drove it away. This journey had taught me that when you are starving, you can think of nothing but where your next bite will come from. When you are sick from thirst, you think only of the next drink.

Even Sister Delia—who once sang as she walked and spoke of Zion with unwavering joy—now trudged forward in silence, eyes fixed on the ground, her voice lost to hunger, thirst, and her worry for Ellie and Olivia. They were too small to help her push, so they usually walked beside her. But they were not well, the hunger and heat had taken such a toll, and Gideon had begun letting them ride on his cart.

One wretchedly hot afternoon, a cry jolted me out of my dazed walking.

"Aunty Delia!" It was one of the twins.

Delia had collapsed, her body half hung over the yoke on her cart. Gideon and Eli ran to her, arriving before Mother and I did.

It seemed no one else noticed. Or if they did, they didn't stop. The sound of shuffling footsteps never ceased. Wagon wheels creaked, voices murmured prayers, and still no one turned back. No one could afford to.

Eli and Gideon pulled Sister Delia's limp body loose from the cart.

"She's burning with fever," said Eli as I approached.

That means she's alive, I thought.

My mother rushed to her, calling out for a cup of water. "The heat has overcome her," Mother said. "Bring me some sugar as well!"

I watched as Mother, cradling Sister Delia's head in her lap, mixed a little sugar into a cup of water. Delia was starting to waken as Mother held the cup to her parched lips.

"Drink, my friend, drink," my mother pleaded. "Do it for the girls."

Ellie and Olivia cried in my arms, their heat burning my body. I held a hand to Ellie's back. Too hot. They had been too hot for days now.

I watched the company move slowly and heard screaming from ahead. Many carts were stopping. Gideon went to see what was going on.

He came running back swiftly. "Rattlesnake," he told us breathlessly. "I need my knife."

The rest of us stayed with Sister Delia, helping her drink, fanning her, praying for her to regain strength.

She slowly revived, but her voice was thick with confusion as she woke: "Girls is oright? Elvia?"

Gideon returned, his face pale and eyes wide with urgency. "A man was bitten by a rattlesnake," he said, his voice hoarse. "His leg swelled up fast—three, four times its normal size. They're cutting the wound, trying to draw the venom. The elders anointed him." He glanced back toward the commotion. "I don't know if he'll make it."

After a pause, he hung his head and added, "He's got four children."

Another man gone, then, I thought.

Though the sun still hung high, President Martin called for camp. Too many had fallen sick today. Too many burned with fever. The man with the rattlesnake bite still clung to life, but barely. We had not made it ten miles, let alone fifteen, as the prophet had planned for us.

At first light we counted four more dead. We also thanked the Lord for two miracles. Sister Delia and the rattlesnake victim were going to live. But even as we rejoiced, my heart ached for the families forced to leave the bodies of their loved ones behind, hidden in shallow graves. Their pain was my pain.

This was becoming the way of things. One day a man would collapse on the trail. Another, a child would be taken by fever, or a woman struck by lightning. We prayed. We anointed them with oil. Some lived, some died. We hastily buried the bodies in shallow graves. Always without markers. As if they had never been.

I rejoiced for the miracles. Of course I did. But I could not help noticing how indiscriminate it all seemed. Who was spared, who was not. Some lived. Some died. I found it hard to thank the Lord for the one without holding him responsible for the other.

I envied those who knew how.

CHAPTER SIXTEEN

We were halfway through Nebraska, making camp at a tranquil spot near the Platte River. The Platte, often our only source of water, was shallow and muddy in most places this time of year. There was rarely enough clean water to quench our miserable thirst.

But President Martin had scouted a clear-running creek that day, and we drank from it greedily before setting up camp.

Eliza and I sat beneath a cottonwood tree, resting our backs and legs before supper preparations began. A few wild sunflowers still bloomed, but they drooped, with only a few bedraggled petals clinging to life. I found myself mesmerized at the way those petals held on as I tied rags around my blistered feet.

Eliza interrupted my thoughts with talk of what we would do when we got to Zion: "I'm going to eat one hundred licorice whips," she said, giggling.

"I'm going to take one hundred baths," I countered.

"Do you think we'll get to go to school again?" she asked.

I wasn't sure. No one ever talked of specifics when they spoke about our future in Zion. They just promised bounty, blessings, and protection from judgment. I wanted to believe the promises.

"I hope there's a library," I said. "Oh, and a park!" I added, thinking of our time in Buffalo.

My mother was tending to Ellie and Olivia, who still burned with fever, steeping a remedy from the last of our precious herbs. She had sent Sister Delia to rest while she sat with the girls.

Around us the familiar evening clatter of metal and wood echoed through the camp as men struggled to repair broken wheels. A few muttered curses. Even the most pious men in our company lost their composure over those wretched handcarts. The whole lot of us had been scolded more than once by President Martin for grumbling about them.

A light breeze rustled the leaves and cooled our bodies. Eliza and I stifled laughter at the men's attempts to vent their frustration while keeping their voices low, wary of Martin's ever-watchful eye. It had been a long time since I felt anything close to ease. The quiet relief made me realize how much suffering I had grown accustomed to.

There was no amount of rest or cool water that could make me forget all that was left behind in Florence. But I told Eliza that if I could find a little shade and drink my fill like this every day, perhaps I could at least endure the rest of the journey.

"We might survive it, but I don't think those handcarts will," she said with a wry smile, nodding her head toward the row of broken carts.

We both laughed. Not in joy, but in exhaustion. In absurdity.

And that's the moment when nature reminded us how little control we really have.

It started with a distant rumbling, then a thunderous roar from the north. The earth began to shake violently beneath our bodies.

Fear rained down like a thunderstorm.

Screaming and bellowing voices all around me:

"What's happening?"

"Run to the river!"

"Buffalo stampede!"

I couldn't see them, but the violent sound overtook me. Somebody grabbed me and Eliza, pulling us into the creek—one arm around me, one around Eliza. Gideon. He was holding us both, pushing us down, under the cover of his body.

Where was Mother? The girls? Sister Delia? Eliza's mother and Elder Monson? These questions came at me quickly, with no time for answers. Everything was happening at once.

I could not have told you what a buffalo looked like, as I had not yet seen one, and I did not that day. What I saw was a blur. A dark brown, rushing wall of fury. Some said there were more than five hundred.

The fringes of the stampede tore through the outer edge of our camp. When it was over—and it was over almost as quickly as it began—several handcarts and one of our supply wagons had been crushed to pieces. Hundreds of pounds of precious flour and rice lay spilled and scattered all over the ground.

And two more men were dead.

I found Mother and collapsed into her trembling arms.

I didn't even know I'd been screaming until I stopped.

"My dear girl," she repeated while stroking my head.

My body racked with sobs, terrorized at the fury of the frontier. At our utter helplessness against it.

I craved this comfort from my mother, and I could not let go. Would not let go. As she held me, I cried and watched members of our company on their hands and knees, using tin cups to scrape flour and rice from the dirt, salvaging what they could.

It was another restless night. Every time I began to sleep, I jolted awake at the thundering sound of buffalo. My body didn't know the difference between memory and reality. Every day thereafter I searched the horizon for buffalo as we pushed and pulled through the Nebraska prairie.

A week passed, and the weather started to cool a little. Other than a couple of evening storms, we had no disasters to speak of. Our hunger, however, remained a relentless foe, gnawing at us more intensely with each passing day. Some nights Gideon shot a rabbit, so we had a little roasted meat to share among our group of friends.

But opportunities to hunt were scarce. President Martin demanded we keep moving, and each evening there were broken carts to tend to.

From time to time we saw a lone buffalo on the prairie. The giant beasts terrified me, but hunger has a way of dulling fear. How many Saints could one buffalo feed? I was certain Gideon and Brother Ashford had the skill to take one down.

But the elders discouraged it. Killing buffalo would antagonize the Indians. It would jeopardize our safety, they warned.

I wasn't sure if I believed them. I thought our hunger and declining rations put us at greater risk. The Indians we'd seen hadn't looked like they wanted to harm us. But my opinion carried no weight, so I said nothing.

~

One afternoon I was helping Sister Delia push her cart while Gideon took my place at ours. We had fallen into this rhythm—shuffling between carts, lending strength to one another when it was needed. Brother Ashford and Gideon, being among the strongest, could each manage a cart alone, which meant they were frequently the ones stepping in to help others keep moving.

Ellie and Olivia were riding in a supply wagon, which was often used as a sickbed for those who could not walk. The girls had been ill for weeks, and we were all worried.

Elder Monson had given them a priesthood blessing and anointed them with oil before we left that morning.

"Some sickness just lingers," he said, trying to encourage us. "I've seen fevers hold on for weeks, burning a child down, and then it breaks and sets them free again."

I heard a twinge of doubt in his voice even as he stood confidently and spoke with faith.

As Delia and I walked, I felt her intense worry. "Ellie barely wakes now," she said. "And when she does, she makes no sense. It's all I can do to get a little water down her."

"Olivia is improving," I said brightly, trying to offer hope. "I saw her sitting up last night, eating."

Her face was grim. "Yes," she said softly. "But the fever doesn't take everyone it inflicts. Not always. One fights it off. The other …" She didn't finish. She didn't have to.

A few moments passed, and she spoke again with deep shame in her voice. "I promised my brother on his deathbed that I would keep them safe," she said. "I gave my word."

And a few moments later, her voice stronger and more confident, she declared, "I trust they will thrive in Zion. I just have to get them there."

We walked in silence the rest of the day.

President Martin said we would push harder that day and into the evening if necessary. As twilight settled over the prairie, I learned why.

All day the trail had stretched endlessly before us, rolling waves of golden grass swaying in the cooling breezes. Dust clung to every part of my clothing and skin. My body ached, hunger made me sick and lightheaded, and thirst consumed me. Then came the first murmurs from ahead. Suddenly, there was excitement where there had been only exhaustion.

"Look ahead!"

The cry rang out from the front of the line, voices rippling through the ranks.

I lifted my head and squinted against the setting sun. At first I saw nothing but open plains and the endless trail. Then, just faintly, a dark shape began to rise on the horizon.

"Chimney Rock!"

The cries rang out all around me, and then a hush fell over the company. There was a collective awe and realization that we had made it to one of the most important landmarks on the trail. After weeks of pushing through the relentless prairie, after heat and mud, hunger and hardship, sorrow and death, we were standing at the foot of one of the grandest and most inspiring sights I had ever seen.

The massive rock jutted into the sky like a solitary church spire, rising from the flatlands, as if it was there to remind us how small we were underneath the heavens. Gold and crimson hues from the sun's fading light cast long shadows across the ground beneath us.

President Martin called camp, and we began to settle in for the night. Everyone moved reverently in wonder of the stone sentinel before us. Prayers of gratitude were offered all around me.

I watched Gideon wade into the muddy Platte, rubbing the dust from his arms before cupping his hands over a bowl and using his fingers to filter dirt from the water. There would be no crystal clear refreshment tonight. But water was water. The best we had.

Mother made a fire and mixed flour, lard, and salt with a little water to make flour cakes for dinner. We would not get meat or rice until tomorrow, and even then it would be a paltry ration.

Sister Delia and several other women tended to Ellie and Olivia, pressing cool rags to fevered foreheads. I knew it wouldn't be enough. Not for Ellie. We all knew.

As the sky darkened, the stars unfurled in brilliant clarity, stretching wide over the lonely prairie. The rock stood silent beneath them.

It felt like a milestone.

It felt like a grave marker.

CHAPTER SEVENTEEN

The unmistakable cries of mourning woke me before sunrise at Chimney Rock. Brokenhearted wailing pierced the darkness, dragged me from sleep, and split open my heart.

It was coming from Sister Delia's tent. I heard Delia's cries, and I heard Olivia's. But I did not hear Ellie.

Precious Ellie. Just six years old. A child whose short life had already been marked by the loss of both parents. Ellie, who found new hope in the faith of her doting Aunty Delia. Ellie, who sat sweetly and obediently, always at her twin sister's side.

Mother lit a candle. We threw on our shawls and crawled into Delia's tent. Olivia lay prostrate over her sister, her sobs shaking her body. Delia knelt beside them, her anguish raw and unbearable.

I placed a hand on Ellie's forehead. Cold. Her small fingers were curled stiffly against her chest.

Outside, I heard the quiet shuffle of feet. Then the rustle of tent flaps.

Gideon stepped in first, followed by Elder and Sister Monson, with Eliza clinging to her mother behind them. More shadows gathered behind, drawn by grief and breaking dawn. Mother's candle flickered, casting an amber glow across Delia's stricken face.

Eliza's mother let out a gasp. "Oh, Delia. No." She dropped to her knees and gathered Delia into an embrace.

Elder Monson exhaled slowly and lowered his head. "God rest her little soul."

From outside, whispers spread. A few more figures gathered at the entrance, reluctant to intrude but unwilling to leave.

Gideon crouched beside Olivia and placed a hand gently on her back. "Come, Livvy," he whispered. "Let's go to the river and get a drink."

But Olivia would not let go.

I stumbled out of the tent, gasping for air. The grief, the candle smoke, the faint smell of death. It was all too suffocating. Tears blurred my vision.

I dropped to my knees in the cold dirt and cried out to God. "Stop the suffering! Stop taking people away! You're supposed to be protecting us! Why are you doing this? *Why? Why? Why?*" I pounded my fists against the ground. My wrists ached, but I didn't stop.

I screamed and sobbed until my body trembled.

My mother came quickly to my side. "Hush, Emmaline, hush," she said softly. "Do not make this harder for Sister Delia and Olivia." She stroked my hair, wiping her own tears with the edge of her sleeve.

I quieted, but the weeping did not stop. Not for Ellie. Not for my father. Not for William. Not for the long list of souls now buried in shallow ground along the trail. All of them gone, and we were still walking. Still calling it God's will.

Gideon came to me with a cup of water. It was gritty, but I drank it. He sat beside me while Mother went to help prepare Ellie's body. We didn't speak. We didn't need to. Gideon understood. Maybe better than anyone.

We buried eight that afternoon.

The funerals were brief, as always. President Martin spoke of restored bodies and eternal reunions, but I kept my head down. I stared at the grass and the dirt, felt the ache in my chest.

Delia and Olivia sat stone-faced by the fire that night. I recognized the look on a face where grief had drained the tears away. I tried not to let their sorrow deepen my own bitterness, but it lingered.

Eliza and I knelt beside Olivia and tried to coax her into playing a game with her lamb. She turned away. It was Gideon who got through to her—lifting her onto his shoulders with a gentle smile. Her eyes brightened, just a little.

The next morning, as we warmed ourselves by the fire, I spoke to Sister Delia. "I'm so sorry," I said, my voice hoarse. "I don't understand."

Delia looked at the flames. Her voice came out flat but steady: "Emmaline, not everything is for us to understand. The Lord provides for us. He blesses us. He tests us. Look at Olivia. He healed her. He is still working among us. We must pass this test of faith."

I wanted to believe her. But I couldn't. Why would God take one child and spare the other? What kind of test demanded a six-year-old's life?

I said none of it aloud. It brought her comfort, and she deserved that.

We departed Chimney Rock the next morning, though no one truly left it behind. Some would remember it as a sign of God's presence on the trail. Others, like me, would remember it as a monument to what we'd lost.

Whatever the reason, we would not forget Chimney Rock.

The miles stretched endlessly over the next week as I kept putting one foot in front of the other. The days blurred. I remember no disasters. Only cold air and gnawing hunger.

One evening Gideon shot another rabbit. We shared it between nine of us: Mother and me, Brother Ashford and Gideon, the Monsons, and Delia and Olivia. One rabbit. A few bites each.

There was little strength left for conversation. We walked mostly in silence, pressing onward toward Fort Laramie.

By the time the fort appeared on the horizon, we had been walking nearly two months. It was the second week of October, and the wind had turned sharp. Cold crept into our clothes and stayed there.

Excitement rippled through the company. Fort Laramie. President Martin had promised we would be met there by supply wagons from Utah. That meant blankets and replenishment of our food stores. The thought of it was the only thing that kept us moving those final days.

But hope is a dangerous thing.

We reached Fort Laramie on the ninth of October and found … nothing. The supply wagons hadn't come. I was never told why. I don't think anybody was. We didn't tarry long. President Martin pushed us forward with the same unshakable conviction he'd held from the start.

The fort had come and gone. And we were nearly out of food. Our flour rations were cut again—now four ounces a day, weighed out like gold dust.

I watched Elder Monson scrape leather from a discarded boot and boil it in a pot, trying to soften it into something we could chew. Others boiled strips of rawhide, cut from cart covers and broken harnesses.

It was no longer hunger we were battling; it was starvation.

~

The Platte had been our lifeline for weeks. We'd followed the river all through Nebraska and into Wyoming. It was our source of water and our guide. We were alive because of the Platte.

But on the nineteenth of October—a day so bitterly cold that the winds bit straight through our bones—the river became our greatest foe.

It ran wide and swift, with ice chunks bobbing over the rough waters. The river cut straight across our path. We had to get to the other side. And the only way past it … was through it.

There was no bridge. No ferry. No choice.

I stood next to Gideon and considered the unforgiving threat before us, our breath hanging like clouds around our heads as we spoke. "There has to be another way," I said.

Then with more urgency, "Don't we have to turn back?"

"We can't," Gideon answered softly, drawing a deep breath as he brought his trembling hands to his face. It was the first time I saw him scared. "If we go back, we'll starve to death. Our only hope now is that the supply wagons will meet us on the other side of the river."

President Martin, looking grave, called us to pray. "Our Father in Heaven," he began, "we are thy servants, gathered in great need. We ask thee to still the waters, to strengthen our bodies, and to deliver us in safety to the other side. Increase our faith, and let thy angels attend us."

Even as he finished, elders began to ford the river, testing its depth and strength. The frigid waters were up to their waists, and light snowflakes began to fall around them.

President Martin, seeing that the depth was passable, began ordering people to go.

Eliza and her mother stood at the front of their cart, with Elder Monson pushing from behind. They descended into the waters. Their cart shifted, swayed, tipping far enough to let water into the cargo bed. Their belongings were now wet, but with Elder Monson's steadying hand, they were secure. Terror seized my chest and limbs as they continued. I could not see Eliza's face, but she was chest deep in the river.

Gideon turned to Sister Delia. "I'll help you and Olivia across and then come back for Pa."

She nodded, clinging tightly to Olivia, whose face was buried in her chest.

Gideon looked me in the eye. "I'll be back for you."

He hoisted Olivia on his shoulders and stood at the yoke of Delia's cart. She grabbed on the back and began pushing. Wagons and oxen crowded the water. Families clung to one another, and women dragged carts through the riverbed alone. I saw one cart float away from its owner, then another.

"Let them go," one of the elders hollered. "Forget the carts and save yourselves."

Women and children slipped under the water, but men were coming back to steady them and get them to shore. Gideon left Delia and Olivia once they were safe and began swimming back to us. His strong, tall body emerged on our side of the river, visibly shaking, but safe.

I watched him cross again with Brother Ashford. Gideon had the same calm assurance with his pa that he had with Olivia. I noticed how much he'd changed during this journey. How tender his strength was. I knew his pa had to be so proud.

He returned to help Mother and me, as he promised.

"You can do it," he told me. "Watch the rocks; many of them are slippery with moss. Take slow steps. Keep hold of the cart, but if it tips over completely, let it go."

I was terrified, but I nodded my understanding.

He spoke again, more emphatically, looking Mother and me both in the eyes. "Save yourselves, not the cart."

I promised him we would.

At the last minute I reached into my satchel under the tarp and retrieved my journal. Its pages were swollen from the dampness but still legible. It held everything I couldn't say aloud.

"Take this," I said, pressing it into Gideon's hand. "You're taller. Maybe you can keep it dry."

He nodded solemnly and tucked it inside his coat. "I'll guard it with my life."

We descended the bank and into the river. The icy water seeped into my boots first, then climbed up my bloomers. My dress grew heavy with water, ice, and mud. Gideon was correct about the rocks; they felt slippery beneath my feet.

My mother called out in prayer, "Lord, give us strength."

I barely heard her as the screams and cries engulfed the air around us.

Next to me, Brother Van Dyke—a gentle, quiet man I knew only by name—reached out and steadied my arm for a moment. His three-year-old, Patrick, sat perched on his shoulders.

An undercurrent caught our cart and it began to tip. Mother screamed. I tried to steady it, but it pulled me down. I turned just in time to see our butter dish floating away, the one my grandfather carved. One of our last remnants of England.

Then the rest of our belongings were swallowed by the river.

The snow was falling heavily now. I couldn't see the bank. I couldn't see anything at all.

"Let go of the cart!" Gideon boomed.

I let go. So did Mother. We stood waist deep in the frigid North Platte River. And we had lost everything.

I turned. Couldn't think about it. Gideon steadied my mother, but my own feet slipped out from under me.

"Emmaline!" he shouted.

His hand caught my arm just in time.

And then, above the noise, one thundering voice cut through it all: "Patrick!"

The little boy had fallen from his father's shoulders. Brother Van Dyke dove after him.

As Mother and I reached the western bank, I turned back and watched them sink into the river.

Nobody ever saw them again. Ripples spread in widening circles from the place where Brother Van Dyke hit the water. I noticed them. I wondered if anyone else did.

There were still dozens waiting to cross, but we were safe—Mother, Gideon, his father, the Monsons. All my friends had made it across.

We stood there together on the western bank, helpless, watching as more people descended into the waters. I thought the screaming lasted for hours, but maybe it was only minutes. Maybe it still hadn't stopped. Maybe it was only the memory echoing. What I know is that I'll never forget it.

As I stood on the west side of the river, watching everyone count the people and belongings they had left, my wet dress stiffened to ice.

CHAPTER EIGHTEEN

We spent the night at Red Butte, just the other side of the river. Everyone tried to make camp, but the light snow that began as we crossed the river grew into a blizzard. The wind howled. The cold was excruciating. Snow fell for hours, so heavy it blinded us.

Mother and I, like most in our company, wore the only clothing we had left. The fabric had frozen against our bodies the moment we stepped out of the water.

Our blankets were gone. Our tent was gone. Our food was gone. Our matches, flint, and steel—gone. If there was any wood to burn, it lay buried beneath the storm's thick white blanket.

We huddled under a hastily rigged tarp with the Monsons, the Ashfords, Sister Delia, and Olivia. And there, in the dark, I had a thought. It was a wicked thought, and I dared not speak it aloud.

The ones who already died are the lucky ones.

We huddled the entire night, all of us encircled around Olivia in a futile attempt to share warmth.

My teeth chattered violently, and I had difficulty keeping my body upright because I could not feel my feet. It was not the way feet feel numb when they are cold. It was as though I didn't have feet at all. I held my burning fingers beneath my arms, but I had no body heat to warm them. They ached as if burning from the inside out.

We didn't say much. It was too cold to talk. The only thing holding us all up was the way we leaned on each other. No one wanted to lie down. President Martin had cautioned everyone to stay upright, to stay awake.

Just as dawn broke, Eli Ashford started to speak. His words were slurred and clumsy as they cut through the frozen air. "Please, Papa, take me down the lane to the fishing hole," he mumbled. "It's such a fine day, innit? Let's have some apples. I like the apples by the fishing hole."

Gideon lifted his head in alarm. "What are you saying, Pa?" he asked.

"I'll catch a big 'un, I will. Won't let her slip off this time. Down by the tree where the apples fall. Can I have one, Papa? Just one? I'm ever so hot. It's scorchin' out, ain't it?"

Gideon grabbed his father by the shoulder and gave him a gentle shake. "Pa, it's me, Gideon. We're going to Zion. Look at me."

But Eli didn't seem to hear him. "Gideon's nappin'," he slurred. "He can have an apple after. He always liked them apples."

"Pa!" Gideon cried.

Eli kept murmuring. It was nonsense now, strung-together words with no connection.

Gideon shook him harder. "Pa! Wake up. You're not at the fishing hole. You're here. With me."

Eliza's mother felt Eli's forehead and face, whispering, "He's burning up. That's not good. That's not good at all."

"He's freezing!" Gideon cried. "Why does he think he's hot?"

Eli began trying to remove clothes.

Gideon fought him. Held his arms apart. "Help me!"

"It's the cold," Elder Monson said. "I've seen this before, in the war. When it gets to this stage, they believe they are hot. I'm sorry, Gideon. It won't be long now."

"No!" Gideon yelled. "Pa, I'm here. Listen to me. It's Gideon. We're going to Zion. You're very cold, but you're going to be fine. Help is on the way." His voice trailed off into a sob.

He knew his father wasn't going to make it to Zion. We all did. Within minutes Eli was slumping to the ground. He was gone. Gideon fell on top of him and wept until the sun came up.

My heart was broken for my friend. He had journeyed all this way in spite of his desire to stay in England—just to get his pa safely to Zion. It was his purpose. The one thing he held on to. And it had been for nothing.

In the light of the morning sun, we counted thirty-four dead bodies. We didn't even bury them this time. They were placed in a pile and covered with a tarp.

"No," cried Gideon, begging for a proper burial. "That won't keep the wolves away."

President Martin wasn't without compassion. "I'm so sorry, son," he said. "There's too much snow. The ground is too hard. The men don't have strength enough right now."

"May I dig a grave for my pa?" Gideon asked with more deference than I'd ever seen him show. "Please, sir."

"You can try, son."

Gideon did try, but President Martin was right: The ground was too hard.

Many more were close to death. Over the next couple of days, we added twenty or thirty more bodies to the pile. I don't know if anyone was counting anymore. The dying continued day after day as we stayed there to regain our strength. Now we knew that when someone started talking nonsense, the end was near.

My body never got used to the cold. The hurting grew worse by the hour. I couldn't use my fingers, so I palmed snow to my mouth to eat. It was all we had.

Despite all odds, the rest of our circle of friends survived the next three days. We mostly sat under the tarp to shield us from the winds. We had found that moving our bodies provided some warmth, but it also caused our frozen clothing to rip away our skin. When this happened, the bleeding and exposed skin brought further suffering. We had no dry clothes to dress the wounds. So we determined to stay as still as possible.

We sat in a circle, as close as we could get to one another, and waited for death to come.

But instead of death, there came a rider on horseback on the third day. His voice cut through the wind, at first unintelligible, and we all searched for its source.

"Help is coming!" the rider yelled. "Rescuers from the valley!"

Everyone surrounded him. He had been sent ahead to tell us that a rescue train was several days out.

I blinked slowly, unable to process the words. Help: I had forgotten that such a thing existed.

The next day we packed up what little was left and began walking west. The farther we could walk, the sooner we could reach help.

We walked arm in arm, trying to stay strong, to protect one another. With help now certainly on the way, we walked with the hope that our bodies would not be among the growing numbers left dead on the trail.

CHAPTER NINETEEN

Perhaps it is a mercy that I don't recall much of the trip to Devil's Gate. My only clear memory is starting the journey holding tightly to Mother and Eliza. Everything after that is a blur. I'm told we walked through the snow for five more days. I'm told many more people died.

The numbness crept from my feet to my thighs. I couldn't feel my lower body. And yet I was too heavy to stand.

I was so tired. So very tired.

"I'm going to rest here now," I said to no one in particular. That would be my last lucid thought for days.

Bursts of memory from that time come back to me now and then, especially in the middle of the night:

Mother screaming, "Stay with me, Emmaline!"

A mumbling voice I didn't recognize saying something about burning with fever.

A hot cup of broth at my lips that smelled like sagebrush and bark.

Being lifted and carried like a baby. Was it Gideon? Maybe Elder Monson? I'm not sure. I saw both of their faces in my dreams.

When we arrived at Devil's Gate on November 2, 1856, I was barely conscious. I knew this place marked a significant point on our journey west. A place I would have wanted to see. But in my fevered state the details blurred. I could not tell you what was there.

While voices murmured about reaching this milestone, I collapsed into the snow. We were a few hundred miles from Salt Lake City, they said. But those words held little meaning. I was more dead than alive.

In my mind I was in Wiltshire again, running the grassy hills with William. Was it memory or dream? I couldn't tell. When fleeting moments of clarity pierced the fog, the biting cold returned, prompting me to close my eyes and wish for death. It seemed inevitable now for all of us. Why was it taking so long?

And then I slept. I don't know how long.

When I awoke, I was in a covered wagon, dressed in dry clothes. A thin straw mattress beneath me, a mountain of quilts over me.

"It's South Pass!" someone shouted outside the wagon. The voice cracked with excitement. As if those words alone could light the sun and melt the snow.

I reached down to feel my clothes. They really were dry. I thought maybe I was dead. Was this the moment before death, my mind playing tricks on me?

Then came a voice I didn't recognize. A man. A soft and steady voice. "Well now, glad to see you're awake, young lady."

"Where am I?" My lips were cracked, my tongue sticky and thick. "Where is … my mother?"

I couldn't understand his full reply. I heard him say his name was Benjamin London. Something about wagons from Salt Lake. I remember the moment when he said my mother was alive.

I tried to sleep again. Benjamin wouldn't allow it. He sat me up, held me, and brought a cup of hot broth to my lips. Real broth. Chicken maybe, not sagebrush and bark. I drank a little, and he handed me some bread. I shook my head and tried to sleep.

"Come now, dear," he coaxed. "You've got to drink and have a little bread."

He broke off tiny pieces and put them in my mouth. As they dissolved on my tongue, he spooned down more broth.

Benjamin's face comes to me in my dreams now too. Thin, ruddy, with an auburn beard and merry smile. I never saw him after those few days at Devil's Gate. Benjamin London, the man who saved my life.

But I was still very sick.

I slept for days, sometimes jostled awake by the rolling wagon. More broth. More bread.

One morning I stirred and realized someone was beside me. A warm body, faintly breathing. It was my mother.

She couldn't speak.

"They won't be able to save her legs," I heard someone whisper. Were they talking about me or Mother? I couldn't feel my legs. I didn't want to know.

She moaned lightly but never spoke. I was just relieved her warm body was alive beside me. I reached for her under the quilts. Her fingers laced in mine.

Voices outside. I heard them say Fort Bridger. I think that meant we were closer. We were still going to Zion.

Where was everybody else? Gideon? Eliza? Were my friends alive? I wanted to ask, but I couldn't string together that many words.

I felt hot and then cold and then hot again.

One morning—I think it was morning because of the way the sun filtered through the side of the wagon's tarp—Eliza knelt by my side. She stroked my face and brushed my curls, working on each tangled knot one at a time. I tried to say hello, to acknowledge her presence. I couldn't find the energy to reach her, but I could hear her. She spoke for a long time.

"Oh, Emmaline, you've just got to wake up," she pleaded. "When my papa died, I thought my whole life had ended. I didn't care about anything. Not Mama's new faith, not the promises of Zion, not even my life. But then I met you."

She paused to smooth a tangle from my hair, her voice trembling as she went on, "You were so full of fire even when you were scared. You made me laugh again even when there was nothing to laugh about. You made me believe I could be anything. We talked about having houses and going to school again, remember? We're almost there. It's really going to come true."

A tear landed on my cheek, and I felt her thumb brush it away.

"Gideon's beside himself. He carried you through the snow, Emmaline, half the way to Devil's Gate. And the rescue wagons—they came. God really did send help. We're almost there. We'll be in Zion tomorrow. But I don't want to see it without you."

Her voice dropped to a whisper. "Please, Emmaline. Come back to me. I love you."

I wanted to answer, to tell her that she was the brave one. That it was she who'd taught me how to smile and laugh again. But I was too tired. I would sleep first.

I went back to Wiltshire and William in my dreams. Father was there. I rode piggyback on his shoulders. I ate cake with William, and we rolled in the grass. I laughed with the innocence of a child who knew no want or loss or cold.

I had to decide whether to stay in Wiltshire or go back to Eliza and my mother.

Then came a chorus of voices outside the wagon, all saying something to the effect of "Look! It's the valley. It's Zion!"

I felt myself awaken, a little life returning to my body. I turned to my mother and found the strength to speak.

"We're here, Mother. We made it."

CHAPTER TWENTY

We arrived in Salt Lake City, Utah Territory, on November 30, 1856. It had been six months and five days since we boarded the *Horizon* in Liverpool. Half my fourteenth year had passed on this voyage to the Promised Land.

I summoned what little strength I had to crawl to the edge of the wagon and peer out as we descended into the valley. At first I felt only disappointment.

Whatever was down there lay covered beneath more snow, like everything else we'd had to survive. After all we'd endured, this was Zion?

But then I lifted my gaze. At the edges of the Great Basin, the mountains came into view. I gasped in wonder.

They rose like a fortress from the earth, encircling the valley in every shade of blue, their peaks capped in white and reaching straight into the heavens. Nothing I'd been told about the Rocky Mountains had prepared me for this. The beauty felt almost holy.

The sky was bright, indifferent to our hunger and our pain. There was the faintest whisper of clouds. The city below was not yet visible in detail, but I felt something shift in me. Hope. It gave me strength to sit for a while.

"Mother, wait until you see the mountains," I whispered.

She moaned softly. I could not tell if it was a response to my voice or the pain of the wagon wheels jolting over the rocky terrain. In this light, I saw more clearly how sick she was. Skin gray, cheeks sunken, her body reduced to half its size. She was a shadow of the strong and determined woman I knew.

Is that what I looked like too?

I kissed her forehead. "We're here. There will be doctors. You're going to feel better soon."

Then, I softly added, "I love you."

I had said similar words of hope to Father before he died, but with him I knew they weren't true. This time I had a mustard seed of faith. I believed she would get better. I believed I would get better. The majesty of the mountains and the glimpse at Zion had changed something in me. Maybe everything Sister Delia, President Martin, and all the others said was true. Maybe the Lord was testing us. Maybe he was with us. I wanted to give it a chance.

The town became clearer as we neared the heart of the valley. I saw mostly wooden homes laid out in neat square streets. Smoke rose from chimneys, and picket fences were dusted with snow. Orchards and farms lined the outskirts of the town. *A home for everyone*, Father had said. Oh how I wished he could see it.

There were people too. A crowd had gathered. They were cheering, singing hymns, calling out names. Some shouted, "Welcome!" Others wept.

Everywhere I had ever gone since becoming a Latter-day Saint, I had been looked upon with scorn. Teased and mocked for simply being a part of a religion that my parents had chosen for me.

But today we entered this city as welcome guests and heroes. Safe, but for the grief and sickness we carried with us.

I felt suddenly dizzy. Overwhelmed by exhaustion.

I lay back down beside my mother, her breath shallow, her mind completely detached. The wagon slowed, then stopped, and I heard footsteps in the snow, voices conferring. I think someone peeked in. A man said, "She can come with us."

Did he mean me or my mother? Where were we going?

I wanted to ask who he was, what was happening, whether Eliza was nearby. But my thoughts came slow and disordered. I couldn't turn them into words.

I'd been awake too long. My body had nothing left to give. I was drifting to sleep.

The last thing I remember was being cradled in someone's strong arms and the quiet sound of boots on snow.

It was dark when I woke. I was in a bed—a real bed. My head sunk into a delightfully soft pillow. The air smelled faintly of fresh bread, and I could hear a fire crackling in another room. I tried to remember the last time I had felt the comfort of a real feather mattress. Not since Wiltshire.

I blinked slowly. Was I dreaming?

A baby cried softly nearby. I heard the sound of a woman's footsteps and a gentle hushing. A door creaked open and closed again.

I tried to sit up, but I couldn't.

That was all right. I felt safe. And, for the first time in months, warm. I closed my eyes and slipped peacefully to sleep.

I awoke again to the face of an angel, bathed in morning light from a nearby window. Her skin was fair, her eyes blue like a summer sky after the rain. Her thick yellow hair was braided and pinned into a twist on the back of her head. She looked a little like Eliza, only twice as old. Her hands were warm and soft as she laid them on my forehead and cheeks. They felt like a mother's hands.

"There now," she said gently. "Your fever's come down nicely. Doctor says your fingers and toes will heal. You're one of the lucky ones. We just need to fatten you up now."

She picked up a tin bowl of porridge from the bedside table. It looked to be topped with peach preserves.

I stared at it, blinking. Maybe this wasn't a dream after all.

"Where am I?" I asked. "Where is my mother?"

The woman smiled, and her soft laugh was pleasant and inviting. "Now that's a fair question, dear. My name is Betsy Green. You're in our home in Salt Lake City. You've been asleep nearly two days. Didn't stir at all—not when I gave you a wash or spooned broth into your mouth. Had us worried, you did. But you're strong. Doctor says your lungs are clear."

"My mother?" I asked weakly.

"She's alive," Betsy said. "Needs a little extra care. But don't fret, sweetheart. She's at the ward house where the midwives can tend to the sickest."

"Ward house?" I echoed.

"The church," she said. "We hold Sunday meetings there, but for now, it's been made into a kind of hospital. All the best midwives in the valley are helping Dr. Phillips care for the worst cases."

I nodded. My worry lingered, but knowing she was in good hands brought some peace.

Betsy settled beside me with the bowl and spoon. "Now, do you think you can hold it yourself? I need to tend to the baby if you're able."

I tried to sit up and found I could, barely.

"I'll try," I said.

She handed me the bowl and watched a moment, making sure I could manage it. Once satisfied, she turned toward the sound of the fussing baby.

"You know," she said over her shoulder, "the first time I saw this valley, I was not much older than you. My family came here from Winter Quarters not long after Brother Brigham. My uncle died on the plains."

She disappeared into the next room, her voice low and soothing as she tended to her baby.

I looked down at the bowl of porridge in my hands. The pale orange preserves glistened in the light. I took a bite. It was warm and sweet and soft. Tears burned my eyes as I ate.

I was alive. I was in Zion. And I was not alone.

There were still many questions, but the answers could come later.

I stayed in bed for two more weeks.

"Dr. Phillips' instructions are firm," Betsy told me. I was to sleep as much as I could. He permitted only six small meals a day. More, he said, could make me ill.

Betsy was a gentle and devoted caretaker. Each time I awoke, fresh water was waiting at my bedside. She prepared simple meals for me— porridge, broth, soft potatoes, and fresh bread. Though they were small, she always found a way to make them special. A dollop of peach preserves, a smear of fresh butter, or a few dried apple slices dusted with cinnamon made me feel like a queen after all I had endured.

Every morning she helped me wash. Then we brushed and braided my hair. My chamber pot always seemed to be emptied the moment it was needed. I rarely saw the baby, Matilda, whom they called Mattie, but I knew she was tenderly cared for. The house was full of quiet warmth and order, and love.

Betsy's husband, Micah, was a blacksmith. I saw him each day after he returned from work. He would come in each evening to offer a priest-hood blessing, always anointing my head with consecrated oil and laying his hands gently on my head. He prayed with quiet fervor for both me and my mother.

One night he spoke this prayer: "Heavenly Father, we thank thee for sparing Emmaline's life. We know her journey has been long and her body weakened by the trials she's endured. But thou art a God of healing. We ask thee now to strengthen her frame, to nourish her soul, and to restore her joy. Bless her mother with comfort and peace, and if it be thy will, let her recover too. Help this household to be a place of refuge while thy work continues in her life. We place her in thy care, with full hearts and grateful spirits. In the name of Jesus Christ, amen."

Usually his prayers comforted me, but this one made me uneasy. I noticed he had added "if it be thy will" to the part about Mother. I was getting better every day, but I feared she was growing worse.

The next morning I asked Betsy when she might take me to see my mother.

Her eyes looked sad as she slowly pulled up the rocking chair to sit beside me. "Emmaline," she said softly, "your mother is not well. Both of her legs were lost to the cold. They were frozen clear through and blackened by the time the wagons reached the valley. The doctor did what he could, but she drifts in and out of consciousness. Her fever still burns. She is not yet in her right mind."

I stared at her, waiting with dread for whatever came next.

Betsy reached for my hand. "She's alive," she said, trying hard to reassure me. "But she's not out of danger."

"She needs me," I pleaded. "I want to see her. I'm strong enough. Please."

"I'll ask Dr. Phillips."

CHAPTER TWENTY-ONE

etsy and I sat in matching oak rocking chairs in front of the stone fireplace, sewing. Steaming mugs of hot cider sat on a small table between us, and a roast in the Dutch oven filled the house with the most comforting aromas I'd ever known. It smelled like happiness. Like warmth and safety and belonging.

Here in this warm home—with the scent of food made with love and not measured out in rations, with people who laughed and sang and gave affection freely, with a warm fire and soft beds—I felt at home. I felt like part of the family I had always dreamed of having.

Betsy's needle was flying as she worked on a small Christmas dress for Mattie, and I was mending Micah's church trousers.

Now that I was strong enough to spend half days out of bed, I had found my mending skills to be a good way to contribute to the household and repay the Greens for the kindness they had shown me. It was also the best way to have conversations with Betsy.

These sewing sessions, while the baby took her afternoon nap in a cradle beside Betsy, had become dear to me. It was nothing like the hours I had spent mending with Mother in our dark, damp room in Liverpool, when we mostly worked in silence or talked about what chores needed doing and what we would buy next at the market.

Betsy hummed when she worked alone and chattered happily when I joined her. She talked about everything—her childhood in Ohio, what Utah looked like in the summer, her favorite recipes, or whatever else was on her mind.

Today she was telling me how she and Micah had first met while walking across the plains when they were about my age, and how they met again at a community dance a few years later. He began courting her, and they were married six months later.

We talked of the wonderful dances and socials the church held, and she said that as long as I was well enough, they would take me to the Christmas Eve dance.

"You can wear my red calico," she said. "It has pearl buttons down the front and a delicate white lace collar that will look beautiful with your dark hair. It might fit a little loose, but we'll take it in. Oh, it's such fun. I can't wait to take you."

Sometimes I told Betsy about growing up in England, about the beauty of Wiltshire and the fun that Eliza and I had at the mission. But Betsy never asked, and I never shared, about my journey to Zion. It was too painful for me to think about, and I believe she sensed that I wasn't ready.

About the time the baby began to stir, Betsy stopped sewing and looked at me. Her needle and thread still pulled taut, she seemed to have forgotten what she was doing. There was a flicker of worry on her face.

I suddenly felt uneasy. What was she afraid to tell me?

"Emmaline," she said finally, "Micah is going to take you to see your mother tomorrow."

That was good news, but I didn't like the anxious look on her face.

"She's been moved to the Thatchers' house right down the road. The doctor thinks you both are ready for a visit."

"So she's doing better?" I asked, my voice trembling.

Betsy twisted the fabric in her hands and let out a little yelp when she accidentally stuck herself with the needle.

"Yes," she said after a moment. "There are improvements. But I want to prepare you. It may be quite difficult to see. Her legs have been amputated above the knee. She's lost more weight, and she may not know you."

"She'll know me," I said with quiet certainty.

Betsy smiled, hopeful, and placed her sewing back into the basket. I couldn't help but wonder if there was more she wasn't saying.

After some hesitation she added, "Micah was there when the doctor came last. She gripped his hand when he spoke your name. I know she has not forgotten you in her heart. It's her mind that is not always clear."

Betsy did not know Mother's determination like I did. I believed—I knew—she could get better.

After Betsy started feeding the baby, I summoned my courage to bring up the next thing weighing on my heart.

"Can I ask you something else?"

She nodded.

"I'd like to find my friend, Eliza. Or at least find out how she's doing. Her mother married Elder Monson while we were in Iowa, so she's likely at his home."

Betsy raised an eyebrow, and her eyes grew wide for a moment. She recovered quickly, but not fast enough to conceal her shock and what I thought was a hint of disapproval.

"He's an important church leader," she said. "With a large family. I didn't know he'd taken a second wife, but I am not surprised."

I could not find the words to respond to that.

"Can you get any information about her?" I asked.

"I'll see what I can do."

〜

I wasn't sure sleep would ever come that night. The excitement of seeing Mother—the fear of seeing Mother—consumed my body and my mind. I tossed this way and that, praying for rest, hoping for peace. I know I eventually fell into a fitful sleep because I had my first nightmare.

I am standing on the banks of the Platte as President Martin gives the order to cross. Snow falls about me, the wind howls, and the cold cuts through my bones. But this time, instead of Mother and Gideon, I am crossing with Father. The water fills my boots and slowly soaks my dress. It is heavy, frozen. We struggle to move against the current.

"Emma …" He is trying to talk to me, but I can't hear.

We make it halfway when he goes down. I watch the cart pull him under the frigid, icy water. I stand in the river, screaming.

"Father! Let go of the cart! Save yourself, not the cart! Save yourself, not the cart! Father!"

And then, just like that, I was back in bed. I knew I wasn't in the river anymore, but I kept screaming, "Father! Father!"

Betsy was at my side. She climbed in next to me. I wasn't cold anymore. I was sweating, soaked straight through my nightdress.

Betsy cradled my head in her lap, stroking my hair and wiping at my tears with a cotton handkerchief.

"You're safe, Emmaline," she whispered. "I'm here."

I cried like a baby until I fell back to sleep.

Sunshine streamed through the small window the next morning, bathing the room in light and announcing that the day I would see Mother had arrived. I felt groggy from my sleep, still shaken from my nightmare.

I shuffled to the bureau near the door and poured water from the crockery pitcher into the matching bowl and splashed water on my face. The smell of crackling bacon drifted in from the kitchen, gnawing at my stomach. I was allowed real food now, and my body knew it. Still, fear lingered before every meal, a habit left by too many hungry years.

After quickly dressing, I brushed my curls and tied them back with the yellow ribbon from Father, letting my fingers linger on the smooth satin. Letting myself miss him. The ribbon was dirty, and a little frayed, but it was still the most beautiful thing I owned. It was the only thing I owned.

After a breakfast of biscuits with preserves, bacon, and cold milk, I rocked Mattie while Betsy cleaned up the dishes. Looking down at her little face with big blue eyes like her mama and a dimple in her chin like her papa, I dreamed about what it would be like to grow up and have a family like Betsy and Micah had.

Plural marriage in Zion had never been fully explained to me. I knew it was practiced here, of course. They called it a sacred principle and spoke of it as a command of the Lord. But I wasn't sure how it worked or if everybody did it. I hadn't been to a Sunday service here or even been outside the house. So far, everything I knew about Zion was what I'd experienced in this home.

Would Micah take a second wife? I couldn't imagine it. He looked at Betsy with great love and devotion, and there was such sweet affection between them when they were together. I was afraid to ask Betsy about it. I didn't want to know the answer.

I turned my thoughts instead to my visit with Mother. I didn't know what I would find. But I had to see her. I had to believe that some part of her remained. I couldn't have come all this way to lose her too.

When I let myself think of the future, fear overtook me. How could we survive? With Father gone and Mother with no legs, everything felt hopeless. I couldn't see a path forward, so I stopped trying. I focused on what was real now: seeing her, reaching her, and somehow restoring her body and her mind.

Before long, Micah came in to announce that the wagon was ready to go. Betsy took a woolen coat from a hook by the door and wrapped it around me, then fixed a scarf snugly at my neck.

She took my hands in hers. "God be with you, Emmaline," she said softly. "I'm praying for you and your mother."

Micah took my arm and helped me into the wagon. He gave Betsy and Mattie each a kiss on the cheek, then climbed up beside me, taking the reins in gloved hands.

As we pulled onto the packed dirt road, the wagon creaked beneath us and the horses snorted in the crisp air. I gasped again when I saw the mountains before me. I had forgotten their magnificent beauty in the weeks I had been convalescing.

For a time we rode in silence. Finally, Micah spoke. His voice was gentle, but certain.

"She's a strong woman, your mother. Stronger than most."

I nodded, my eyes fixed on the mountains.

"Whatever you find today, just remember—our Heavenly Father doesn't leave us halfway. He finishes what he starts. He doesn't waste suffering."

I swallowed hard, a well of tears threatening to spill down my cheeks. I wasn't sure if I believed that. But I held on to the words anyway.

Micah gave the reins a gentle flick and looked ahead. Soon we were stopping in front of a small wooden house almost identical to the Greens' home. Smoke rose from the chimney, and it smelled like someone had baked a buttermilk pie.

"You ready?" Micah asked.

I nodded.

Micah knocked on the front door, and an older couple answered it together. They looked like they belonged to each other. Neither was too much taller than me, and both were round and soft around the edges. They had silver hair that reminded me of my grandmother's. I liked them immediately.

"Brother and Sister Thatcher," Micah said, "please meet Emmaline Kendall."

"Pleased to meet you, dear. I'm Sister Thatcher," the woman said as she ushered us into the home.

Brother Thatcher was silent, but he had a welcoming look on his weather-worn face.

Sister Thatcher took our coats and offered us cups of water. I appreciated the kindness, but I only wanted to see my mother.

"May I see her?" I whispered.

"Of course, child." She opened a door off the kitchen and guided me in.

Micah and Brother Thatcher did not follow. I couldn't help but look back at Micah for reassurance. He gave me a knowing look with eyes that said, *"You can do this."*

The room was dark and sparsely furnished. There was a bed, a bedside table with an unlit oil lamp, and a small wardrobe. The walls were white-washed, and a small window let in filtered gray light on this cloudy day.

My mother lay in the bed, covered in quilts, so I could not see her legs. I walked to her slowly, wiping silent tears from my cheeks as her emaciated face came into view. Her hair had grown longer than I realized and was beginning to gray around her face. She looked like she had aged ten years. Her eyes were closed, and her breath was labored.

"Mother," I whispered.

Then louder, "I'm here. It's me, Emmaline."

She stirred but did not open her eyes. I reached under the quilts and found her hand. She laced her fingers in mine. She did know.

I could not keep the tears from coming now. I bent close, pressing the back of her hand to my cheek. "I'm here, Mother. I made it. And so did you."

Her lips moved slightly, but no sound came. Her hand, though frail, held mine tightly.

"I wanted to come sooner," I went on, summoning all the courage to make my voice strong. "I've been ill too. But I'm getting stronger. I'm so much better now. I have wonderful people caring for me. I'm safe. I don't want you to worry about me. I just want you to get better, Mother. We'll get a small place of our own, and I'll take care of you. The houses are so nice here. And wait until you see the mountains. It's all so beautiful. You are going to make it, Mother. You have to. I need you to come back to me."

Standing there in that dark room with my Mother looking so sick, so weak, I didn't know if anything I said was true.

I kissed her forehead and left the room, walking into Sister Thatcher's waiting arms. I could no longer hold back the waves of choking sobs that had been building inside me.

As Micah and I left, I overheard Sister Thatcher speaking softly to her husband. "She's been through too much for one so young."

CHAPTER TWENTY-TWO

continued to visit my mother most every day for the next two weeks. Dr. Phillips said I did her more good than any tonic he could prescribe.

"Everyone needs a reason to live," he told me. "You're her reason."

He had no idea what those words meant to me. I had never thought I was enough for my mother. I wasn't sure if she had truly seen me since William died. This journey had taught me what we meant to one another, and that was the one treasure I held in my heart after all we had lost.

She started saying my name each time I came. At first it was faint and difficult to hear, but her voice grew stronger by the day. Sister Thatcher let me feed her the afternoon broth, and within a week she was sitting up on her own, steadying her head as I spooned it in.

As we worked on getting the broth down, I would tell her all about life with the Greens, the beauty of the mountains, and the excitement of the upcoming Christmas holiday.

"Oh, Mother, you should see the baby. She's starting to crawl. And she reaches for me now when I come in the room. And, Mother, I can't wait for you to taste Betsy's apple cake. She's teaching me to make it myself."

I carried on about these things each day until Sister Thatcher said it was time for Mother's nap. About that time, Micah would pick me up, or Brother Thatcher would drive me home. *Home.* That's what I'd begun calling the Greens' house in my mind.

One afternoon before Christmas, Micah said Betsy had a surprise for me. I tried to guess what it would be. Maybe she had taken in the red calico for the Christmas dance, or perhaps she had borrowed some of the books I'd been asking for. Maybe Dr. Phillips was clearing me for more activity. I went out only to see Mother.

Micah laughed at each guess and said, "You'll just have to see."

We got home, and I anxiously waited for Micah to assist me out of the wagon, eager to know what was happening inside. Before I reached the walk, the door flew open—and there she was. Eliza.

I ran to her and wrapped my arms around her. My Eliza had come to supper.

She looked worn, much thinner, and her hair was twisted up and pinned on top of her head instead of in its customary braids. But she was unmistakably Eliza. As we embraced, I felt I would never let go of her.

"How are you?" we both cried in unison, making Micah and Betsy laugh.

"You two have some catching up to do," Betsy said with a smile. "Why don't you sit and visit while I finish getting supper ready."

We sat in the rocking chairs, and Betsy served us two mugs of warm milk.

"I really thought you were dead," Eliza said. "I asked Elder Mon—I mean my father—to find you. But it took him weeks to learn where you had been placed."

"I've been asking about you too," I said.

We talked about our mothers and our recovery and what we thought of Utah. Both Eliza and her mother were doing better. They spent a couple of weeks in bed like I did, and her mother had a toe that might not recover, but the doctor was watching it. They had been cared for by Elder Monson's first wife.

I leaned in to whisper, "What's it like?"

She sighed heavily. "Oh, Emmaline, it's so strange. They have a really big house—and seven children. Seven! I'm the same age as the oldest daughter, and she hates me. I don't think any of them like us. Mother and I each have our own chamber upstairs. His children call my mama Mother Martha, and I am to call the first wife Mother Agnes."

The first wife.

My face grew hot as she spoke.

"Oh my," I said, not sure how to respond.

"Every night we have family prayers, and he talks about how we are a chosen family, following the prophet and God's holy ordinance."

Holy. It didn't sound holy to me. It sounded confusing and chaotic and wrong.

"And Mother Agnes did this to my hair," she added, wrinkling her eyes and frowning.

I laughed a little. The style looked stiff and awkward on her, like she was a child pretending to be grown.

"Have you heard from Sister Delia or Gideon?" I asked. I had been sick with worry for all my friends.

She frowned and looked down at her lap.

"I know nothing about Gideon," she said sadly. "I haven't seen him since Fort Bridger. I don't know if he even made it to the valley."

I gasped. Gideon was so strong. He'd saved me. How could I be alive and not Gideon? I couldn't believe it. Wouldn't believe it.

"Delia and Olivia?"

"They made it." Eliza drew out a long pause and lowered her voice. "I've seen her."

I tried to read her serious expression but could not.

"She's been married," Eliza said.

"Married? I haven't even been allowed out of the house yet except to see my mother. How could she have had time to meet someone and get married?"

Eliza shook her head and frowned. "It's a church leader in southern Utah. She and Olivia were sent there last week. Mama said she's his fifth wife; that's what Father told her."

My stomach turned over. Five wives.

"He said Delia's young and has a child, and this is the best way to care for her."

I tried to picture Delia and Olivia in a house like that, tried to imagine what Delia's face must have looked like when she was told. I couldn't. But I knew she would have been faithful to do anything the church asked of her.

"Brigham Young has *dozens* of wives!" Eliza said. "He'll probably get more. I've driven by his home. There are so many children. Some of them live in other houses. His family could be a whole town."

Betsy glanced at us as she set the table. There was a flicker of disapproval on her face as she placed the last dish. We stopped talking.

"Supper's ready, girls," she said, her voice a little too bright.

~

On Christmas Eve I stood before the looking glass in Betsy's dress. I felt the delicate pearl buttons and ran my hand over the lace. Who was the girl staring back at me?

My thick brown curls had begun to regain their shine with regular brushing. But my face was still so thin, and the freckles that I had inherited from Father were fading away, giving me an older, almost unfamiliar look. Betsy had been right—the dark red calico with ivory sprigs did suit my hair and complexion, but it hung loosely on my fragile frame.

"You look lovely," Betsy said, coming up behind me.

She placed her hands on my shoulders and smiled proudly, and then she gathered my curls behind my neck and tied them with Father's yellow ribbon. Just the way Mother had.

This would be my first time in public since the journey, and I felt no small measure of unease. I did not yet understand the American way of things—let alone how one was expected to behave in Zion. Betsy assured me the evening would be festive and full of cheer, that I had nothing to fret over. Even so, I felt the weight of stepping into society for the first time.

Micah, Betsy, Mattie, and I went to the ward house together. It was a short walk, only half a block. When the dark, cold night air hit my face, I froze with fear. I had to remind myself that there were warm buildings all around me. This wasn't Wyoming. The dark, cold night could not trap me.

As we neared the building, I heard music. A piano. Strings. The fiddles made me think of Brother Ashford and the lonesome version of "Amazing Grace" he'd played the night before we left Iowa City. A tear rolled down my cheek. I was beginning to understand that reminders of this year's suffering would be everywhere I went.

Light spilled from the ward house windows and flickered across the snow. I followed the Greens through the front doors and into a world I did not expect.

The room was warm and full of the scents of Christmas. Pine needles, nutmeg, cinnamon, fresh baked rolls.

Evergreen branches were strung across the rafters with red ribbon, and a Christmas tree stood at the far end of the room. Children placed handmade ornaments and strings of popcorn on the tree, while mothers oohed and awed. Other little ones ran about, their laughter ringing above the music and the hum of conversation

"Come, Emmaline," Betsy said gently, her hand on the small of my back as she guided me through the crowd.

We walked past long tables covered with roasted meats, winter vegetables, pies, breads, and cider jugs, through clusters of neighbors joyfully greeting one another. People turned to look at me—some with curiosity, others with warm smiles. I fixed a smile on my face and kept my head high.

A group of young people stood near the hearth, where the fire popped and hissed. Girls about my age were whispering and giggling, adjusting their hair ribbons and smoothing their skirts. I suddenly felt unsure of every part of myself. Did the dress fit? Was I standing properly? What was the polite way to respond when introduced?

Micah brought mugs of warm cider. The heat of the cup soothed my cold hands, and the scent of cinnamon calmed my nerves.

The piano began to play "Joy to the World," a Christmas hymn I knew from England, and I hummed along a little. I felt out of place yet awed by the joy all around me. I was introduced to many neighbors and church members, though I remembered few names.

Then I noticed Eliza. She stood across the room, holding her mother's hand. Her face lit up when she saw me, and I returned her smile. It brought me so much comfort to be where she was. We were here. We had made it.

But so many had not. How was I to celebrate my life when hundreds of bodies were left buried on the plains? I wondered if others felt this way. I didn't know because we didn't speak of it.

I closed my eyes for a moment and saw Gideon's face as he passed me the last bite of rabbit. I saw Ellie, so sweet and full of life. I saw my father, hoisting our family trunk up the gangplank of the *Horizon*.

"Emmaline," Betsy said softly. "Would you like to sit with the girls your age? You don't have to, but they're very kind."

I looked again at the group by the fire. One of the girls whispered into the ear of another, and they both burst out laughing. I was envious of their innocent, unburdened joy.

"I don't think I'm ready," I said.

She nodded. "You don't have to be. There's time."

When the dance music started, Micah asked me to hold Mattie while he took Betsy to the floor. Across the room couples began to form lines. The fiddler tapped his bow against the strings, and the pianist joined in with a lively reel—cheerful, clapping music, perfect for laughter, celebration, and twirling skirts.

I'd never seen anything like it. The men bowed; the women curtsied. Then the music started in earnest with fiddles quick and light, boots thudding softly on the wooden floor. Betsy laughed as Micah spun her across the room.

No one seemed burdened by the weight of winter or hunger or death. Not tonight.

I held Mattie close, breathing in her milky baby scent. She gurgled and smiled and kicked her little satin slippers. I closed my eyes and gave in to the melody, swaying lightly to the rhythm.

Suddenly, a man's voice cut through the music. "Is she yours?"

I opened my eyes to see a tall man, older than I'd expected—perhaps thirty or thirty-five—standing over me. His hair was dark, almost black, and matched his closely trimmed beard. He wore a formal black coat, and his boots shined.

What kind of a question was that?

"No, she's Betsy's daughter," I said quickly.

His steely eyes didn't match the softness of his smile. Betsy was at my side in an instant, breathless from dancing, and Micah was right behind her.

The tall man chuckled as though he had told a joke. "Of course," he said. "You're the young lady staying with the Greens."

Micah stepped slightly forward, his posture friendly but firm. "Emmaline, this is Brother Samuel Sandbury. He serves on the bishop's council. Samuel, this is Emmaline Kendall."

I dipped my head in greeting, unsure whether I was supposed to curtsy. Betsy reached for Mattie, making me feel more exposed.

"She's had a long recovery," Betsy added, placing a hand gently on my shoulder. "And this is her first outing, so we're easing her in slowly."

Samuel smiled again. "Then I'm honored to be among the first to welcome you, Emmaline."

I nodded but said nothing. Something about his expression made me uncomfortable.

"How are your little ones, Brother Sandbury?" Betsy asked, shifting the conversation.

"Growing like weeds," he said. "My Mary turned nine last week. Sarah's expecting again. Could be any day now."

"Oh my," Betsy said. "That'll be four?"

"Five, God willing."

Micah gave a low whistle. "And still time to attend the Christmas dance."

Samuel smiled at that. "Evenings like this are rare. We make time for what matters." He looked at me again as he said it, and my sense of unease deepened.

"Well," Betsy said brightly as though she sensed it too, "we're glad you stopped by. I promised Emmaline I'd help her find a seat near the fire."

"Of course," he said with a nod, lingering a moment before turning back to the crowd.

Betsy led me away, and I dared a glance back. He was watching us.

"Who was that?" I whispered.

"Samuel Sandbury is one of the bishop's men," Betsy said softly. "Respected. Married. But ..." She paused. "... keep your distance, sweetheart."

I didn't understand what she meant, but I could tell it was not good.

Betsy and I sat with Mattie near the fire, meeting more people and enjoying the music. We left the gathering early. But before we did, I noticed Micah speaking with Brother Sandbury.

Micah's arms were folded. His face looked serious. Cross, even. I wondered what it was about this man that had us all so unsettled.

Later that night, lying in bed, I heard voices from the other side of the house. Quarreling. Why? Betsy and Micah never quarreled. I slipped slowly to the door and tried to listen. I could only make out a few words.

"We never should have taken her," Betsy said, anger in her tone.

Micah sighed. "It was going to happen eventually."

What was going to happen? What were they quarreling about?

CHAPTER TWENTY-THREE

At night my body forgot that it was warm and safe. I was no longer at the Greens' house, tucked into a feather bed with a full stomach and a crackling fire across the room. The always-present cup of water on the bedside table was forgotten once my body gave way to the dark.

Instead, my dreams carried me back to Wyoming—back to the banks of the Platte, starving, thirsty, freezing to death.

I am on the far bank of the river, my dress frozen solid to my skin. Blinding snow falls all around me, the flakes gathering at the toes of my boots, rising inch by inch.

I look into the water and see a hundred bodies. Every one of them is Gideon. Each face turns toward me. Each one reaches, calls out, just before the undercurrent pulls him below the surface.

A hundred terrified voices cry, "Help me, Emmaline!"

I scream his name. "Gideon! Gideon!"

But the river sweeps them all away, and I am alone in the desolate Wyoming wilderness. Gideon is gone. I look for the others. There is no one. Snow, there is only snow. I collapse to the frozen ground like a sack of flour and weep. My tears form icicles down my cheeks. The snow covers me up until I am gone too.

I woke, trembling and screaming. Sweat-soaked curls matted to the back of my neck.

"There, there, honey. You're safe. I'm here."

Betsy's voice. Calming, soothing. Always there in the night when I needed her.

The next morning Dr. Phillips called to examine me.

"Your lungs are strong, and your fingers and toes look right as rain," he said as he hung his stethoscope around his neck.

He turned to Betsy. "She appears to be gaining weight. How is she eating?"

I wasn't sure why he addressed Betsy rather than me.

"Appetite like a horse," Betsy said brightly. "She eats everything we eat, and more."

"Excellent," he said. "I think she's ready for a sacrament meeting. I would not have her out in the cold air longer than necessary, but gathering with the Saints in church is the best way to nourish her soul now that her body is healing."

As he turned to leave, Betsy spoke again. "Doctor, the nightmares …"

"These are not uncommon," he said. "A return to church will do her good. She needs to be reminded that the Lord's purpose is greater than her suffering."

Dr. Phillips' words stayed with me long after he left. *"Greater than her suffering."* Is that truly what church leaders believed about the horror we had lived through?

Part of me wanted to go to church—was curious, even. I had taken the sacrament and attended Sunday services for years in England, but this would certainly be different. I wondered what worship in Zion looked like.

And yet, another part of me wanted to resist. Church had always been something I did because my parents had chosen it for me. Now I would do it because Dr. Phillips had chosen it. He hadn't even addressed me, hadn't seemed to care whether I felt ready to go.

The more I recovered, the more I realized that every decision was made for me. When had I last done something because I chose it? Even the pleasures I had were borrowed, arranged by others, fit into their days, not mine.

Still, I said nothing when Betsy came in on Saturday night and laid out a dress for Sunday. I didn't want to disappoint her. She worked so hard to care for me.

So I nodded and said, "Thank you," then I folded the dress carefully over my arm.

On Sunday morning the four of us headed toward the ward house again. It wasn't quite as cold as Christmas Eve, but I pulled my coat around me tightly. The sun, unshielded by a cloudless sky, made my eyes water. I wanted to enjoy the view as we walked. The mountains always gave me such peace, but I had to look down to avoid the sun.

My stomach lurched the closer we got. Church was something I did with my parents. I felt their absence more in that moment than ever before.

"I feel sick," I whispered to Betsy. "I don't know if I can."

She gave my hand a gentle squeeze. "You'll be fine, sweetheart. I'm with you."

Micah held the door open as we stepped inside. The air was warm and fragrant, with the pine boughs from Christmas still hanging from the rafters. But the atmosphere was much more reverent than it was at the Christmas Eve social.

People sat in narrow rows and spoke in low murmurs. The only sounds rising above a whisper were the cries of fussing infants and small children. Micah led us to a bench in the middle, where we got settled in time for the meeting to begin.

A short, portly man whom I recognized from the Christmas social rose to begin the service with a prayer. He then called out the name of a hymn, and voices rose in worship. I recognized the tune but not the words. None of the hymns were familiar to me, not until we closed with "Come, Come, Ye Saints."

"And should we die before our journey's through,
Happy day! All is well!
We then are free from toil and sorrow, too;
With the just we shall dwell!
But if our lives are spared again
To see the saints their rest obtain,
O how we'll make this chorus swell—
All is well! All is well!"

Everyone around me appeared to have great affection for the song. I once liked it too, but I did not anymore. I could not sing it. My father's death did not bring me happiness. Toil and sorrow were no longer just words. The song took me back to Iowa City. I saw a company of six hundred voices singing with joy as we prepared to push those miserable handcarts out of camp. And I heard Gideon's voice: *"We ain't ready, Emmaline … if we go now, some of us ain't going to make it."*

After the sacrament was given—bread and homemade wine—Elder Monson rose to speak.

Eliza and I exchanged a glance. She was sitting with her mother and another woman, older with wrinkles in her forehead and sad eyes. I assumed she was Mother Agnes. A whole row of children sat on the bench next to them. Two towheaded little boys fidgeted, and Elder Monson gave them a stern look before he began speaking. The boys sat up straight. I noticed a few other families with two or three adult women sitting together. I assumed they were plural families like Eliza's, but I wasn't sure.

"Brethren and sisters," he began in a lofty tone that I had never heard him use before, "the Lord will have a *tried* people. Not a weak people, nor a people who murmur at adversity, but a faithful, covenant-keeping people. A people willing to lay everything upon the altar of Zion, even their very lives."

People around me nodded in agreement, and I felt my heart beating in my ears as he continued to speak about what that meant.

"The sufferings of the Saints are not a tragedy. They are a testament. A testament that the Lord chastens whom he loves. That he proves his people through fire. Did he not send Abraham to the mountaintop? Did he not allow Satan to cover Job in ashes and boils?"

Was Ellie's death not a tragedy? Brother Ashford? My father? We left hundreds of bodies on the trail. My mother lay in bed without legs. Was that not a tragedy?

"I tell you now: Those who have arrived in this valley, weary and broken, are the chosen of God. For he hath brought them here to be made holy. And what will they do with their trials? Will they complain? Will they shrink from the holy ordinances? Or will they submit for the sake of Christ? Ye must submit, my brethren and sisters, as a child submits to his father. There is no Zion without obedience."

Chosen. Why would God choose me and not my father? His faith was zealous, without question. Mine was not.

I was not hearing everything Elder Monson said anymore. I kept my eyes on the fire in the stone fireplace behind him and felt anger burning in my chest, like the hot red coals that smoldered and hissed.

I was enraged at his dismissal of all the suffering and death. Confused by his statement that what we endured was not a tragedy. How could this church still ask more of us? He had made the journey. He had suffered. He had watched others die. How could he say the Lord had done this on purpose? I did not accept it. The God he spoke of was not a God I wanted to follow.

"There is no Zion without obedience."

Betsy seemed to sense my discomfort. She put her arm around me protectively. Her touch was comforting, but not enough to quiet the growing anger in my heart.

I don't remember much of the rest of the meeting. I was deep in my thoughts as we walked out of the building.

As we reached the steps, I heard a voice behind us: "Good morning, Miss Kendall. How are you? I trust your recovery is going well?"

It was Brother Sandbury. He placed a hand on my upper arm. His touch was light but strangely possessive.

"The Lord must be smiling on this beautiful Sabbath."

I flinched, and he let go, but not before giving a gentle squeeze. I took a step back. He pretended not to notice my revulsion and turned instead to Micah and Betsy.

"Brother and Sister Green, good day. I hope you are well."

I noticed that Betsy did not meet his eyes, but Micah shook his hand. "Brother Sandbury," he said with a nod. "We are well, but we do have to get Mattie home now. It is quite past her nap time."

Brother Sandbury then addressed Micah directly. "I trust you'll be at the priesthood meeting tonight. Brother Brigham will be addressing us."

"I'll be there," Micah replied, a hint of irritation in his voice. He was already walking away as he said it.

We passed by Eliza on the walk outside, but I couldn't meet her eyes. I wasn't angry with her; if anything, I needed her comfort. But I felt too sick, too shaken, to talk to anyone.

We walked away in silence.

"I need to lie down," I told Betsy once we got home.

She nodded, understanding. "Let me help you out of your dress and get you settled."

"No," I said, too sharply.

She looked taken aback, and I immediately regretted the harshness.

I softened my voice. "I can do it. I just need to rest awhile."

She nodded again and let me go. Hot tears slipped down my cheeks as I climbed into bed and hid beneath the quilts. I did not like the way I felt—alone in a country that seemed to believe it possessed me, at the mercy of a God who wanted me to suffer, and helpless to change anything for myself or my mother.

CHAPTER TWENTY-FOUR

woke the next morning groggy and hungry—and still in my church dress. The events of Sunday slowly came back to me. I still felt sickened by my first sacrament meeting in Zion, the dismissive words Elder Monson spoke about our suffering, and Brother Sandbury's uncomfortable touch.

Betsy had to be worried. She'd left me alone and let me sleep through supper. I felt she deserved an explanation or an apology. But something held me back, as if part of me blamed her for taking me to church, for being a part of this world that I was starting to feel trapped in.

I knew it wasn't fair. She was the best thing that had happened to me in Zion. But somehow I had lost a little trust in everyone.

At breakfast I tried to be pleasant, focusing my attention mostly on Mattie. We ate porridge and small slices of ham. The porridge had gone cold and lumpy waiting for me to wake. But Betsy did not mention it. Instead, she spoke brightly about the weather, the baby's new tooth, and a calf due this spring—everything but what had happened yesterday. I loved her for not making me explain.

Later that afternoon Brother Thatcher picked me up for a visit with my mother. We rode silently at first. The clouds were low and heavy, and the air was gray. The wind howled and hinted at a coming storm. I focused on the sound of the wagon wheels creaking over the frozen ground and wrapped my shawl tighter. The scratch of the wool on my neck was more irritating than usual.

After a while Brother Thatcher spoke. "The Lord is working, Emmaline," he said. "He strengtheneth the feeble and restoreth the broken."

I silently fumed. So many feeble and broken were left dead on the trail. Why wasn't the Lord working then, when we had begged him for help? I was still very young, but I felt it was wrong to celebrate the living without mourning the dead. I felt that the indiscriminate protection of God—if it was true—was cruel, not loving.

I trusted what I had seen with my own eyes: Death and survival were not indiscriminate. No, death on the trail came first to the weak, the sick, the old, or the very young. It spared those who began the journey stronger and healthier. It hurt to hear survival attributed to God's favor, while suffering and death were dismissed as nothing more than a test or a trial.

These thoughts I kept to myself, of course. Brother Thatcher was just a caring man taking me to see my mother. I could see he was sincere in his belief.

But then he said something that caught my attention: "Your mother sat up on her own this morning and ate porridge. It was a tender mercy to witness."

I turned to him, unsure I'd understood him correctly. "She ate by herself?" I asked.

"That she did, dear. And then she asked for you."

A smile escaped my clenched jaw. These were the words I had been waiting to hear.

I found Mother sitting up when I walked in her room.

"Emmaline," she said softly.

I ran to her and kissed her forehead. She was smiling at me, her eyes full of love and glistening with tears.

When I sat down next to her, she reached for my hands and took them both in hers. Her grip was weak but purposeful.

She peered at me for a long moment before she spoke—softly and deliberately, with no small effort. "I … love … you … proud … Emma."

Mother had called me Emma. The way Father used to.

I could only say one word before my tears choked out my voice. "Mama."

I lay my head in her lap and cried. Her hands rested on my back, lightly stroking my curls that surely reminded her of Father. I wanted her to know everything. How the doctor dismissed my nightmares. How these people glorified suffering and said Father's death was not a tragedy. How uncomfortable I felt around the strange Brother Sandbury. How afraid I was that she and I couldn't take care of ourselves anymore.

But I could not make words from any of it. Only tears.

We sat like that for a long time before Sister Thatcher gently opened the door and said it was time for my mother to have some soup. She had a bowl for each of us. It wasn't broth, but a hearty chicken stew.

The warmth of the bowls and the scent of garlic and onion comforted me. I dried my cheeks and helped Mother eat. Maybe next time I could find the words to explain my tears to her.

Micah came soon to pick me up. "Best get home before the storm sets in," he told me.

I kissed Mother and tucked the quilts around her, assuring her I'd be back the next day.

Micah spoke about his work at the forge, of a mule's thrown shoe and a wagon wheel needing repair, but his words were nearly lost to the wind. It howled around us like a warning, wild and bitter cold. I huddled closer to his side, trembling at the thought of being caught outside in another winter storm.

For dinner that night we sat down to a warm meal of stewed beans and salt pork while the wind roared outside. Betsy served a skillet of rich corn bread with creamy butter that ran down my chin. Though the coming storm scared me, I felt warmed by the loving care that Betsy put into the meal. I couldn't help but think of all the nights I had gone without.

Micah was heartily enjoying it as well. "I think I'll have to go for another helping, darlin'," he said, planting a kiss on Betsy's cheek.

"Well you might not have room for pie if you do that!" she teased.

After dinner I sat by the fire mending socks while Betsy put the baby to bed. I thought how lucky I was to be living in this loving household after everything that had happened.

"Emmaline," Micah called, interrupting my thoughts. "Can you come join us?"

Betsy and Micah were sitting at the table across from each other—something I'd never seen outside of mealtimes. They looked serious, and my stomach felt the nervous edge to Micah's voice.

"We'd like to talk to you."

They're mad at me. They want to talk about last night.

But Betsy's face did not look angry. It looked sad. I put my mending back in the basket and joined them. Under the table my legs were shaking, and my hands were sweaty.

"I'm sorry about yesterday," I said timidly. "I shouldn't have spoken to you harshly. I am sorry that I missed supper. I didn't intend to fall asleep. I promise it won't happen again."

"Emmaline, honey, this isn't about that," said Betsy gently, reaching across my lap to hold my hand.

Micah began, "When the handcart companies came to the valley, the prophet asked for volunteers to help assist and house all the sick. Of course we volunteered right off."

"We were so fortunate to get you," Betsy interjected. "We have loved having you in our home."

Have loved. Past-tense.

"If it were up to us, you would stay here until your mother was well enough for you both to get your own home," Micah went on.

"But it's not up to you?" I asked.

"No, I'm afraid it is not," he said. "The prophet has made new assignments for those who are improving. New homes where you can continue to convalesce while also helping families who need help."

"What kind of help?" I asked, tears welling in my eyes as the understanding that I would leave the Greens came over me.

"Larger households," he said gently. "Families with many children who need help keeping up with chores. They said you were strong enough now, that your primary need is simply a place to stay until your mother is well."

"But I like it here," I said, tears spilling over. "I like helping you. I can help more. I promise."

Betsy's chin quivered, and she twirled her hair around her index finger. "Sweetheart, you've been a tremendous help. And we don't expect any more of you. It's just that the prophet decided you can be more help elsewhere."

"Where?"

Micah hesitated. He ran a hand through his hair and leaned his forehead on his hands for a moment.

"You've been assigned to the Sandbury household," he finally said, matter-of-factly.

We all let that news settle for a moment.

"Brother Sandbury?" I asked. "From church?"

His touch on my arm. That uncomfortable way he looked at me.

"Yes," Betsy whispered. If she was trying to hide her disdain for the man, it was not working.

"No," I said quietly.

And then I stood up. "No!"

"Emmaline," said Micah.

"No, I don't want to go there. I want to stay here. I like it here." Desperation rose in my voice as I spoke.

They looked at me. The weight of the moment, of this terrible news, began to suffocate me. I needed to escape. There had to be somewhere to go to outrun this.

I ran out of the house and bent over sobbing on the front walk. The cold air hit me like a wall of ice. It was snowing hard—like Wyoming. I couldn't even see as far as the barn. Was it the cold or the fear causing me to tremble so?

That's when it hit me. If I left, if I ran, I would be completely on my own. Without shelter, money, or food. It would be even worse than Wyoming. I was completely at the mercy of the prophet.

"There is no Zion without obedience."

The front door opened, and Micah came out. He knelt down and scooped me off the ground and carried me inside. Snow fell off my body and piled in clumps on the floor as he set me down. I quaked with cold, and my toes were starting to numb.

I didn't say another word that night. Betsy helped me dry off and brought a cup of warm milk to my room. I didn't touch it.

I climbed into bed and cried myself to sleep. Again.

CHAPTER TWENTY-FIVE

The sun rose on January 25, 1857, because you can't stop a day from coming.

The storm outside had ended, but the one in my heart still raged. I woke with a pounding headache, as I always did after a nightmare, and I was exhausted from several nights of sleeping poorly.

I'd had only a few days to prepare for my move to the Sandburys' house. No amount of crying and begging had changed my circumstances. I finally just quit talking. I had nothing left to say. Not to them. Not to anyone.

Even my last few visits with Mother had been quiet. I did not want to worry her, so I said nothing except that I would be moving to a different home. She patted my hand when I told her, as if she'd been told already. She wasn't capable of a discussion yet, even if I had wanted to talk to her about everything. So I purposed in my heart to endure what I had to until the two of us could live together again.

A light knock came at the door. Betsy pushed it open. We had just sat through a silent meal of cornmeal porridge with cream and molasses. I could tell she had tried to make the breakfast special, and I did not make it easy for her. I didn't have much appetite, but I tried to eat a little.

"I've brought a bag for you." She walked into the room, her voice too bright for the moment.

The navy-blue carpetbag had rich leather handles and a brass latch. It looked like it had been in her family for decades. I wondered if she had traveled across the plains with it from Winter Quarters. But I did not ask.

"I've packed the red calico and your church dress. I want you to keep them. They don't fit me anymore, and they suit you perfectly."

She set the bag down at the foot of the bed and opened it, smoothing the fabric as she spoke. "There's also an extra pair of stockings and a clean chemise. I took it in a little, so it should fit well enough."

I said nothing. Not even a nod.

Betsy glanced up at me, her hands shaking for a moment before she continued, "I tucked your hairbrush in too—and a needle and thread with a few buttons in case anything comes loose. And here's my ribbon that you admired at Christmas. The blue one. I know you usually wear your yellow ribbon, but you might want another color sometime."

She didn't know anything about my yellow ribbon. I might have told her someday, but not now. Not like this.

"Here's a handkerchief of mine," she said as she folded a small piece of fabric. "I'm sorry it has my initials on it, but it's all I have."

Still, I said nothing. But my heart softened. I looked at the embroidered B.G. and knew I would be glad to have something with her initials. Something of Betsy.

Finally, she picked up my scriptures from the night table, which had been her Christmas gift to me, and silently placed them in the bag.

"Micah will be home to pick us up shortly, and we'll all ride together." Her tone had a note of false cheer. As she walked out of the room, I found my voice.

"Betsy—"

She turned around, surprised.

"Thank you. For everything."

She came back and gave me a hug. Her body was warm, and her touch comforting. She smelled like molasses and cinnamon. I inhaled her scent so that I might never forget it. Dear, sweet Betsy, the angel who had nursed me back to life. The angel who had made me want to live again. My chest ached with the loss of her.

When she pulled away, her shoulder was wet with my tears. Would there ever be a day I stopped crying?

Micah soon arrived and said it was time to leave. "May I give you a priesthood blessing before we go?"

I nodded.

Micah placed his hands gently upon my head. His voice was gentle and caring. "Heavenly Father, in the name of Jesus Christ and by the authority of the holy Melchizedek Priesthood, I lay my hands upon the head of Emmaline Kendall to bless her in this time of trial.

"Emmaline, the Lord knows your heart. He has seen your suffering and gathered your tears. He knows the weight you carry, and he will not forsake you. I bless you with strength to endure the road ahead. I bless you with courage when you feel alone and with peace in your heart, even in the midst of sorrow.

"You will not be forgotten. Angels are round about you, and the Lord will make a way, in his time, for healing and for hope. I bless you to remember who you are—a daughter of God—and to know that his love is constant, even when the world feels cold."

Mattie fussed, and Micah picked her up after the amens were said. Betsy wrapped a shawl around my shoulders. We all walked outside together, maybe for the last time, and climbed into the wagon. Micah helped Betsy onto the bench seat and placed Mattie in her lap, tucking blankets around them.

He handed me a thick wool blanket as I climbed onto the wagon bed. I held my carpetbag close and soon heard the wheels creak to life. We were rolling down the road, taking me once again toward an unknown future.

~

The Sandbury home was a couple of miles from the Greens, and my sense of dread grew steadily as we drove through wheel ruts in the packed snow. The crisp air was colder when we were moving, and the light breeze burned my cheeks and ears. We traveled east, in the direction of the mountains, and they looked stunning.

The brilliant blue was striking against the fresh white covering of snow. But today they stood not as a monument of peace, but a painful reminder of the life I longed for: a home like Betsy and Micah had, but with my own mother and father.

That's why we had come here.

Quicker than I had hoped, we were pulling into the drive at a two-story adobe home with a thatched roof and covered porch. Two chimneys stood on opposite ends of the home. My first thought was that four families could have lived in this home in Liverpool. It seemed too large, even for their family of seven, and I realized that I did not know how Brother Sandbury earned his living. I wasn't sure I cared.

I stayed in the wagon while Betsy and Micah got down. Micah came round to help me, but I pulled back from his extended hand.

"Please," I said, trying one more time. "Let me stay with you. Tell them no. You could do it if you wanted to. It's your house. Please. I'll do anything."

Micah looked only at the ground.

"Sweetheart, the prophet has ordained this," Betsy said. "It's what the Lord wants for you. Even when we don't understand his ways, we must trust, and we must obey."

"There is no Zion without obedience."

I climbed out of the wagon only because I had no other choice.

About that time, the front door opened, and Brother Sandbury exited the home with a woman following behind him, a newborn baby in her arms. Several more children peered out curiously behind her.

Sarah Sandbury was Brother Sandbury's wife. Betsy had told me they both came from England like I did. But they had arrived in 1853 and established a home in Zion with their oldest two children. Three more had been born since. Perhaps I would feel more at home with an English family, she had said brightly. I doubted it then, and I doubted it now.

Sarah was tall, like Brother Sandbury. While he stood about six feet, I guessed her to be around five foot nine. She was thin, with a severe face and dark blonde hair pulled into a tight knot. She wore a cotton dress the color of the mountains, with a matching bonnet hanging around her neck.

Samuel approached Micah and shook his hand, saying, "Brother Green, thank you for bringing her."

Micah nodded.

Betsy hurried up the walk to see Sarah and the baby. "Congratulations on the new little one," she said kindly. "How did it all go?"

"We're well," Sarah said firmly, not really answering the question.

Betsy rubbed her thumb over the baby's cheek. "What's his name?" she asked sweetly.

"Seth." She paused. Then, "After my father."

"Oh, he must be so proud to have his grandson named after him," Betsy said.

"He died," Sarah responded. "Last year. In England." She still spoke with a mild British accent.

Betsy looked ashamed, realizing she had accidentally said something that caused Sarah pain, not knowing how to repair the damage.

Sarah turned her attention to me. "Best come inside now," she said. "Before the baby catches cold."

Betsy was not quite ready for this. She put her hand on my shoulder. "You're going to love Emmaline. She's sweet as can be, she has magic fingers with a needle, and she's been a great help with Mattie."

Sarah nodded. "Come along, then."

Brother Sandbury, who had been talking with Micah, then turned his attention to me. "Welcome to our home, Miss Kendall." He smiled. "We trust you'll be very happy here."

He stared at me with that gaze—too intense, too familiar—that made me so uneasy.

He ushered me up the walk and into the house behind Sarah. Before I walked over the threshold, I stole a glance at Betsy. She was watching me, still in the same place I had left her. Micah put an arm around her and led her away. She looked as sad as I felt.

The home smelled like woodsmoke and fresh paint. I already missed the scent of Betsy's kitchen. The Greens' house always smelled like apples and cinnamon and fresh bread. Smells that made me feel like the house itself was giving me a warm hug. This felt colder, despite the crackling fire.

I found myself standing in the parlor, which was finer than any home I'd ever seen. An oval woven rug covered much of the wood-plank floor, and it was furnished with a matching red velvet settee and stuffed armchair. Two straight-backed chairs sat across from the settee. A large painting of the Nauvoo temple hung above the fireplace, and scriptures were placed prominently on the table between the chairs. A piano stood against the opposite wall. My eyes fell to a book sitting on top of the piano: *The Poetical Works of William Wordsworth*. It was the first book I'd seen since leaving England, and it struck me like a lifeline thrown across a stormy sea. Just knowing it was there steadied something inside me for a moment.

I turned to the plate-glass window and watched as Micah, Betsy, and Mattie drove away.

"Let me show you to your chambers," Brother Sandbury said.

Sarah quickly stepped in. "I'll take her," she said, handing him the baby.

She turned to me but did not meet my eyes as she spoke. "Follow me. Your room is to the left at the top of the stairs."

My room was nicer than the one at the Greens' house. The bed was larger, made for two, and lace curtains hung at the window, bathing the room in filtered golden sun.

A washstand with a basin and pitcher stood opposite the bed, and a simple wardrobe sat in the corner. There was a bedside table with a single drawer. Above the bed hung a framed sampler in red thread: "Endure in the faith, that ye may be found worthy." I wondered whose hands had stitched it, but I did not ask.

The bed was neatly made, covered by an exquisite quilt so beautiful that I paused at the door.

It was unlike anything I'd seen before. Deep red pansies curved on stems of faded green, all stitched by hand onto creamy muslin blocks. The corners were bordered in delicate vines and leaves of red and deep yellow. This was a quilt made for beauty—for display—not for a girl's bedroom.

Sarah watched me finger the leaves as she said, "Samuel bought it back East on a business trip. Baltimore, I think. Or Philadelphia."

"It's beautiful," I said.

"Yes, well," she said. "Do take care to keep it nice. Now unpack your things and come down to the kitchen. There's work to be done to get dinner on for the children."

I hung my dresses in the wardrobe and unpacked my few belongings, arranging them around the room, trying to find a configuration that felt personal to me. I finally put everything but the clothing in the little drawer in the nightstand. The fact was I had so few things, and this room was not personal. I didn't know how to make it mine. Didn't want to make it mine.

I walked downstairs and found the kitchen. Sarah was serving johnnycakes and apple butter to four children. Each had a small tin cup of milk. I stood in the doorway and watched, unsure what to do.

"Letty, mind yourself, you almost spilled your milk," Sarah said to one of the girls who was barely old enough to hold her own spoon. Her tone was not harsh, but it lacked the gentleness with which Betsy spoke.

She seemed surprised to see me and stiffened a little.

For a moment she opened her mouth and then paused. Was she unsure what to do with me? I thought I was here because she needed help.

"Well then, let's get to work," she said, nodding at me. "You don't expect to be served, do you?"

It was not really a question.

"No ma'am," I said, wanting to cry but determined not to. "I want to help."

"Can you peel a potato?"

It was an absurd question.

"Yes, ma'am."

"Please call me Sister Sandbury."

There was no sharpness in her tone, but no warmth either.

She handed me a knife and gestured toward a pile of potatoes. "There's an apron on the hook by the door."

I found the apron and tied it behind my back. Then I set to work peeling potatoes. Sister Sandbury left to go care for the baby, who was fussing in another room.

Before long, Letty did spill her milk. She began to cry.

I found a rag and knelt by her side. "Hush, sweetheart, it's okay. We can clean it up."

"Mama be angry," she said, then sniffed.

"We don't have to tell her," I said, leaning in to whisper. "It will be our secret."

I looked around at all the children to see if they were willing to share our little secret. They all giggled as I wiped up the spill and wrung the rag out in the bucket of water by the door. There was a little less tension in the air.

When I went back to peeling potatoes, feeling a bit lighter, I looked out the window and saw Brother and Sister Sandbury. She must have settled the baby back down. I watched closely and saw that they were quarreling. I could not make out any of the words, but she was obviously crying. He put his hands on her shoulders, trying to draw her into a hug, but she pulled away and ran off.

The front door soon opened and someone ran through the house. A bedroom door slammed.

I had the strong feeling that I was not the only one unhappy with my presence at the Sandbury home.

CHAPTER TWENTY-SIX

At first, life at the Sandbury home wasn't so much bad as it was strange. By the end of the first day, I realized no one had introduced me to the children. I'd spent several hours with them, helping at mealtime and tidying up, because their mother had disappeared to her room after quarreling with their father. I'd pieced together their names—Mary, Samuel, Lucy, Letty, and baby Seth—by listening and watching. But no one had ever told me outright.

They called me Sister Emmaline. So I knew they'd been told something. It felt oddly impersonal, as though I'd been placed in their lives without being welcomed into them.

I had to learn the house rules by quietly observing, stumbling into them by accidentally breaking one, or asking when there was no other way to figure things out. One thing I learned: If I needed something, I had to ask Brother Sandbury. Sarah was usually unapproachable. This was so different from the Greens, where Betsy had been my lifeline.

I finally got up the courage to approach him about my biggest concern one evening after family prayers. He was sitting in his red chair by the fire, reading scriptures, while Sarah settled the children into bed.

I began to head up the stairs to my room, hesitated on the fourth step, and turned around to face him.

I spoke timidly, barely above a whisper. "Brother Sandbury?"

He looked up, surprised, and for a moment he said nothing. Then he called me to him.

I stood before him, and he smiled. I felt he was pleased that I had come to him.

It took all my courage to speak. "I wondered—That is, I would like to ask when might I go see my mother."

He smiled that same unsettling smile—an expression that filled me with hatred. But I realized he had the power to grant or deny my request, so I smiled back as sweetly as I could.

"Emmaline," he said, drawing out the last syllable a little too long. "Are you happy here?"

I considered how he wanted me to respond. "Your home is lovely. I am grateful for the hospitality, sir."

"You don't have to call me sir."

"Brother Sandbury," I corrected.

"I asked if you were happy here."

"It's been—It's only been a week," I stammered. "I am enjoying the children. I am very happy to have a place to stay while my mother recuperates."

He nodded, still smiling. "Um-hm." He paused for a few moments and then continued, "About your mother … I have spoken to Dr. Phillips. He feels that your visits may be too frequent for her. They are overstim-ulating. She tires too easily and is not recovering as fast as he'd like."

This didn't sound anything like the Dr. Phillips who told me I was better than any tonic he could prescribe.

"He thinks limiting visits to once a week for now would be best for both of you."

My knees buckled underneath me. My dinner backed up into my

throat. He was going to keep me from my mother. But why? Did Sarah need so much help that they couldn't spare me for two hours in the afternoons? She didn't act like she wanted help.

I had to think. Had to fix this.

"I could have shorter visits," I offered. "Brother Thatcher offered to pick me up and bring me back each day. I'll just go and check on her and help a little and be right back here to start supper. I can do it."

He gazed so intently at me as I spoke, I'm not sure he blinked.

"I've spoken to Brother Thatcher," he said. "I will take you."

He picked up his scriptures. The conversation was over. I tried to understand what was happening, but I could not make sense of it. I was meant to be here until Mother recovered. I could help her recover. The sooner I left here, the happier this household would be.

I went upstairs, confused and angry. I put on my nightdress and sat on the bed without pulling back the elegant quilt, then fell over, sobbing. I must have drifted off to sleep, still curled on the quilt.

I am free-falling into the dark night as the ground trembles beneath me with the thunderous roar of a buffalo stampede. I land in the Nebraska prairie.

Carts and people and body parts fly all around me. I duck my head and clutch Father's arm, trying not to let go. But the buffalo are coming right for us in a blur of coffee-colored fury. And then a screeching halt as the buffalo quit running and start moving slowly through thick fog and quicksand. I am face-to-face with a bull. His dark, menacing eyes, his nostrils the size of eggs, snorting and blowing hot air on my neck. I could wrap my palms around his thick horns, and my fingertips wouldn't even meet.

Then in a clap of thunder, the stampede starts again and I am separated from Father. He vanishes into a herd of five hundred buffalo. The entire company disappears with him, and I am alone on the Nebraska prairie. I spin around looking for signs of life. There are none. Even the trees were taken by the buffalo. Desolation stretches as far as my eye can see.

"Come back! Don't leave me! Please don't leave me! Father! Mother!"

I woke on the floor, gasping between sobs. Where was I? The room was so dark, cold, and suffocating. I shivered through my sweat-soaked nightdress as the truth slowly came back to me. I was waking from another nightmare. But Betsy did not come to my side. I was alone this time. My heart still beat wildly in my chest; choking sobs still racked my body.

The floorboards creaked outside my door. A figure pushed it open. The oil lamp Sarah held bathed light across the room. She stood in the doorway in her nightdress, her hair falling long and wild around her shoulders. I'd never seen her hair down. She scanned the room and found me on the floor.

"What is all the noise up here?" she asked. "You've woken the baby."

I couldn't speak. Couldn't catch enough air to explain. I sat up and wiped my tears.

Her face softened, just a touch, and she set the lamp on the wash table. I watched as she pulled back the quilt and settled the pillows.

She extended a hand. "Get back in bed. You need to rest."

After pulling me up and seeing that I'd gotten into bed, she walked away without a word, shutting the door behind her.

I rose early the next morning, eager to leave that room. *I'll make the porridge for breakfast*, I thought. *They'll see I can be helpful and understand they can do without me in the afternoons.*

I slowed at the kitchen door. Voices. The room was not empty. Sarah was speaking in a low and desperate tone. I inched closer, eager to hear what was being said.

"She's still a child, Samuel. Please don't do this."

"She will be fifteen next week," he responded.

They were talking about me.

"You should have seen her last night. She is suffering. She's lost nearly everything. This is not right."

"That's why she needs us," he said. "That's why it is right."

"Please, no," she said, not demanding this time but pleading.

"Darling, this is the Lord's desire for our family. When we follow the prophet, when we submit to a duty out of obedience, the Lord blesses us with understanding, with abundance. We are only protected from evil and judgment when we are under submission to his holy ordinances."

"There is no Zion without obedience."

My whole world turned dark. Ice crawled through my veins as their meaning became clear. I could only hope that I was wrong.

I tiptoed through the next few days in quiet horror, performing my duties with care, finding ways to help while remaining unseen, playing with the children when I could. All the while I tried desperately to think of some way to change my circumstances. I kept my deepest fears hidden even from my own thoughts, not daring to form the words in my mind. But they loomed over me like the sooty fog on a Liverpool morning.

On Friday I rose to find Sarah in the kitchen, dressing two chickens to roast. She had wrung the necks of two older hens that morning—too tough for frying, she said, but they'd roast up fine with herbs and root vegetables.

She asked me to fetch apples from the cellar to make a pie. It all seemed extravagant compared to what I'd come to expect in the Sandbury household. The baby whined, and she picked him up to feed while continuing to bark at me about how to peel and slice the apples just so.

We would bake a loaf of bread next, she said. I paused for a moment, finding that to be odd. Today was Friday. She usually baked bread on Saturdays. I wondered what all the fuss was about, but I did not ask.

Somewhere between kneading the bread and dusting the top of the pie with cinnamon, Sarah spoke. "The prophet will be dining with us for supper." There was no excitement in her voice.

"Brigham Young?" I asked with surprise.

"Yes, and you must be on your best behavior."

That was a strange comment. I always behaved well. Kind and compliant, on the outside at least.

"It's wiser for us to submit," she said cryptically. For a moment she looked like she wanted to say more, but she did not.

Later I considered how to dress for the prophet. The importance of the evening was not lost on me. I did not wish to wear the red calico. It was too beautiful, too festive, too special to me. But my everyday woolen frocks would not do.

I finally settled on my church dress, a simple but elegant brown print. There was no lace at the collar, but the fabric was gathered and fastened with brass buttons. I brushed out my curls and braided my hair behind my neck. A few curls fell about my forehead, but they would not be tamed. I fastened the braid with Betsy's blue ribbon. I would not wear my father's precious gift to a dinner that felt like the beginning of a future I could not escape.

When the prophet arrived, I was sitting in the parlor. I rose as he entered. He was tall and broad-built, with graying hair and a full beard. Dressed in a dark wool suit with a high-collared white shirt and long coat, he seemed to fill the entire room. I was, at once, frightened and in awe. Part of me hoped God had sent his prophet to deliver me from my trials.

He took my hands in his and looked at me with the type of measured politeness that does not really try to see you, does not meet your eyes.

"Sister Kendall," he said. "I am glad to see you well. I thank the Lord for your healing and strength." The words implied warmth, but his voice lacked it.

Brother Sandbury was exceedingly proud to have the prophet in his home, and I winced at his show of false humility.

"It is no small thing, Prophet, to have you sit at our table," Samuel said, clasping his hands reverently. "I only pray that our simple fare is not beneath so great a servant of the Lord."

He carried on this way through the meal, more insufferable than usual all evening.

After supper we moved to the parlor. The dishes had been cleared, the table wiped clean, and the children sent to bed, except for baby Seth, who fussed in Sarah's arms. She cradled him gently, her eyes low. The room was dim but warm from the heat of the stove, the shadows from the oil lamp flickering against the walls.

I sat straight-backed in a chair next to Sarah, hands folded tightly in my lap, trying not to fidget. My heart had not stopped racing since Sarah uttered the words that the prophet would be dining with us.

Brigham Young had removed his coat and sat now with one ankle resting atop the other knee, wholly at ease. He praised the bread, the pie, the roasted chicken and thanked Sarah for her hospitality, though he did not look at her when he spoke.

"She's a wonderful cook," Samuel said.

Sarah said nothing.

The prophet turned to me. "You're a quiet one, Sister Kendall."

I looked up, startled to be addressed. "Yes, sir. I mean, thank you, sir." It sounded absurd, but I had no idea what to say.

He chuckled lightly, folding his hands over his stomach. "A quiet girl is often a thoughtful one. And a thoughtful girl makes a faithful woman."

I smiled faintly, uncertain if I was meant to respond. I tried to hide my trembling hands in the folds of my skirt. His reference to "woman" did not help. I could feel Sarah's gaze on me, though when I glanced her way, her eyes were fixed on Seth.

The prophet leaned forward. "I've come tonight with a sacred purpose." His eyes flicked between Sarah and me.

I felt the air sucked out of the room.

He spoke slowly, with a kind of solemn reverence. "The Lord is gathering his people in these latter days. He is preparing a generation of

Saints who will carry Zion forward in purity and power. But Zion is not built by ease. It is built by obedience."

Samuel nodded along, silently projecting his approval.

"Sometimes," the prophet continued, "the Lord asks hard things. But through obedience, he pours out blessings—upon families, upon nations, upon generations."

The heat from the fire burned my face though my body felt ice cold.

He then looked directly at me with his soft gray eyes and took a dramatic pause.

"Sister Kendall," he said, "the Lord has revealed to me that Brother Sandbury is to take you into his household under the covenant of celestial marriage."

There it was. The thing I had feared all week.

"He is a righteous man. A priesthood holder. And you are a virtuous girl from a faithful family. Your mother is recovering. Your path is uncertain. But the Lord provides. This is provision. This is blessing."

The sound dulled around me, like I was sinking underwater. I stared at the brass buttons on Samuel's waistcoat. The second one from the top was crooked.

The prophet's voice softened. "We do not compel. The Lord does not compel. He invites."

Sarah's arms tightened around the baby. He squirmed and whimpered. She patted his back gently. Her voice, when it came, was almost too soft to hear. "She's fourteen."

Samuel's jaw tightened. His glare cut across the room. She fell silent under it.

"She will be fifteen next week," Samuel said.

Sarah nodded. Slowly. Sadly.

The prophet turned back to me. "Sister Emmaline. Are you willing?"

One thing I knew: That was not a question.

I opened my mouth, but no sound came. My thoughts screamed, *No.*

No, I am not. I am a child. I do not want this. Not marriage. Not this man. But the words would not come.

Samuel spoke gently. "You'll be safe here. Loved. Honored. That's what the Lord wants for you."

I looked to Sarah. Her jaw was trembling. She would not meet my eyes.

"I …" My voice was barely a whisper. "I want to see my mother."

Brigham Young nodded. "You shall."

And then he rose. "It is settled."

He placed a hand briefly on my shoulder. His palm was warm. Heavy.

"The Lord will bless you, dear. Zion has need of strong daughters." He turned to Samuel. "We will speak again tomorrow."

Then he was gone, with Samuel walking him out and looking pleased.

Sarah stood, the baby asleep on her shoulder, and carried him to her room without a word.

I remained seated long after the room had gone quiet. I stared at my hands, knuckles white, clenched so tightly they ached.

I had not said yes. But I had not said no.

And now it was done.

About the time I found my legs and dared to stand, Brother Sandbury came back into the room. He walked to me and placed his hand on my arm.

His touch was revolting.

"Emmaline," he began, his voice soft and assured, "this sealing isn't only about you. It's about your mother too. Her healing depends on your obedience, don't you see?"

I stared at him, frozen.

"When a household aligns with the Lord's will, blessings flow. But when a daughter resists her calling …" He paused, squeezing my arm slightly. "Well. Judgment doesn't always wait for the next life."

I registered the threat and took a step backward.

Then something inside me cracked open. The final thread that had held me in place.

"No," I said, my voice low but steady. "Do not touch me. And do not ask this of me again."

And with that, I ran upstairs and slammed the door to my room.

I pushed my back against the door, chest heaving, heart thundering in my ears. I wanted to collapse, to disappear, to scream. Instead, I stood perfectly still, staring at the brass knob wondering if he might try to turn it.

But the hallway remained silent.

Only then did I let myself sink to the floor, pulling my knees tight to my chest. I rocked slowly in the darkness, my fingers gripping the hem of my dress, afraid to even cry.

I had stood up to him.

But I had no idea what would happen now.

CHAPTER TWENTY-SEVEN

did not leave my room the next morning. I was prepared to stay there all day, all week if necessary. I would not eat. I would not speak. Not until they took me to my mother.

I had not considered every part of my plan before executing it. They could not know my mind if they did not come seeking me. But there was no help for it. I would remain in that room until someone noticed, and then I would speak.

But to my surprise they did not notice. Or at least no one came looking.

I sat through breakfast as the smells of sizzling salt bacon wafted through the house and made my stomach growl. It was uncomfortable, but I had known hunger before, and I could endure it. There was water in my pitcher for now.

Getting to the outhouse was another matter I had not considered. But there was a porcelain chamber pot under the bed meant for illness that would have to do.

Throughout the morning hours I heard the familiar sounds of Saturday in the Sandbury home—the children running and playing, the baby crying, Mary practicing the piano, and Samuel's heavy boots pacing in the study below.

Someone came to the front door, and I heard Samuel's voice but not his words as he spoke to the visitor. I longed to know who it was and what they were saying. But I would not open the door to satisfy my curiosity.

By mid-morning my hunger was eating at me intensely. My sense of isolation was growing, and I seethed with anger over being ignored. Perhaps that's how they wanted it. That's about the time I was hit with the smells of baking bread. I had forgotten that Saturday was bread-baking day.

This was not going as I'd wanted.

I decided I had to come up with some way to pass the time. The only reading material in my possession was my scriptures. I opened my drawer and took out the beautiful leather-bound books that Betsy had given me for Christmas.

As I flipped through the Book of Mormon, a note fell out. I could see that it was in Betsy's careful hand. She must have tucked it in when she was packing my bag.

Emmaline,

I don't know what lies ahead, but I know you. You are brave and bright and full of life, even when you feel weak. The Lord loves you, and so do I. If things grow too heavy, remember that there are people who will help you carry the weight. You are never truly alone.

—Betsy

I wiped a tear from my cheek and folded the note in my hands. Betsy loved me. She would not let this happen.

And yet my thoughts paused as I fingered the note; Betsy *had* let this happen. She must have known what was coming. Memories that made no sense at the time now became crystal clear—the quarreling after the Christmas social, Betsy telling Micah that they shouldn't have taken me. How had Micah responded? Something about how this would have happened eventually. Was this what he meant? Betsy and Micah behaved as if they were saddened to see me go, but they still packed me up and brought me here. I could tell they didn't like Brother Sandbury. So why had they done it? Understanding flushed my face like heat from the parlor fire. This was why:

"There is no Zion without obedience."

I set the scriptures back in my drawer and noticed a newspaper clipping that I had never seen before. It wasn't mine. Someone had placed it there. Alarmed but also curious, I picked it up.

The clipping was from the September 14, 1852, edition of *The Deseret News*, the newspaper published by the church. The title read, "REVELATION: Given to Joseph Smith, Nauvoo, July 12, 1843."

I skimmed the words and realized this was the revelation so often spoken of when plural marriage was discussed: "For behold, I reveal unto you a new and an everlasting covenant; and if ye abide not that covenant, then are ye damned; for no one can reject this covenant and be permitted to enter into my glory."

I continued reading about this covenant, the rejection of which would lead to my damnation. It only got worse: "And again, as pertaining to the law of the priesthood—if any man espouse a virgin, and desire to espouse another, and the first give her consent, and if he espouse the second, and they are virgins, and have vowed to no other man, then is he justified."

This suggested that Brother Sandbury could have me only with Sarah's consent. But she did not seem to want this. In fact, I had overheard her say it was wrong. *So what then?* I wondered.

I read on: "And again, verily, verily, I say unto you, if any man have a wife, who holds the keys of this power, and he teaches unto her the law of my priesthood, as pertaining to these things, then shall she believe and administer unto him, or she shall be destroyed, saith the Lord your God; for I will destroy her; for I will magnify my name upon all those who receive and abide in my law."

The Lord would destroy her. Not punish. Destroy. The power of God's wrath, it seemed, belonged to Brother Sandbury.

Although I could have stepped outside of my room at any time, my confinement began to feel involuntary.

Afternoon turned to evening as dusk fell. The scent of supper made my stomach growl. I heard the drone of family prayers downstairs. They would all go to bed soon.

I changed into my nightdress and prepared to go to bed with a growling stomach. And then I heard it. Creaking on the floorboards outside my room. A light tapping at the door. I sat up straight, stayed silent, and did not answer the door. Instead, I waited to see what would happen.

"Emmaline ..." It was Sarah's voice. She barely spoke above a whisper. "I understand why you are upset, but you are acting like a child. This tantrum will not move Samuel or the prophet."

There was a long pause. Was she waiting for me to speak? I kept quiet.

"Samuel does not want me up here. I have to hurry back. But I'm leaving you a tray."

I ignored the tray and went to sleep. Scared, lonely, and hungry, I slept fitfully. But I did not have any nightmares, which was a mercy.

Pounding on the door woke me with a start. Morning sun peeked through the window. This did not sound like Sarah at the door. I pulled my knees to my shoulders and wrapped the quilt up around my neck.

More pounding on the door. "Emmaline!" It was Samuel's voice, laced with exasperation. "Open this door or I am coming in."

I pulled my knees in closer, trying to fold into myself.

The door opened. He stood there, dressed in a dark Sunday suit, filling the entire doorway. His eyes were impatient, but not quite angry.

"Get up and get dressed. You're going to church."

"I want to see my mother." The words barely came out.

"You're not in any position to make demands of me right now." His expression grew more angry.

"I want to see my mother," I repeated, a little louder this time.

He sighed. He appeared to be unsure about his next move. Would he pick me up? Force me to get dressed?

"You come to church, and then I will take you to the Thatchers'," he finally said.

"Today?" I asked.

"Today."

I had no other move, no other choice. I would have to trust him if I wanted to see her. I nodded my agreement.

Sunday services were a blur. I heard nothing but an echo of waves pounding in my ears. I noticed Betsy glance my way several times, trying to meet my eyes, but I would not look at her. As we walked out of the ward house, Brother Sandbury kept a hand firmly around my upper arm. Sarah walked with the children in front of us.

Samuel drove the family home, and everybody piled out of the wagon. I stayed. Samuel walked back to the wagon and looked at me, arms crossed.

"Come. We eat Sunday supper first."

"I want to see my mother." I did not move.

Suddenly, there was fury in his eyes. I could see that my refusal to comply angered him. I don't think Sarah defied him in this way, and he appeared unsure how to exert his control. It occurred to me that this anger made him dangerous.

"We eat Sunday supper first." He seethed.

I remained in the wagon. We stared at each other.

"Have it your way," he said. "But you'll wait."

With that, he walked back into the house.

By the time we arrived at the Thatchers' home, I was weak with hunger and cold to my bones because I'd sat outside in the wagon after Samuel had gone in, resisting the urge to follow him and join the family for supper. I simply would not give the Sandburys the satisfaction of my presence or cooperation. I'd gone to church; I'd fulfilled my end of the bargain. Samuel eventually came back out to fulfill his. But he had certainly made me wait for it.

Brother and Sister Thatcher greeted me warmly when we entered their home, as they always did. I resisted Sister Thatcher's hug and went straight to see my mother. The room was warm from the fire, and the window was cracked a little to let in fresh air. She was sitting up, her hair brushed and braided, alert and expecting me.

I had not cried for the last two days. They had been the first two days in weeks that I hadn't cried. Rage had been my primary emotion, and it kept the tears at bay. But when I saw my mother, every wall I had put up came tumbling down.

I fell on top of her and sobbed uncontrollably.

"Emma," she said softly, stroking my face with one hand and wrapping the end of my braid around the fingers on her other hand.

I tried to sit up and talk after a while, but I could not do it. Could not get enough oxygen in my lungs to speak. My body shook with uncontrollable grief, and the choking sobs kept coming.

She continued to caress me and whisper my name, and eventually, I ran out of tears. I sat up and looked at her face. Her expression was stricken with worry. Suddenly, I wanted to spare her from the truth of what was happening, but I knew I could not.

"Mother," I finally said, choking on each syllable. "Oh, Mother."

The tears came again, but I kept speaking. I told her everything. About leaving Betsy and Micah's, about Brother Sandbury's unsettling behavior and his wife's cold treatment, about the prophet and the unthinkable proposal, and about everything I had read in Joseph Smith's revelation on plural marriage.

She watched me as I said everything. There was concern in her eyes, but not surprise. Had they told her already?

"Oh, Mother, what are we going to do?"

She was silent for a minute. Then she reached for my hands, took them both in hers. I waited in agony for her response.

Finally, she softly whispered, "Emmaline, obey."

She might have slapped me across the face and I would have been less shaken.

"Obey?" I repeated in horror. "You *want* me to marry him?"

Her face darkened. She looked the way she did when Father died. But she did not waver.

"Obey." She patted my hands.

I ripped them away. That's when I understood that not only had she already known, but she had consented to this as well.

I suddenly recalled her vision in Liverpool.

"Sorrow awaits those who turn away. Woe to any who reject the principle."

Panic rose in me. I needed to escape. I looked at the open window, cracked to let in fresh air. I glanced back at the door, making sure it was still closed. I pushed the window open, swung my legs over the sill, and jumped into the snow below.

And then I ran.

CHAPTER TWENTY-EIGHT

When I first started running, I had no destination in mind. The plan had been conceived thirty seconds before I climbed out of the window. Once I was on the ground, I hitched up my dress and ran as fast as my boots would take me in the snow.

If they were following me, I didn't know. I never looked back.

By the time I reached the end of the street, I realized where I was going—the only place in town I knew: Betsy and Micah's house.

I turned right on Thirteenth East like I had done dozens of times before on the way home from visiting Mother. And then I took a left on Third South. Minutes later I was in front of the little brown house that was a quarter the size of the Sandburys' home but one hundred percent more full of love.

I ran straight into the house without knocking. Betsy, scared half to death by the intrusion, dropped a bowl of eggs on the floor.

"Emmaline!" she gasped. "Mercy me, child, what is wrong? What did they do to you?"

I stood shaking in the doorway. Betsy's eyes scanned me from boots to braid. She stepped toward me as my knees gave out.

I sucked in air that burned my lungs while tears fell down my wind-chapped cheeks. I tried to speak but once again found myself unable to get the words out. Betsy picked me up and walked me to her rocking chair, then went into the kitchen to pour me a cup of water. She sat by me as I gulped it down, waiting for me to be ready to talk.

With my breath and heartbeat settled a bit, I tried to speak. I looked at her and said, "She … She told me …"

"What, honey? Who told you what?"

"My mother," I cried. "She told me to obey."

A knowing look came over Betsy's face, and I had the feeling she knew what I was talking about. She reached for my hand. "Tell me everything."

I told Betsy the story, just like I'd told my mother. She did not respond with words. Instead, she pulled me to her—right into her lap—and cried with me until we both ran out of tears.

Micah walked through the front door a few minutes later, his coat still dirty from working in the barn, and found us that way.

"Emmaline!" he exclaimed. "What's going on?"

Betsy told him everything. His eyes darted between us as she spoke. He looked at me with compassion, but I also noted fear on his face. He sighed deeply.

"He is going to come looking for you," he said. "He's probably on his way now."

I fell to the floor and looked up at them both. "Please," I said. "Please don't make me go back."

Betsy looked at Micah, and Micah looked at the ceiling.

That's when the knock came at the door. I knew without a doubt it was the pounding fist of Brother Sandbury. Micah went to the door while Betsy sat on the floor with me, holding my hand.

"Emmaline." Brother Sandbury spoke my name with a concerned tone that I knew was meant for the Greens, not for me. "Thank the Lord you are safe. I've been out of my mind with worry. It's time to come with me now. We'll talk about this at home."

He took a step toward me, but Micah stepped in front of him.

"Brother Sandbury, she's going to stay with us tonight."

"Micah, you don't want to do this," Brother Sandbury said, his voice now stripped of its warmth. There was no concern anymore. Only warning.

I knew the use of Micah's first name was meant to intimidate him … and me. I watched them both as the tension in the room reached a boiling point.

"Let's speak outside," Micah said.

As the two men walked out the door, I turned to Betsy and finally exhaled. "Are you really going to let me stay?"

"Let's see what happens," she answered.

The baby fussed about that time, and Betsy got up to tend to her.

Micah came in and looked at me with his usual gentleness. "You'll stay here tonight," he said. "Brother Sandbury will come back in the morning. I think it's best everyone calm their nerves right now."

I stood and smoothed my dress, which was now damp from the melting snow. Betsy stepped back into the room with Mattie.

"Let's get you into some dry clothes," she said brightly. "Then I think you need a meal and some rest."

I sat at the table and ate a plate of leftover sausage and buttered bread, with a glass of fresh milk. It was the first food I'd had in almost two days, and I was ravenous now that I felt safe. Betsy and Micah went out to the barn while I ate, and I knew they had to be talking about me, but I didn't mind that as long as they let me stay.

After I ate, Betsy sent me back to my old room to lie down. "Have a little rest and then we'll talk."

The sun was already down. I feared if I slept, I would not wake back up. So I lay quietly in the dark and considered my situation. I would only cause trouble if I stayed there, I could not go to my mother's, and the Sandburys' was unthinkable. I had no means to run. And even if I did, where would I go?

The world was closing in on me. My only hope was that Betsy and Micah had a plan.

I cautiously walked out the bedroom and found Betsy and Micah by the fire. They looked deep in conversation.

"May we speak now?" I asked.

"Of course," Betsy said.

Micah jumped up and brought me a kitchen chair. We sat in awkward silence for a few minutes, and then Micah began to speak.

"Emmaline," he said, his voice gentle and slow. "I know what the prophet has asked of you. I know it is a difficult calling. May I ask if you have prayed about it?"

My mouth dropped open. *Pray about it?* I was about to turn fifteen years old. I was half Brother Sandbury's age. He was already married. I didn't need to pray about it.

"No," I said.

Betsy reached out to hold my hand. "Sweetheart, celestial marriage is a higher law. A virtuous one."

Anger crept into my voice. "You are not living it," I said, feeling the heat in my cheeks. "Why has Micah not taken a second wife?"

"The Lord does not call everyone to it," she whispered, as if she didn't believe her own voice. "It is most often the leaders of the church who are called."

I looked at Micah and asked, "If the prophet calls you to this, will you do it?"

Micah and Betsy looked at one another. I knew my questions were piercing and uncomfortable. I didn't care.

"We trust the prophet," Micah said finally. "We believe in the restored gospel. If the Lord asks us to live the law of celestial marriage, we will obey."

He paused and swallowed hard, running his hand through his hair. "Sometimes obedience comes before understanding."

"There is no Zion without obedience."

I watched Betsy as she listened to her husband. I could tell she was trying to support him, but her eyes betrayed her. She would not take so kindly to it—of that, I was sure.

She finally spoke. "All we're asking, Emmaline, is for you to pray about it. The Lord will reveal his will to you." Her voice broke as she continued, "We do understand. This is not what we would have for you, but the Lord's ways are not always our ways."

I looked at the floor as she said this. After a few moments I quietly walked into the bedroom and closed the door. There was nothing more to be said. Betsy and Micah were not going to help me.

Once in the bedroom, I slowly changed into the nightdress that Betsy had laid out for me. And then I knelt on the floor beside the bed, and I did pray.

I prayed for God to save me. I cried out to the God of Zion and begged him to save me from the people of Zion.

I woke early the next morning and dressed back into my brown church dress, which had dried by the fire. I combed my fingers through my hair and quickly braided it. My head pounded like always after a night of crying, and I felt sick to my stomach. I wished that I had died on the plains with my father.

I walked to the kitchen and found little Mattie happily playing in her high chair while Betsy made a pot of porridge. I picked her up and held her to me, trying to draw comfort from her velvet cheeks and innocent smile.

Betsy set three bowls on the table, which told me Micah had not gone to work early as he usually did. Milk was heating on the stove, and I silently poured it into three tin cups. She set out a jar of apple butter while I set out the spoons. Betsy and I had a familiar working rhythm in the kitchen. We were quiet but not tense.

Micah came in from the barn, and we all sat down at the table. He bowed his head and prayed: "Heavenly Father, we thank thee this morning for the food before us and for the hands that prepared it. We're grateful for the blessings thou hast given, for health, for safety, and shelter. Please guide our hearts this day that we may walk in obedience and peace. And bless Emmaline, Lord, with comfort and courage for the path ahead. We ask these things in the name of thy Son, Jesus Christ. Amen."

After we cleaned up the dishes, I went instinctively to Betsy's sewing basket and picked up a sock to mend. I wondered if God had heard my prayer—if he heard any prayers.

Before long a knock came at the front door.

The knock was firm, but not aggressive. Micah opened the door, and in walked Brother Sandbury, flanked by Bishop Theodore Grayson. I had met him at the Christmas social and heard him speak several times at church.

He smiled warmly, but his eyes were sharp and discerning. He was a large man, younger than Brigham Young. But he dressed and styled his beard to resemble the prophet.

Brother Sandbury addressed Micah. "The bishop would like to speak with Emmaline."

Micah ushered them in. Brother Sandbury and Bishop Grayson took the rocking chairs, and Micah brought the kitchen chairs for the rest of us.

The bishop removed his hat. "Good morning, Sister Kendall. I hope you'll allow a few minutes of your time for us to speak together?"

I nodded, barely. Like all requests posed by religious leaders in Zion, I knew this was not really a request.

The bishop began speaking in that lofty, authoritative tone they use in church. "Emmaline, I understand you've been through much in these past months. The hand of the Lord has been heavy on many of us. You've borne it with strength and great courage."

I said nothing.

"You are at a sacred threshold, dear. You have been given the opportunity to enter into the new and everlasting covenant. This is not a burden. It is a blessing. One reserved for the elect."

I kept my eyes on my hands, folded tightly in my lap.

"I know it may seem frightening. But fear is not of God. Faith is. And obedience is. The Prophet Joseph Smith taught that those who reject this covenant cannot enter into the highest glory. I would be failing in my stewardship if I did not remind you of that."

He paused, let his words settle, then went on, "You may think this decision is only about you. But we are never alone in bearing the consequences of our choices. Your mother is a widow, afflicted and dependent upon the mercy of the Saints. You understand that."

It was a statement, not a question. But then he softened his voice and spoke in an almost pleasing melody that made my blood run cold: "You are her only daughter. A sealing to Brother Sandbury will ensure not only your eternal salvation, but hers as well."

That was the moment I felt the trap close around me.

His voice was still melodic. "Do you understand me, Emmaline?"

My mouth was dry. I knew it was over. I could not abandon my mother. As long as they had her, they had me. And they knew it.

The bishop leaned forward slightly; the softness in his voice had gone. "I know the Lord has great purpose for you, Emmaline. But the adversary is near, whispering doubts and stirring up a spirit of rebellion. That is what he does best. He deceives the purest souls. If you turn away from this covenant, the sorrow you feel now will be nothing compared to what is to come."

I looked up and saw every eye in the room watching me.

"I know this is difficult. But the Lord asks hard things of his disciples.

He asked Abraham to sacrifice Isaac. He asked the Saints to cross the plains. And he is asking you now to enter into a covenant that will exalt you beyond your understanding. This is not the end of your story, Sister. It is the beginning."

He stood, nodded to Brother Sandbury, and laid a hand on my shoulder. "Take time to pray. But do not delay long. The Lord has spoken."

I had no more words. I had no more tears. I had no more fight left in me.

"Are you ready to go home, Emmaline?" Brother Sandbury asked.

I do not remember what happened after that. I must have nodded. I must have climbed into the wagon. We must have driven across town. Because thirty minutes later I was walking back into the Sandbury home.

CHAPTER TWENTY-NINE

Have you ever seen a gentle dog backed into a corner? Not a mean or wild one. A faithful dog, the kind that loves and wants to please. At first it growls. Barks. Tries to show it still has teeth.

Then it cowers.

It pulls itself deeper into the corner, ears down, eyes wide. Whines. Whimpers. And then, finally, it lies down. It goes quiet. Beaten. It will now do whatever the master wants.

That's what they did to me.

I moved about the Sandbury house in quiet submission for the next few days. Nothing was said about the marriage, but there was a knowing on everyone's faces.

Once, as Sarah and I washed and scrubbed the children's clothing in wooden buckets on the kitchen floor, she started speaking to me, which was rare.

Her voice sounded tight and her words flat. "It is not so bad for you," she said, scrubbing Mary's dress a little too hard. "He is a good provider. You'll not lack for anything here. That is not true of many people in this valley."

She was speaking of the drought and cricket plagues that had devastated the Saints' crops in the Utah Territory the summers before I came. Many of the Saints had suffered, and provisions were limited this winter. But Samuel was a businessman, a mill superintendent. He did important work for the prophet. This home was one of plenty, if not one of warmth.

I didn't answer her. She didn't mean for me to.

The following week, on February eighth, I turned fifteen.

The whole family was seated at the table when I entered the kitchen for breakfast, including Samuel, who usually had left for the mills by now.

"Happy birthday, Emmaline," he said as I entered the room.

"Thank you," I said politely.

Sarah put a plate of steaming griddle cakes on the table, a rare treat. There was maple syrup and bacon and canned peaches with cream. All were favorites of mine, though I wasn't sure how they could have known. It was a lovely meal. I knew Sarah had worked hard to make it special, but I couldn't tell if she did it because she wanted to or because she was told to.

Later that morning I was putting away clean clothes in my room when a knock came at the door. I opened it, and Brother Sandbury walked in carrying three packages wrapped in brown paper and tied with string. He looked very pleased with himself.

I took a step back. He took a step forward.

"Birthday gifts," he said. "Take them."

I took the packages and said, "Thank you, Brother Sandbury."

"You can call me Samuel now. You're going to be my wife."

I swallowed hard but said nothing. It was the first open acknowledgement of the arrangement since we left the Greens' house.

"Go on now, open them."

I did not want to. I did not like this man in my room and did not want his gifts. But I was a cornered pup.

After he offered to hold two of the packages, I opened the large box first. It was a pair of new black leather boots. They were not everyday boots. They were boots for a lady, with small heels and laces that threaded all the way to the top.

"A wife should not have to wear borrowed shoes. Not a wife of mine."

He waited for me to thank him. I did not. After a moment he handed me a soft wrapped package. I slowly ripped the paper and saw that it was a boughten dress. It was the finest dress I had ever seen up close, made of soft cotton. The color was a deep shade of plum, with a fitted bodice and gathered sleeves trimmed in delicate black velvet. The skirt was full, with fine pleating at the waist.

The buttons down the front were jet black. Shiny and cold to the touch. He watched me run my hands over the velvet and finger the thin row of lace at the collar. Just enough to soften the neckline without adding fuss.

It would have taken weeks to order from back East. How long had he been planning this?

"It's your wedding dress," he said. "You'll wear it next Monday. That gives you and Sarah time for alterations."

All I could focus on was "wedding" and "Monday."

There was one more gift. A small black box. He placed it in my hands. When his fingers touched mine, I flinched and stepped back. He ignored this.

"Open it," he said. "It was my mother's."

Nestled on a bed of black silk was a small, oval cameo brooch, no larger than a walnut. The carved-ivory face of a woman—serene, Greco-Roman in style—was set against a background of deep coral. A ring of filigreed gold framed the cameo, and the clasp on the back was worn smooth with time.

"My father bought it in France. He gave it to my mother on their wedding day."

He looked proud. It was that insufferable expression he often wore, and it was becoming too familiar to me. I knew he expected deep gratitude in return for these gifts, but I couldn't help but think these gifts weren't really for me. They were for him. To transform me into the woman he wanted.

I said, "Thank you," not because I was thankful, but because it was expected.

As he left the room, he turned to me and said, "I have also ordered fabric for you to make some new dresses. I don't want you wearing borrowed clothes anymore."

"Yes, sir," I replied. It was an automatic response.

Later that afternoon, Sarah came to me and asked me to put on the dress so we could measure for alterations. Her taut expression told me she dreaded this task as much as I did. I asked her to leave me alone so I could change. The dress fit almost perfectly. It would only need to be hemmed.

In this fine, boughten dress, the girl in the looking glass appeared more like a young woman. My body had been changing while I was enduring the horror of my fourteenth year. I practiced twisting my hair and piling it on top of my head, which would certainly be expected after the marriage. I hated everything about my reflection. The dress, my body, my hair. I looked ridiculous. Like I was in a costume. I let my hair fall back down around my shoulders and sighed.

About that time, I heard a man's voice at the front door. He was talking to Samuel, and I thought I heard my name. I stepped out to the top of the stairs.

"What business do you have with Emmaline?" Brother Sandbury asked.

I took a step downstairs for a look, and for a moment I thought my eyes deceived me. Was it real? I leaned in farther.

"Gideon!" I squealed, ran to him, and jumped in his arms. "I thought you were dead."

"I've been trying to find you and Eliza for weeks," he said. "I came from her home. She told me I could find you here."

Brother Sandbury stepped forward, placing a hand on my shoulder and lightly pulling me away from Gideon.

"Who are you?" he asked, his voice laced with the sound of possession.

Gideon extended a hand to Brother Sandbury.

"Name's Gideon Ashford," he said politely. "I was in the handcart company with Emmaline. I'm here to return this."

He held out a small parcel wrapped in cloth—my journal.

"Oh, Gideon," I cried. "I thought it was lost. You have no idea how much this means to me." I hugged it to my chest as tears fell down my cheeks.

Brother Sandbury stepped between us. "Alright, you've returned it. You best go on now."

I couldn't bear to see Gideon leave. I had to think of something to keep him close a little longer.

"Samuel," I said, knowing he would like this use of his first name. "Gideon saved my life. I would be dead without him. May we please have a little time to speak?"

He stared at Gideon for a moment and finally agreed. "You may visit in the parlor. I'll be in my study."

He walked into the study but did not close the door.

I showed Gideon into the parlor and took a seat on the settee. He faced me in a straight-backed chair.

"I would offer you a drink, but I don't know how much time we have," I said, glancing back at the study. "Where have you been? What have you been doing?"

"I've been around," he said, shrugging. "I was sick for a while, recovered at a home near here. They sent me south in a wagon train with Delia and Olivia. I was meant to be working farms. I won't do it. I'm heading west. Going to California. There's land out there—and wages. This place is not for me."

He was back and already leaving again. That fragile sense of safety he brought with him was already slipping away.

"You're not going back to England?"

He looked down. "There's nothing for me in England."

I knew he was thinking about his pa, the only family he had left—until Wyoming had happened.

"What are you doing in that dress?" he asked, changing the subject. "It looks ridiculous."

Leave it to Gideon to speak his mind.

I lowered my voice. "It's my wedding dress."

His gasp was almost audible, but he caught it just in time. "You're getting married? To who? Tell me it's not that man," he whispered, gesturing toward the study.

I nodded.

He looked around the house, saw the signs of children. The baby's cradle. Lucy's shoes. Samuel Junior's baseball bat. He understood exactly what was going on.

"Emmaline, you don't have to do this."

"I do," I said, another tear falling down my cheek. "They have my mother." There was no way to really explain. Gideon would never understand.

"You're still a girl," he said.

I just looked at him. There was nothing I could say.

"Come with me," he said, barely above a whisper.

"I can't," I cried.

Samuel stepped out of his study and told Gideon it was time for him to go.

Gideon glared at him. "She's just a girl."

"We're done here," Samuel said. "You need to leave my home now."

Gideon looked back at me as Samuel pushed him out the door.

"You don't belong to him," he called out. "You're not his. You're not theirs. You're still Emmaline."

His words settled into my heart. And I knew they would stay there forever.

Samuel slammed the door. He turned to me and said coldly, "See that Sarah hems your wedding dress."

PART TWO

EMMALINE SANDBURY

CHAPTER THIRTY

lay on my bed Sunday afternoon, wondering how I had gotten here. I closed my eyes and fell into a lifetime of memories.

The lush, rolling hills and stone churches of Wiltshire, a small elm coffin lowered into the earth, buried with my brother's body and my parents' joy.

The dirty cobblestone streets of Liverpool, lined with fishmongers and newsboys. Missionaries in the courtyard. Baptism in the River Mersey. The great expanse of the deep blue sea. Celebrating America's birthday in a park in Buffalo, New York.

Buffalo. That was the last place I could remember being happy. Eliza and I had sat among the trees and flowers, surrounded by cheerful families, enjoying the taste of street food and freedom. We were happy, just for a couple of hours. I remember the band and choir, filling the gazebo strung with red, white, and blue bunting and American flags. I believed in freedom that day. But I had not found it since.

After the picnic I boarded a train and rolled down the tracks toward a life that stole my safety, my security, my comfort, my family, my childhood, and the very freedom we had come here to find.

Within twenty-four hours I would be a wife. A plural wife. I wasn't even sure what that meant for me. Sarah had let me know, without saying it directly, that this was her home, not mine. I wasn't sure that Brother Sandbury thought the same thing, but it was Sarah I would spend my days with. It was Sarah who would keep me in my place.

All this I pondered that Sunday afternoon. My thoughts were interrupted by a commotion in the parlor. I got up to see what the fuss was about.

Samuel was at the door, arguing with Betsy and Micah. Why were Betsy and Micah here? Hadn't they done enough? I could not even meet Betsy's eyes in church that morning.

"I will not leave until I speak with Emmaline," Betsy said. She was standing her ground, head raised, eye to eye with Samuel.

I couldn't imagine what she would have to say to me. I was following the virtuous path she wanted me to follow. It was all but done.

Samuel and Micah spoke quietly for a few minutes, with Betsy and Sarah both looking uncomfortable. Micah eventually turned to Betsy and said something, then she started up the stairs.

Would there ever be a time when the people in this place stopped talking about me and making decisions for me? It seemed the only person who never got a say in what happened to me … was me.

I did not welcome Betsy in, but neither did I turn her away. What choice did I have? I sat down on my bed, and she sat beside me. I moved away—enough to let her know I was angry—and pulled back my hand when she tried to hold it.

"Emmaline," she began, nervously. "I want to ask you something."

I looked at her, waiting.

She started and stopped a few times and finally asked, "Did you and your mother ever speak about marriage?"

I was curious now, but I didn't know how to answer. My mother once told me how my parents met and fell in love. I knew they were married at St. Patrick's church in Wiltshire. That had been recorded in the family Bible. Is that what she meant?

That was not what she meant.

"Did she talk to you about … about what husbands and … and wives do together *privately*?" she said, emphasizing the word "privately" in a way that made me nervous.

After a pause Betsy asked, "Did she ever explain why you have your monthly courses?"

No, my mother had not spoken to me about any of that. The last time I had a real conversation with my mother, I was barely fourteen years old, spending my days mending for a few shillings a week. What need did we have to speak of such things?

And so Betsy told me.

She told me what it meant to be married. What would happen in the night. Destroying every part of my soul that was left.

~

The morning of our marriage, our "sealing" they called it, started out like any other day. Sarah and I made breakfast, fed the children, and put on a roast for supper. She swept the house, and I dusted while Mary practiced piano. The little ones ran in and out, and the baby fussed. We tended to them as we went about our chores. I'm not sure I ever spoke, except to the children. I might have doubted it was happening, except that Samuel did not go to the mill that day.

At eleven Samuel came in and told us both to start getting ready. A ward member would be there in an hour to stay with the children.

I had never been to a wedding before, but I had often seen wedding parties coming out of the churches in Wiltshire and Liverpool. The brides usually wore white gowns that made them look like princesses, with long veils trailing down their backs. What I noticed most were the big smiles on the faces of the brides, the grooms, and all the friends and family who joined them to celebrate. Joy and laughter and love surrounded these occasions, as far as I could tell.

This was not how it happened in Zion. Sealings were private ceremonies conducted in an unmarked building called the Endowment House. I had never been there before. It was a place where the sacred rites of Mormonism were performed. These sacred rites included the secretive endowment ceremony and plural marriages. Women usually went only to be sealed.

I put on my new dress and boots and considered what to do with my hair. I knew I would have to wear it up after the sealing, but I wasn't sure about now. In the end I tied it behind my head with Betsy's blue ribbon. Samuel came to inspect me and asked for his mother's brooch. He affixed it to my bodice and told me that I looked lovely. This display— his nearness, his touch—nearly made me sick. All I could think about were the things Betsy had told me.

We rode to the Endowment House in silence, then Samuel ushered us both inside. There were no flowers. No celebration. No music or procession. Just rooms where women were separated from men, stripped of their outer garments, and told to prepare themselves for holiness.

I was told to remove my shoes before I stepped inside, for the floors were too sacred to be touched by the dust of the world. My name was written in a ledger, along with the names of my parents and the date of my baptism. Then I was handed over to a Sister Ellen Robins, who led me behind a curtain to where the other women waited.

It was there I learned I would have to remove my dress and undergarments and step into a basin to be washed.

The bath water was cold. I was washed, slowly and thoroughly, while Sister Robins murmured prayers over me, words I could not quite understand. Oil was poured down my body, soaking my scalp, dripping into my eyes. I was anointed from head to toe, every part of me claimed for a purpose I did not choose: my head to wear a crown, my breasts to nourish children, my loins to bear a righteous race. My body, I was told, had now become a temple.

I was given the garments of the holy priesthood, which I would wear under my clothing every day henceforth to signify my covenant with God and protect me from all harm. I did not feel protected. I felt itchy and constricted.

I also received new clothing to wear for the rest of the ceremony. White, shapeless, sacred. A gown. A linen robe. A sash tied across my chest. A veil for my head. Each piece whispered obedience.

I did not understand why I'd been gifted a beautiful new wedding dress if I wasn't to wear it for the ceremony. I would have pondered this longer, but everything got even more strange.

Once dressed in my white endowment clothing, I was led into the next room, where Sarah was waiting for me.

She did not touch me, but she adjusted my sash and smoothed my veil as if dressing a child. "You look ready," she said.

I did not answer.

It was not yet time for the sealing. We moved through rooms, watching actors portray a drama about the creation of the world. I was taught signs and tokens for the afterlife and made many promises I did not understand. I floated through this experience as if disembodied and could not tell you precisely what happened.

And then Sarah led me into the sealing room.

It was quiet—"sacred," they would say. The prophet's counselor stood beside a narrow altar, a ledger open before him, ink glistening on the tip of his pen. Brother Sandbury waited to one side, hands clasped behind his back.

Sarah led me forward.

She did not hold my hand, but she guided me with a firm touch at my elbow, her palm ice cold through the fabric of my robe. When we reached the altar, she turned to me slowly and then reached for my hand.

I hesitated and thought about pulling back, but I was paralyzed. Sarah paused, and I thought she might run. But instead, she took my hand and placed it into her husband's.

Her hand was there only a second as a bridge between us before she stepped back. Even as my world was falling apart, I could not help but feel a little sad for her as she was forced to participate in her own betrayal. This woman who had married a man she loved in England, discovered a new faith with him, and crossed an ocean, only to learn she would face damnation if she did not consent to sharing him with a fifteen-year-old girl.

The officiator spoke. I heard only some of the words: "covenant … obedience … eternity." I heard my name. His. The word "sealed."

I repeated what I was told to say. I stood still when his fingers closed around mine.

Brother Sandbury leaned toward me then, close enough for him to smell the oil still clinging to my skin. He whispered something I would try to forget for the rest of my life: my new name. The name by which he would one day call me from the grave. It was a secret between us now. A secret I wished he did not hold.

And then it was done.

I was not kissed. Not embraced. I was simply given to him. To be his priestess for time and all eternity.

That night before family prayers, Samuel told the children: "We are a chosen people," he began, his voice full of reverence. "The Lord has smiled upon this family and poured out his blessings in abundance. Not all are called to this path, but we are. We are his peculiar people, a royal priesthood, set apart for a great and eternal work."

He looked around the room, his gaze settling on each of them in turn. "Today our family has grown in righteousness. Sister Emmaline has entered the holy covenant of celestial marriage. She is now sealed to me, not only for this life, but for all eternity. She has stepped into a sacred role, one that carries weight and honor in the eyes of God."

He paused and nodded toward me. "From this day forward you are to call her Mother Emmaline, for she is not a guest in this house, but your new mother. For you now have two mothers. Her heart and hands will help raise this righteous generation."

The children sat silently, eyes wide. Silent tears ran down Sarah's cheeks.

Samuel folded his hands and lifted his face toward heaven. "May the Lord continue to multiply our blessings. May we walk in obedience, in humility, and in love. May this house be a house of order, a house of faith, a house of joy. And may our posterity rise up and call us blessed."

Sarah stood up with the baby and left the room. I heard the door slam behind her. Samuel asked me to put the children to bed. He followed Sarah, and I heard crying and loud voices. Our home was anything but a house of joy.

I prepared myself for bed, thankful it was over and thankful that Sarah was taking up Samuel's attention tonight. I blew out the lamp and climbed in bed, praying to never wake.

But before I slept, a knock came at the door. It was him.

And there in the dark, in the little room above the stairs, I found out that every awful thing Betsy had told me about marriage was true.

CHAPTER THIRTY-ONE

stand waist-deep in the frigid waters of the river. Chunks of ice pelt my body while snow falls thick, blinding my view. I try not to fall as an undercurrent hits my knees. The relentless, bitter cold bites through my bones.

I am alone. I look up and down the flow of the river, but I see no one. Nothing. No handcarts. No wagons. No oxen. No other Saints. Suddenly, the icy water turns red. Deep red. It isn't water anymore. It is blood. Thick, dark, freezing. The blood of my friends, my family, everyone who made the journey.

"Noooooooo!" I scream. "Mother! Father! Eliza! Delia! Olivia! Ellie! Gideon!"

I am screaming their names again and again, hoping someone will hear me. The blood is thick and cold, and I can't move through it. I'm not going forward. Not sinking. Just spinning in the freezing blood.

"Help!" I scream. "Help!"

A voice cuts through the piercing wind. It's a male voice. I can't see him, but I hear him.

"Walk in obedience, Emmaline. The blessings are westward. Walk toward my voice."

It is the voice of Samuel Sandbury. Calm. Steady. Powerful.

And then another voice: "Don't go, Emmaline! Turn around now. The only safe way is back."

It's Gideon. He's on the east side of the river. He sounds desperate to stop me.

I keep turning. I cannot step either way. The wind is howling. The snow is blinding. The bloody river is consuming me. I look down and see I am wearing my endowment clothes. Pure white—stained by the blood of my family and friends.

I scream, "Help me!"

"Hush, Emmaline, hush. You're safe. I'm right here."

I jolted awake, gasping, tangled in sweat-soaked sheets, and found myself in the Sandbury home. In Samuel's arms.

"What is it? What's wrong?" he asked. He tried to comfort me, to caress my arms and stroke my hair and whisper that everything would be all right.

I gasped and cried and tried to resist his touch; there was no escape. I collapsed against his chest and sobbed. For a moment I pretended I was being held by my father. But then I remembered where I was.

It was the early-morning hours of my fourth day as a wife. He hadn't come to me the second night, but I'd lain awake for hours, bracing for the sound of his steps, not knowing how often he would come. By the third night, when his boots thudded up the stairs, I was sick with exhaustion and nerves. After the door shut behind him, I learned that what Betsy told me about marriage happened more than once and despite my resistance. It was not the first time I prayed to die in my sleep. It would not be the last.

When I woke again, he was gone and the morning sun through my window was turning into afternoon sun. The late hour panicked me. Sarah would not be happy. I jumped out of bed, hurriedly dressed, and ran downstairs. Mary was already practicing the piano, and Sarah was churning butter.

She glanced at me with scorn as I entered the kitchen. "I suppose a new bride needs her rest," she muttered, not trying to hide the jealousy in her voice. "All that attention …"

I didn't say anything, so she continued, "We've been churning and practicing and making ourselves useful. But I'm sure your rest was more important."

Did she think I wanted his attention? Did she think I was well? Her words felt cruel, considering how complicit she had been in my marriage. I understood that she had protested, but didn't she understand that I had too?

The baby started crying.

"I'll feed him," I offered as I began to make a bottle.

"He's my baby. I'll feed him." She took the bottle from me and sat down with him to nurse. "Remember your place," she said, her voice now openly hateful.

What was my place? I had no idea what she wanted of me, let alone what Samuel wanted of me.

Letty and Lucy came in the room, both crying and fussing over the same toy. She looked at me, waiting for me to intervene.

I thought for a moment and shrugged. "They are *your* children."

If that's the way she wanted it, so be it.

I walked out of the kitchen and sat down in the parlor. I was hungry but too angry to go back in the kitchen to eat. I silently fumed for a while before I noticed a brown paper package next to me on the little table with the scriptures. My name was written in black ink on the paper.

I opened the package. This was the fabric he'd told me had been ordered for my new dresses. Three beautiful pieces of calico—navy, burgundy, and yellow. Making dresses seemed like as safe an activity as any. I got supplies out of the sewing basket and set to work, starting with the yellow.

Sarah came through the parlor later, holding both Letty and Seth. She paused to watch me. "It must be nice to have all new dresses," she said.

Still seething from our interaction that morning, I chose my words carefully. "I had my own dresses," I said. And then, looking her straight in the eye, "I lost them when I pulled our handcart through the river during a blizzard."

I turned back to my stitching, so I did not see her face when she softly said, "I'm sorry."

I didn't want to be Sarah's friend, but neither did I want to be her enemy. I didn't want to be her anything. But I would not be the one she punished.

On Sunday morning I rose early to dress for sacrament meeting. I knew this would be important to Samuel. I dreaded stepping out into society as his wife, but I didn't want to upset him because that only made my life more difficult.

I stood in front of the wardrobe and considered my options. He liked to say I should look "befitting of a wife." I chose the red calico. It was the nicest thing I had that was appropriate for church.

I braided my hair and pinned it up. The way Betsy wore hers. And then I laced up the new boots. I stepped into the kitchen, hoping to receive approval. Or at least avoid rebuke.

Samuel and Sarah were standing at the stove. I hesitated in the doorway, afraid I was interrupting something. She was wiping tears with one hand and stirring porridge with the other. He stood behind her with his hands on her shoulders.

"That will be enough of this," he said impatiently. "I don't love you less than I did last week. In fact, I love you more. A woman living in obedience to the Lord's law is to be highly praised. He approves of you, and so do I."

I cleared my throat to make my presence known. They both spun around.

"What are you doing in that dress?" he asked. "I told you, a wife of mine does not ever wear borrowed clothes."

"It's not borrowed," I said. "She gave it to me."

"Well then, I will give it back," he said. "You'll wear your wedding dress today."

The wedding dress? That was not appropriate for church. It was meant for a ball. I would make a spectacle of myself at church in that dress.

"Go on now—change," he said.

I went. There was nothing else to be done about it.

The church was near full when we arrived. Boots shuffled on the wooden floors, echoing under the murmur of men quietly greeting one another while women settled restless children in the pews.

Sarah walked ahead with the girls, baby Seth in her arms. She held her head high, but her shoulders told the truth. She walked slowly. I could feel her shame, not only because it clung to her like wet wool, but also because it clung to me. Samuel Junior walked on one side of his father, and I stood on the other. I did not try to hold my head high the way Sarah did.

Samuel placed his hand on the small of my back, guiding me forward with enough pressure to let me know he was in control.

Heads turned at our entrance. I felt eyes on me, on my dress, in that way people have of looking past you while seeing everything. A few women smiled at me. Others had pity on their faces. Some men nodded in approval. It felt as though my skin was folding in on itself to escape the stares.

We took our seats in the second row. I sat between Samuel and Sarah. She kept space between us, holding the baby and trying to pretend I wasn't there. He held my hand tightly, as if he was afraid I would run.

Betsy and Micah sat farther down our row. She held Mattie on her lap and smiled warmly at me. I looked away, missing her terribly but unable to forgive her. I scanned the room for Eliza, but my vantage point from the second row did not give me the best view.

The meeting began. Hymns were sung. Prayers were offered. I did not hear them. I heard only the pounding of my own heart. I looked down when Bishop Grayson rose to speak. All I could hear were the words he had said to me at Betsy and Micah's house: *"The adversary is near, whispering doubts and stirring up a spirit of rebellion. That is what he does best. He deceives the purest souls. If you turn away from this covenant, the sorrow you feel now will be nothing compared to what is to come."*

Was the bishop pleased with me now? Did he still think I was a pure soul? He must have known what happened in the nights. When Samuel held my wrists down so tightly that I feared they would break.

The bishop gave the closing prayer and people rose slowly. Samuel turned to speak with Brother Cartwright, a neighbor who was also the overseer at one of the mills. Sarah gathered the children and began making her way toward the door. I lingered. My eyes swept the room again and found Eliza standing by the far wall near the stove.

I looked at Samuel. He was not watching me, so I took the chance to run to Eliza and swept her into a hug.

"Oh, Emmaline, I heard," she said, then stopped, as if there was too much to say. Too much to ask.

"Are you all right?" I asked, ignoring her curiosity about my situation.

"They asked me to teach school," she said.

That shocked me. "You're not old enough to teach school."

"Well you're not old enough to be married."

We both laughed, but not with the same innocence we had last year.

"I saw Gideon," I said. "He brought my journal. He says he's going to California."

"Yes, I saw him too. I told him you were at the Sandburys'. I offered to take the journal and give it to you, but he said he wouldn't leave until he found you and saw that you were safe."

"I hope he makes it out of here," I said.

She nodded. She knew what I meant. He wasn't in the kind of danger young girls were. But I didn't want to see another strong, independent spirit crushed by the weight of Zion.

"Come, Emmaline." Samuel had found me. He guided me out to the wagon without another word, and we all went home for Sunday supper.

CHAPTER THIRTY-TWO

Samuel was true to his word about taking me to visit Mother on Saturday mornings. Everything about the visits distressed me. From the tense family breakfasts when Sarah sulked about Samuel taking me out alone to the uncomfortable ride to the Thatchers' when I had to endure being alone with him.

But the worst part was how things had changed with my mother, how our relationship had slipped back in time. Except now I was the one locked up in grief. Like Betsy and everyone else in Zion, she had betrayed me. But she was my mother, and I had done this for her. I was determined to protect her in the only way I was able.

The first Saturday in April, we were running late because Sarah wouldn't get out of bed. She had carried on about feeling unwell, though I suspected she just didn't want Samuel leaving the house with me again. He paced the floor between the fire and the piano, trying to decide whether to force her or wait for her to get up.

Finally, he turned to me and said, "Go hitch the wagon."

By the time we left, the frost had melted from the rooftops and Mary was already practicing the piano. The road to the Thatchers' home was muddy from a late spring snow, but it was sunny and pleasant outside. Spring was coming to the valley. Fruit trees bloomed with puffy white flowers like popped corn, and bright yellow daffodils cut through the many shades of Rocky Mountain blue.

I allowed myself a moment of pleasure with the warm breeze and beauty around me. Until he said my new yellow dress matched the daffodils. I did not want Samuel Sandbury comparing me to my favorite flower. The moment of respite vanished as quickly as it came.

Then he switched to fretting about how the overnight frost might kill the budding fruit. "We must pray for protection of the crops this year," he said.

I stayed quiet through all this.

We rode in silence for a few more minutes, the wheels of the wagon moving slowly, grinding through the thawing mud. Then, as he always did, Samuel began to speak about the mills.

"There's talk of opening a third grist mill," he said, adjusting the reins. "Down south. The prophet says they are producing enough grain now to justify it."

Every Saturday he gave me a full report on grain yields, millstones, and shipments. Always recited with the same quiet pride. There was usually a hint of insecurity in his voice, as if he were hoping to impress me or make me proud.

"You know, when I was in England," he said, "I studied the work of the old millwrights. The ancient Greeks and Romans. Centuries of labor that fed civilizations. There's a sacredness in making a good meal from rough grain. Most people don't see that. Grain becomes bread, bread sustains life, life sustains Zion."

He'd practically made himself a prophet of flour and meal carrying on so.

I did not give him the satisfaction of a reply. He could compel my presence but not my attention. That was mine to give. My thoughts were on my mother. I never knew what state I would find her in, if she would know me, or if she would be lost in her mind again.

Brother Thatcher greeted us at the door. "Sister Sandbury, pleasure to see you. Your mother is having a fine day; anxious to see you she is."

"*Sister Sandbury.*" Every time I heard those words, I looked around for Sarah. When I realized they were meant for me, I had to fight to quell the retching of my stomach.

I nodded, then walked straight into my mother's room and sat down without kissing her on the forehead. I had not been able to greet her affectionately since the sealing. Sister Thatcher had set a bowl of canned peaches on her night table, and I began feeding them to her.

She ran her hand over my new yellow calico and fingered the stitching. A smile and nod told me she was proud of my work. I could see she felt all those years sewing together had been worthwhile. But I felt all the years sewing meant the same thing as this dress: a childhood lost.

I told her about the navy and burgundy fabrics and said I would be working on those next. She smiled proudly.

"They asked Eliza to be a schoolteacher," I said. "Isn't that peculiar? A fourteen-year-old schoolteacher? Think of it. She hasn't been to school herself in two years. It seems young to me. But age is different in Zion, I suppose." I trailed off and looked out the window as I said that last part.

I spooned another bite of peach in her mouth, and she patted my hand. I wondered whether I wanted her to believe I was happy or know that I was sad. I wondered if she knew what happened in the night to her daughter. She surely had to.

Samuel came in then. "You look good today, Mother."

I startled and looked at him with ice-cold eyes. How dare he call her Mother? It was the first time I heard it, and I guessed he was trying it out to see how we both responded. Her smile in return was tight-lipped, as though maybe in that moment—with him taking liberties—she felt a little of what I felt.

He then offered a priesthood blessing, which he did each time we came, signaling that the visit was over and it was time to go home.

"Goodbye, Mother," I said.

"Emmaline," she responded, squeezing my hand. And then she wiped a single tear off her cheek.

I burned with fury on the ride back, sliding as far away from him as I could get on the buckboard. He glanced at me but otherwise ignored this.

"What did you and your mother talk about?" he asked.

"Sewing," I answered, afraid to ignore a direct question.

Samuel left to go to bishopric meetings on Saturday afternoons, and that's when Sarah usually made me pay for the mornings. She would make life difficult however she could. Leaving unpleasant chores for me, making hostile comments about my inexperience with some skill like quilting or cooking, or leaving me out of visits when sisters from the ward came to call.

That day I walked past her and up the stairs to my room and took a nap. She could treat me however she wanted; it didn't lessen the time Samuel spent with me. This was of little value to me other than in the way I had grown to enjoy it a little bit when she sulked. It was the only power against her that I had.

Samuel had just come home from the mills on a Thursday evening when a knock came at the door. I didn't see who it was because I was in the kitchen peeling carrots while Sarah fried sausages. She worked in silence except when she talked to the children. That was how she communicated with me now—by talking through them to me.

"Tell Mother Emmaline you need your britches patched," she'd say right in front of me.

I did not play this game. I'd respond with something like, "Have him put his britches on the mending pile, and I'll be happy to do it tomorrow." This made her angrier, but I didn't care.

The kitchen door burst open and Samuel handed me my shawl. "I'm taking Emmaline to see her mother," he said.

"Samuel, no!" Sarah cried. "This is my night."

He ignored her protests. "I'm not sure when we'll be back."

I barely had time to understand what was happening before we were on the road to the Thatchers'. I chilled while the sun disappeared behind the Wasatch Mountains.

"What is it?" I asked. "Why are we going now?"

"She's taken a turn," he said.

"A turn?"

"Fever, delirium. Dr. Phillips said this might be her time. He urged us to go quickly."

I jumped off the wagon and ran through the door before Samuel was able to put the brakes on the wagon.

"How is she?" I cried as I ran to her room.

Sister Thatcher stopped me. "Emmaline, she's not well. Burning up with fever. Doctor says she's full of infection. Not been in her right mind all day."

I walked into the room and fell to my knees when I saw her purple-and-red mottled skin and heard her shallow, labored breaths. Samuel helped me off the floor, but I couldn't find my legs. He sat me on the bed next to her. When I leaned over to kiss her, I felt the heat of her fever reach through her gown to me.

"Mother, I'm here."

I kissed her. Again and then again. I felt ashamed for withholding my love. How could I have carried my unforgiveness for so long? I kissed her again.

"I love you, Mama. I love you. Don't leave me. Please."

Her eyes were gray and vacant. She looked right through me. "William … James."

"No, Mama, William and Father are dead. I'm here. I'm Emmaline. I'm right here."

How could one body be so hot? I yelled for ice, and Samuel said he would go find some. I heard him leave in the wagon and hoped he knew where to find an icehouse.

Mother kept repeating William and Father's names until I believed she really was seeing them. I had been through this before. I knew what it meant.

Dr. Phillips came in and placed his satchel by the bed and lifted her forearm with careful, compassionate hands. He placed his fingers to her wrist. A moment passed. Then another.

He set her hand down gently and looked me in the eye, his face grave but compassionate. "The fever has taken firm hold, Emmaline. I'm afraid her strength is near spent."

I covered my mouth with my hands and shut my eyes, trying not to hear the words I already knew were coming.

"She's beyond the reach of medicines now. What comfort we can give her will come from love and presence, not ice or tonics."

I nodded and a quiet understanding came over me.

He lowered himself into the wooden chair by the window, the lamplight catching in the silver at his temples. "You may speak to her still. The spirit often lingers even when the body fades away. Say what you need to say." Then he rose softly. "I'll be in the next room should there be need."

As the doctor stepped out, Samuel stepped in, breathless, his arms empty. "There's no ice to be had. The house was locked, and no one answered."

I shook my head. "It's all right. Dr. Phillips says it wouldn't have made a difference."

Samuel looked at me, then at Mother, and the sorrow in his eyes told me he understood. He crossed the room without a word and rested his hand lightly on my shoulder.

"Can I be alone with her?" I asked.

"Of course. I'll be in the parlor with the others."

I took her hand again, surprised to find the skin that was hot before the doctor came in the room was now clammy and cool.

She looked at me now. Her eyes locked with mine.

"Emmaline."

It was the last thing she said.

In that moment I didn't cry. I didn't do anything but hold her icy hands and watch quietly as the strained expression on her face melted away. For the first time in my memory, she looked at peace.

I rejoiced that she was free, not yet comprehending that I was utterly alone. A long time passed before I finally decided to leave the room.

When I was ready, I kissed her forehead one more time. "Goodbye, Mother."

I walked into the parlor. "She's gone."

CHAPTER THIRTY-THREE

We buried my mother at the Salt Lake City Cemetery on a quiet, rainy Tuesday in April.

It rarely rained in the desert, and I heard more quiet murmurs from ward members about the blessing of the moisture than about the loss of my faithful mother who'd crossed an ocean and a continent in pursuit of Zion, gave up her husband, her legs, her health, her daughter, and then her life—in order to be obedient to her God.

They didn't know her. They didn't know what she lost or what she surrendered in this life. They didn't know the quiet way she loved me, despite her grief, all my fifteen years. They didn't know how she could talk a fishmonger out of a fresh haddock for three pence or how she could feed us on day-old bread and potatoes for a week. They didn't know the way Father called her Ruthie, kissed her cheeks, made her smile even when she didn't want to.

They didn't know the way she stroked my curls, her touch telling me she loved me when her words could not.

No, they did not know Ruth Ann Hensley Kendall of Melksham, Wiltshire, England. She was mine, not theirs. *Let them talk of rain,* I thought. It was better than empty platitudes about my mother. This was my loss. This was the end of my family. I didn't care what anybody had to say. Not Betsy, not Sister Thatcher, not Eliza or her mother, and certainly not Samuel Sandbury.

Samuel tried to show some kindness. Or at least make a show of it for others. He even paid for a notice in *The Deseret News*:

DEATH OF HANDCART COMPANY SAINT

Ruth Ann Hensley Kendall died on April 16, 1857, in the home of Robert and Helen Thatcher, having succumbed to blood poisoning following the amputation of her legs. Ruth Ann was born to Lawrence and Elizabeth Barton Hensley in Melksham, Wiltshire, England, on December 12, 1810. The son and husband of the deceased preceded her in death. She is survived by one daughter, Emmaline Sandbury, wife of Samuel Sandbury.

I don't remember much of the service, but I remember standing at her grave singing her favorite hymns. I once loved them too, but the meaning of so many of the words had changed for me. Too much had happened. I had seen the veil lifted from Zion's face.

As they lowered her pine box into the ground, I thought about the hundreds of dead left on the trail. My father, buried in a shallow grave. Gideon's father, left in the snow for the wolves. So many bodies discarded as we had to move on. I was glad at least she had a proper burying. She would have liked that. I wondered if she was with William and Father. I believed she was.

Still, I didn't cry. I was all locked up. Since the day of the sealing, I had not shed a tear outside of my nightmares.

We went home and ate a silent dinner that Sarah had prepared. The children were quiet, no fussing or quarreling like usual. I could tell they had been warned to be on their best behavior. It was meant to make me feel better, I supposed, but it made me more uncomfortable. I picked at the stew for a while and drank a little milk. The food tasted bitter. I felt as if I might never eat again.

"If you'll pardon me, I believe I'll retire now. My head aches something awful," I said, hoping they would not require me to return for family prayers.

Lying in bed, I thought about Bishop Grayson's prayer at the funeral:

"Our Father in Heaven, we bow our heads in humility and gratitude as we lay to rest thy handmaiden, Sister Ruth Ann Kendall, who hath given all in obedience to thy will. We thank thee for her faith, her long-suffering, and her steadfast desire to build up Zion upon this land.

"She hath crossed the sea and the plains, suffered the loss of her husband, her health, and her limbs, and hath endured all things in righteousness. Receive her spirit with gladness, O Lord, and bless those she leaves behind that they may honor her sacrifice by continuing in faith...."

The words beat in my head like a drum: *"Given. All. In. Obedience."*

How was Zion better because of her obedience? My father suffered and died. My mother suffered and died. Their daughter was a fifteen-year-old plural wife. Why does God need us to suffer and die to accomplish his will?

I had been asking this question for two years and felt only further from an answer.

I was almost asleep when I heard the all-too-familiar footsteps and knock at the door. Samuel opened it.

My legs trembled. My chin quivered. My mouth went dry. "Please go," I said hoarsely. "Please not tonight."

I felt waves of emotion welling up in me, threatening to spill out and drown me. My chest collapsed in on itself.

"I'm only here to ask if you're all right," he said.

Was I all right? I didn't even know what that meant anymore. He sat on the bed and reached for my hand. I leapt away from him.

"I don't desire your comfort!" I yelled. "You did this! You all did this!"

He put his hands on my shoulders. "Emmaline."

"No!" I shouted.

I spun and struck him in the chest, hitting wildly, wherever my fists could land. Hard, with both hands. Pounding on him again and again.

He did not stop me. He did not defend himself.

When I finally collapsed, shaking, I realized I'd drawn blood on his bottom lip.

"Do you feel better?" he asked, wiping at the blood.

"No," I cried.

Curled on the rug beside my bed, I sobbed so violently I thought I might come apart, knew I had come apart.

He backed out of the room and down the stairs.

And that's when I determined I would leave Zion. Some way, somehow, I would figure out a plan.

It was time for me to go. I would not die here the way my mother had.

CHAPTER THIRTY-FOUR

After church on Sunday, I waited near the stove for Samuel and Sarah to finish speaking with Bishop Grayson. Samuel Junior asked me if he could go outside with some of the other boys, and I nodded yes. Mary stood by her mother, and the little girls clung to her skirt. I looked for Eliza, but didn't see any of the Monsons. I felt isolated and alone, but that was better than standing at Samuel's side and playing the role of Sister Sandbury.

Sister Thatcher saw me alone and crossed the room to approach me. "Good morning, Emmaline. How are you, dear?"

"I'm sad," I said honestly, trusting she would understand.

She did. "We miss your mother. As little as she could say, she had a way of communicating faithfulness and love every day."

I nodded. I knew what she meant. She didn't know that even before my mother's mind was taken by illness, she communicated mostly in silent ways.

She looked around, then leaned in closely, lowering her voice to a whisper. "Emmaline, your mother left something for you."

I wondered what she could mean. We'd lost everything in the river.

Sister Thatcher reached for my hand and placed two small handkerchiefs into it. I recognized them both as my father's. One was small, and I could feel something hard and round inside. The other felt heavy and bulky.

"These were sewn into the fabric of her dress when she first came to us," she said. "They belong to you, not to the church." She looked around before saying that last part, as if she were taking a risk of disobedience.

"Thank you," I said.

She patted my hand. "They're yours, not his," she said softly, then hurried away.

I resisted the urge to look now, shoving the small pouches up my sleeve. But later, alone in my room, I carefully unwrapped them. The first held three small coins.

One quarter and two dimes. Forty-five cents.

It could get me a ride out of town, maybe a meal or two. Three small coins. A chance at freedom. My heart fluttered with excitement.

Mother and Father didn't know it, but with their careful saving, they might have provided the one thing I needed most. They had left me with hope.

My knees buckled when I saw the contents of the second pouch. Mother had still hidden away the pocket watch and brooch. They had belonged to my great-grandparents and were carefully saved through all of our travels and trials. I had a piece of my parents, my heritage, my country. I held them to my cheeks and wiped away tears. I felt a little less alone in that moment.

"Thank you, Mother."

I wrapped the treasures again and hid them far beneath my feather mattress.

I would wait until the time was right. Maybe I would go out West like Gideon. Maybe I would go back East and earn my passage back to England. I hadn't decided yet. But one thing I knew for sure: I would leave.

One Saturday in early June, Samuel planned a fishing trip with Samuel Junior. Now that his Saturdays were not so busy taking me to see my mother, he spent more time with the children. I couldn't help but notice how they thrived with his attention. It was my opinion, after having observed things in Zion for many months now, that the more wives a man had, the less time he had with his children.

Samuel Junior was alight with excitement. He was up with the roosters, outside digging in the mud for worms, and continually asking his father when it would be time to go.

"Where will you take him?" Sarah asked with more than a little jealousy that she had not been invited along.

I wished she was going as well so that I might have a peaceful day.

"We'll go up City Creek Canyon," he said. "Near the mill."

I cut thick slices of bread and covered them in butter for the picnic basket that Samuel would take. Sarah handed me a piece of brown paper to wrap the bread, as well as some salt pork and fried doughnuts. Samuel filled the canteen, and with that, they were ready to leave and head up the canyon.

Sarah looked at me and said, "Sister Grayson will be coming to pick me up for a Relief Society meeting. I'll take the baby. You'll need to put Letty and Lucy down for their naps."

She barked the orders at me as though I were the hired help. When Sarah finally left with Sister Grayson, I breathed a sigh of relief. I still didn't understand why she hated me so much.

I put down my dust rag and looked at the girls. "Shall we have a walk?" I asked.

"Yes," all three squealed—especially the little ones who were given the gift of a nap delayed.

We didn't go far, just to the edge of a nearby field where the grass had grown tall and white field daisies bloomed in clusters along the fence line. Letty and Lucy ran ahead, their bonnets bobbing, while Mary walked more slowly beside me, watching for butterflies.

Letty dropped to her knees, gathering daisies in both hands. That gave me an idea.

"Sit down, girls," I said.

We sat right in the middle of the tall green grass. Butterflies fluttered around us while meadowlarks, sparrows, and robins all sang the songs of summer. It was warm but not hot. A near perfect, early June day.

"Have you ever made daisy chains?" I asked.

They looked at me with blank faces.

I showed them how to split the stems and weave one flower into the next. Their fingers fumbled at first, but soon each girl had her own crown.

Mary laid hers gently on my lap. "It's for you," she said sweetly.

A wave of emotion washed over me, and I smiled in spite of myself. I would miss these girls when I left. They were loving and innocent children. Too innocent for Zion. They would one day become its victims. Mary was nine now. In just over five years she could be given away as a plural wife.

I placed the crown I made on Mary's head. "And this one is for you," I said.

We all laughed.

"Well, we best go have some of those doughnuts and get you girls down for your naps," I said, then sighed.

No one wanted to go back indoors, but I didn't want to press my luck with Sarah.

While the younger girls napped and Mary sat by the sewing basket quietly working on a sampler, I settled into the parlor and rocked gently as I read from Samuel's worn volume of Wordsworth. The house was finally quiet, the air still. I wouldn't have called it contentment. Too much had been lost for that. But for one hour I could simply exist in a fragile safety. Just me, a book, and the sound of my own thoughts.

Samuel and his son came home that evening with enough trout for supper, and Sarah was beginning to fry them up when I stepped into the kitchen with a bucket of fresh milk.

I unexpectedly recoiled at the odor of the fish. My stomach lurched, and I felt like I was inside out. I dropped the bucket and ran back outside, the milk splashing on the floor behind me. I was doubled over heaving the contents of my lunch all over the grass when Samuel found me.

"Emmaline, what happened? Are you ill? When did this start?"

I flopped over into the grass, holding my stomach. "Just now," I said. "I'm so sorry. It was the smell of the fish. It came over me suddenly."

"Let's get you upstairs," he said. "I'll go fetch Dr. Phillips."

"I don't think that's necessary," I said. "I just need to rest."

"Nevertheless, I'd feel better if the doctor looks you over."

He scooped me up and carried me all the way to my bed upstairs. I felt he was making a ridiculous fuss. I was already feeling better. It was just something that could come over a person sometimes.

Dr. Phillips came and gave me a thorough examination. He asked a lot of strange questions for a stomachache. Finally, he handed me a glass of water and patted me on the head.

"Everything looks normal. You take care of yourself."

A few minutes later I heard him talking to Samuel and Sarah downstairs in the parlor. I crept to the top of the stairs to listen but could only hear low murmurs. Samuel sounded happy, maybe even excited.

Then Sarah's voice was loud and clear. "Well that explains it," she said.

Suddenly, like a thunderclap in my soul, I understood exactly what was happening. In one instant everything had changed—again.

CHAPTER THIRTY-FIVE

t was not long before Samuel came up to deliver the good news. Because in that world the news *was* good. And it was his to deliver.

I hadn't ten minutes to sit with the reality of becoming a fifteen-year-old mother without a mother before his boots were pounding up the stairs, two at a time, and he burst in without even knocking to find me sitting on my bed under the covers like before.

"Well now," he said, grinning like he'd won a prize calf, "Dr. Phillips confirms it: You're with child. The Lord has blessed our union already. A baby, Emmaline. Our baby. Just imagine. You'll make a fine mother. I always knew you would. Knew it from the first time I laid eyes on you."

"Isn't it a little soon?" I asked.

The words felt foolish the moment they left my mouth. What did it matter whether I thought it too soon? The baby was already growing inside me. I was going to be a mother.

But when?

I cleared my throat and tried again. "I mean, did he say when?"

"He expects it in February."

February.

My birthday month.

I had hoped to be gone by then.

But this changed everything. I had seen mothers and newborns die on the trail. One woman had bled out before the baby was delivered. I could not be reckless enough to go where there might not be a midwife, a doctor, some sort of help. Not when I did have that here.

Besides, I hadn't a plan yet. No idea where to go or how to keep an infant safe. How to feed her. How to keep her warm.

All these thoughts whirled in my mind while he stood there, grinning at me like a child on his birthday.

I placed a hand over my stomach and left it there. But I said nothing.

"Sarah's fixing your supper—no fish," he said with a wink. "Doctor's orders. Get into bed, and I'll bring it up soon. We'll go to bed early. You need to get plenty of rest."

"We'll go to bed."

I had hoped he would stay away tonight. I had counted on it. On having a little time to think, to be alone with this news.

"Samuel," I said. I always used his name when I wanted something. Usually, it worked. "I still feel ill. May I rest alone tonight? Can we celebrate tomorrow?"

"You can rest," he said, his smile wearing thin. "But I'll be by your side. If you're ill, that's all the more reason you shouldn't be alone."

A soft knock interrupted us, too soft for Samuel to have heard it or cared. The door creaked open, and Sarah stepped inside with a tray.

"I brought her supper," she said, her eyes fixed somewhere near my shoulder. "Bread, broth, and some of the stewed apples."

"Exactly what she needs," Samuel said. "Thank you, Sarah."

She crossed the room and set the tray on the bedside table. Her movements were brisk and efficient, but not compassionate. Then she turned to go, but not before her gaze flicked down to my stomach.

She said nothing.

But she knew.

And I knew she knew.

When the door clicked shut behind her, I suddenly felt very small beneath the covers. I felt the most alone when Samuel was next to me.

He fell asleep with his arm draped over my back, as if he feared I would slip away in the dark. The night drug on, and every breath he took felt slower and deeper than the one before. My eyes were still open when the first rays of sunlight shown through the lace curtains.

The next night after supper, I approached him, careful to keep my voice sweet. "Samuel—I wondered if I might call on my friend Eliza to share our blessed news."

He paused, watching me longer than I could bear. I held his gaze, then looked away as if shy.

"Please?" I added softly. I didn't like to beg. But I needed this.

"Brother and Sister Monson will rejoice," I said, steadying my voice. "They'll be so pleased to hear."

He seemed to consider it. I caught Sarah's eyes across the room. She knew I was lying.

But Samuel didn't. "I'll take you Saturday," he said. "I've got some ward business to discuss with Brother Monson anyway."

Sarah narrowed her eyes at me, turned on her heel, and left the room without a word.

She didn't like that I'd dared to assert myself with Samuel. And she especially didn't like that it worked.

The Monson place was similar in size and build to the Sandburys' home, but it was made of dark red brick rather than adobe. It sat next to a small orchard of peach trees, and one large apricot tree stood in the front yard. On Saturday morning several young children were fussing about taking turns on a single wooden swing that hung from the branches.

As Samuel and I pulled up the lane, I saw Eliza and her mother hanging laundry on the lines outside. They both looked our way.

"Eliza!" I hollered.

She dropped a wet patchwork quilt into the grass and came running to me. I started to climb down.

"Wait," Samuel instructed. He tied the horses to the hitching post and came around to help me down. "Don't hurry. You're not a child. And you mustn't run in your condition."

I waved and waited for Eliza to reach me. We embraced, and I whispered in her ear, "I must speak to you alone."

Sister Monson was right behind Eliza, and Brother Monson stepped out of the house to greet us.

"Oh what a marvelous surprise!" Sister Monson said. "How wonderful of you to call. Won't you come in for some cookies? I believe Agnes has just made some."

Samuel was shaking Brother Monson's hand and already carrying on about the new mill in Iron County.

"I spoke to the prophet last week," Brother Monson said. "He's pleased with your work. Says the mill will help make the desert bloom."

Samuel seemed to stand two inches taller and grinned from ear to ear.

Sister Monson invited us all into the parlor. "Eliza," she said. "Come now and help me."

They returned in a few minutes with cups of water and a plate of molasses cookies. Brother Monson sat down with Eliza's mother and Mother Agnes on either side of him.

Samuel took a sip and then lightly clapped his hands together, beaming. "We have some wonderful news."

He rested a hand on my shoulder as though to present me. "The Lord has blessed our union. Emmaline is with child."

Eliza's eyes grew wide, and Sister Monson gasped, then clapped her hands in delight. "Oh what a joy! A true blessing from above!"

Brother Monson nodded solemnly. "A reward for righteousness."

Samuel took another sip of water. "She'll make a fine mother. I'm so proud of her and thankful for the Lord's abundant blessings."

I smiled as Eliza reached for my hand and gave it a tender squeeze. We listened to the men talk mill business far longer than anyone would want to—especially two young ladies with private matters to discuss.

Eliza took the opportunity when a break came in the conversation. "Oh, I'd just love to take Emmaline out to show her the orchard," she said. "May we excuse ourselves and take a short walk?"

Samuel hesitated. "She is in a delicate condition," he said, and I wondered if he'd been this protective with all of Sarah's pregnancies.

Eliza shot her mother a pleading look.

"A bit of fresh air is very good for her right now," Eliza's mother said. "And it is a lovely day. There's a nice bench among the trees if Emmaline tires."

Brother Monson spoke up as well. "I would like to speak to you about some priesthood business," he told Samuel.

"Well then, that settles it," Eliza's mother said brightly.

Eliza led me down a narrow footpath between rows of peach trees, the early June sun warm on our backs. We passed the swing and walked beyond the sight of the house, toward the bench her mother had mentioned. It was a simple wooden seat nestled beneath the trees. I drank in their sweet scent and watched blossoms floating to the ground.

She sat first and waited for me to join her.

After a moment she turned toward me, her voice low and hesitant. "What's it like?" she asked. "Being with child?"

I tried to answer, but nothing came out. I opened my mouth, closed it again, and stared down at my hands folded in my lap. I felt the tears begin before I could stop them.

"I'm scared," I whispered. "I don't know what to do. I can't talk to

Sarah. I—I don't even want to be in that house, Eliza. I feel like I'm losing myself a little more each day."

She was quiet for a moment, then gently tucked a piece of hair behind my ear. "Talk to Betsy," she said. "She loves you. She can help you through this."

"I can't forgive her," I said, wiping at my cheeks. "She knew what they were going to do. She knew, and she didn't stop it."

Eliza's gaze didn't falter. "She may not have had the power to stop it. But I know she tried. And I know she cares for you."

I looked away, ashamed of how long I'd carried the bitterness. "Maybe. But I don't know if I can trust her again."

"I think it's time to try," Eliza said gently. "You can't do this alone, Emmaline. You shouldn't have to."

We sat in silence then, the wind rustling through the trees like a soft blanket falling over the orchard. For the first time in weeks, I let myself lean against someone else's strength.

That night in bed, I resolved to speak to Betsy at church the next morning.

CHAPTER THIRTY-SIX

My daughter, Genevieve Ruth Sandbury, turned one year old on February 20, 1859, shortly after I turned seventeen.

In a polygamist household crowded with wives and children, birthdays were modest affairs. We usually marked the day with a nice family meal and whatever small gestures we could manage to make the day feel special.

But Ginny—I mostly called her Ginny—and I had survived a full year. And that felt like a miracle worth celebrating. So I determined to invite my friends and make the day memorable.

As it happened, Samuel and Sarah were away for the week, overseeing construction on the mill in Cedar City. They had taken their new baby, George, with them, leaving me in charge of the household. Managing Seth and Ginny was the most difficult part, but the older ones helped. Samuel said they would be back by Saturday afternoon for Ginny's birthday.

After sacrament meeting the Sunday before, I had pulled Betsy aside. "Would you help me?" I asked. "I'd like to do something for her. A little gathering of friends."

She didn't hesitate. "Of course," she said, smiling. "We'll come—Micah and Mattie too. I'll come early and help you bake an apple cake. We'll manage all the children together."

Even at eight months along now, Betsy never stopped giving. She had a way of showing up with exactly what I needed—steady hands, a kind word, or something warm from her kitchen. Especially for Ginny and me.

"Oh, thank you," I said, shifting Ginny from my right hip to my left and rubbing my hands through her dark brown hair. She had inherited my father's curls and freckles, just as I had. But she was tall and lean like her father. I softened my shoulders in relief. "Could you also tell Eliza? I haven't seen her in several weeks."

Betsy's brow creased. "They've missed three Sundays, haven't they?"

I nodded. "I've been worried."

"I should see her mother tomorrow," she said. "I'll do what I can to make sure they come." She reached for my hand and gave it a squeeze. "Emmaline, I'm so proud of you. I know this hasn't been easy, but Ginny is such an angel. You're doing a beautiful job."

"She saved me," I whispered.

And she had saved me. The pregnancy was filled with sickness, grief, and despair. My desperate love for the child growing inside me was my only comfort. It was also my motivation for everything I did. I had not forgotten my plan to leave Zion; I only delayed it. I kept it hidden in my heart, just as I kept my mother's coins hidden under my feather mattress and added a penny or nickel sometimes when I had access to a little extra household change.

Betsy arrived early on Saturday morning, her cheeks pink from the cold. She unloaded apples for the cake and a basket of fresh-baked ginger cookies. Mary and Samuel Junior entertained the little ones in the parlor while we baked.

"Brother and Sister Monson will be here," Betsy said, peeling apples at the kitchen table. "But Eliza won't be able to come."

I looked up from the mixing bowl. "Is she not well? Has something happened?"

Betsy hesitated, her hands pausing mid-peel. She set the knife down and reached across the table for my hand.

"Eliza's been married," she said gently. "She has moved to Ogden. She's attending her new ward there. Her parents went with her to help her settle; that's why they've been gone."

I stared at her. *Married?*

"She didn't tell me," I said, my voice barely audible. "She didn't say goodbye."

"I don't think she was given the time."

No, it couldn't be. Ogden was at least two days away by wagon—a world away from our corner of Zion. I knew because Samuel talked about the grain shipments from Ogden constantly.

"Who did she marry?" I asked.

"He's a bishop," Betsy said.

I closed my eyes for a moment. A bishop. Then it was almost certain: Eliza was a plural wife.

"Are there … other wives?"

"She's the third," Betsy said softly.

I didn't speak. Couldn't speak.

"She's not quite seventeen," I said at last. "How old is he?"

Betsy's hand tightened around mine. "In his fifties, I believe."

Fifties. Our fathers had not even been that old. I turned back to the batter and stirred it blindly, my hands trembling. I felt sick. Not only for Eliza, but for all of us.

Samuel had surely known. He was close to the prophet. He attended the priesthood meetings. The ones women weren't allowed to enter. Decisions were made in those rooms. Assignments given. Marriages arranged.

He would have known I would want to say goodbye. I buried my rage, as I so often did.

We finished the cake and placed the refreshments on the kitchen table and sat down in the two new rockers that Samuel had bought for Christmas. One for me and one for Sarah. Betsy picked up Seth and rocked him while I held Ginny and kissed her little head.

She was still a baby but trying to be so big. Earlier that week she took three wobbly steps toward me, and she babbled, "Mama, Mama, Mama," throughout the day. The freckles on her rosy cheeks made me ache with the memory of my father. Ginny gave me the strength to endure, and every time I held her, I became more determined to get us both out of this life.

Micah and Mattie arrived right as Samuel and Sarah returned from their trip. Brother and Sister Monson pulled up right behind them in their wagon, bundled in scarves against the bitter February air.

Samuel stepped inside first, stamping the snow from his boots, his expression caught somewhere between surprise and aggravation. His gaze moved from the crowded parlor to the refreshments laid out in the kitchen.

"I didn't realize we were hosting a party," he said to me, hanging his coat with deliberate slowness.

I stood, shifting Ginny to my hip. "It's just a small gathering," I said. "A few friends for Ginny's birthday."

He glanced toward the table as the children came running in excitedly to greet him. But he barely acknowledged them. His eyes landed instead on Micah and Betsy, then lingered on Brother Monson. Whatever disapproval Samuel carried into the room was quickly tucked away behind the superiority of a priesthood smile.

"Well now," he said, clapping his hands once. "A full house! Happy birthday to our little Ginny." He reached for her hand, giving it a perfunctory kiss. "You've grown so much, haven't you? Just look at you."

Ginny buried her face in my shoulder. Samuel let out a small chuckle for the room, then turned to greet the guests, playing the part of the generous patriarch.

I watched him closely. He shifted so easily from annoyance to affability when someone was watching. But I knew that look from before the smile. He hadn't wanted a big celebration. He didn't like me making plans independently.

But now, with guests already seated and cake already cooling, there was no graceful way to object. And so Samuel did what he always did: He became the host.

When he came to me that night, he said I shouldn't have done it. That we hadn't had such a party for Seth's birthday and that it had caused trouble with Sarah. "You've caused contention," he said.

"Oh, Samuel," I said, feigning surprise at his rebuke. "I only thought it would please you to celebrate her. She is such a blessing. Isn't it proper we gather to thank the Lord at such a time? There was nothing to stop Sarah from doing the same for Seth."

He studied me, trying to decide whether I was being sincere or sly.

"Of course I'm pleased and proud to celebrate the children," he said at last. "But we are one household. One family. That spirit must be preserved. I'll expect you and Sarah to plan future birthdays together, in unity."

"I understand," I said, lowering my eyes.

He softened, emboldened by what he saw as my obedience.

"And speaking of our baby …" He leaned in, his body warm against my back, his fingers finding my buttons. "Don't you think it's time for another one?"

I felt the familiar chill spread through my body. I closed my eyes and went to that place. That place where I saw nothing, felt nothing, knew nothing.

In the morning, before he left my bed, I decided to confront him about Eliza. It was a risk. If I angered him, I would learn nothing.

But I was getting better at finding the edges of what I could say with him.

I waited until he stood to dress, his back to me, buttoning his shirt slowly.

"Samuel," I said quietly. "Did you know Eliza had married?"

He paused for a second before going on with his buttons. "I heard it was being arranged."

"But you didn't tell me." I reached for his hand. "She is my closest friend. I would have wanted to say goodbye."

He turned slightly, not facing me fully. "It wasn't my place."

"You're in those meetings," I said gently. "You knew. You knew what was happening. You knew I would want to know."

"She's been sealed to a bishop. It's an honor and a blessing from the Lord. Her family was pleased."

"I'm glad they were," I said, my voice steady, though my heart beat fast. "Still, it hurt. That I didn't get to say goodbye. That no one thought I should."

He looked at me then, only briefly. "She's in Ogden now. That's all I know."

I nodded, keeping my tone soft. "Would you find out where? I'd like to send her a letter. To congratulate her."

He hesitated as if weighing the request.

"She was like a sister to me," I added. "Surely there's no harm in that."

"I'll see what I can do," he said.

Which meant maybe. Or nothing. But it was more than I had before.

A week later he came home from priesthood meeting with the address. I held the slip of paper to my chest, and before I realized what I was doing, I hugged him. Sarah looked on with fury as Samuel and I had a nearly genuine moment of tenderness. It surprised me as much as it did her.

I stepped back slowly, composed myself, and thanked him. Then I carried my precious paper to my room. Let Sarah rage. She was going to do it anyway.

CHAPTER THIRTY-SEVEN

t was early March when the first glimmer of hope began to take shape. I hadn't imagined that the Saints' troubles with the US government might open a door for me. But quietly, unexpectedly, they did.

One Sunday evening the children were unusually still, curled on the rug in the glow of the fire, looking at picture books and humming a tune they'd sung at church that morning. Samuel sat in his chair, polishing his boots for the coming week. It was, by all accounts, a peaceful Sabbath evening.

"They say the troops are still posted near Fairfield," he said, continuing out loud a conversation he seemed to have been having in his head. "Camp Floyd, they're calling it."

Sarah looked up from her mending. "I thought the trouble was over."

He grunted. "It is, mostly. The prophet brought peace, not Washington. We bent so there'd be no bloodshed, but don't mistake that for weakness. This people will not be overpowered by Gentiles again."

I said nothing, just rocked Ginny gently in my lap. Her hair was damp with sweat from sleep, and I kissed her temple out of habit. I had little interest in skirmishes between Zion and the United States government.

"They thought they could scare us into obedience," Samuel went on, his voice deepening. "Sent their army marching through the mountains with no sense and less preparation. Froze out before they even saw Salt Lake."

"And now they sit idle?" Sarah asked, threading her needle.

"They sit where they're told," Samuel said. "The Saints outmaneuvered them at every turn. That's the Lord's protection."

He turned to me then. "There are rumors they'll be passing through again come spring. Supply trains and peacekeepers, maybe."

I kept my expression neutral. "You mean they'll come into town?"

He gave me a look of superiority. "I don't think they want to provoke us further. But I wouldn't worry yourself, Emmaline. The priesthood is shouldering these concerns."

I nodded, as I'd learned to do.

But I tucked the information away—troops moving, supply trains, spring. They were the kind of details a woman wasn't meant to be concerned with. But suddenly, I was. I began listening anytime the troops were mentioned. At home, at church, and especially when Samuel let his guard down in bed, speaking more freely than he realized. I learned the men really were more concerned about the government than they were letting on. There was even talk of moving more Saints south.

When the weather warmed up a little, Sarah and I walked to town on Mondays. The older kids were in school, and we took turns pulling the ones who couldn't walk in a small wagon that Samuel had built for Sarah after baby Seth was born. Seth now toddled alongside while Ginny and George rode, George bundled in blankets and Ginny sitting up behind him.

The wagon was compact, but it had pine slats tall enough to keep the babies safe and sturdy wheels trimmed in iron. It was nicer than most women had, and I wished it wasn't. Samuel Sandbury wanted his wives to stand out. I wanted us to be invisible.

That day we had several letters to post and needed to pick up some fabric and thread at the dry goods store. There was also a list of staples to be purchased from the mercantile: sugar, molasses, salt, thread, lamp oil, and such.

It was a beautiful spring day, and I would have enjoyed the outing had I been with anybody other than Sarah. As it was, we walked in silence, speaking only to the children now and then.

On the outskirts of town, Sarah turned to me out of the blue and snapped, "He doesn't love you, you know."

I paused and looked at her for a moment, trying to decide what had sparked this outburst. She was jealous; that much I knew. I might've been half her age, but I saw the situation more clearly than she did. I had the benefit of emotional detachment. The benefit of not loving him. I could have used this moment to stir her jealousy. To tell her what he said to me in my bedroom. And part of me wanted to.

But when I looked at her, all I saw was a woman in pain. She was a victim of this system, just like I was. She had loved Samuel Sandbury for almost as long as I had been alive, but she was utterly powerless to control what happened in her marriage. When I saw myself through her eyes, I understood the pain. And I wished for us both that we were not sharing her husband.

"I know, Sarah, I know."

And we continued walking in silence.

When we reached town, I picked up Ginny and announced that I would take the mail. I had a letter for Eliza, and I wanted to see to it myself that it was posted. Sarah ignored me and took the other children to the dry goods store. She trusted I'd meet her there. And I would. But I waited patiently for the day when I could take advantage of that trust.

~

I saw the government soldier as I approached the post office.

He was standing off to the side of the doorway, in full uniform, as if he didn't care who saw him. Or maybe he wanted to be seen. That was probably the point.

The soldier was tall. Taller than any man I had ever seen. He had honey-blond hair and a clean-shaven face. I guessed he was younger than Samuel but older than Gideon. His coat was buttoned high, the brass buttons reflecting the late morning sun. A pistol rested at his side. His boots were polished. He stood with his hands behind his back, still as a statue but for the flicker of his eyes as people passed.

I stepped aside to let a man with a parcel come out first, then shifted Ginny on my hip and walked through the door as if I hadn't seen him at all.

But I had.

And I think he'd seen me too.

Inside, I stood in line behind two women and a thin man with a lopsided hat. My heart wasn't pounding, but it was awake. Alert. My mind was spinning with questions and ideas. I wasn't sure how to make a move, but I was paying attention.

The letter to Eliza was warm in my hand. When I stepped up to the counter, I handed it over and paid the postage with the money Samuel had given me. The clerk didn't look up as he handed me a few coins in change. I dropped one penny into the waistband of my dress, as I often did. Samuel and Sarah would not miss one penny.

Something about letting go of that letter made my eyes fill up with tears. They threatened to spill over as memories of Eliza flashed before my eyes, images from our friendship imprinted on a picture book in my mind.

When I came outside again, I was distracted and wiping away soft tears. I bumped right into the soldier.

He looked at me—not like the men in Zion looked, measuring righteousness or obedience. Not like Samuel. Not like the boys on the streets of Liverpool. He looked at me like I was there. Like I had weight and presence. Like I was another human.

"Pardon me, ma'am," he said. "Are you all right now?"

I didn't move at first. Ginny stirred against my chest and started to cry, more from the startle of the collision than from pain.

The soldier bent his knees to look Ginny in the eye. "Hey there, little 'un. Let's wipe those tears. Your mama has you safe and sound."

She gave him a half-hearted grin.

Then, turning to me, he said, "Pardon me, ma'am, I do apologize."

"That's quite all right," I said. "Thank you. We are fine. I am so sorry. I'm much too clumsy."

I hurried off, afraid someone might tell Samuel they saw me talking to a soldier.

"Good day, ma'am," he called out.

As Ginny and I left to find Sarah and the children, I felt more alive than I had in months. I didn't yet know if this encounter with the soldier would change my life; I only felt that it could.

That night Sarah and I shuffled through our normal dance in the kitchen. Rehearsed steps, memorized lines, the occasional foot stepped on. A family was meant to have one mother, and never was this more apparent than in a small kitchen during supper preparation.

But out of necessity we had figured out a way to work together effectively most of the time. Sarah peeled the last of the winter carrots while I stirred a pot of ham and pinto beans that I had put on the fire that morning. She lined up the tin plates and cups on the table, and I looked over at the salt I needed on the shelf behind the table.

Sarah noticed this. Our eyes met for a moment and there was a different look on her face. Kindness? No. Maybe just sadness. Whatever it was, it was softer than I was used to. She grabbed the salt and handed it to me. Something about this gesture felt like her way of apologizing for the morning's outburst. I nodded and took the salt. The moment was over.

We all sat at the supper table as a family. Like usual Samuel talked about the mills and the children fussed with one another. I finished my plate quickly and picked Ginny up to help her eat the rest of her food.

Sarah surprised me, and everyone else at the table, by speaking directly to me. "Emmaline, you did a fine job on the beans."

I stopped chewing. Sarah Sandbury had not only spoken to me, but she'd complimented me. She must have felt a lot of shame about what she had said this morning.

I nodded a thank-you. And then thought I ought to return kindness for kindness.

So I spoke to her too. "Thank you. Your corn bread suits them nicely."

Had something melted between us? Probably not. But I had seen, if only for a moment, a softer side. I wondered if the hateful words while we were alone showed the true Sarah while this softer side was an act for Samuel. Perhaps the outburst this morning was her resentment at him asking her to treat me more kindly. Or perhaps she truly felt badly about her behavior. Maybe it was both. I would never know for sure because she tightened back up immediately.

If only she understood that I wanted myself removed from her world as much as she wanted it.

Samuel, for his part, seemed amused by the entire exchange. He said nothing but eyed us both. His arrogant smirk infuriated me.

I did not like being his plaything—some prize goat trotted out at fair, admired for my compliance and the novelty of my presence at his table. There was satisfaction in his eyes. To him our strained civility was proof of his success. Two wives. One kitchen. One long table with children lined up on either side, eating quietly. He saw harmony where there was only suppression. He saw order where there was only obedience.

He thought he had won something.

But I was not his to win. And I did not exist for his amusement.

I looked down at Ginny in my lap, her small hand wrapped around my thumb. The warmth of her cheek against my arm grounded me. I would endure what I must, but only for a time.

One day soon I intended to wipe that smirk off his face.

CHAPTER THIRTY-EIGHT

I t is a sleepless night at Chimney Rock. My body trembles and aches with relentless hunger. Mother and I try to rest, our hands laced together beneath the quilts, but sleep won't come. I glance at my free hand. It is ghostlike and papery, like a wet, threadbare sheet hanging from the clothesline. I am disappearing. I try to scream, but my tongue is sealed to the roof of my mouth with the sticky glue of toxic thirst.

Now I am floating, hovering over our pallets. Watching as we slowly starve to death.

A raw and mournful scream pierces the night. I know it is Delia. I know what comes next.

It is Ellie's death.

No. No, I can't live it again. I try to force myself awake, clawing toward consciousness, but the dream traps me, like a cart sinking in prairie mud. The scream sharpens.

It isn't Delia's voice anymore.

It is mine.

I am inside Delia's tent now, hovering still, but forced to witness what I cannot bear. I see myself crouched over a child's body—wailing, shaking, *soaked in sweat.*

But the dead child is no longer Ellie.

It is Ginny.

My baby, limp in my arms. Her brown curls matted, her mouth slack, her warmth gone.

This journey, this holy trek to the land of milk and honey has now taken my child.

"Ginny! No, not Ginny! Please help my baby!" I am screaming, choking, struggling for air. My throat burns. My chest heaves. The tent is closing in like a tomb.

Arms wrapped around me.

Samuel.

He held me down. Not harsh, but firm. "Hush, darling. Hush. It's another nightmare. Ginny is asleep. She's safe. You're dreaming." His mouth at my hairline, his hand stroked my back.

I flinched. His unwanted embrace was suffocating. I twisted against him, still gasping, still caught between two worlds. Once fully awake, I had only one thought: *This place will not take my child.*

Later that morning Sarah and I walked to town with the children. She pulled the wagon with baby George, while I held Ginny in one arm and wrangled Seth down the road with the other.

My eyes were swollen with tears, my curls disheveled. The fear from my dream clung to me, and I knew I must look a sight.

There was a long list of items to purchase from the mercantile, and Sarah preferred to select the items herself, so I offered to post the letters again. It gave me comfort to personally see Eliza's letter mailed. I hadn't received a reply yet, but I continued sending letters every Monday.

I approached the post office with Ginny, kicking up dust as I walked, paying little attention to where I was going. My mind was still shaken, and I wiped at the occasional tear with the back of my hand.

Ginny, sensing my sadness, had patted my cheek earlier and said,

"Okay, Mama. Okay." She was only one year old, but she cared about me more deeply than anyone ever had. I loved her without reason and was twice as determined to escape with her as I'd been before the nightmare.

All these thoughts swirled in my head when I bumped right into him—the tall, honey-blond soldier I had seen several weeks ago. Samuel liked to talk about the soldiers as if they were evil. Here to intimidate us all. But this soldier had become a familiar, friendly face in town. I didn't fear the army like the others did.

"Well, there's that little 'un nearly knocked me over a while back," he said with a twinkle in his eye and a gentle tap on Ginny's nose.

"Oh sir, excuse me," I fumbled. "I'm so sorry."

"Ma'am, are you all right?" he asked, his voice lowering. "Do you need help?"

He must have noticed my puffy, tear-stained face.

I nodded, then pushed my way past him, eager to post Eliza's letter. But as I stood at the counter waiting for the postmaster, an idea struck me.

And suddenly, I had the beginning of a plan.

If this idea was going to work, I would have to trust this soldier. And that was a huge risk. My heart rate quickened, and my palms grew sweaty as I counted out change.

I took a deep breath and, before I could think again, made my decision.

"May I buy a single envelope?" I asked the postmaster.

"Two cents," he replied.

Two cents that cut into my savings, but I had to do it. I bought the envelope, borrowed a pencil, and scrawled a few words.

As I passed the soldier on my way out, I stopped and looked up at him urgently, holding his gaze for a moment, then quickly placed the envelope into his hand.

As I walked toward the mercantile, I glanced back.

He was reading my note:

"I need help. Meet me here next Monday. Same time."

He tipped his hat at me. I turned away before I could see anything else. Now came the hardest part: waiting.

That night at supper, Samuel remarked about the army in town, and I nearly choked on a potato.

"Saw another pair of them strutting past the ward house today." He shook his head. "Soldiers, sent by Buchanan to keep us in line, same way they'd handle Indians. As if we're no better than savages."

I wanted to say that the soldiers I had seen were kind, that I didn't think we had to be afraid as long as we didn't cause trouble. But I didn't dare call attention to myself on the matter. And I really didn't understand the conflict well enough to get involved. I stayed silent and fed Ginny.

Every morning that week I stood in front of the mirror and practiced what I would say to the soldier. I tried to look older. Wiser. Someone he'd take seriously, not just a desperate girl. I would have only a moment, and I had to make it count. I had to convince him to help.

On Monday morning Sarah woke up ill. She did that a lot.

"I don't think I can do the shopping today," she said. "We can go tomorrow."

I tried not to react. I couldn't let her see my desperation.

"I can go," I said. "Let me take the list. Ginny and I can handle it."

The look she gave me said she didn't think I could tell the difference between sugar and soap.

"We'll go tomorrow," she repeated curtly. The matter, as far as she was concerned, was settled.

I turned to Samuel. "If the shopping doesn't get done today, we'll run out of lamp oil by morning. I really don't mind going alone. I'm happy to let Sarah rest."

I had no idea how much lamp oil we had. I realized the folly of the statement the moment it left my mouth.

But neither of them questioned it. Samuel looked from Sarah to me and back again.

"I think it's best we keep the household on schedule," he said. "Emmaline can go. That's one of the blessings of plural marriage. The Lord designed it so no one wife is left to carry the burden alone."

For a while I was giddy with the luck of it. Any day I could leave that house alone was a small freedom. But today—today—I was nearly dizzy with relief.

Sarah, for her part, either couldn't abide the thought of me doing the household shopping alone or she was suddenly cured.

Because two hours later we all set out for town.

"I'll take the letters," I said calmly and slowly. I was full of hope that I was about to have the most important conversation of my life.

He was there when I arrived, as if he hadn't moved an inch all week. His eyes found mine instantly, and this time I didn't look away.

I didn't speak either. Not at first.

Ginny stirred against me, her face buried in my shoulder, and I adjusted my grip on her.

He took one step forward. "You came."

I nodded, heart racing. "I said I would."

A pause passed between us, heavy with everything I couldn't say aloud.

"I don't have much time," I said quietly. "She's expecting me back at the mercantile."

He glanced toward the store. "You want to tell me what you meant?"

"I need to leave. I can't explain everything. I just … I need to get out of here. Anywhere east or west. I don't care."

He studied me. "How old are you?"

"Seventeen."

He glanced at Ginny. "You running from a man?"

"Yes."

"Is he dangerous?"

"He could be."

He gave a slow nod. His jaw tightened, and a look of anger passed his face. I could feel his desire to help. "You have a plan?"

"No," I said. "Just a few belongings and a child. A little money. Less than a dollar. That's all I've got."

"We've been able to assist a few girls like you. I'd like to help if I can."

After thinking a minute he said, "Your name?"

I had to decide in that moment to put our fate in his hands. "Emmaline. And this is Ginny."

"Nice to meet you, Emmaline. I'm Sergeant Levi Allison."

He looked down at Ginny, then back at me. "There's a supply wagon headed for Fort Kearny next Monday. I can get you in. No promises how comfortable it'll be."

"I don't care about comfort."

"You sure about this?"

"I'm sure I can't stay."

He considered that. Then, "Where's your house?"

"East. Edge of town. He'll be at the mill. She'll be waiting for me in the store."

"You can get in and out quickly when they're gone to grab your belongings?"

"If you give me a few minutes."

He hesitated, then gave a short nod. "Be here same time next week. I'll do the rest."

I blinked and smiled. "Thank you."

He didn't tip his hat this time. He just said, "Don't tell anyone."

Then he turned and walked away.

CHAPTER THIRTY-NINE

Six days later I sat in the second row at the ward house, hoping it would be my final sacrament meeting. Ginny sat on my lap, George on Sarah's, and Samuel between us, holding himself with the confidence of a king on his throne.

I mouthed the words to "Come, Come, Ye Saints," weighing their meaning against my own journey.

"And should we die before our journey's through,
Happy day! All is well!"

Rage rose in me as the congregation sang with joy.

Was I the only one in the room who thought it absurd to sing joyful songs about tragic, unnecessary deaths? I had watched hundreds of our people die on our death march between Iowa City and Salt Lake City. I myself had nearly died from starvation and the elements. My mother was stripped of her dignity as she slowly lost her fight for life. To me this was madness; to them it was worship.

"Happy day! All is well!"

Girls like Eliza and me were forced into marriages we never wanted, into households that resented us, with first wives who freely "gave us" to their husbands and then punished us with their bitterness every day after. I had been a fifteen-year-old bride and a sixteen-year-old mother, all under the threat of eternal damnation for me and my family.

No, all was not well in Zion. And it didn't matter how joyfully they sang.

But I was no longer the fourteen-year-old girl who came here with no voice and no power. I was a seventeen-year-old, and I was capable of saving myself and my child. I was scared, but I believed in myself now. Maybe for the first time in my life.

The one good thing I had in this city—refuge in Betsy and Micah's home—had been stripped from me. I watched them now, Micah with Mattie in his lap and Betsy holding her new infant, Katie, named for Betsy's mother, Katherine. I knew they were true believers, raised from birth in this faith.

But they had not been called to plural marriage—yet—and I feared if it happened to them, it would tear their tender lives apart. Betsy and Micah were wonderful people. They represented all that I thought I'd wanted. Except that they were believers in an order that had entrapped me and held me against my will.

No matter how righteous they believed it to be, I knew it was wrong. I knew it when I didn't have a choice in my marriage. I knew it when Samuel came to me in the night and held my wrists down, despite my cries of "No."

Betsy and Micah knew this would happen, and they had not stopped it. Though Betsy had tried to prepare me and make it easier for me, she and Micah had not stood up against it. I knew they never would. The cost for them would be too high.

This was the reason I could not say goodbye. It tore my heart out to lose Betsy, to miss seeing the girls grow up, to think of her worrying about where we had gone and whether we were safe. But it was the only way.

I scanned the room and found others who had been good to me in Zion. There was Eliza's mother, who had loved me since I was twelve. And Brother and Sister Thatcher, to whom I owed a great debt of gratitude for the loving care given to my mother. I could not tell any of them goodbye, but as I watched them that morning, I prayed for them. I prayed the way I had as a child. I prayed from my heart.

A member of the bishopric rose to speak, and I squirmed as he began to talk about the trouble between the Saints and the US Army.

"Brothers and sisters," he said, pausing to sweep the congregation with his eyes. "As you know, federal troops continue to encroach upon this valley. Sent here not to protect us, but to subdue us. They call it peacekeeping. We know what it is: persecution in uniform."

A few murmurs of agreement moved through the room.

"The prophet has counseled us to stand strong. Prepare but not provoke. We do not seek war, but we will not bow to Gentile tyranny. We are a covenant people. The Lord has led us here, and the Lord will protect us, just as he parted the Red Sea for Moses. These soldiers may ride through our towns, but they do not ride with authority in Zion."

He straightened the papers in his hands, voice solemn now. "There may come a time when we must make sacrifices for our faith. Not only of comfort, or labor, or even of land, but of our very safety. But we do so willingly. We do so joyfully. Because we know this is the only true church upon the face of the earth, and no army of men can shake that truth."

One more afternoon. That's all I needed to survive. One more evening of keeping my face blank, my hands calm, my voice light. If I could do that, Ginny and I would have a chance at a real life. I would have to build it myself, but we could be free. The thought both steadied and shook me. I could almost see the clock ticking down. But what if I missed my moment? What if I broke before the morning came?

It was an endless night. By God's grace Samuel didn't come to me.

The next morning I made preparations quickly. I couldn't pack my bag yet—couldn't risk it being discovered. But I arranged everything I planned to take so it would be easy to grab when the time came.

I wrapped the coins in Father's old handkerchief and sewed them into the lining of my dress, along with the pocket watch and brooch, just as Mother once had. My sweaty, trembling hands made crooked stitches, but I trusted they were strong enough to hold. I took the cameo from Samuel's mother and pinned it inside my dress where Sarah wouldn't notice. I had no sentimentality for it, but I would trade or sell it in Fort Kearny without hesitation if Ginny and I needed food or shelter or medicine.

I tied Father's yellow ribbon in my hair.

Everything else that mattered I sorted into neat stacks in my drawer or wardrobe: My journal. Betsy's handkerchief and the blue ribbon she'd given me. A copy of the newspaper announcement of Mother's death. I also set aside my scriptures because they held the only record of Ginny's birth date, written carefully by Samuel in the opening pages.

The few practical dresses Ginny and I owned hung in the wardrobe, and the empty carpetbag waited at the bottom, ready to be filled. I had come to Zion with nothing. God willing, I would not leave that way.

Sarah was ready to leave for what she thought was our weekly trip to town. She called for me impatiently, and I scooped Ginny into my arms. Wrapping her close was my best cover for trembling hands. And holding her while I walked gave me an excuse for my short breaths, so I declined Sarah's offer to make room for her in the wagon.

Ginny objected. "Wagon, Mama! Wagon!"

"Mama wants to hold you right now," I said, kissing her cheek. "Wagon later."

She fussed but eventually settled into my arms and fell asleep. From that point on, everything had to go perfectly. One misstep and it could all fall apart.

Fear rattled through me, and I jumped when a wagon clattered by.

"Are you all right?" Sarah asked.

I nodded. "It just startled me. Head's in the clouds, I s'pose."

We arrived in town, and I was about to take the letters to post when Sarah complicated my plan.

"Samuel would like me to show you how to shop at the mercantile," she said, her voice laced with irritation. "In case I get sick again."

Panic flooded my chest. As if I didn't know how to buy basic goods at a mercantile. But for the plan to work, I needed her distracted in another building. I thought quickly, knowing only one thing would work—her pride.

"Oh, Sarah, I could do it if needed," I said lightly. "But you're so much better at selecting the right things. And you can do it more quickly. Let's just get through our errands today and get the children home to nap."

Sarah nodded, eager to agree that she could do the job better.

I waved the envelopes at her. "I'll go post the letters, and then I'll meet you at the mercantile. You can show me a few things there."

That seemed to satisfy her. Having overcome that obstacle, Ginny and I crossed the street toward the post office. I scanned the view in every direction.

Sergeant Allison was not there.

My mind spiraled. *He changed his mind. He lied. He turned me in. He's not coming.*

I had trusted him, and he let me down. I should have expected this. I should have known it would never work. The world spun around me, and I wasn't sure what to do. I wanted to die. How could I face Samuel when he found out what I had tried to do? I knew there was nothing I could say that would save me.

I marched into the post office, eyes stinging with tears of defeat.

But when I stepped back outside, I heard a low, urgent voice: "Emmaline!"

I turned, startled.

He was out of uniform, half hidden behind a maple tree. His eyes found mine. He pointed to the back of the building.

"Quickly," he whispered.

I looked once over my shoulder, then ran. I didn't think anyone had seen me, but I couldn't be sure.

Behind the post office, I saw what he had pointed toward.

A covered wagon.

Notable in its plainness, it looked like any other on the road. The canvas was yellowed with dust and age, the wooden sides unpainted. Nothing marked it as military. No flag, no seal, no sign of the government it served. Only the driver in partial uniform gave it away.

I approached the back, and from within, a man's voice called softly, "You goin' east, ma'am?"

I hesitated, glanced behind me. "Yes," I whispered.

He offered his arms, and I handed Ginny to him. He set her gently down, then reached out a hand for me. I climbed in quickly and gathered my daughter, who was crying now and confused.

"We're going for a ride, baby. Mama's here."

We scooted to the side of the wagon. I was trembling so hard I spilled the cup of water he handed me. The cold dampness crawled up my leg.

"Hello, Emmaline. I'm Private Lawrence Edward. We're going to move fast," he said. "Tell me where your house is, and I'll speak to the driver."

I gave him the directions. He spoke quickly to the other soldier and settled in the back of the wagon with us.

"Is Sergeant Allison coming?" I asked.

"No, ma'am. He doesn't do supply runs. But he gave me this envelope for you."

Inside were two silver dollars and a note that read simply: *Godspeed, Emmaline.*

I clutched it to my chest. My heart was pounding. Ginny still whimpered. The wagon lurched forward. We were on our way.

I expected relief but felt only terror.

Then a sharp whistle cut the air. The wagon jolted to a halt. I froze. Covered Ginny's mouth.

Two men on horseback pulled up beside the wagon. I saw out through a thin crevice in the gathered canvas. One was older, one barely more than a boy. Both wore broad hats and dark coats, the insignia of Brigham's Nauvoo Legion hidden but unmistakable. Private Edward tossed a blanket over Ginny and me.

"Where you headed?" the older man called out with all the bravado of Brigham himself, thinking he could overpower the US government. I'd heard Samuel talk about it. I was afraid they'd try if they thought they were being threatened. I suspected that's why the wagon was unmarked.

"Just a delivery, sirs," the driver answered. "Seed grain and supplies for Camp Floyd."

I gripped Ginny tighter and bent my head low.

"You're Buchanan's men?"

"Yes, sir. Army. Quartermaster detail."

"You carryin' anything else? Brigham's only given you permission for supplies."

The driver gave a long pause and spat casually on the dirt. "No, sir. Just supplies."

"Move along," the older man said. "I don't want to see you back in town."

The wagon began to roll again.

I let out a shaky breath.

"They could've looked back here," I whispered.

"But they didn't," the private said.

"Why not?"

"Sometimes bluffing's enough," he said. "And for all their arrogance, they really don't want trouble."

As we neared the Sandbury house, my fear surged again.

"Let's just leave," I said. "I'm afraid he'll come back. I'll never make it if he does."

"Samuel Sandbury's being held for questioning," he said.

"But why? How? I didn't even give my last name."

"We can find things out," he said, adding a shrug and a wink. "He thinks he's being accused of interfering with federal operations. They won't keep him. It's just to tie him up long enough to make sure the house is clear and give us a head start."

Relief washed over me. Sergeant Allison had thought of everything.

Even so, when the wagon pulled up in front of the house, I thought I would be sick.

"I can't do it," I said.

"You can," Private Edward said gently. "You don't want to leave with nothing. Go quickly."

I looked at Ginny. She was crying and afraid. I wasn't sure about leaving her, even for a minute. How did I know I could trust these men?

Then I thought of Sergeant Allison's note.

I had already decided to trust them. I had to follow through.

We couldn't afford to leave with nothing.

I kissed Ginny and promised I'd be right back. I hurried into the house and bolted up the stairs, struggling to turn the doorknob with my sweaty hands. I grabbed a handful of my skirt and used the cloth to turn it. I burst into the room, shoved everything into the blue carpetbag, and ran back down the stairs.

At the bottom step I stopped cold. I heard something. *The back door? Or just the wind?* I couldn't be sure.

What if the wagon was gone?

What if someone had seen?

What if Samuel had come home early?

What if this was the part of the dream where it always went wrong? Where I woke up?

"Please, God," I whispered, then flung the door open.

The wagon was still there.

Ginny cried out, "Mama!"

I ran.

Within seconds I heard the driver shout, "Giddyup!"

We were heading east. Ginny and I were safe.

I did not even look back.

PART THREE

EMMALINE

CHAPTER FORTY

MAY 1859

The first time I traveled over the Rocky Mountains, I'd been half dead—delirious with fever, burning with pain in my fingers, and unable to feel my legs. I remembered little. Sometimes the sound of wagon wheels grinding against the rocky path, the crack of harness leather, and my mother's soft groans come back to me in my nightmares. But I never saw what was outside the wagon then.

This time I saw the mountains the way they were meant to be seen.

The wagon climbed slowly through a narrow canyon, pine trees crowding close on either side. My senses came alive with the fragrance of pine, sagebrush, and crisp mountain air. Above us rocky ridges rose steep and uneven, catching the light where the sun slipped through the trees. The trail wound its way up the slope in long switchbacks.

There were boulders as tall as houses, and little waterfalls spilled everywhere through crevices of melting ice. It was quiet, save for the scrape of hooves and the wind in the trees. The higher we climbed, the farther away we were from Zion and its hold on me. And with each turn of the wagon, my tension eased and was slowly replaced by a fragile sense of safety.

A stout army wagon could travel two or three times faster than a handcart company, and our driver, Private David Scott, was determined to make good time.

David and Lawrence—that's what they asked me to call them—were friendly men who treated Ginny and me with a gentleness I hadn't expected. They didn't prod me with questions or speak in hushed tones about the girl with the baby. When we gathered around the fire at night, they talked about their own lives instead. I enjoyed their tales from the army and mishaps on the trail. The more they talked, the less I had to.

David especially took to Ginny. He said he had a little one, Beckah, about Ginny's age back home in Tennessee. Ginny was fifteen months; his Beckah was about eighteen months. I often caught him watching Ginny when she played, a distant look in his eyes like he was seeing someone else.

"Beckah's hair looks like that," David said one night as Ginny sat combing her fingers through the dust. "Gets wild the minute she steps outside. My wife says it's got its own opinions."

Lawrence chuckled, stirring the supper pot. "That's how you know she'll run the household one day."

"You think?" David asked. "I was hoping she'd go easy on her old man."

"Not a chance," Lawrence said, grinning. "My Ann says she's marrying me for my cooking. That, and I follow orders."

We all laughed. I couldn't believe these men were real, talking about following orders from women and showing such tenderness toward the ones they loved. I was on the same trail that had taken me to Utah, often camping in the same places. But away from the Saints, I might as well have been in a different world.

I never said much. I wanted to trust them, but I couldn't go that far. Still, they knew where I'd come from, and I got the sense they understood.

Lawrence was from Massachusetts. He didn't have a family yet, but he liked to talk about Ann and their plans to marry once his service was up next year. He'd been a cook in the army before he started running supply wagons, and he took great pride in feeding us well.

Truth be told, we mostly ate the same kinds of food I'd eaten on the handcart trail—wheat porridge, johnnycakes, beans, salt pork—but there was more of it, and Lawrence served it with flair when he could. They even had a crate of oranges from California, and each night we shared one between us. I hadn't tasted citrus since Buffalo. Ginny bounced with excitement each time the orange came out, and she was usually successful at getting an extra slice from David.

In the long, slow days that followed, the rhythm of trail life settled into us. There was comfort in the routine of it. Days of movement, nights of firelight, and the slow unwinding of fear.

Ginny and I slept in the wagon, and the men slept in a tent outside. For the first time in years, I felt free and, though I hardly dared admit it to myself, almost safe. Part of me, though, stayed alert. I was always listening, always watching. I didn't know if we had been seen leaving or, worse yet, followed. I wasn't ready to trust anyone.

We reached Fort Bridger the first week of June 1859. The plan was to stay there a few days to meet up with a regiment coming from Fort Laramie. This caused me a good deal of fear. More people meant more chances to be recognized. More time for Samuel to find us, if he had come looking.

We sat around the fire the second night and watched Lawrence cook up a mess of trout he'd caught that afternoon. Ginny had been fascinated by the shiny, wiggling fish, and I felt a sudden pang for Wiltshire. For days beside the river, watching my father fish. They were slivers of memory, maybe not even real. But they saddened me all the same.

Suddenly, I noticed a man on horseback approaching.

My first thought always was whether we had been found. I grabbed Ginny and climbed into the wagon. We often stayed hidden like that when other travelers passed near our camp.

But it turned out to be a mail courier with the army. He had a sack of mail for Fort Kearny and a handful specifically for David and Lawrence.

After a few minutes Lawrence came to me and handed me a letter. "I think this one will be of interest to you," he said.

I opened it slowly and then shut my eyes before reading it. Whatever it said, I was afraid.

Lawrence—

E. made it out clean, but not quiet. They turned the town upside down when they found the girl and baby were gone. Sent men looking into the hills, worried she might have wandered or been taken.

It didn't take long before they figured otherwise. Her satchel was missing. And all her personal effects. Word got around quick. I got questioned. Said I saw her at the post office a few times. Just a girl with a baby mailing a letter. Told them she climbed into a wagon, but that's all I saw.

Word is, they think she went west with a man named Gideon. California, maybe.

I'll be gone from Salt Lake soon. Tell her it worked. She bought herself some time. Give her my best.

—L. Allison

My mouth hung open as I read. I pictured Sarah getting impatient, then confused, then panicking when we didn't show up at the mercantile. I pictured Samuel going through my room and then setting out to look for me. He would go to Betsy and Micah first. I felt a deep pang of shame for worrying Betsy.

Sergeant Allison had thrown them off our trail. Sent them looking in California. But how did Gideon's name come into it? I didn't want to cause trouble for him.

And yet, I felt that Gideon would be proud of me. I remembered the last time I saw him, the last words he said:

"You don't belong to him. You're not his. You're not theirs. You're still Emmaline."

I had kept those words hidden in my heart, and I prayed that someday I would get to tell him how they helped me.

That night, long after David and Lawrence had settled into their tent and the fire had gone to coals, I lay awake with Ginny snuggled beside me. Her slow breaths whistled faintly and tickled the space beneath my chin. She slept with one hand tucked against my ribs, the other curled up by her cheek.

It was a full moon, and the light glowed through the canvas just enough to softly illuminate her face. It was long like Samuel's, but she had my olive skin and dark curls. I saw Mother in her round green eyes and Father in her cheekbones and freckles. She knew no fear or want; her face was the picture of peace.

I didn't question taking her away from Samuel, but I did feel sorrow that she didn't have a father. He thought of her as a reward for righteousness, something to parade before the ward as evidence of his standing with God and the prophet. It was hard to tell which he wanted to please more. He liked to say his children were arrows in his quiver, blessings from God, but he rarely spent time with them. Especially the girls.

And one day, I knew, he would likely have married Ginny off as a plural wife, for that was his intention for all his daughters. Not my child. That would not be her future. I didn't know how yet, but I would give her a life of safety and freedom. And when she was old enough, she would chart her own path. Just as I was doing now.

She stirred as the sound of something howled outside of camp. Coyotes? Wolves? I wasn't sure, but the sound sent shivers down my spine. I held her closer and stroked her cheek.

"Hush, baby, Mama's here."

It was a reminder of how vulnerable we were out on the open trail. My sense of safety dropped out from under me as I thought of all the wild things outside the wagon. There was nothing but a sheet of canvas between us and the wind, rain, and glowing eyes that lurked in the darkness.

When the sound faded, I sat up and looked outside. There was nothing to see but silence and stars. I hadn't experienced the night like this before. The sky was soft velvet black with resplendent clusters of light that stretched on forever. I felt both small and large and somehow … connected. I was the most alone I had been in years. But I didn't feel alone.

This feeling. It meant something. I believed it was a sign from the heavens. I didn't understand exactly what it meant, but I held on to what I did know.

I knew there was beauty in nature and in people. I knew that whoever created these stars created me too, and maybe even loved me. I didn't know if I believed in God the way I used to, but I believed in goodness. I had seen it in Eliza, Gideon, Betsy, Levi, David, and Lawrence. Each one of them was an angel in their own way. I had survived only with their help.

I also knew I was strong enough to walk away from what was wrong.

It was wrong to intentionally give others false hope in order to control them. It was wrong to be careless with desperate people's lives. It was wrong to threaten souls with the wrath of God in order to control them. And it was wrong to send fourteen-year-old girls into the homes of married men in order to make them young plural brides.

These things I knew, and for now, that was enough.

I fixed my eyes on the heavens and whispered, "Thank you." Then I laid down next to my daughter and fell asleep.

CHAPTER FORTY-ONE

The creek water was cold, but the rhythm of scrubbing helped settle my nerves. Ginny sat at my feet, happily stacking rocks and playing in the dirt. I'd nearly finished the last dress in the pile when I heard voices on the other side of the creek.

Two soldiers stood beside their wagon, arms crossed, spitting brown streams of tobacco juice at the ground. Their coats were dusty, their boots caked with the road. I could only see one of their faces from where I knelt at the water's edge, but I could hear them both.

"Fort Laramie says to hold until the Second Battalion clears the trail," one of the men said. "They want to avoid another standoff with Brigham."

The other snorted. "Whole place is ready to blow. He's holed up there with thirty wives and counting, and he's got his boys blockadin' supplies and torchin' our wagons."

Were the Saints really setting fire to army wagons?

"He ain't the only one with all them wives," the first replied. "Seems the holier you are, the more wives he hands out. Blessings with bonnets."

The other soldier scoffed. "More like bodies with bonnets," he said.

"Three women for every man, I hear."

They both laughed.

I stopped scrubbing. Water ran down my wrists and soaked into my sleeves, but I didn't feel the cold anymore.

My cheeks burned. To them, we were a joke. Brigham, the wives, girls like me.

Zion had been my family's dream, our greatest ambition, ever since I was twelve. My father's life was lost in pursuit of it. My mother surrendered her dignity and her daughter to it before she died. We had crossed oceans and mountains because, like everyone we knew, we believed it was the New Jerusalem.

Of course I saw it differently now. I had found it oppressive and coercive. Life there was untenable for me. But it was also my story. My life.

And now I was listening to strangers laugh at it. Laughing at girls like me. If they knew what I had given—what it had taken from me—they wouldn't laugh. The next morning we moved on. But their ridicule followed me long after we'd left the creek behind.

The journey became more difficult after we left Fort Bridger. I had lost the sense of comfort and safety I felt when we were alone with David and Lawrence. The new men looked at me with curiosity and sometimes derision. I saw in their eyes what I really was: a seventeen-year-old with a child, from a peculiar religion, with no support and not even a hint of a plan for our future.

I didn't feel regret, and I hadn't lost hope. But I did feel fear. Where would we go? What would we do? I had spent more than a year planning to escape. I knew what I was running from, but I had no idea what I was running to.

"I know you hear talk," David said to me one night as we sat by the fire. "Don't let it get to you. Them soldiers seen a lot, but they don't really understand. You're brave. You're stronger than any young woman I've ever met. You and Ginny are gonna make it."

I nodded but kept my eyes on the flames. "What's Fort Kearny like?"

David poked at the fire with a stick. "It's not much to look at. Just a cluster of low buildings and a palisade along the river. Officers' quarters, a mess hall, some storehouses."

I wondered what we'd do when we got there. It didn't sound like a place for a young mother and child.

"But they've got regular traffic. Army wagons, emigrant trains, even the Pony Express comes through."

He looked at me and paused. I sensed he knew what I was worried about. "You might be able to find work in a kitchen or laundry."

I glanced at him hopefully.

"It ain't a place to settle, but it's a place to rest a spell," he said. "Get your bearings. You'll hear news from all over, maybe even get word to someone if you've got people out East."

I didn't tell him we had no people. I didn't speak at all. But the tightness in my shoulders and back eased a little. A place to get my bearings. That sounded like exactly what I needed. If I could rest and get a little work, I could come up with a plan.

I traveled more lightly after that. At least for a little while.

We were halfway across Nebraska on a beautiful day in the middle of June when one of my nightmares roared back to life. The wagon train was stopped along the Platte for a short water break for the horses and oxen. Ginny and I drank our fill from the river and explored the wild prairie violets that grew along the bank.

It reminded me of the few tranquil moments I'd spent with Eliza along the Platte. My eyes brimmed as I remembered Eliza's carefree laugh and innocent dreams of candy stores and school houses in Zion.

Biting my lip to stop the tears, I pushed those thoughts away. No sense in looking back. The future was about me and Ginny.

I decorated her hair with the blossoms and then tucked one behind my ear.

She giggled and exclaimed, "Pretty Mama!"

I tucked another flower into her curls. "Pretty Ginny," I said, grinning at her laugh.

A low, distant rumble interrupted our play. I looked up at the sky. Bright and blue. Not a cloud in sight. That wasn't thunder. My stomach dropped. I'd heard that sound before.

"Buffalo stampede!" someone yelled.

Men shouted in reply. Horses were pulled to the creek. Chaos erupted around me.

I threw myself over Ginny's body, shielding her with my own.

It was over almost as quickly as it began. The herd didn't strike our party. This one was smaller than the stampede I had experienced on the handcart trek. But it was enough to take me back to that day when the buffalo took two Saints, several handcarts, and a supply wagon. A day I visited often in my nightmares.

I found myself on my hands and knees, shaking and gasping, unable to catch my breath or comfort my daughter, who sobbed beside me. Was I dreaming again? I couldn't tell.

Strong arms lifted me from the dirt. My mind flashed. Samuel? No. David.

He handed me a cup of water. "Emmaline, have a drink." His voice was gentle and steady.

I blinked and looked around wildly. "Where's Ginny?"

"She's safe," he said. He pointed to Lawrence, who was holding her protectively.

"These stampedes happen sometimes out on the open prairie," David said. "You never get used to them."

My sobs slowed into gulping breaths and my body still trembled, but with our friends around us, I felt safer. A little less broken.

"I … I've seen one before," I said.

It was all I could manage, but it was enough. He understood.

"Let's get you girls settled in the wagon," Lawrence said. "It's time to get moving again."

It took a long time to calm Ginny down and even longer to settle myself into sleep that night. I knew we were still on the right path, but I had a greater awareness of how difficult that path would be.

Between the forces of nature and the judgment of others, I feared Ginny and I faced a more uncertain future on the American frontier than I had realized.

CHAPTER FORTY-TWO

The first thing I saw as we approached Fort Kearny was the American flag. It rose tall above a cluster of white clapboard buildings and canvas tents, rippling in the breeze with its thirteen stripes and thirty-two stars.

I had last seen the US flag in Buffalo, New York, when Eliza and I joined the Independence Day crowd and feasted on street food with Brother Monson's fifty-cent piece. I remembered the laughter, the music, the smell of roasting sausages and corn. I held Ginny up so she could see out of the wagon and pointed toward the flag.

"See, baby? See that special flag?" I said softly, though I was really talking to myself. "That flag means we're free now."

The Saints in Zion didn't want to be part of the United States. Brigham Young had tried to build a kingdom of his own, and for years the church and the government had been at odds. But I didn't want a kingdom. I wanted a country. I wanted laws that protected, not controlled. I wanted choices. That flag reminded me it was still possible, that I wasn't trapped anymore.

I sat up straighter, my back aching but my heart lifting. The road ahead was still unknown, but something was stirring in me that I hadn't felt in a long time. It was hope, but it was also the sense that I could choose what came next. That flag, and the memory of Buffalo, gave me a reason to believe in something better. I bounced with excitement as we neared the fort.

But to my surprise we didn't go through Fort Kearny itself. David said civilians weren't permitted inside unless invited. Instead, we made camp by the river beyond the fort's edge. I hadn't expected to be turned away, not after coming all this way.

I sat silent at dinner, eating johnnycakes and stewing in frustration. We were so close to our destination, and suddenly, it felt as if the door had been slammed shut. What would this mean for us?

After dinner I washed the tin plates and found David standing alone. A younger Emmaline would have stayed quiet and waited to see what happened. But not now. Ginny and I needed a plan, and this might be our only chance to make one. I was done letting things just happen to me while I sat by helplessly.

"What happens if we're not allowed inside?" I asked. "You and Lawrence will resupply and head back West. But what about Ginny and me?"

"There are several boardinghouses in the area," he said. "Lawrence and I will report at first light tomorrow. We'll make inquiries as soon as we can."

"You said there might be work for me in the fort," I said, working hard to keep accusation out of my voice.

He tried to reassure me. "That's still a possibility. Let us ask some questions tomorrow."

His vague answers angered me. I clenched my teeth and blinked hard to keep in the tears. "You said this was a place to rest. To start over. And we can't even get inside."

Perhaps he realized how he'd set my expectations too high—and how quickly fear could rise up in the silence that followed—because he gently replied, "Emmaline, Lawrence and I are going to find a place for you and Ginny to start over. I promise. And if you don't like anything here, there are wagon trains coming through every day. You'll be able to get a ride going east if that's what you want."

With a nod I climbed into the wagon bed. I was still disappointed but mollified for the night. Maybe I wouldn't get answers until tomorrow, or even the next day. Maybe this next chapter would be harder than I imagined. But I was here, I had my daughter, and we were going to make it. Because we had to.

David and Lawrence were already gone by the time Ginny and I stirred the next morning. I made wheat porridge over the hot coals while watching the fiery sun rise over Fort Kearny. Nebraska was still as beautiful as I remembered from my first trip through it. Tall prairie grasses swayed in a light breeze as rich verdant hues danced on their blades.

David's words, his vague plans, turned over in my head, and I couldn't help but fight off fears that had resurfaced with the morning light. Had I brought my daughter all this way to languish on the Nebraska prairie? I had no plan. No means to support her. What was I thinking running away with her?

I tried to fight back these feelings. I knew the fear did not serve me, but there was a small voice in my head that asked, *Isn't this what your parents did? Bringing you across the sea with no real idea what would happen?* Was I leading Ginny into trouble the way my parents had done with me?

No, I told myself, *it's not the same.*

Ginny and I sat in the grass, wrapped in our woolen shawls against the light morning chill, eating porridge from tin bowls. I picked at mine, struggling to recover the confidence that seemed to drift away with the steam. Why couldn't I reclaim the resolve I'd felt so strongly the afternoon before? This journey felt frustratingly full of stops and starts.

Ahead of us a single wagon passed by. Its canvas tarp flapped in the wind as it rolled west—back along the very road that had brought us here.

I watched it go, wondering who they were and where they might be headed. And with that, a memory surfaced. A memory that seemed a lifetime ago.

I was back on the *Horizon*, the day Captain Reed invited Eliza and me up to the quarterdeck to view a passing ship through his spyglass. I could suddenly taste the salt in the air, feel the wind whip through my curls, and see nothing but blue in every direction. With a twist of the spyglass, the ship's billowing sails came into focus.

"Sometimes the sea feels endless," I had said. "Like we're just drifting or even going backward."

The captain had pointed toward the other vessel. "But you see that ship? When the sea swallows the world around you, look for another traveler. You may not feel yourself moving forward, but if you fix your eyes on a ship sailing the other direction, you'll begin to feel the motion."

In that moment the motion of the other ship had given our ship movement again. I'd felt it beneath my feet.

Now, watching that wagon roll west, I felt the same shift. I realized how far I had come, how much ground I'd covered. I didn't know what was ahead. But I wasn't going backward.

Thank you, Captain Reed. Wherever you are.

David and Lawrence came back that afternoon with news.

"Spoke to Sergeant McGraw about your situation," David began.

I looked up from my sewing curiously, almost sticking my thumb. Ginny had been growing like a weed, and I was letting out the hem of her yellow calico frock. I had made it from leftover fabric from the birthday dresses Samuel had given me when I turned fifteen.

I studied David's face for clues, but it gave away nothing.

"There's a place about two miles north of here. A boardinghouse. It's run by a widow named Abigail Prentiss. She's got a farm as well and may need some help. If not, it will be a place to rest for a few weeks."

I thought of the $2.61 sewn into my dress and wondered how much this would cost.

"He says she's tough but fair," David said. "It will be a safe place for you and Ginny."

Lawrence went back to the fort, and David and I rode to the Prentiss home in silence. Ginny slept in my lap, and David fidgeted with the reins while I smoothed my skirt repeatedly and twisted my buttons. I sensed he was as anxious about our destination as I was.

We followed a well-worn trail a mile or two north, passing scattered wagons, a crude livery, and a blacksmith's shed with smoke billowing from a tall, bent chimney.

The wagon turned off the main road onto a narrow dirt track, rutted and dry. I saw a tidy farm and knew that this had to be it.

Young corn stood in neat rows, the stalks still low, about as tall as Ginny. Their bright green leaves rustled in the breeze. Beyond the fields rose a tired, whitewashed farmhouse that needed a coat of fresh paint. It was two stories tall, with a simple porch that stretched across the front.

The porch sagged slightly at the middle and held two rocking chairs, one rocking gently as if someone had just been sitting in it. Or maybe it was rocked by the breeze. A yellow sign with black block letters that read "BOARDING" was tacked to the right of the front door.

To the left a faded red barn with wide double doors stood open to the air. A coop leaned against one side, hens pecking in the grass nearby. A young man, maybe early twenties, hauled two buckets of water toward the barn. He wore canvas overalls and a cowboy hat, like he'd wandered off the cover of one of Eliza's dime novels.

Several small garden plots were fenced off near the house, the largest of which grew thick leafy vegetables. A tall, thin man with a trim gray beard worked a hoe into the dirt between rows. Small, round stones framed a kitchen garden in front of the house. The farm was teeming with growth and life. It seemed like a place with stories to tell.

"Looks just as they described," David said, applying the brakes. He jumped down and came around to assist me with Ginny and the blue carpetbag.

We knocked on the door several times before a woman answered. A tall brunette with a streak of gray in her tightly wound hair, she was an imposing figure. Pearls of sweat formed on her forehead and cheeks. The flour on her arms and apron told me we had interrupted her bread baking, and her face told me she didn't take kindly to being interrupted.

"Are you Abigail Prentiss?" David asked.

"Yes." She wasn't making it easy.

I stepped up. "I'm Emmaline Kendall," I said, dropping Samuel's last name, which I did not consider to be legitimately mine. "This is my daughter, Ginny. We need a place to board."

She looked me up and down, clearly sizing up the single teenager with a baby. "You can pay?" she asked.

"I have $2.61."

David shifted beside me, and I immediately felt his disapproval. Maybe I shouldn't have told her how much I had.

She thought for a moment that seemed to go on too long. "There's a room in the attic," she finally said. "It has a feather mattress on the floor. A month will be $1.75 for room and board if you help me wash the supper dishes."

I looked at David. He nodded.

"I can do that," I said.

"The attic is upstairs. Take the door at the end of the hall. Steps are narrow and loud, so don't go creeping around at night. I've got to get back to my bread."

David took Ginny from me and gave her a long hug. He ran his fingers through his hair and let out a long sigh.

"We'll be at Fort Kearny until Friday," he said. "If you need anything. If you change your mind …" his voice trailed off.

"We're going to be okay," I said, wiping away tears. "I don't know what we would have done without you and Lawrence. I'll never forget you."

He handed Ginny back to me and tipped his hat.

I stood on the weather-worn porch at Abigail Prentiss' boardinghouse with my daughter and watched our last tether to the past drive away.

CHAPTER FORTY-THREE

t didn't take Ginny and me long to settle into our attic room. There was, as we had been told, one feather mattress on the floor. A small pitcher and washbasin sat atop a crate. There were no drawers. I kept our things inside the carpetbag, as there was nowhere else to put them.

The ceiling was low, and the floor creaked with each step. But it was swept clean, and everything was meticulously dusted. The wall opposite the bed was lined with shelves full of canned fruits and vegetables. So many beautiful glass jars of peaches, apples, plums, jams, tomatoes, green beans, onions, and relishes, all stacked several rows deep. There was no doubt that Abigail Prentiss was an industrious woman.

Bundles of dried herbs hung about the room, mingling the scent of sage and mint with mustiness and age. Several crates of old quilts and fabrics were stacked on top of an old steamer trunk. I couldn't help but wonder how many places that trunk had been.

The one small dormer window did not appear to open, so the room was poorly ventilated. I expected the nights to be hot. Even so, I knew they would be far more comfortable than any night I'd spent at the Sandbury residence.

I was starting over again in an unknown place with an unknown future. It was an all-too-familiar feeling. Looking back at each home I'd had, each place where I'd laid my head, I couldn't help but feel how this sparse, clean attic room represented the most independence I'd ever known. I could pay for it myself. We would be safe, dry, and obviously well fed. That was no small thing.

I glanced at Ginny, and her innocent eyes looked at me with complete trust. I would show her she was right to trust me.

"Shall we go see the garden?" I asked, maybe too brightly, eager to begin our new life. I knew nothing of what it held, and my hands trembled in spite of themselves.

I took $1.75 from the pouch sewn into my dress. Then I lifted Ginny onto my hip and carried her down the narrow attic stairs to find Mrs. Prentiss and pay for our lodging. We searched the kitchen but found only the rich, tangy smell of cooling sourdough loaves.

Finding the house empty, we stepped outside and saw her pulling weeds in the kitchen garden.

"Mrs. Prentiss," I called. "I've brought the money."

"Everyone calls me Miss Abigail," she said in a tone that implied I should have known. She wiped her hands on her apron and took the money. Sweat dripped down her brow and darkened the sides of her cotton shift.

"Miss Abigail," I corrected. "May we explore the farm? It's all so lovely."

She nodded. "Supper's at six."

Ginny toddled beside me, her hands clutching the folds of my skirt as we followed the path around the side of the house. The garden was larger than I'd realized, stretching well beyond the kitchen plot into rows of hearty vegetables. Beets, carrots, beans, tomatoes, and squash were neatly tended.

The thin, gray-bearded man I'd noticed earlier still worked the earth, his hoe slicing between rows in a slow, steady rhythm. His straw hat shaded most of his face, but I guessed him to be about sixty. His sleeves were rolled to the elbows, and his hands looked soft, like he had not spent a lifetime working with tools.

He glanced up as we approached and gave us a small nod and warm smile. "Afternoon, miss."

I returned the gesture with a polite smile. "It's a beautiful garden."

He leaned on his hoe. "Miss Abigail makes a good deal on the board if you're willing to work. I'm too old for the heavy lifting, but I can keep the weeds at bay."

Ginny let go of my skirt and plopped down in the grass nearby, busying herself with a clump of clover. She babbled to herself, utterly content.

"I'm Emmaline," I said. "And this is Ginny."

He removed his hat, revealing thinning hair and a sun-reddened forehead. "Abner Pike. Folks call me Reverend."

Reverend. The word alone stirred up a familiar trembling in my legs. I'd learned too well what power in the name of God could do.

"I see," I said carefully.

He glanced at me, then at Ginny. I imagined his curiosity. His judgment.

But he tilted his head slightly. "Don't worry, I'm not here to preach. And I don't judge. Just earn my supper and keep my joints moving. And anyway, my ministry has always been about Christ's love."

That earned the smallest smile from me. We stood in companionable quiet for a moment, watching Ginny chase a grasshopper through the weeds with total abandon.

"Miss Abigail seems a little … tough," I dared to say.

"Aww, old goat is gruff on the outside but soft as oatmeal on the inside," he said. "She's had a hard life. A lot of loss. She doesn't trust easily. Once you earn it, she's as loyal as an old country hound."

"You've been here a long time, then?" I asked.

"I come through a lot," he said. "I do a fair bit of itinerant preaching these days. This is a good place to lay my head during my travels. It's also a good place to stay and write for a while."

He nodded toward the barn. "Careful with the little one near the animals. Elias is usually good about keeping the barn clean, but livestock don't care who's underfoot."

"Elias?"

"Elias Emberton," he said. "One of the other boarders. Works as an apprentice at the blacksmith shop. Nice kid. Engaged to a young woman back East."

Blacksmith. It made me think of Micah and dear Betsy. A wave of sadness came over me.

"Thank you," I said. "We'll be careful."

He returned to his work with no further word, as if the conversation had never happened. I gathered Ginny into my arms and started toward the barn, feeling oddly comforted by the exchange.

The Reverend hadn't pried. He hadn't preached. And he hadn't looked at me with suspicion or pity. He was just a man keeping weeds out of the beans.

There was something so beautiful about his kind and nonjudgmental presence. I felt we could be good friends, the Reverend and I.

At six we gathered for dinner. The dining table was long, carved of sturdy oak. Best I could tell, there was room for twelve, but tonight it sat seven: Miss Abigail; me and Ginny, who sat on my lap; the Reverend; Elias the blacksmith; and a mother and daughter I hadn't yet met. The Reverend, who seemed to take it upon himself to make everyone feel comfortable, introduced us.

"Emmaline, this is Naomi Beckett and her daughter, Lydia," he said. "They are from Boston."

I didn't say I had been to Boston. I wasn't ready to tell that story.

Looking at Lydia and Naomi, he continued, "And this is Emmaline and her daughter, Ginny." He paused, turning to me. "I'm afraid I don't know where you are from."

I didn't know what to say.

"England," I finally said. "I've lived in Wiltshire and Liverpool."

"Well now, how interesting," the Reverend said. "We'll look forward to hearing all about that."

"You seem awful young to have a baby," Lydia said.

She wasn't being rude. It was a fact. I was young to have a baby, especially on my own.

"Hush," her mother said. But her look said she agreed, and her eyes were full of the judgment her daughter lacked.

"The cow's near to calving," Elias offered, clearly trying to change the subject.

There seemed to be an abject lack of curiosity about the calf's impending arrival, and we all ate our stew and bread in silence after that.

I studied the room while we ate, partly to avoid meeting anyone's eyes. The dining table took up most of the space. Though it was well made, it was timeworn, its surface scarred by decades of meals and daily use. A handmade china cabinet stood along the far wall, but instead of fine dishes, it held stacks of tinware and plain serving pieces, all carefully arranged.

To the right hung a small wooden cross and a faded bit of embroidery that read, "Give us this day our daily bread." I wondered if anyone else in the room could appreciate the beauty of simply asking God for provision, rather than earning it through obedience to earthly leaders. I stared at the words for a long moment and whispered the prayer in my head. Nearby, an almanac page for June was pinned crookedly to the wall, its edges curled and yellowing with age. Two oil lamps burned from built-in shelves, casting flickering light that couldn't quite reach the corners.

There wasn't much else. Just a pair of extra chairs pushed against the wall and a silence that felt heavier than the stew in my stomach. Everything in the room seemed to belong. To have its place.

I wasn't sure I did, but I was new. I understood why people might judge. I was willing to work to earn their trust.

I pondered this until the end of the meal. Then I rose and began clearing dishes, as per my deal with Miss Abigail. I set Ginny in the corner with the first few clean plates and spoons—something I'd always done to entertain her at the Sandbury home—and got to work.

When Miss Abigail started to help, I gently waved her off. "Please don't trouble yourself," I said. "I'm used to cleaning for a larger family. I can do this easily."

She hesitated, then gave a short nod and left me to it.

By the time I finished and turned down the lamps in the kitchen and dining room, I found her asleep in her rocking chair, a skein of yarn and a crochet hook resting in her lap.

"Miss Abigail," I whispered.

She stirred, blinking in the dim light but didn't speak.

"The kitchen's finished. Ginny and I are going to bed."

She nodded without opening her eyes.

Back in the attic Ginny curled into me without protest. The day hadn't been easy. But neither had it been too hard. I fell asleep believing that what lay ahead wasn't meant to break me, but to make me stronger.

CHAPTER FORTY-FOUR

There was a high chair at the table in the morning.

I surprised myself by tearing up at this small gesture of hospitality. Something seemed to have shifted since the evening meal, when I had been expected to hold Ginny on my lap. The chair wasn't new. Its paint was chipped, and one leg looked slightly uneven. Many babies had eaten there before. But it had been scrubbed clean and pushed up to the table like it belonged there. Like we belonged there.

What a change I felt in twelve hours.

Miss Abigail didn't mention it. She just nodded at me when I entered the room and poured my coffee. Ginny, sleepy-eyed and barefoot, reached for the chair and clambered in with the wobbly determination of a toddler who believed herself entirely capable of managing on her own.

I laughed and gave her a little boost. The Reverend also grinned over his coffee cup as Ginny worked her way into the chair.

My smile was wide, genuine. I hadn't felt that in a while—the ease of sharing a moment of uncomplicated, innocent joy with another human being.

The rest of the table still was empty, though two more places were set.

"Where are the others this morning?" I asked.

"Elias leaves early for the shop," the Reverend said. "I expect we'll see Lydia and Naomi anytime now."

As if on cue, Lydia walked in the door, her mother behind her. Both wiped at tired, puffy eyes and seemed to have been quarreling. Miss Abigail set down cups of milk for Ginny and Lydia and poured a cup of coffee for Naomi.

After we finished a quiet breakfast of cornmeal mush and fresh berries, which Ginny devoured like she hadn't eaten before—and I wasn't sure if she'd ever had a fresh berry—I got up to clear the breakfast dishes.

"No, dear," Miss Abigail said. "I've only asked you to do the supper dishes."

"I'd like to do them if you don't mind," I said. "I need to keep my hands busy, and it's really no bother."

She twisted her mouth, thinking it over. It was only a few dishes.

"All right, then," she finally said. "I do have much work on the farm that needs my attention. Thank you."

I sat Ginny to play in the corner again and had the dishes done in no time. I was grateful for something to do. I wasn't sure how else to spend the day.

In the dining room Lydia was bent over a slate, her head resting in both hands. Her chalk sat idle beside her, and she seemed to have given up in frustration.

I dried my hands on my apron, scooped up Ginny, and lingered in the doorway. "Are your lessons giving you trouble?"

She didn't look up. "I hate them."

"What are you working on?"

She lifted her head and scowled. Not at me, I thought, but at the slate. "Copying a poem. Only I keep smudging it, and it's dumb, and it doesn't even rhyme."

I stepped closer. Her handwriting was uneven, but I recognized the first lines: "The stately homes of England / How beautiful they stand."

"Felicia Hemans," I said before I could stop myself.

Lydia looked surprised. "You know it?"

I nodded. "I had a book of her poems. Back in England."

She seemed surprised. "You like poetry?"

"Very much." I pulled out a chair and sat beside her with Ginny in my lap. "May I?"

She slid the slate toward me.

"It doesn't have to rhyme to be beautiful," I said. "Sometimes it just has to feel true. Do you want to know a trick I used when I had to copy a hard piece?"

She shrugged but didn't say no.

"Read it aloud once. Let your voice help your hand find the rhythm. You'd be surprised how much that changes things."

Lydia gave me a skeptical look, but after a moment she picked up the slate and read the first two lines aloud, a little stiffly. Her voice cracked on the second one.

I smiled. "That's it. Try again."

She did. And this time the cadence was better.

We sat like that for several minutes. Her reading, me quietly helping, the room slowly warming with late morning sun. I hadn't taught anything in my life, but I knew what it felt like to be stuck, and I knew the joy of having someone see you trying.

When she got through the whole verse without a smudge, Lydia grinned. Not at me, at the slate.

"That's much better," she said.

"Yes," I agreed. "It is."

Naomi stood in the hallway, arms crossed, watching us without expression. I wasn't sure how long she'd been there. She didn't say a word. But when Lydia stood and carried her slate to the other room,

Naomi gave me the smallest nod I'd ever seen.

I nodded back.

Ginny was getting sleepy, and I thought a morning nap would do her good. I took her to the parlor and sat in a rocking chair and nestled her to me. It was the first time I really got a look at Miss Abigail's parlor.

It was the finest-looking room in the house, though nothing in it was fancy. Just thoughtfully decorated and well cared for. The wallpaper was an old-fashioned gold-and-blue print, faded in spots but clean. A brown braided rug with a simple border covered most of the floor. A blue velvet settee, threadbare along the arms but still soft, sat opposite two sturdy oak rocking chairs near the woodstove.

In one corner stood a game table and benches with a checkerboard mid-play and a tin box that likely held cards or dominoes, probably both. In the other a small bookshelf leaned slightly to one side, flanked by a worn reading chair with a cushion that had clearly been restuffed more than once. I couldn't imagine ever getting bored in a room like this.

I softly hummed "Lavender's Blue" as I rocked Ginny and thought about the small successes of the morning. For the first time in a long time, I was beginning to feel content.

That's when Naomi walked into the room. Her dark eyes found me, and she took a seat on the blue settee. She wrung her hands and didn't meet my gaze. Her thin lips were pursed. She had carried a chill into the parlor, and I immediately sat up straighter.

"Emmaline," she began.

I stared at her, sensing unkindness in her voice and judgment in the words that would follow.

"It isn't that I'm not grateful to you for helping Lydia."

I said nothing.

"It's just that she's starting to admire you." She paused. "She's impressionable, only twelve years old. And I'm not sure a girl like you is a good influence on her."

There it was: *A girl like me.*

I hadn't decided if I would tell anyone my story, but if I did, it wouldn't be this woman.

"Are you done?" I asked.

"Do we have an understanding?"

"I'm not here to win your approval, Mrs. Beckett," I said quietly. "And I didn't seek your daughter's admiration. She is old enough to have her own mind."

She stiffened.

I didn't stop. "Nevertheless, if it would put your mind at ease, I'll do my best to stay out of Lydia's way. But don't mistake your assumptions about me for truth. You don't know me or my story."

Her mouth opened and then closed. She seemed unsure what to say next, and I gave her nothing.

I buried my face in Ginny's soft head, damp with sleep, and resumed humming. Naomi walked away. I was shaken but proud.

I was no longer the child carried across the Atlantic on the *Horizon*. No longer the girl married off like property.

I was the one who walked away. I was making my own life. Too young perhaps, but doing it all the same. Let them think what they would. Let them whisper what they wanted. They didn't know me. And women like Naomi didn't deserve to.

That evening before bed, Ginny and I wandered through the yard chasing fireflies. Neither of us had ever seen one before, and the flickering lights felt like something out of a fairy tale. We ran and laughed and tumbled in the grass until we were breathless with wonder.

I stopped short when I nearly rolled into the Reverend and Miss Abigail, who were out walking the property. I started to apologize, but then I saw it: an honest-to-goodness smile on Miss Abigail's face. I hadn't seen that before.

I wasn't sure who had put it there. But something told me it hadn't come from me or Ginny. There was more happening in this house than I realized.

I gathered Ginny into my arms and offered them both a quiet good-night. As we headed back inside, I heard quiet laughter in the distance and felt the warm hum of something unfamiliar. Joy? Could it be joy?

It had been an interesting day. Full of more kindness than cruelty, more hope than fear. For our second day in a new life, that felt like something close to a new beginning.

CHAPTER FORTY-FIVE

Wednesday afternoon Ginny and I were in the kitchen fixing a midday snack when Miss Abigail came in with a chicken.

"Are you planning to fry it or roast it tonight?" I asked.

"Do you have a preference?" she replied, as if my question had been impertinent.

"No, ma'am," I said. "It's just that I make a good roasted chicken. I was going to offer to put it on for you. I enjoy working in the kitchen. Do you have any rosemary?"

"Well, ain't you something?" Miss Abigail shook her head.

I went on, "I noticed you have a lot of canned apples in the attic. Would you mind if I make an apple cake? I have a special recipe. I don't like sitting idle, and Ginny likes to help me."

"Suit yourself." She threw up her hands as if exasperated, but there was a grin on her face.

~

Later, as the cake cooled and the chicken roasted, Ginny and I rocked on the front porch and worked on a nursery rhyme.

"Little Bo-Peep has lost her …"

"Sheep!" Ginny finished it for me.

"She doesn't know where to …"

"Find them, Mama," Ginny laughed as she said her part.

The late afternoon sun was at its hottest, and despite the shade, sweat trickled down my back. I took a moment to be grateful I was no longer confined by the so-called sacred undergarments I'd been forced to wear in Zion.

About that time a wagon rumbled down the dusty road.

I had lived with fear of being found since the day we left Salt Lake. Every wagon wheel, every unknown face, rattled me. I scooped Ginny into my arms and carried her inside.

Within minutes the Reverend stepped into the kitchen.

"You've got a caller," he said.

My stomach clenched. Sweat prickled along my skin. "Who is it?"

"I believe it's the private who brought you here."

"David!" I ran outside.

It was him. I threw my arms around him, and he caught me in an embrace of relief.

"What are you doing here?" I asked. But the moment the joy of seeing him passed, I tensed. Had he brought bad news?

"Lawrence and I wanted to check on you and Ginny," he said. "Make sure the arrangement is suiting you. We leave on Friday."

"It's going as well as can be expected," I said. "Maybe better."

He smiled.

"I don't know how everything will work out," I admitted. "But most of the people are so nice. I'll figure out a plan."

"You want to stay, then?"

"Yes."

He nodded, then hesitated. "I guess the other question is—do you want us to take back any letters?"

"Do you think that's a good idea?" I asked. "Would someone be able to tell where they came from?"

"We wouldn't post it," David said. "Since they already think you went to California, I'd have them carried east by a soldier who's been stationed farther west. There are men we trust. If you want it done, we can manage it. Happens all the time."

I considered it, but the answer didn't come easily. "Can I have some time to think?"

"I'll come back tomorrow."

He tipped his hat and drove off, leaving me standing in the still air. I was grateful but unsettled.

I let the question simmer for the rest of the day. There were four letters I desired to send, but if I was going to do so, there was someone I wanted to speak to first, and that had to wait.

At dinner I presented a meal of roasted chicken and carrots, mashed potatoes, Betsy's apple cake, and Miss Abigail's buttered sourdough bread.

I don't remember the taste of the meal, but I will never forget the smiles on the faces around the table, the compliments from the people I shared it with, and particularly one exclamation from Miss Abigail: "I don't know where you learned to cook, dear, but this is the best meal I've had in a very long time."

Naomi remained silent, but that didn't keep her from eating.

After cleaning up the dishes, I finally made up my mind to seek out the Reverend. I found him sitting under the apple tree on a bench beside Miss Abigail. I'd hoped to find him alone, but the conversation couldn't wait.

I spent a good ten minutes working up the courage to approach. In the end it was Ginny chasing a firefly in front of the tree that forced me to act. I found myself standing before them with no more time to stall.

I took a deep, unsteady breath. "Reverend," I began, "may I ask you something about right and wrong?"

"Of course, Emmaline."

Miss Abigail looked at me with interest. She made no move to leave, and I got the sense she didn't intend to.

My words came out awkwardly. "If someone leaves … escapes … a terrible situation … I mean, something where terrible things are done to them against their will …"

He nodded gently. "Go on."

"Well … if another person tells a lie to help them get away … one lie, to protect them … is it wrong to let others go on believing it?"

There was so much grace in his voice as he chose his next words. "Emmaline, are you ready to tell us what brought you here?"

My voice broke. "I'm sorry," I cried. "I ca-can't."

"It's alright," he said. "I don't have to know what happened to know that God loves you and Ginny. He sees you. As for your question, let me say this:

"There are times when truth is sacred. And there are times when mercy is. The letter of the law is not always the spirit of it. Jesus himself once broke Sabbath law to heal a man. He told the Pharisees that mercy mattered more than sacrifice.

"If someone tells a lie to protect a soul in danger, to deliver them from harm, well, I believe the Lord sees the heart behind it, as he did with the Hebrew midwives and Rahab in the Old Testament. And he judges not by man's rules, but by divine love.

"So if you're asking whether God would condemn a person for protecting the innocent, I believe the answer is no. I believe he blesses that kind of courage."

Before I knew what I was doing, I threw my arms around the Reverend in a hug. His shoulder was wet when I pulled away.

"Thank you," I said. "Thank you so much."

When David came back the following day, I had four letters for him, each written on a torn page from my journal. I had carefully written extra copies of the first two letters for my own records as well.

June 1859

To Brigham Young, Church of Jesus Christ of Latter-day Saints:

I write to make my intentions known, though they have long been settled in my heart.

I hereby revoke my membership in your church. I do not recognize your doctrine, your authority, or the marriage you claimed to arrange on my behalf.

I was a child when I was brought to your valley. I was a child when I was forced into a plural marriage I did not consent to, with a man twice my age, whom I did not choose. What you called obedience, I now know to be control. What you called faith, I call fear.

Let me say this clearly: Religion is good and pure when it is chosen out of love for Christ and serving others. It is evil when it is sold with lies and forced upon a desperate people out of fear of damnation.

For these reasons I fled your valley. I have not looked back. But I send this letter so there will be no confusion: I renounce all affiliation with your church and demand that my name be stricken from your records.

—Emmaline Lucille Kendall

June 1859

Samuel,

You may have wondered if I survived. I did. You may have told yourself I would come to ruin without you. I did not.

Let us be clear: The so-called marriage you and your church claimed to sanctify was no marriage at all. I did not choose it. I did not consent to it. I do not recognize it now. You were never my husband in any way that matters. Most certainly not in my heart.

I left because I had to. I will stay gone because I want to. And I write now only to say this plainly: You have no hold over me. You have no claim to me, or to the child you never cared about but would have kept for appearances and control.

She is well, and she is free, as am I. She will never know your name unless she asks for it when she is grown.

I have sent separate correspondence to Brigham Young renouncing my membership in the church. Let this be the final word on the matter.

Do not seek us. You will not find us.

I hope, for your soul's sake, that you someday understand what you did to me.

—Emmaline Lucille Kendall

June 1859

My dearest Betsy,

I write to tell you we are safe. I am sorry if our departure caused you worry or pain. I hope that one day you will understand why we had to leave.

I would be remiss if I didn't tell you it was you who saved me. I could never thank you enough for breathing life back into me. I love you, and Micah, and the girls.

Please be true to yourself. Protect your heart.

One day, if it is safe, I will send an address where you can write back. For now, I only wish to convey my love and let you know we are well.

With love,

Emmaline

June 1859

Eliza, my sister, my best friend—

I do not know what you were told about my disappearance, and I imagine you have wondered. I want you to know that we are safe and well. You, more than anyone, will understand why I left.

There are pieces of my heart I will never get back. One of them is the loss of you, the kind of friend a girl never expects to find more than once in a lifetime.

But I could not stay. Not even for you. You know what I lost. You know what they did to me. You know what they expected of me.

You may be warned against me. Let them say what they like. You knew me before they claimed me, and you will remember who I really am. I hope, in your most honest moments, you can understand why I ran. I did what I had to do for Ginny, and for myself.

I pray for you every day. Take care of yourself. When it is safe, I will send word of where I am. And if you ever need to leave, know you have someone in this world who will always open the door to you.

With all my love,
Emmaline

CHAPTER FORTY-SIX

By mid-October the heat of summer had given way to a crisp fall. If Nebraska was pretty in the summer, it was otherworldly in the autumn. The golden prairie grasses and leaves of dark red and orange painted the world the color of sunset. I had lived at Miss Abigail's for four months and been in her employ since the third week.

The rhythms of the house felt as natural as the sunrise. I knew when the hens laid best; how to coax Gussie, the most stubborn cow, to let me milk her; how long the stove took to heat; and exactly how Miss Abigail liked her coffee—scalding hot with cream and no sugar. I knew the Reverend stayed more weeks than he was gone, and that Miss Abigail was easiest to get along with when he was around.

Elias had finished his apprenticeship in September and gone back East to marry his girl. People like Naomi came and went, each carrying secrets of their own. I never did learn Naomi and Lydia's story, and they never learned mine. But that was the way of a prairie boardinghouse. I liked having a few trusted friends nearby and offering kindness and a hot meal to the strangers who passed through. Some stories were shared, but most were left to the prairie winds. And that was just fine with me.

Miss Abigail hired me on when she realized I was a better cook than she was, handier with a needle and thread, and didn't mind the cleaning. She preferred to be outside, working the earth. And she could certainly get a better yield and a better price when she spent more time tending the farm. Charlie, the hired hand, worked harder when she was out there too.

She even taught me to keep the books. I had always been good with numbers, and it came easily. She only paid me fifty cents a week, but the room and board were free.

Sometimes in the evening when we sat in the parlor, she would tell me about her son, Daniel, who was in the army and serving out West. He was twenty, and she always kept his bedroom open for him. That's why Ginny and I still slept in the attic. I didn't mind. The Reverend had built us some shelves and a small wardrobe, and I made a rag rug for the floor. The space felt homey enough to me.

It was a Wednesday afternoon when Miss Abigail came running back from town worked into a frenzy. Half of her hair had fallen out of her bun and bounced wildly behind her as she zigzagged down the road like she didn't know which way she was going. When she reached the house, she bent over, nearly falling to her knees.

The Reverend, Charlie, and I came running, half worried she was having a stroke. She lowered herself to the ground gasping. But there was a wide smile on her face.

"What in the world is going on, Abigail?" the Reverend asked.

I thought I should get her some water, but I didn't want to miss the answer.

"Daniel is—" she gasped.

"Is Daniel all right?" I asked.

She bobbed her head. Tears ran down her cheeks. "He's coming home!"

We all clapped and cheered.

"Did you run all the way from town?" I asked.

"Crazy old goat," the Reverend teased.

"Let me get you a drink of water and you can tell us all about it," I said.

Once she'd caught her breath and had some water, Miss Abigail read Daniel's letter aloud at the kitchen table:

Dear Ma,

Leave granted at last. I'll be home by the twenty-seventh if the weather holds and the wagons run on time.

Bringing a friend, a corporal from my unit. Good man, about my age. He's got no family and could use some warm meals and a quiet place to rest. Hope there's room.

Tell the Reverend he still owes me a game of checkers.

Your son,

Daniel

P.S. We're still posted out of Fort Laramie, but I hear there may be movement toward Kearny soon. I'll know more after I get back.

"The twenty-seventh," I said. "That's a week."

"Not nearly long enough," Miss Abigail muttered, already on her feet. "His room needs dusting, the rugs need to be beat, and we'll need a roast for a proper supper."

She moved with the sudden energy of a woman ten years younger, flinging open the pantry door and scanning the jars with a critical eye.

Noticing Charlie had already gone back outside, Miss Abigail hurried to the kitchen window and called out, "Charlie! You'll want to split enough wood for the stove and the guest rooms by Friday. And check the roof over the porch. If it leaks on Daniel, I'll tan your hide."

She turned back to me, hands on her hips. "Emmaline, we've got work to do. Tomorrow I'll need you to help with the laundry. I want a pie on the table when he walks through that door. Custard is his favorite."

I smiled. "Consider it done."

She gave a sharp nod, then paused at the table, running her hand over the worn surface. Her mouth tightened the way it did when she was holding something in.

"'Course," she said, a little quieter now, "he's bringing a friend. House needs to be respectable."

Truth be told, the house was always respectable. That's why we had paying guests every day of the year. But I understood what she meant. She wanted warmth. A place that felt like home for Daniel and his friend.

I stood, already forming a list in my mind: linens, windows, boots to polish. "Will you want biscuits too?" I asked.

Miss Abigail gave a small grunt, but a smile tugged at her cheek. I knew she liked how I understood that it was important to make everything special.

"Well, we can't have a homecoming without biscuits."

We began right away and worked hard all week. I loved the busy days. But at night the sadness visited.

There would never be a family reunion for me. My parents were dead. My only brother's death had come so early I barely remembered him. And my extended family had passed before we ever left England. Worst yet, I could never even pay my respects or place flowers on their graves.

Sometimes I physically hurt with the grief of leaving my mother's body behind in Utah. And now, in Nebraska, I was still nearly two hundred miles from my father's burial place. Even if I could reach Florence, I would likely never find the spot.

No, Ginny was my family now. The life we'd have would be the one I made for us. Most of the time I had made peace with that. But in the excitement of someone else's family reunion, the intensity of my isolation returned. The grief of what Zion had taken from us filled my body in waves.

∽

The twenty-seventh came sooner and cooler than expected, with frost crusting the edges of the garden in the early morning hours. We had just finished polishing the brass on the entry lantern when I heard the wagon wheels. I was in my burgundy calico, Ginny in her yellow. I hadn't yet taken off my blue apron or scarf when footsteps sounded on the porch.

Miss Abigail ran out the door shouting Daniel's name while I tucked the feather duster behind the bench and turned to straighten the books on the shelf.

I had a copy of *Pilgrim's Progress* in my hands, still looking for the perfect spot, when something stopped me.

A voice. Low. Steady. English.

The ground shifted beneath me, gooseflesh rising along my arms before I could even register the words. That voice. That accent. That confidence.

But it couldn't be. Could it?

I yanked off my scarf and patted down my curls with my free hand, glancing toward the hallway where I knew there was no mirror. No use.

And no time to do anything about my apron because the door opened.

They were inside. And there he was.

Gideon.

He looked taller than I remembered. His blue army coat was dusty from the trail, his hair neatly trimmed, and several days' beard shadowed his jaw.

His eyes met mine the moment he stepped inside. He stopped cold. So did I.

For a heartbeat the world stopped turning.

Then he dropped his bag. I dropped *Pilgrim's Progress*. And he crossed the room in three strides, swept me into his arms, and spun me around as if no one else existed.

Everyone was watching. Miss Abigail, Daniel, the Reverend, Charlie, Ginny, and half the boarders. But I saw no one else.

He cried. I cried. Others wiped their eyes, though they didn't know why.

He set me down.

"Emmaline! How did you get here?" He lowered his voice. "How did you get out?"

"Later," I whispered.

He nodded.

Then I started laughing. "The army?" I said. "The *American* army?"

"Later," he repeated.

Everyone laughed.

Ginny walked over and clutched my skirts. "Mama?"

She must have been confused by all this. I scooped her up. "Gideon, I'd like you to meet my daughter, Ginny."

He crouched slightly and reached for her hand, giving it an exaggerated kiss. "You're as pretty as your mama, Miss Ginny."

She giggled, bashful but pleased.

Then he gave me a sheepish look and patted his coat pocket. "I've got nothing fit for a proper introduction, but ..."

He pulled out a small, smooth stone. It was the size of Ginny's palm. Pale gray with a stripe of white running through it.

"I picked this treasure up a few weeks back, right outside Fort Laramie. Didn't know why I kept it." He turned it over in his hand. "Guess maybe I do now."

He held it out to her.

Ginny took it with both hands like it was the finest jewel she'd ever seen.

"Is somebody going to tell us how you two know each other?" Miss Abigail asked.

Gideon and I looked at each other and laughed. Then I sighed. It was such a long story, and there was so much of it I didn't want to tell.

But Gideon rescued me. "We both sailed from England on the same ship when we were just kids," he said. "It's been several years since we've seen each other."

That seemed to satisfy everyone's curiosity for now, and the attention turned to Daniel and his mother.

That night, long after the supper dishes were cleared and the excitement of the day had faded to a warm hush, Ginny and I lay curled together beneath the attic eaves. Her little body relaxed as I stroked her curls, but right before sleep claimed her, she whispered, "Mama, I like him."

I smiled into the dark. "I do too," I said.

As she slept, I pried the stone from her little hand and held it in my own.

Gideon and I had a lot of talking to do. And as I drifted off to sleep, I wondered what those conversations might bring.

CHAPTER FORTY-SEVEN

dressed in my yellow calico the next morning and brushed through my curls. It was the first day I regretted not having a mirror in the attic. Most mornings I simply braided my hair, wrapped it behind my head, and checked my appearance in the dining room mirror sometime before breakfast. It usually didn't matter. My scarf covered the worst of it, and my cheeks were often dusted with flour before any boarders were seated.

But today felt different. I didn't want a scarf. I didn't want to be caked in flour.

Still, I had a job to do. I tied my curls back with my yellow satin ribbon, then worried it made me look too young and twisted it up at the last minute. I dressed Ginny in a blue cotton dress that suited her eyes, and together we headed downstairs to start the griddle cakes. They were Daniel's favorite, and Miss Abigail had requested them.

When I darted into the dining room to take a quick peek in the mirror, I found Miss Abigail and Daniel already at the table, sipping coffee. The smell of bacon wafted in from the kitchen. Panic rose in my chest.

"Am I late?"

"Nonsense, dear. We just woke early and got things started," Miss Abigail said.

I nodded, still uneasy. "I'll go start the griddle cakes."

"Emmaline."

I stopped short in the doorway and held my breath, afraid my fretting over my appearance had made me late and ruined her morning with Daniel.

"After breakfast I thought you might like to take the day off," she said.

The day off? My mind spiraled with worry. I had worked every day for nearly four months. I couldn't afford to lose this job.

"You haven't had a day off since I hired you," she added gently. "With an old friend in town, I thought you might like a little time to catch up. Maybe take a picnic. I'll even keep Ginny if you'd like."

I stiffened. I had never been away from Ginny for more than an hour, and even then it was only because Sarah had once sent me on an errand.

"Daniel's already spoken to Gideon. You can take the buckboard. There's a lovely spot near the river just past the Cantrell place."

Had I seen her wink? Surely not. My cheeks burned.

"Thank you for the offer, ma'am. We'll take Ginny," I said. I didn't want even the hint of anything improper. I turned quickly before anyone could see how flustered I felt.

By the time I set out the griddle cakes, bacon, and peaches with cream, the table was full. Gideon sat between Daniel and Ginny, clean-shaven and wearing civilian clothes. He and Ginny played keep-away with the stone, and her sweet giggles filled the room.

My hands trembled as I poured the coffee, but I didn't spill a drop.

～

The grass was still dewy where the shadows fell, but the sun had warmed a patch near the riverbank. We spread one of Miss Abigail's old quilts. Ginny wandered a few feet away, collecting pebbles and placing them in a neat little pile, humming to herself.

We laid out the fruit and bread and cheese like every place we put it mattered. Gideon didn't say anything at first. He watched the water as though he'd never seen a river before.

Finally, he turned to me. "Emmaline … how is your mother?"

I looked down at my hands, at the threadbare edges of the quilt. I had wondered when he'd ask. I was surprised it took this long.

"She passed," I said quietly. "About a year before Ginny was born. In Utah."

He closed his eyes briefly. "I'm sorry. I admired her."

"She never recovered from the trek," I said. "She was sick a long time. It wasn't peaceful, but it was final. She's not in pain anymore, and I'm grateful for that." I didn't explain further. I couldn't.

Gideon reached for a piece of bread and tore it in half.

He didn't speak, but I felt him watching me. I didn't want to tell him more about Zion. Not yet.

I cleared my throat. "What happened to California?"

A small smile touched his mouth. "Didn't take to it," he said. "Too many people looking for something. I didn't even know what I was looking for."

"So you joined the army?"

He nodded. "Seemed like the best way to be useful, I suppose. They sent me east, then west again. It's a hard life, but good work. It gives you time to think."

I glanced at him, wondering what he'd spent so much time thinking about.

"I never stopped thinking about you," he said, as if he knew my thoughts.

I looked down again. The sun danced off the water, and Ginny came over to show me a rock shaped like a heart.

"That's lovely," I said, brushing a curl off her forehead.

She nestled against me and sat on my lap.

"I knew you were trapped with him," Gideon said, softer now. "I hated myself for walking away. I felt so helpless."

"I did too," I said.

I wanted to ease his mind. But there wasn't anything about the situation that wasn't terrible.

"It wasn't your problem to fix," I said at last. "You couldn't have done anything. They would have stopped you."

"I know," he said. "But you're here now. You found a way out. How did you do it?"

"That's a story for another day," I said. "Today I just want to enjoy the sunshine and the company. Is that okay?"

"Absolutely," he said. "But only if this little one will help me collect some leaves."

He tickled Ginny, and she doubled over with laughter.

I watched him take her hand and lead her down the riverbank, where they picked up golden cottonwood leaves and spread them out in a line. She showed him her pebble collection, and they methodically placed one stone on each leaf.

In the past Gideon had been a friend, someone I cared for deeply; but when he left for California, I never thought I'd see him again. I certainly never imagined a future with him.

But today, watching him with my daughter, I did.

$\sim$

"Daniel, the porch really needs to be replaced," Miss Abigail said the next morning at breakfast. It was the kind of hint a son was supposed to understand.

He laughed. "Do you have the wood, Ma?"

"Charlie picked it up last summer," she said. "Just hasn't had time to get to it."

"If Gideon will help me, we should be able to get it done in a couple of days," Daniel said, glancing at him.

I could see that mother and son were both skilled in the art of dropping hints that couldn't be refused.

Gideon smiled. "Sounds like a fun project. Let's do it."

I enjoyed watching him work. He held nails in his mouth while he measured, sawed, and pounded planks into place like a journeyman carpenter. Daniel seemed to look to him for guidance. In two days they had built a beautiful new front porch. Miss Abigail beamed with pride.

A week later Gideon told Ginny he had a surprise for her. She bounced up and down.

"A 'prise, Mama, a 'prise!" she squealed.

I raised my eyebrows at him, as curious as she was.

He dramatically wrapped a handkerchief around her eyes and took us both out to the front porch, where an old quilt covered a mysterious small structure.

Gideon took off the handkerchief. "Okay, Ginny, you can remove the quilt now."

She tugged and grunted and struggled to set her surprise free. "Help, Mama," she said.

I looked at him, and he nodded. Together, Ginny and I pulled back the quilt. I'm not sure whether Ginny or I smiled bigger when we uncovered the little white rocking chair Gideon had made. It was small enough for her now, but big enough for her to grow into.

As she climbed into it excitedly, I threw my arms around him. "Oh my! Thank you," I said, tears pricking my eyes. "This is so special. How did you learn to do this?"

"Did you know my father was a carpenter?" he asked.

"No." I touched his arm. "His work lives on in you beautifully."

He looked sad and unsure how to respond.

"Thank you for what you did for Ginny. I'll never forget."

We turned to see her happily rocking.

We laughed.

"And neither will she," I said.

Over the remaining week of Gideon's leave, we spent almost all of our free time together. More of our stories came out each day. I held back the hardest parts but told him many things. He helped me with my chores. We walked in the garden and looked at the stars at night.

Ginny grew more attached to him each day. And so did I.

Sometimes his hands lingered on my shoulders when he wrapped my shawl around my neck. Sometimes I brushed his fingertips a little too long when I poured his coffee.

One November evening, when the moon was full and a few remaining leaves rustled in the breeze, he stood behind me, close enough for me to feel his breath on the back of my neck as he reached around to button my shawl.

"Are you warm enough?" he asked, patting my arm.

Every part of me was warm, but I didn't say so. I only nodded.

"Emmaline, I want to tell you something." His voice was shaky, lacking its usual confidence.

I turned and looked at him, praying for good news but half afraid it would be bad. The last two weeks had felt like a dream. How could I be so lucky as to hold on to it?

"This morning Daniel and I received new orders," he said.

There it was.

He met my eyes. "We're being reassigned to Fort Kearny."

My lips parted, but no words came.

"It's not temporary. We're being stationed here."

Daniel had mentioned this possibility in his letter to Miss Abigail, but I hadn't dared think about it really happening. A breeze stirred the brown, brittle cornstalks and carried their earthen scent our way.

"So you'll be … here?"

He nodded. "Just a couple miles away."

"And for how long?"

"Could be months. Could be longer." He shifted his weight. "I wanted you to hear it from me. I didn't want it to feel like something was decided without you."

I wrung my hands together. "How do you feel about it?" I asked.

He gave a small nod. "Honestly? I hoped for this. But if it makes you uncomfortable, I can ask for another assignment. They might consider it."

I looked into his eyes. "Don't do that."

He reached for my hand, lightly holding my fingers, and held my gaze. "That's all I needed to hear."

CHAPTER FORTY-EIGHT

hristmas was the perfect time for a wedding at the boardinghouse. There were fewer boarders, so the work was lighter, the parlor was lit with the soft glow of advent candles and moonlight on fresh-fallen snow, and Daniel and Gideon had a few days' leave.

The only trouble I saw was the matter of the officiant since the only minister we had was also the groom. But that was solved easily enough by inviting the army chaplain from Fort Kearny to lead the ceremony.

I was up all night baking, and Ginny was even asked to be a flower girl. She looked like a dream in her new red velvet Christmas dress with delicate white lace at the collar. It turned out to be a perfect day for the celebration of the union of Miss Abigail and Reverend Pike, which had been such a long time coming that most people never expected it to happen.

But I always knew it would. Those two were as content and happy as hens in sunshine when they were together, and I only hoped to one day be as happy as Miss Abigail looked that Christmas Day 1859.

That evening, long after the wedding ceremony was over and the Christmas goose was eaten, Ginny and I sat with Gideon in the parlor. She was sleepy and getting fussy, but she hadn't forgotten there was one more present coming. And she wasn't about to fall asleep in my arms until she had it.

"Well, little miss," Gideon said, patting his coat pocket, "what's this I've got here?"

He pulled out a small brown paper package, neatly tied with a piece of red string.

Ginny sat up straight and looked at me, grinning wide. Her blue eyes sparkled with excitement, and her curls were still tousled from where she'd pulled her bonnet off. She smelled like pumpkin pie and lavender soap. And she looked like an angel. My angel. My chest ached with love for her, and I loved Gideon for loving her.

She grabbed the package with both hands and tore into it with clumsy fingers.

Inside was a delicately carved bunny, about the length of Gideon's palm, sanded smooth and finished with beeswax. Its ears were long and slightly uneven, its back legs tucked close as though ready to spring.

Ginny gasped. "It's a rabbit!" she cried, turning it over in her hands. "He's jumpin'!"

She held it up for me to see, her voice reverent now. "He's got little feet, Mama."

"I see," I said softly, brushing a curl off her forehead. "And he's beautiful."

She clutched it to her chest like it was the finest gift she'd ever received. And it was.

Gideon didn't say anything, but his eyes met mine and his smile said everything about how he felt about her.

I looked down at Ginny a few moments later, and she was already asleep.

"I'll never get that bunny out of her hands," I said, laughing.

"There's something for you too," he said.

"Wait," I said, laying Ginny down on the settee.

I stood up and retrieved my gift for him off the tree. "You go first."

He unwrapped my package and ran his fingers over the gray-wool crocheted scarf and stocking cap. He immediately put on the cap and wrapped the scarf around his neck.

"My, my, who's the most handsome soldier in all of Nebraska Territory?" he asked with a wink.

I laughed. "You didn't need my hat and scarf for that."

I opened my gift next. It was a lovely new leather-bound journal. He had fastened it with a leather strap tied around wooden bobs. I ran my hands over the crisp white pages.

"Oh, Gideon," I cried. "It's beautiful."

"Figured the old one was about full by now."

"It is."

"And I hope you have happier things to write these days."

A single tear fell from my eye. A happy tear. Gideon reached over and brushed it away with his thumb. I couldn't wipe the smile off my face. I felt as if I would never stop smiling.

"Do you know when I first saw that smile?" he asked.

I shook my head, not remembering many smiles in the old days.

"It was in Buffalo, New York," he said. "The Fourth of July."

"Oh, you mean the day you refused to come celebrate America's birthday? I remember you that day too. It was one of my happiest days. But you sat and sulked the whole time at the train station," I teased.

"I was still so angry about leaving England," he said. "I wanted to keep Pa safe, but I couldn't believe I had to follow his fool ideas that the church put in his head. I had such a bad feeling about them."

"Well you were right about that."

"I wish I wasn't. So much needless suffering and death. My pa and your parents and so many others should be alive today. I don't know how to stop being angry about that."

"Come here," I said.

We stood together in front of the Christmas tree. I took the cap off his head and smoothed down his mussed blond hair, then reached for his hands. I was close enough to smell the faint scent of beeswax on his skin, still lingering from the bunny.

"I'm angry too," I said softly. "I've been hurting and angry my entire life. There are things that happened to me there I still haven't told you about."

He squeezed my hands a little tighter.

"I've had nightmares for years, and sometimes I still have them. But there's another side to all of it. I'm standing here with you tonight. I have Ginny. And for the first time in a long time, it feels like we could be happy. It makes me want to let the anger go."

He lifted one hand to my cheek. His palm was rough and calloused from work, but his touch was gentle.

"You're an amazing woman, Emmaline," he said. "Where does your strength come from?"

"I'd be lying if I didn't say part of it came from you. The day you stood in that doorway and told me I didn't belong to them. That I was still me."

"That was one of the worst days of my life," he said quietly.

"Mine too. But it was also one of the most important. Because your words reminded me that even if they took my body, they couldn't take my soul. You helped me remember who I was. And that helped give me the strength to leave when the time came."

"I'm so proud of you."

"I'm proud of you too."

We stood there for a while, saying nothing more. His hand on my cheek, our breath rising and falling in rhythm. Ginny's light little snores broke the silence, and we both smiled at the sweetness of them.

"Emmaline," he whispered.

I looked into his eyes and waited.

"I love you. I've loved you since I was seventeen. I want to be with you forever. I want to change your name to Ashford, have babies with you, and be the one to keep that smile on your face for the rest of your life."

I didn't think my smile could get any bigger, but it did. "Is that a proposal, Gideon Ashford?"

"It is if you want it to be."

"That's exactly what I want."

And then, for the first time, he kissed me. Softly and gently and full of promise. And I knew that we belonged to each other, now and forever.

CHAPTER FORTY-NINE

A week later Gideon and I joined the Reverend and Miss Abigail in the dining room after breakfast. We had asked to speak with them privately. After Gideon took a seat with the two of them, I poured coffee with trembling hands, trying to ignore the knot in my stomach. There were things I needed to say. Hard things. Unspeakable things.

Even Gideon didn't know all that I would share today. But I didn't want to begin our marriage with secrets buried inside me. I needed to release them. And, truth be told, we weren't entirely sure of the legalities of our situation. We needed some guidance from someone who would know.

I was deeply grateful for the friendship and wisdom of both Miss Abigail and the Reverend. If anyone could help us face what needed saying with grace, it was them.

Ginny played in the parlor with Daniel as a January storm raged outside. Most of the boarders were tucked away in their rooms or reading by the fire. I knew this might be our only quiet chance to speak with them, and I intended to use it well.

Snow fell thickly outside, ridging the dining room windows. The stove took the edge off the cold, but there was still a chill in the room. Gideon motioned for me to sit, then placed his hand over mine to steady it.

"We want to get married," he began.

"I knew it!" Miss Abigail brought her hands to her cheeks with a wide smile. "Knew you were meant for each other the moment you walked into my parlor, young man." She patted Gideon's hand. "You couldn't find a better woman than Emmaline in all of Nebraska Territory."

I grinned, remembering the way she'd looked me up and down the first day I arrived. Miss Abigail didn't give praise lightly.

The Reverend smiled warmly. "How wonderful." After a pause: "But I sense something more on your minds."

"It's a little complicated," Gideon said.

I looked down at the table, tracing a dark crevice in the wood with my fingertip. "I might have been married before," I whispered. "I might already be married. I'm honestly not sure."

Gideon gripped my hand more tightly.

"Why don't you start at the beginning," the Reverend said.

"Emmaline and I both came from England," Gideon said. "Our parents were converted to the Latter-day Saints—the Mormons."

"I see," the Reverend said.

"Are you familiar with them?" Gideon asked.

"I am," he replied. "I was in Nauvoo when Joseph Smith led the church. He was known to have many wives—some very young ones, I understand. It's an abomination. And it's one reason that church is always running afoul of the government."

We both nodded, and tears welled in my eyes.

"What happened after you arrived in the States?" Miss Abigail asked.

"We were part of a handcart company that pulled our belongings on foot to the Utah Territory," Gideon said.

"You *walked* to Utah?" she asked. "On foot?"

"Yes," I said. "From Iowa City. We landed in Boston and took the rail west. From there, we walked. It took about four months."

"We got caught in a blizzard in Wyoming," Gideon added. "No shelter. Many died. Neither of our fathers survived the trek."

"Dear God," the Reverend said.

"Emmaline barely survived," Gideon continued. "She was half dead when we reached Salt Lake."

"Gideon saved me," I said. "He saved a lot of people."

"What happened when you got there?" Miss Abigail asked, looking at me.

"At first I was sent to a kind family. They nursed me back to health. I loved them. I would have been content to stay while my mother recovered. She was much sicker than I was."

"But that's not what happened," Gideon said.

They both leaned in, listening closely.

"I was sent to a new home and told to help care for their children until my mother recovered. I was fourteen, almost fifteen. The man and his wife were around thirty. They had five children. After two weeks the prophet Brigham Young came to dinner and said he'd received a prophecy from God: I was to marry that man as his second wife. They called it the covenant of celestial marriage. I was told it was an honor and a blessing."

"What did your mother say?" the Reverend asked.

"She was still very ill. She'd lost both her legs. I went to her and begged her to stop it. She told me to obey. She was a true believer to the end. I ran. I tried to refuse. But they said they wouldn't take care of my mother. They said God would heal her if I obeyed but he might not if I didn't. They said we'd both be damned. They didn't use those words exactly, but that's what they said. They broke me."

Soft tears ran down my cheeks. Miss Abigail and the Reverend wiped at their own.

"I just gave in," I said. "I shouldn't have, but I did."

Gideon wrapped an arm around me. His body trembled.

The Reverend leaned forward, voice low and steady. "Emmaline, let me speak plainly. You did nothing wrong. You were a child. They isolated you and frightened you and gave you no choice. That's called coercion. What they demanded of you was not love. It was not marriage. It was spiritual manipulation and abuse wrapped in the name of God."

Miss Abigail spoke gently. "No man of God would ask a girl to sacrifice her body or soul to prove her faith. A marriage born of fear is no covenant. Not in the eyes of heaven."

The Reverend nodded. "That so-called union was never sanctified by God. You are not bound to it, nor marked by it."

For a long moment I had no words. Just tears. Miss Abigail reached across the table and held my hand. The Reverend bowed his head in silence.

"There's more," I said.

I looked at Gideon. I gripped his hand tightly, and then I voiced the hardest part. "I will never be sorry to have Ginny," I said carefully. "But I never welcomed him into my room. He forced his way in. He held down my wrists. Many times."

"Bastard," Gideon said through clenched teeth.

"It was legal, though, wasn't it?" I asked, not waiting for an answer. "I intend to marry Gideon, but will I be sinning against God? Will I be bringing shame to Gideon?"

"No," Gideon whispered before anyone else could speak.

The Reverend looked at me, not with pity, but with sorrow and holy anger. "No," he said firmly. "What that man did to you was not union and was not legal by the laws of this country. It was violence. It was his sin, not yours. He defiled what God made sacred. The shame is in what he did to you, Emmaline. God sees only your clean, pure heart."

He looked between the two of us, his voice softening. "The Lord sees the heart. And I have no doubt yours is clean."

"You and Gideon love one another freely," Miss Abigail said. "That's what God honors. That's the covenant he blesses. And, yes, you can enter it with clean hearts."

I glanced at Gideon. His eyes were red and swollen.

The Reverend reached across the table and laid a hand on each of ours. "May I pray with you?"

We both nodded.

He closed his eyes, voice gentle. "Gideon, Emmaline … you have walked long, hard roads to find each other again. You've come through fire. And today you stand not as broken people, but as survivors. As two souls still capable of choosing love, when the world gave you every reason not to. That is holy."

He bowed his head and prayed a prayer of healing and blessing over us.

The room was still. Miss Abigail and Gideon each held one of my hands. But Gideon slowly pulled his away and stood. His chair scraped softly against the floor.

He didn't speak. Didn't look at me. Just walked out into the cold, coatless, his boots shuffling across the frozen porch.

Miss Abigail looked at me with compassion. "He'll be back," she said softly. "Sometimes a man has to cry alone."

I nodded. I knew that already.

Not knowing what else to do, I cleared the coffee cups and washed them. I stood too long with my hands in the water, forgetting what I was doing, wondering when he would return. Ginny laughed in the distance. The house went on.

~

The sun had dipped low behind the trees before I heard the front door open again while I was in the kitchen preparing supper. I didn't turn.

I was afraid that if I saw his face, I'd start sobbing all over again. And I had nothing left.

His boots creaked on the floorboards. He stood behind me in silence.

"I couldn't—" he started, then stopped.

I turned slowly. His cheeks were red from the cold. His eyes raw. Snow clung to his hair.

"I know," I said.

He looked down at his hands, flexing them like he didn't trust them.

"I wanted to be enough to stop it. Even now I want to go back and take you out of that place. I don't know how to forgive myself for leaving you."

I stepped forward and took his face in my hands. "They had all the power then, Gideon. You couldn't have saved me. I made a decision. I wasn't going to leave my mother."

His eyes filled again, but he didn't look away.

"But you did help me save myself," I said. "Not with fists. With words. You reminded me who I was. That's what gave me the strength to leave."

He swallowed hard. Placed his hands on my shoulders. "I'm here now," he said. "And I'm not going anywhere. I swear to you, Emmaline, whatever healing takes, whatever trust you still have to rebuild, I'll walk through it with you."

"I know," I said. "I don't need to be saved anymore. I only need you beside me."

"I will be."

He pulled me into his arms, and this time we stood there without words.

There was nothing left to say.

We held each other and shared the silence that proves love is stronger than what tried to destroy you.

# CHAPTER FIFTY

The January days were cold and long. Gideon and Daniel had been sent west on assignment. All they were told was that it might be one or two months, so we didn't know how long we'd be separated. A short patrol, in truth, unless you were young and in love.

I hoped he'd return for my birthday on February eighth, or at least Ginny's on the twentieth, but I didn't mention them in my letters. I didn't want to pressure him. Besides, I had no way of knowing if my letters were reaching him. So far, I'd received only one:

January 12, 1860

Emmaline,

The army used to feel like an exciting life, before there was someone special to come home to. Before there was you. It's cold and lonely out here, and every day I think of being with you and Ginny. I hope you're busy planning our wedding, because I'm coming home soon to build a house and marry you.

All my love,

Gideon

I understood what he meant. I had once been content at Miss Abigail's. But Gideon's return had turned contentment into restlessness. His heart had become my home, and now I was homesick.

That night I rocked Ginny to sleep in the parlor, the letter laced through my fingers, dreaming of spring when the daffodils would bloom and Gideon and I would say our vows in the garden.

"That must be a special letter," Miss Abigail said, smiling.

I grinned back.

She sat on the settee, a quiet seriousness in her face. "I just want you to know that I am so proud of you," she said. "Watching you grow since you arrived has been an honor. I think you're the bravest young lady I've ever met. I hope you feel that in your heart."

She stood, patted my shoulder, and left me in silence.

My mouth fell slightly open. I loosened my grip on Ginny and sank deeper into the chair, eyes brimming. In that moment I felt my mother's presence. If Miss Abigail was proud, could my mother be too?

But maybe that didn't matter.

My mother had loved me as best she could. She once told me she was proud, near the end. She'd seen the girl I was then. And now I had Miss Abigail, who'd seen the woman I'd become. She saw me, and she was proud.

Most importantly, I was proud of myself. I had found a way out. I had found a way to survive. I had earned my keep, saved money, learned new skills. I did this all before Gideon came back into my life.

In some ways, healing would take a lifetime. In others, I was already healed.

I looked down at my sleeping daughter. My chest ached, not from pain, but from awe. Usually, I noticed features in her face that reminded me of others from my past—Samuel, my mother, my father. But tonight all I saw was me. The brown curls, the freckles. The way her soft mouth curled upward even when she wasn't smiling. The fierce determination

I knew lived in her spirit.

"I love you, baby girl," I whispered. "I'm proud of us."

The next morning I cleaned the attic and organized our growing collection of belongings. A few items remained in the carpetbag, and I moved them to the small chest Gideon had built. My fingers brushed against the cameo that had belonged to Samuel's mother.

I'd forgotten how beautiful it was. If it hadn't come at such a cost, I might have worn it with pride. I fingered the delicate ivory carving and gold filigree. I'd kept it only in case I ever needed to trade it for food or shelter. It had been a gift, yes, but one I would have used to keep Ginny alive.

But now Ginny was safe. We had a roof, food, care. I had money saved. And soon she would have a father. We didn't need it. And I didn't want a penny of our future tainted by Samuel.

I considered what to do with it.

I could save it for hard times. But if I didn't want Samuel's help now, I wouldn't want it then. This life's trials would be mine and Gideon's, and we would face them together.

I could keep it for Ginny someday. He was, technically, her father. Maybe she would want a piece of him. But the thought made me sick. He didn't deserve a place in her life. Gideon had already filled that space, in love and in presence.

I could toss it in the river. That would be satisfying. Maybe I'd go alone. Maybe with Gideon. I'd think on that.

But the more I moved through my chores, the more one thought took hold: *I should send it back to Samuel.* Not because he deserved it. But because it was his mother's. Returning it for his children's sake, not his, felt like the choice that would set me free.

The only question was how. I couldn't post it directly. It would have to go with someone discreet, someone I trusted to keep our location unknown. I was confident now that Samuel had no claim on me. But Ginny? I wasn't so sure. He didn't need to know where we were. Not for a very long time.

I would wait and talk to Gideon when he returned.

In the end, he didn't make it back for our birthdays. I turned eighteen without him at my side. But that was all right. We had a lifetime of birthdays ahead. And this year I had Ginny and the family we had found in Nebraska.

On February 20, as we sat around the table eating chocolate cake for Ginny's second birthday, there was a knock at the door, so I hurried over to open it.

It wasn't Gideon or Daniel, but rather another surprise.

"David!" I said.

How wonderful it was to see him.

Stepping just inside the door, he said he'd seen Gideon at Fort Laramie and brought a stack of letters and packages for us.

"All that man does is talk about the two of you girls," he teased. "His regiment's about a week behind mine. I'd say you'll be seeing him soon."

"And Daniel?" Miss Abigail asked.

"Yes, ma'am. Some of those letters are for you, and the two of them will be returning together."

She smiled and wiped her cheeks. Nothing brought that woman to tears but chopping onions and word from Daniel.

I invited David to join us for cake and coffee.

"You won't believe how Ginny's grown," I said. "She'll be thrilled to see you."

"Well now, chocolate cake and time with Miss Ginny? That's an offer I can't refuse," he said with a wink.

Ginny and I opened our packages from Gideon and found birthday gifts: a small bottle of perfume for me and a carved bear that matched the bunny for her. We were both delighted. David brought lightness to the day. It didn't make up for Gideon's absence, but it was special just the same.

Before he left, I pulled David aside and asked if he could discreetly return a small package to the Sandbury home. He understood the need for caution and said he could handle it. He'd be heading back to the Utah Territory in the spring.

I ran to the attic, wrapped the cameo in the brown paper and string from my perfume, and wrote one word on it: "Sandbury."

No note. No explanation.

I watched David ride off down the frozen road.

It was done. I felt the weight from my past lift and float away.

CHAPTER FIFTY-ONE

t was May 1, a year since I had left Utah and two days before I would marry Gideon. He still hadn't let me see the house. He'd worked on it every spare minute. Daniel, the Reverend, and a few hired hands had helped when they could.

All I heard from him was "one room," "too small," and "I'll build on later, don't you worry."

I always laughed and said I'd live in a tent with him if I had to. And I would have. Gladly. But every day I pictured the timbers going up, a roof taking shape, the space inside. I didn't know what it would be, only that I already loved it.

I was told it stood only half a mile from Miss Abigail's, near the creek around the bend from the Kerr place. Gideon said I could still work at Miss Abigail's if I wanted, but I'd decided to start a garden and focus on housekeeping and schooling Ginny at home. We dreamed of having our own boardinghouse someday, once he was out of the army.

After lunch he came running through the door, breathless. "Come on!"

"What's the matter?"

"Nothing," he said, slowing his voice. "I'm sorry. Just excited. The house is ready for you."

He turned to Miss Abigail. "Would you keep Ginny for us for a while?"

She laughed. "Of course. As long as you need."

He helped me into the buckboard and immediately started apologizing for what I was about to see.

"It's not as big as I wanted, Emmaline," he said. "You deserve so much more."

"Stop the wagon," I demanded.

He looked a little shocked, but the wagon lurched to a halt.

I held my finger to his lips. "Do not apologize one more time for building me a house. For building us a house. You are about to show me the place where we are going to start our life. I am excited, and I am going to love it, and I don't want to hear another apology, Gideon Ashford. Do you hear me?"

He laughed. "Yes, dear."

The wagon bumped along the rutted trail that curved behind the Kerr place and followed the gentle slope toward the creek. The trees were full of blossoms, and the air held that sweet, wet smell of springtime. The closer we got, the more nervous Gideon looked. I was smiling so hard my cheeks ached.

We turned a bend, and there it was.

Nestled beyond a grove of cottonwoods stood a small house. It was modest and square, its freshly hewn walls still the pale gold of raw wood. A thin trail of smoke curled from the chimney, and the windows—there were two—reflected the afternoon sun, which was unfiltered by the cloudless day. The roof sloped steeply on each side, and the front door had no paint on it yet, just a simple handle and hinges that still shone silver from the blacksmith shop.

The porch was barely more than a platform, with two rough-hewn steps and a rail on one side. But beside the steps, growing proudly from the earth, were six daffodils. They bloomed bright yellow against the gray-brown grass. They weren't native. Someone had planted them.

I put a hand over my mouth. He knew they were my favorite flowers.

"The Reverend got six bulbs from Miss Abigail's," Gideon said quickly. "I didn't know if they'd take. We buried them before the last snow."

I climbed down without a word and walked slowly toward the house. The wood creaked under my boots as I stepped onto the porch. The door opened with a gentle push.

Inside was one room, just like he'd said. But it was more than I'd imagined.

A stone hearth had been built into the far wall, and the stove was already lit, giving off the faint scent of pine smoke and iron. There was a bed in one corner, with a patchwork quilt folded neatly at the foot. A washstand stood near the window, with a pitcher and basin already in place. A table with three simple but sturdy chairs sat near the stove. Beside it, on a shelf he must have made himself, was the leather-bound journal he had given me at Christmas. Ginny's bunny and bear sat beside the journal. I wondered when he'd snuck in to get those things.

There was a small bed for Ginny in the corner.

I turned to him, unable to speak.

"I know it's plain," he said, shoving his hands in his pockets. "And I still want to add another room on the back. And I know you want a chicken coop …"

"Gideon."

He stopped.

I crossed the room and took his face in my hands. "This is the most beautiful home I've ever seen."

He exhaled deeply and wiped away a single tear. His vulnerability touched my soul and made me ache with love for him.

"It's ours," he said quietly.

I nodded. "It's home."

"There's one more thing I want to show you," he said, taking my hand and leading me outside.

We walked down to the creek where it widened into a perfect wading pool. He had built a bench under a beautiful shade tree. And a little wooden swing hung for Ginny. I was overcome with the love he had shown in every detail. I put my hands over my mouth again. I had no words.

He sat on the bench and patted the seat next to him. I sat and laid my head on his shoulder. He kissed my forehead. I thought I would never be so happy as I was in that moment.

We sat there a long time, talking about the wedding, the house, and the memories we would make together.

After a while he said something that surprised me. "Do you ever think about going west again? Not soon. I mean, someday?"

I had thought about it. I loved the mountains more than any other land I'd seen, but I didn't want to be in Utah. And California didn't interest me.

"Where would we go? You know I love the mountains, but we can't go back to Zion."

"No, I don't mean that," he said. "The army has sent me all over the Kansas Territory and New Mexico Territory. I've seen the Front Range of the Rockies, Emmaline. It's extraordinary. I want to show you someday."

"As long as you're there," I said.

Then I looked out over the water and told him something I hadn't said aloud before. "What I dream of is a place in the mountains, but like Buffalo. For years I've not been able to get that park out of my mind—the one with all the families gathered to picnic and laugh and sing together. The gazebo and the band captured my heart."

"Are you sure it wasn't just your hunger and the hand pies?" he teased.

I laughed at first but then grew serious. "It was the community that made it so beautiful. The people were so free and happy. I loved the way they came together. I want a place like that. Where families are able to gather and celebrate."

I turned to him. "I want to build that someday, with you."

EPILOGUE

Aspen Lake, Colorado, is the kind of place that looks like paradise despite its bloodstained past. Stories still circulate—half truth, half legend—of Doc Holliday, Butch Cassidy, even the Espinosa brothers stirring up trouble in the region's saloons and mining camps. The stories grow like fish tales around campfires each year.

But now the town is quieter. The saloons are gone. The gold rush never yielded much more than broken dreams. These days, families and travelers come for the clean mountain air, the deep blue lake, the golden sweep of aspens in the fall, and the otherworldly peace found in the Rocky Mountains.

It's a place to return to year after year. Many stay at Ashford Lodge, built near the edge of the lake by Gideon and Emmaline Ashford in the waning days of the mines. Gideon passed in 1925. Emmaline died last July. But their legacy endures.

On this warm Saturday in mid-July, more than forty Ashfords gather for the dedication of the Emmaline Ashford City Park, established 1929. The new sign gleams in the sun. Children race past it, laughing, their shoes pounding fresh dirt paths and thumping down the new metal slide.

"She would've loved this day," says Ginny, Emmaline's eldest, her fingers absently twirling the stem of a blue columbine her granddaughter, Audrey, handed her.

"She would've hated the attention," says her brother, Jack, the town's Methodist minister.

The two share a knowing smile. Everyone knows Emmaline would've relished the attention while pretending to shoo it away.

The scent of apple pie and fried chicken drifts on the breeze. Ponderosa pines edge the walking path. Beneath the bunting-strung gazebo, the mayor waits to speak. It is the kind of day Emmaline always imagined for her town. She designed the park, lobbied the town council, and led the fundraising efforts.

At first nobody notices the strangers who appear at the park's edge. A young man in a stiff black suit. An elderly woman in a prairie dress and bonnet. Their clothing is formal, too hot for the weather, and their hesitation marks them clearly as outsiders in the tight-knit Aspen Lake community, where even the tourists look like they belong.

The strangers approach the Ashford siblings. "Excuse me," the man says as his eyes fall to the sign. "We're looking for Miss Emmaline."

Jack steps forward. "I'm Reverend Jack Ashford. Emmaline was my mother. She passed away last year."

The woman, taken aback, blinks away tears. "I wondered that I hadn't received a letter this year."

"I'm sorry, how did you know her?" Ginny asks.

The woman steadies herself. "I'm a friend from many years ago. Eliza Pickett."

The name does not register with most of the group. Only Ginny looks rattled. She steps forward quickly and takes the woman by the arm.

"You're Eliza?" she asks. "How did you find us?"

"Your mother sent me her address years ago. We've exchanged letters most of our lives. My grandson had a business trip in Denver. I asked him to bring me. I wanted to see her one last time."

Ginny glances toward the gazebo. "The speakers are about to go on. Then we'll talk. But, Eliza, the rest of the family doesn't know. Not about Utah. Only England and Nebraska."

"I understand," she says. "This park, it reminds me so much of a day I spent with your mother in Buffalo, New York, many years ago."

Ginny smiles widely. How her mother would have loved that comment.

Mayor Wayne Craig begins. He speaks of Emmaline and Gideon's arrival in 1879, their dream of the Rockies, the lodge they built with their own hands, the first school, the first library, the suffrage meetings. He calls Emmaline the backbone of the town, the beating heart behind its progress.

Ginny hears none of it. Her thoughts are with Eliza, the ghost from her mother's past.

When Jack rises to speak, Ginny studies him. Her brother is used to public speaking, confident like their father. But the weight of the day is written in the lines around his eyes. His voice is strong but laced with emotion as he thanks the town, speaks of their parents' devotion, of hard winters and shared tables, of the way Emmaline could make something out of nothing.

"She would have loved to see you all gathered here," he says in closing. "That was her dream for this park, for our community."

After the speeches Ginny leans toward Eliza. "Where are you staying?"

"The Greenwood Hotel. Just across the street."

"I'll meet you there in thirty minutes," Ginny says.

She watches them leave, then turns back toward the gazebo, wondering what she's doing. Mama buried that story for a reason.

But curiosity wins. As it always does.

Barely twenty-five minutes later, she crosses to the Greenwood, pauses with her hand on the heavy door, then enters.

They are waiting in the lobby, seated near a ticking grandfather clock.

Eliza rises and takes Ginny into her arms. "The last time I saw you, you were a baby," she says. "Maybe eleven months old. That was the last time I saw your mother too."

As they all sit down, Ginny asks, "What happened?"

"I was supposed to come to your first birthday, but I was sent away to be married just weeks before. I never saw her again."

"You stayed in the church?" Ginny's voice is curious, not judgmental.

"I did," Eliza says softly. "My family was there. My husband was good to me, and my faith held meaning for me. There were difficult times; there were good times too. But I always admired your mother's courage to walk away. She had lost so much. The church was not a good experience for her. She gave me strength to find my own voice. I raised my children differently because she showed me it was possible. I wanted them to know they had choices. They did not always hear that in the church."

Eliza's grandson nods in agreement. His wide eyes tell Ginny that his life was better because of Emmaline's influence.

"She talked about you," Ginny says. "On quiet days. She told me about Liverpool. About the *Horizon*. She missed you."

"I missed her too. Our letters were a lifeline."

Ginny pauses, considers whether she wants to ask the next question. "Eliza … what happened to Samuel?"

Eliza reaches into her bag and removes a folded newspaper clipping. "Your mother never wanted to know, but I've kept this through the years because I thought you might like to have it someday."

Ginny opens it slowly and reads it:

DEATH OF S. J. SANDBURY
WELL-KNOWN MILL SUPERINTENDENT
PERISHES IN BLAZE

Samuel J. Sandbury died in the early-morning hours of March 30, 1908, in a tragic fire at the Empire Flouring Mill in City Creek

Canyon. He was 81 years old. Mr. Sandbury had long served as Brigham Young's mill superintendent, overseeing operations at several mills throughout the Salt Lake Valley and in southern Utah. He was widely known for his skill in millwork and his unwavering devotion to the Church of Jesus Christ of Latter-day Saints.

Mr. Sandbury was born on January 1, 1827, in Egmanton, Nottinghamshire, England. He emigrated to Utah in the early days of the settlement and played a key role in the development of the territory's milling infrastructure.

He is survived by three wives, Sarah, Emmaline, and Henrietta, and by fourteen children. He was a man of firm convictions, respected for his work ethic and the loyalty he inspired in those who labored under his direction.

Burial took place at the Salt Lake City Cemetery on Thursday, April 2.

Ginny rises to her feet. Heat fills her body. She is trembling. Her voice rises, filled with fury. "They used her name?" she says. "They used my mother's name? They had no right. No right."

Eliza stands and places a hand on Ginny's arm. "I'm sorry," she says. "Maybe I shouldn't have shown you. I don't agree with it, but in our church, sealings are considered eternal. A woman cannot release herself if the husband does not consent."

"Well, that's absurd," Ginny nearly spits out the words.

"I agree," says Eliza's grandson. "And I don't think it really means anything. It's just what these men believe. Still, it's a violation against your mother, and you have every right to be angry."

The women retake their seats, and the three sit in silence for a while.

Then Eliza asks, "Ginny … why doesn't the rest of the family know about your parents' lives before Nebraska?"

Ginny thinks about it. "They never said it was a secret," she says.

"They just didn't like to speak of it. My mother talked to me sometimes, told me some of the old stories when she was feeling sad. She and my father took me to Florence to find my grandfather's grave once when I was a little girl. But until the day I asked her about Samuel, it mostly stayed locked up. They built a good life outside of all that. I just don't think they ever wanted to relive it or be defined by it."

Eliza places a hand on Ginny's. "Do you think it's time the rest of your family knew the truth now? Your mother's story, her courage, is part of their legacy."

Ginny looks out the window at the park. The blue columbine is still in her hand, crumpled slightly now from the heat of her grip. "I've thought about telling them," she says. "But I never knew how."

She looks into Eliza's eyes. "Would you help me?"

Eliza nods. "I'd be honored to."

"We'll all be at the lodge tonight. Can you come at seven?"

"Yes, we will be there."

Afterward, Ginny walks around the park to the lodge and slips into the Ashford, looking behind her to make sure she is unseen. She searches the storage room until she finds her father's old army trunk. Her mama had used it for years as personal storage. No one had the heart to go through it after she died. Ginny isn't sure she has the heart now. But it is time.

She slowly opens the lid, coughing as years of dust is stirred up. The scent hits her first. Aged leather, old paper, cedar dust. She spends the rest of the afternoon sorting through the items. There are dozens of letters from Eliza, maybe more than a hundred. Letters from her father during the Civil War. A yellow hair ribbon. A brittle handkerchief that is embroidered with the initials "B. G." Two loose letters that appear to be handwritten copies—one to Samuel Sandbury, one to Brigham Young. And then she picks up an old journal. Beautiful, aged leather. Someone has carved "E. Kendall" into the cover. She opens the journal.

"I am Emmaline …" it begins.

She had a brother? Ginny has a hard time reading as tears cloud her eyes.

At seven that evening she meets her family in the lobby of the Ashford Lodge, the army trunk at her side. When Eliza and her grandson arrive, Ginny gathers the family. With the journal in hand, and with Eliza's help, a story unfolds. Not the story of a mother. Not the story of a grandmother. Not the story of a town matriarch.

The story of Emmaline.

Thank you for reading Emmaline. If you enjoyed the story, a rating or short review on Amazon, Goodreads, or your favorite book site will help other readers discover it. If you would like to share it with your book club, a list of book club questions can be found at ashlioconnell.com.

AUTHOR'S NOTE

Emmaline is a novel inspired by my own family history. My father un-covered it during genealogical research over a decade ago, and I knew the first time I heard it that the story needed to be told. Parts of our family legacy are difficult to face, but they demand reckoning. That reckoning is what drove me to write this book.

I am the great-great-granddaughter of Samuel Sudbury, a polyga-mist with three wives during the early Mormon settlement of Utah. I descend from his third wife. But this novel draws its inspiration from his second: Lydia.

Samuel truly was Brigham Young's mill superintendent. Lydia truly was a fourteen-year-old member of the Martin Handcart Company who was brought into Samuel's home under the pretense of rest and recovery, only to be told—within two weeks—that she was expected to become his second wife.

Here is an excerpt from Lydia's own writings:

"I said no.... I desired to go home and cried and desired my mother to take me home, but she seemed as though she was under some mysterious deliriums or nightmares, and I was so influenced that my mind was in such a state that I just could not seem to think for myself. Remember, I was taught that the church was my only salvation, and if I disobeyed the servants of the Lord, it would be my eternal damnation.[1]"

The major historical beats in this novel are true. I have meticulously endeavored to be accurate with all dates; however, many primary accounts have discrepancies. Where the record is inconsistent or silent, I have filled in the gaps. Also, as a novelist, I have added and adapted details to fill out the narrative. It was never to distort the history, but to tell a story that gives dignity to all the girls and women who lived it.

Lydia's life was the seed from which this novel grew, but this is not meant to be a direct retelling. Still, I am confident that her legacy is honored here.

The following are a few ways in which Lydia's life differed from Emmaline's, which may interest readers:

Lydia, like Emmaline, was born in Wiltshire, but she moved frequently as a child and, so far as we know, never lived in Liverpool. I placed Emmaline there because Liverpool was a major center of LDS missionary activity and thus it allowed a fuller portrayal of the religious and social climate of the time.

We believe Lydia lost two younger siblings, though the circumstances are unknown. That space in the historical record gave rise to William's character and shaped Emmaline's emotional journey.

In reality, Lydia had two children with Samuel and was caught and returned to him three times before her final escape. She eventually returned to Utah to secure a divorce from Brigham Young personally. These events, while extraordinary, would have significantly expanded the novel. I chose a more streamlined narrative, but I want readers to know that Lydia's courage far exceeded what I was able to portray on the page.

---

[1] Untitled and unpublished Lydia F. Goodaker autobiography, compiled by Lloyd Case (1983), from the Lydia Franklin Sudbury Goodaker Collection at the Stephen H. Hart Research Center of the History Colorado Center (Denver).

Some characters—Samuel and Emmaline among them—are inspired by real people, but most are fictional unless they are public figures. And for those of you who, like me, love Gideon: I'm sorry to say he is fictional. But I'm glad to report that Lydia did find real love with a quartermaster sergeant in the US Army and eventually settled in Colorado.

As the story developed, Emmaline became more than one girl. She came to be a composite character who represented every underage girl forced into marriage or held against her will, especially when trapped within a weaponized faith system. Accordingly, Samuel also became a composite character, representing the many older men who took young girls as plural brides, often against their will. Though this story takes place in early Mormonism, the pattern is not unique to that culture. Around the world today, girls are denied autonomy over their bodies and futures. And too often it is not only men who silence them, but also women who uphold the systems that demand girls surrender their agency and their voices for the sake of others' comfort.

I wrote this book for all of these girls.

My wish is that we might consider the ways we contribute to systemic injustice. That we notice how often we expect young girls to be quiet and accommodating. That we learn to hear their questions, their fears, and their bright, bold ideas for changing the world.

This book also grew out of a desire to share the story of the Martin Handcart Company more widely, arguably the deadliest tragedy in westward migration—far deadlier than what happened to the Donner Party, which most Americans are familiar with.

The Mormon Handcart Movement, conceived by Brigham Young and active from 1856 to 1860, was designed to move thousands of impoverished European converts to the Utah Territory as cheaply as possible. Missionary efforts in Great Britain had been enormously successful among the poor, and Young wanted the converts to reach Zion quickly. Funding, however, was scarce. Young established the Perpetual

Emigration Fund to finance their journeys, with the expectation that emigrants would repay the debt upon arrival.

Five handcart companies traveled in 1856; the first three reached their destination without major tragedy. The last two—the Willie and Martin companies—did not. The handcarts were not ready when emigrants arrived. Supplies were inadequate. The departures were dangerously late. Leaders ignored multiple warnings and refused opportunities to winter over safely. Pressures from church authorities to keep moving outweighed basic prudence.

The result was catastrophic. The Mormon Trail is scattered with the bones of men, women, and children who trusted the promise of a better life, only to be pushed past all reason and perish before the dream could be realized. Estimates place the death toll of the Martin Company alone between two and three hundred. Many of those names are forgotten because records were lost, destroyed, or never kept.

Like Emmaline, I am left asking why so many lives were deemed expendable for a cause later reframed as evidence of divine protection. Would a good God truly intend such suffering in the name of saving time and money? Can we truly speak of miraculous deliverance when hundreds were not delivered? These are questions worth weighing against the church's traditional narrative.

Polygamy was renounced by the Church of Jesus Christ of Latter-day Saints in 1890 under pressure from the US government. At that time, many went underground or moved to Mexico or Canada to continue practicing freely. Today polygamists are excommunicated from the mainstream church, but many splinter LDS groups continue to practice it, with girls as young as twelve still coerced into the practice. Joseph Smith's revelation on plural marriage, which Emmaline reads in part in Chapter Twenty-Seven, is now canonized in LDS Scripture as Doctrine and Covenants 132. Many scholars understand this to mean that Mormons will live in polygamy in heaven, although there is not consensus on this interpretation.

If you would like to learn more about the handcart migration and early Mormon plural marriage, I highly recommend the following sources, which informed both my research and my imagination:

- *Devil's Gate: Brigham Young and the Great Mormon Handcart Tragedy* by David Roberts
- *In Sacred Loneliness: The Plural Wives of Joseph Smith* by Todd Compton
- *Wife No. 19* by Ann Eliza Young (novelized by David Ebershoff in *The 19th Wife*)
- *The Polygamous Wives Writing Club: From the Diaries of Mormon Pioneer Women* by Paula Kelly Harline
- *The Year of Polygamy* podcast, hosted by Lindsay Hansen Park

ACKNOWLEDGEMENTS

When I first considered writing a novel, there was only one person to whom I dared say it aloud: my husband, Brian. He has been my best friend and unconditional support for thirty years. His belief in me gave me the courage to begin, and his confidence in my work made me believe I could finish. He was the first to hear every chapter, point out anachronisms and plot holes, and cheer me on endlessly. Honey, I am in awe of your endurance through the most difficult season of our lives. I am so proud of your courage and quiet strength. This journey would mean nothing if we were not walking it together.

I am also fortunate to have an entire family who stood behind this project. My daughters, Abigail and Allison, were early beta readers who offered invaluable feedback on both plot and prose. My son, Benjamin—himself a budding author—is my favorite writing buddy. We have spent hours talking about process, story elements, and our shared writing ambitions. I want to be just like my kids when I grow up.

My parents, Larry and Phyllis, to whom this book is dedicated, have always championed my creative pursuits. Their belief in this story helped make it real. Mom and Dad, I am who I am because of your love. My brothers, Craig and Eddie, were also early readers who offered thoughtful feedback and enthusiasm. I love you both.

To the rest of my family and close friends, thank you for being a part of my world. I hope you enjoy the little Easter eggs tucked throughout the story just for you.

I also felt it important to reach beyond my circle of loved ones to find readers willing to give the kind of honest, constructive feedback that truly strengthens a manuscript. I was lucky to have a group of beta readers who made this book better. My deepest gratitude to Audrey Davis, David Dinger, Sarah Peterson, and Chesca Ornelas. Your insight and generosity were invaluable in shaping the final story. Thanks also to the writing community at Scribophile for help with crafting the early chapters.

My author advisory group provided guidance on marketing, messaging, and presentation. Thank you to Melinda Booze, Kerri Cox, Erica Huinda, Judi Murphy, Sarah Nessel and Jan Peterson. I count each of you as dear friends, and it was a gift to have your insight during the final stretch of this journey.

I am deeply grateful to the Stephen H. Hart Research Center in Denver's History Colorado Center for granting access to the unpublished autobiography of Lydia Franklin Sudbury Goodaker, which informed my understanding of the woman who inspired this story. I also wish to acknowledge the scholars in Mormon studies whose work preserves the history of frontier Utah and the women who lived nineteenth-century polygamy.

Finally, I would like to thank my editor and designer. John David Kudrick helped me refine and revise the final drafts. I am so fortunate to have found a gifted and talented wordsmith who genuinely understood both me and Emmaline. He made the editing process collaborative and joyful, which is a rare gift in an editor. Stewart A. Williams provided all the design work, from cover and layout to marketing assets. His experience was invaluable early on in the process as this rookie novelist learned how to turn a story into an actual book. Thank you both for helping me bring *Emmaline* to life.

This book exists because of the people who believed in it and stood beside me, and I am deeply honored by all who contributed.

LYRIC ACKNOWLEDGEMENTS

"Come, Come, Ye Saints" was written by William Clayton in 1846 and was set to the music of the English folk melody, "All Is Well."

"The Handcart Song" is a traditional pioneer folk song.

ABOUT THE AUTHOR

ASHLI O'CONNELL is the debut author of *Emmaline*. A lifelong storyteller, she began writing as a young girl in Utah and later spent more than twenty-five years crafting narratives in journalism, public relations, and marketing. She has an undergraduate degree in journalism and a master's degree in communication. Ashli now lives in Missouri with her husband and three children.

For more information, visit her website at ashlioconnell.com.